HALﾝ®
THE FLOOD

NOVELS IN THE *NEW YORK TIMES* BESTSELLING
HALO® SERIES

HALO®
THE FLOOD

WILLIAM C. DIETZ

TOR

A TOM DOHERTY ASSOCIATES BOOK
NEW YORK

This is a work of fiction. All of the characters, organizations, and events portrayed in this novel are either products of the author's imagination or are used fictitiously.

HALO®: THE FLOOD

Copyright © 2003, 2010 by Microsoft Corporation

Originally published by Del Rey, The Random House Publishing Group

Microsoft, Halo, the Halo logo, Xbox, and the Xbox logo are trademarks of the Microsoft group of companies.

A Tor Book
Published by Tom Doherty Associates, LLC
175 Fifth Avenue
New York, NY 10010

www.tor-forge.com

Tor® is a registered trademark of Tom Doherty Associates, LLC.

ISBN 978-0-7653-6730-3

First Tor Trade Paperback Edition: October 2010
First Tor Mass Market Edition: March 2012

Printed in the United States of America

0 9 8 7 6

For Marjorie, with love and gratitude

ACKNOWLEDGMENTS TO THE
2010 EDITION

None of this would have been possible without Microsoft staffers Jacob Benton, Nicolas "Sparth" Bouvier, Alicia Brattin, Gabriel "Robogabo" Garza, Jon Goff, Kevin Grace, Tyler Jeffers, Frank O'Connor, Jeremy Patenaude, Kenneth Scott, and Kiki Wolfkill.

Nor without the efforts of the staff at Tor Books: Tom Doherty, Eric Raab, Whitney Ross, Seth Lerner, Megan Barnard, Theresa DeLucci, Jim Kapp, Lauren Hougen, Heather Saunders, Nathan Weaver, Justin Golenbock, and Patty Garcia.

343 Industries would like to thank Bungie Studios, Scott Dell'Osso, Nick Dimitrov, David Figatner, Nancy Figatner, Josh Kerwin, Bryan Koski, William C. Dietz, Bonnie Ross-Ziegler, Phil Spencer, and Carla Woo.

This edition features early drafts of the new cover art, which have been included periodically throughout the book. These images give a small insight into the process of creating the new cover from artists within 343 Industries.

FOREWORD

If, by some chance, you're not familiar with the story in these pages, then skip this foreword and move on to the main course. You've been warned.

The Flood. It's the third-act twist. It's the creeping horror. It's the boogeyman that lurks in dark Forerunner corners. It's a compelling and unexpected bad guy. It's an ancient shame. It's a forgotten sin. And in some ways, it's the icky, sticky glue that holds the Halo universe together.

The Flood is also the first and only Halo novel that's actually based on a game. We enjoy the luxury of an expanded universe that gives us permission to go off on highly exploratory adventures. We can visit distant worlds, move back and forward through an immense chronology, and flit from place to place like a butterfly. But *The Flood* is centered squarely in the vents of the first game—and is unique for that.

Certainly for gamers, it has a mixed reception. Some players enjoy the perverse nightmare of slogging through the Library on Legendary, blasting through putrescent forms with a shotgun and an ever-diminishing ammo supply. Others go into shock at the mere mention of that challenge, wishing for daylight and the bright vistas and the relief of Halo's friendlier climes.

But Bill Dietz, who performed yet another Herculean task in the Halo canon, was able to take a narrative structure from a nascent game universe and turn it into compelling fiction and adventure, often by taking the same detours that we, in Halo fiction, are often tempted by.

Dietz explores a lot of the stuff that was simply inferred during the game. He unravels some mysteries that were never explicitly explained. And he has fun in the corridors and confines of Installation 04, taking us on an underground tour of a place we thought we were familiar with, but that continually surprises us with its alien enigma.

In hindsight, knowing what we know about the Gravemind, the long-ago Forerunner war with the Flood and the very purpose of the Halo array, Dietz's compelling vision of the events of *Halo: Combat Evolved* takes on a fresh new resonance and holds surprises still, even for the cognoscenti. Enjoy it, and enjoy the other little surprises we've scattered among these pages.

Frank O'Connor
Redmond, Washington
July 2010

HALO

THE FLOOD

_____ PROLOGUE _____

Tech Officer (3rd Class) Sam Marcus swore as the intercom roused him from fitful sleep. He rubbed his blurry eyes and glanced at the Mission Clock bolted to the wall above his bunk. He'd been asleep for three hours—his first sleep cycle in thirty-six hours, damn it. Worse, this was the first time since the ship had jumped that he'd been able to fall asleep *at all*.

"Jesus," he muttered, "this better be good."

The Old Man had put the tech crews on triple shifts after the *Pillar of Autumn* jumped away from Reach. The ship was a mess after the battle, and what was left of the engineering crews worked around the clock to keep the aging cruiser in one piece. Nearly one third of the tech staff had died during the flight from Reach, and every department was running a skeleton crew.

Everyone else went into the freezer, of course—nonessential personnel always got an ice-nap during a Slipspace jump. In over two hundred combat cruises, Marcus had clocked fewer than seventy-two hours in cryostorage. Right now, though, he was so tired that even the discomfort of cryorevival sounded appealing if it meant that he could manage some uninterrupted sleep.

Of course, it was difficult to complain; Captain Keyes was a brilliant tactician—and everyone aboard the *Autumn* knew just how close they'd come to destruction when Reach fell to the enemy. A major naval base destroyed, millions dead or dying as the Covenant burned the planet to a cinder—and one of Earth's few remaining defenses transformed into corpses and molten slag.

All in all, they'd been damned lucky to get away—but Sam couldn't help but feel that everyone on the *Autumn* was living on borrowed time.

The intercom buzzed again, and Sam swung himself out of the bunk. He jabbed at the comm control. "Marcus here," he growled.

"I'm sorry to wake you, Sam, but I need you down in Cryo Two." Tech Chief Shephard sounded exhausted. "It's important."

"Cryo Two?" Sam repeated, puzzled. "What's the emergency, Thom? I'm not a cryo specialist."

"I can't give you specifics, Sam. The Captain wants it kept off the comm," Shephard replied, his voice almost a whisper. "Just in case we have eavesdroppers."

Sam winced at the tone in his superior's voice. He'd known Thom Shephard since the Academy and had never heard the man sound so grim.

"Look," Shephard said, "I need someone I can depend on. Like it or not, that's you, pal. You've cross-checked on cryo systems."

Sam sighed. "Months ago . . . but yes."

"I'm sending a feed to your terminal, Sam," Shephard continued. "It'll answer some of your questions anyway. Dump it to a portable 'pad, grab your gear and get down here."

"Roger," Sam said. He stood, shrugged into his uniform tunic, and stepped over to his terminal. He activated the computer and waited for the upload from Shephard.

As he waited, his eyes locked on a small 2-D photograph taped to the edge of the screen. Sam brushed his fingers against the photo. The pretty young woman frozen in the picture smiled back at him.

The terminal chimed as the feed from Shephard appeared in Sam's message queue. "Receiving the feed, Chief," he called out to the intercom pickup.

He opened the file. A frown creased his tired features as a new message scrolled across his screen.

```
>FILE ENCRYPTED/EYES ONLY/MARCUS,
  SAMUEL N./SN:18827318209-M.
>DECRYPTION KEY: [PERSONALIZED:
  "ELLEN'S ANNIVERSARY"]
```

He glanced back at the picture of his wife. He hadn't seen Ellen in almost three years—since his last shore leave on Earth, in fact. He didn't know anyone on active duty who'd been able to see their loved ones for years. The war simply didn't allow for it.

Sam's frown deepened. UNSC personnel generally avoided talking about the people back home. The war had been going badly for so long that morale was rock-bottom. Thinking about the home front only made things worse. The fact that Thom had personalized the security encoding was unusual enough; reminding Sam of his wife in the process was completely out of character for Chief Shephard. Someone was being security-conscious to the point of paranoia.

He punched in a series of numbers—the date of his wedding—and enabled the decryption suite. In seconds, the screen filled with schematics and tech readouts. His practiced eye scanned the file—and adrenaline suddenly spiked through his fatigue like a bolt of lightning.

"Christ," he said, his voice suddenly hoarse. "Thom, is this what . . . who I *think* it is?"

"Damn right. Get down to Cryo Two on the double, Sam. We've got an important package to thaw out—and we drop back into real space soon."

"On my way," he said. He killed the intercom connection, his exhaustion forgotten.

Sam quickly dumped the tech file to his portable compad and deleted the original from his computer. He strode toward the door to his cabin, then stopped. He snatched Ellen's picture from the workstation—almost as an afterthought—and shoved it into his pocket.

He sprinted for the lift. If the Captain wanted the inhabitant of Cryo Two revived, it meant that Keyes believed that the situation was about to go from bad to worse . . . or it already had.

Unlike vessels designed by humans—in which the command area was almost always located toward the ship's bow—Covenant ships were constructed in a more logical fashion, which meant that their control rooms were buried deep within heavily armored hulls, making them impervious to anything less than a mortal blow.

The differences did not end there. Rather than surround themselves with all manner of control interfaces, plus the lesser beings required to staff them, the Elites preferred to command from the center of an ascetically barren platform held in place by a latticework of opposing gravity beams.

However, none of these things were at the forefront of Ship Master Orna 'Fulsamee's mind as he stood at the center of his destroyer's control room and stared at the data projections which appeared to float in front of him. One showed the ringworld, Halo. Near that, a tiny arrow tracked the interloper's course. The second projection displayed a schematic titled HUMAN ATTACK SHIP, TYPE C-II. A third scrolled a constant flow of targeting data and sensor readouts.

He fought a moment of revulsion. That these filthy primates somehow merited an actual name—let alone names for their inferior constructs—galled him to his core. It was perverse. Names implied legitimacy, and the vermin deserved only extermination.

The humans had "names" for his own kind—"Elites"—as well as the lesser races of the Covenant: "Jackals," "Grunts," "Hunters." The appalling temerity of the filthy creatures, that they would dare *name his people* with their harsh, barbaric tongue, was beyond the pale.

He paused, and regained his composure. 'Fulsamee clicked his lower mandibles—the equivalent of a shrug—and mentally recited one of the True Sayings. *Such is the Prophets' decree,* he thought. One didn't question such things, even when one was a Ship Master. The Prophets had assigned names to the enemy craft, and he would honor their decrees. Any less was a disgraceful dereliction of duty.

Like all of his kind, the Covenant officer appeared to be larger than he actually was, due to the armor that he wore. It gave him an angular, somewhat hunched appearance which, when combined with a heavy, pugnacious jaw, caused him to look like what he was: a very dangerous warrior.

The being who floated next to 'Fulsamee bobbed slightly as a gust of air nudged his heavily swathed body. He wore a tall, ornate headpiece made of metal and set with amber panels. The Prophet had a serpentine neck, a triangular skull, and two bright green eyes which glittered with malevolent intelligence. He wore a red overrobe, a gold underrobe, and beneath the fabric, an anti-grav throne which served to keep him suspended one full unit off the deck. Though only a Minor Prophet, he still outranked 'Fulsamee, as his bearing made clear.

True Sayings aside, the Ship Master couldn't help but be reminded of the tiny, squealing rodents he had hunted in his childhood. He immediately banished the memory of blood on his claws and returned his attention to the Prophet, and his tiresome assistant.

The assistant, a lower-rank Elite named Bako 'Ikaporamee, stepped forward to speak on the Prophet's behalf. He had an annoying tendency to use the royal "we," a habit that angered 'Fulsamee.

Even his demeanor dripped with condescension, a fact which made the Ship Master angry, but couldn't be addressed. Not directly, and certainly not with the Prophet present, although 'Fulsamee wasn't willing to cave in completely. "So," 'Fulsamee said, careful to direct his comment to 'Ikaporamee alone, "you would have me believe that the interlopers arrived here entirely by *chance*?"

"No, of course not," 'Ikaporamee replied loftily. "Though primitive by our standards, the creatures *are* sentient, and like all sentient beings, they are unconsciously drawn to the glory of the ancients' truth and knowledge."

Like all the members of his caste, 'Fulsamee knew that the Prophets had evolved on a planet which the mysterious truth-givers had previously inhabited, and then, for reasons known only to the ancients themselves, subsequently abandoned. This ringworld was an excellent example of the ancients' power . . . and inscrutability.

'Fulsamee found it hard to believe that mere humans

would be drawn here, the ancients' wisdom notwith-standing, but 'Ikaporamee spoke for the Prophet, so it must be true. 'Fulsamee touched the light panel in front of him. A symbol glowed red. "Prepare to fire plasma torpedoes. Launch on my command."

'Ikaporamee raised both hands in alarm. "*No!* We forbid it. The human vessel is much too close to the con-struct! What if your weapons were to damage the holy relic? Pursue the ship, board it, and seize control. Any-thing else is far too dangerous."

Angered by what he saw as 'Ikaporamee's interfer-ence, 'Fulsamee spoke through gritted teeth. "The course of action that the holy one recommends is likely to result in a high number of casualties. Is this accept-able?"

"The opportunity to transcend the physical is a gift to be sought after," the other responded. "The humans are willing to spend *their* lives—can we do less?"

No, 'Fulsamee thought, *but we should aspire to more.* He again clicked his lower mandibles, and touched the light panel. "Cancel the previous order. Load four trans-ports with troops, and launch another flight of fighters. Neutralize the interloper's weaponry before the board-ing craft reach their target."

A hundred units aft, sealed within the destroyer's fire control center, a half-commander acknowledged the order and issued instructions of his own. Lights began to strobe, the decks transmitted a low frequency vibra-tion, and more than three hundred battle-ready Cove-nant warriors—a mix of what the humans called Elites, Jackals, and Grunts—rushed to board their assigned transports. There were humans to kill.

None of them wanted to miss this opportunity.

SECTION I

PILLAR OF AUTUMN

INVASION

CHAPTER

ONE

The *Pillar of Autumn* shuddered as her Titanium-A armor took a direct hit.

Just another item in the Covenant's bottomless arsenal, Captain Jacob Keyes thought. *Not a plasma torpedo, or we'd already be free-floating molecules.*

The warship had taken a beating from Covenant forces off Reach and it was a miracle that the hull remained intact and even more remarkable that they'd been able to make a jump into Slipspace at all.

"Status!" Keyes barked. "What just hit us?"

"Covenant fighter, sir. Seraph-class," the tactical officer, Lieutenant Hikowa, replied. Her porcelain features darkened. "Tricky bastard must have powered down and slipped past our sentry ships."

A humorless grin tugged at Keyes' mouth. Hikowa was a first-rate tactical officer, utterly ruthless in a fight. She seemed to take the Covenant fighter pilot's actions as a personal insult. "Teach him a lesson, Lieutenant," he said.

She nodded and tapped a series of orders into her panel—new orders for the *Autumn's* fighter squadron.

A moment later, there was radio chatter as one of the *Autumn*'s C709 Longsword fighters went after the Seraph, followed by a cheer as the tiny alien ship transformed into a momentary sun, complete with its own system of co-orbiting debris.

Keyes wiped a trickle of sweat from his forehead. He checked his display—they'd reverted back into real space twenty minutes ago. *Twenty minutes*, and the Covenant picket patrols had already found them and started shooting.

He turned to the bridge's main viewport, a large transparent bubble slung beneath the *Autumn*'s bow superstructure. A massive purple gas giant—Threshold—dominated the spectacular view. One of the Longsword fighters glided past as it continued its patrol.

When Keyes had been given command of the *Pillar of Autumn*, he'd been skeptical of the large, domed viewport. "The Covenant are tough enough," he had argued to Vice Admiral Stanforth. "Why give them an easy shot into my bridge?"

He'd lost the argument—captains don't win debates with admirals, and in any case there simply hadn't been time to armor the viewport. He had to admit, though, the view was almost worth the risk. Almost.

He absently toyed with the pipe he habitually carried, lost in thought. It ran completely counter to his nature to slink around in the shadow of a gas giant. He respected the Covenant as a dangerous, deadly enemy, and hated them for their savage butchery of human colonists and fellow soldiers alike. He had never feared them, however. Soldiers didn't hide from the enemy—they met the enemy head-on.

He moved back to the command station and activated his navigation suite. He plotted a course deeper in-system, and fed the data to Ensign Lovell, the navigator.

"Captain," Hikowa piped up. "Sensors paint a squadron of enemy fighters inbound. Looks like boarding craft are right behind them."

"It was just a matter of time, Lieutenant." He sighed. "We can't hide here forever."

The *Autumn* seemed to glide out of the shadow cast by the gas giant, and into bright sunlight.

Keyes' eyes widened with surprise as the ship cleared the gas giant. He had expected to see a Covenant cruiser, Seraph fighters, or some other military threat.

He hadn't expected to see the massive object floating in a Lagrange point between Threshold and its moon, Basis.

The construct was enormous—a ring-shaped object that shimmered and glowed with reflected starlight, like a jewel lit from within.

The outer surface was metallic and seemed to be engraved with deep geometric patterns. "Cortana," Captain Keyes said. "What *is* that?"

A thirty-centimeter-high hologram faded into view above a small holopad near the captain's station. Cortana—the ship's powerful artificial intelligence— frowned as she activated the ship's long-range detection gear. Long lines of digits scrolled across the sensor displays and rippled the length of Cortana's "body" as well.

"The ring is ten thousand kilometers in diameter," Cortana announced, "and twenty-two point three kilometers thick. Spectroscopic analysis is inconclusive, but patterns do not match any known Covenant materials, sir."

Keyes nodded. The preliminary finding was interesting, *very* interesting, since Covenant ships had already been present when the *Autumn* dropped out of Slip-space and right into their laps. When he first saw the ring, Keyes had a sinking feeling that the construct was a large Covenant installation—one far beyond the scope of human engineering. The thought that the construct might also be beyond *Covenant* engineering held some small comfort.

It also made him nervous.

Under intense pressure from enemy warships in the Epsilon Eridani system—the location of the UNSC's last major naval base, Reach—Cortana had been forced to launch the ship toward a random set of coordinates, a standard procedure to lead the Covenant forces away from Earth.

Now it appeared that the men and women aboard the *Pillar of Autumn* had not succeeded in leaving their original pursuers behind. The Covenant had followed them *here*. Wherever "here" was.

Cortana aimed a long-range camera array at the ring and a close-up snapped into focus. Keyes let out a long, slow whistle. The construct's inner surface was a mosaic of greens, blues, and browns—trackless desert, jungles, glaciers, and oceans. Streaks of white clouds cast deep shadows on the terrain below. The ring rotated and brought a new feature into view: a tremendous hurricane forming over a large body of water.

Equations again scrolled across the AI's semitransparent body as she continued to evaluate the incoming data. "Captain," Cortana said, "the object is clearly artificial. There's a gravity field that controls the ring's spin and keeps the atmosphere inside. I can't say with one hundred percent certainty, but it appears that the ring has an oxygen-nitrogen atmosphere, and Earth-normal gravity."

Keyes raised an eyebrow. "If it's artificial, who the hell built it, and what in God's name is it?"

Cortana processed the question for a full three seconds. "I don't know, sir."

Regulations be damned, Keyes thought. He took out his pipe, used an old-fashioned match to light it, and produced a puff of fragrant smoke. The ringworld shimmered on the status monitors. "Then we'd better find out."

Sam Marcus rubbed his aching neck with hands that trembled with fatigue. The rush of adrenaline that had flooded him when he'd received Tech Chief Shephard's instructions had worn off. Now he just felt tired, strung out, and more than a little afraid.

He shook his head to clear it and surveyed the small observation theater. Each cryostorage bay was equipped with such a station, a central monitoring facility for the hundreds of cryotubes the storage bays held. By shipboard standards, the Cryo Two Observation Theater was large, but the proliferation of life-sign monitors, diagnostic gauges, and computer terminals—tied directly into the individual cryotubes stored in the bay below—made the room seem cramped and uncomfortable.

A chime sounded and Sam's eyes swept across the status monitors. There was only one active cryotube in this bay, and its monitor pinged for his attention. He double-checked the main instrument panel, then keyed the intercom. "He's coming around, sir," he said. He turned and looked out the observation bay's window.

Tech Chief Thom Shephard waved up at Sam from the floor of Cryostorage Unit Two. "Good work, Sam," he called back. "Almost time to pop the seal."

The status monitors continued to feed information to the observation theater. The subject's body temperature was approaching normal—at least, Sam assumed it was normal; he'd never awakened a Spartan before—and most of the chemicals had already been flushed out of his system.

"He's in a REM cycle now, Chief," Sam called out, "and his brainwave activity shows he's dreaming—that means he's pretty much thawed. Shouldn't be long now."

"Good," Shephard replied. "Keep an eye on those neuro readings. We packed him in wearing his combat armor. There may be some feedback effects to watch out for."

"Acknowledged."

A red light winked to life on the security terminal, and a new series of codes flashed across the screen:

```
>WAKE-UP SERIES STANDBY. SECURITY LOCK
  [PRIORITY ALPHA] ENGAGED.
>x-CORTANA.1.0-CRYOSTOR.23.4.7
```

"What the hell?" Sam muttered. He keyed the bay intercom again. "Thom? There's something weird here . . . some kind of security lockout from the bridge."

"Acknowledged." There was a static-spotted click as Shephard looped in the bridge channel. "Cryo Two to Bridge."

"Go ahead, Cryo Two," a female voice replied, laced with the telltale warble of synthesized speech.

"We're ready to pop the seal on our . . . guest, Cortana," Shephard explained. "We need—"

"—the security code," the AI finished. "Transmitting. Bridge out."

Almost instantly, a new line of text scrolled across the security screen:

```
>UNSEAL THE HUSHED CASKET.
```

Sam hit the execute command, the security lockout dropped away, and a countdown timer began marking time until the wake-up sequence would be completed.

The soldier was coming around. Respiration was up, ditto his heart rate, as both returned to normal levels. *Here he is,* Sam thought, *a real honest-to-god Spartan.* Not just any Spartan, but maybe the *last* Spartan. The shipboard scuttlebutt said that the rest of them had bought the farm at Reach.

Like his fellow techs, Sam had heard of the program, though he'd never seen an *actual* Spartan in person. In order to deal with increasing civil turmoil the Colonial Military Administration had secretly launched Project ORION back in 2491. The purpose of the program was to develop super-soldiers, who would receive special training and physical augmentation.

The initial effort was successful, and in 2517 a new group of Spartans, the II-series, had been selected as the next generation of super-soldier. The project had been intended to remain secret, but the Covenant War had changed all that.

It was no secret that the human race was on the verge of defeat. The Covenant's ships and space technology were just too advanced. While human forces could hold their own in a ground engagement, the Covenant would simply fall back into space and glass the planet from orbit.

As the situation grew increasingly grim, the Admiralty was faced with the ugly prospect of fighting a two-front war—one against the Covenant in space, and another against the collapsing human society on the ground. The general public and the rank-and-file in the military needed a morale boost, so the existence of the SPARTAN-II project was revealed.

There were now successful heroes to rally behind, men and women who had taken the fight to the enemy and won several decisive battles. Even the Covenant seemed to fear the Spartans.

Except they were gone now, all but one, sacrificed to protect the human race from the Covenant and the very real possibility of extinction. Sam gazed on the soldier in front of him with something akin to awe. Here, about to rise as if from a grave, was a true hero. It was a moment to remember, and if he was lucky enough to survive, to tell his children about.

It didn't make him any less afraid, however. If the stories were true, the man gradually regaining consciousness in the bay below was almost as alien, and certainly as dangerous, as the Covenant.

He was floating in the never-never land somewhere between cryo and full consciousness when the dream began.

It was a familiar dream, a pleasant dream, and one which had nothing to do with war. He was on Eridanus II—the colony world he'd been born on, long since destroyed by the Covenant. He heard laughter all around.

A female voice called him by name—John. A moment later, arms held him, and he recognized the familiar scent of soap. The woman said something nice to him, and he wanted to say something nice in return, but the words wouldn't come. He tried to *see* her, tried to penetrate the haze that obscured her face, and was rewarded with the image of a woman with large eyes, a straight nose, and full lips.

The picture wavered, indistinct, like a reflection in a pond. In an eyeblink, the woman who held him transformed. Now she had dark hair, piercing blue eyes, and pale skin.

He knew her name: Dr. Halsey.

Dr. Catherine Halsey had selected him for the SPARTAN-II project. While most believed that the Spartans had been culled from the best of the UNSC military, only a handful of people knew the truth.

Halsey's program involved the actual abduction of specially-screened children. The children were flash-cloned—which made the duplicates prone to neurological disorders—and the clones covertly returned to the parents, who never suspected that their sons and daughters were duplicates. In many ways, Dr. Halsey was the only "mother" that he had ever known.

But Dr. Halsey *wasn't* his mother, nor was the pale semi-translucent image of Cortana that appeared to replace her.

The dream changed. A dark, nebulous shape loomed behind the Mother/Halsey/Cortana figure. He didn't know what it was, but it was a threat—of that he was certain.

His combat instincts kicked in, and adrenaline coursed through him. He quickly surveyed the area— some kind of playground, with high wooden poles, distantly familiar—and decided on the best route to flank the new threat. He spied an assault rifle, a powerful MA5B, nearby. If he placed himself between the woman and the threat, his armor could take the brunt of an attack, and he could return fire.

He moved quickly, and the dark shape howled at him—a fierce and terrifying war cry.

The beast was impossibly fast. It was on him in seconds.

He grabbed the assault rifle and turned to open fire—and discovered to his horror that he couldn't lift the weapon. His arms were small, underdeveloped. His armor was gone, and his body was that of a six-year-old child.

He was powerless in the face of the threat. He roared back at the beast in rage and fear—angry not just at the threat, but at his own sudden powerlessness . . .

The dream started to fade, and light appeared in front of the Spartan's eyes. Vapor vented, swirled, and began to dissipate. A voice came, as if from a great distance. It was male and matter-of-fact.

"Sorry for the quick thaw, Master Chief—but things are a bit hectic right now. The disorientation should pass quickly."

A second voice welcomed him back and it took the Spartan a moment to remember where he'd been prior to entering the cryotube. There had been a battle, a terrible battle, in which most if not all of his Spartan brothers and sisters had been killed. Men and women with whom he had been raised and trained since the age of six, and who, unlike the dimly remembered woman of his dreams, constituted his *real* family.

With the memory, plus subtle changes to the gas mix that filled his lungs, came strength. He flexed his stiff limbs. The Spartan heard the tech say something about "freezer burn," and pushed himself up and out of the cryotube's chilly embrace.

"God in heaven," Sam whispered.

The Spartan was huge, nearly two-and-a-half meters tall. Encased in pearlescent green battle armor, the man looked like a figure from mythology—otherworldly and terrifying. Master Chief Spartan 117 stepped from his tube and surveyed the cryo bay. The mirrored visor on his helmet made him all the more fearsome, a faceless, impassive soldier built for destruction and death.

Sam was glad that he was up here in the observation theater, rather than down on the Cryo Two main floor with the Spartan.

He realized that Thom was waiting for diagnostic data. He checked the displays—neural pathways clear, no fluctuations in heartbeat or brainwave activity. He opened an intercom channel. "I'm bringing his health monitors online now."

Sam watched as Thom led the Spartan to the various test stations in the bay, pitching in where he was required. In short order, the soldier's gear had been brought online—recharging shield system, real-time health monitors, targeting and optical systems all read in the green.

The suit—code-named MJOLNIR armor—was a marvel of engineering, Sam had to admit. According to the specs he'd received, the suit's shell consisted of a multilayered alloy of remarkable strength, a refractive coating that could disperse a fair amount of directed energy, a crystalline storage matrix that could support the same level of artificial intelligence usually reserved for a starship, and a layer of gel which conformed to the wearer's skin and functioned to regulate temperature.

Additional memory packets and signal conduits had been implanted into the Spartan's body, and two externally accessible input slots had been installed near the base of his skull. Taken together, the combined systems served to double his strength, enhance his already lightning-fast reflexes, and make it possible for him to navigate through the intricacies of any high-tech battlefield.

There were substantial life-support systems built into the MJOLNIR gear. Most soldiers went into cryo naked, since covered skin generally reacted badly to the cryo process. Sam had once worn a bandage into the freezer and discovered the affected skin blistered and raw when he woke up.

The Spartan's skin must have hurt like hell, he realized. Through it all, though, the soldier remained silent, simply nodding when asked questions or quietly complying with requests from Thom. It was eerie—he moved with mechanistic efficiency from one test to the next, like a robot.

Cortana's voice rang from the shipwide com: "Sensors show inbound Covenant boarding craft. Stand by to repel boarders."

Sam felt a pang of fear—and sorrow for the Covenant troops that would have to face this Spartan in combat.

The neural interface which linked the Master Chief to his MJOLNIR armor was working perfectly, and immediately fed data to his helmet's heads-up display on the inside surface of his visor.

It felt good to move around, and the Master Chief quietly flexed his fingers. His skin itched and stung, a side effect of the cryo gases, but he quickly banished the pain from his awareness. He had long ago learned how to disassociate himself from physical discomfort.

He'd heard Cortana's announcement. The Covenant were on their way. Good. He scanned the room for weapons, but there was no arms locker present. The lack of weapons wasn't of great concern to him; he'd taken weapons away from Covenant soldiers before.

The intercom crackled again: "Bridge to Cryo Two—

this is Captain Keyes. Send the Master Chief to the bridge immediately."

One of the techs started to object, pointing out that more tests were required, when Keyes cut in. He said, "On the double, crewman," and the rating gave the only reply he could.

"Aye, aye, sir."

The tech chief turned and faced him. "We'll find weapons later."

The Master Chief nodded and was about to move for the door when an explosion echoed through the cryo bay.

The first blasts slammed into the observation theater's door with a noise that made Sam jump. His heart pounded as he quickly hit the door controls, engaging an emergency lockout. A heavy metal barrier slammed into place with a crash—then began to glow red as Covenant energy weapons burned their way through.

"They're trying to get through the door!" he yelled.

He glanced down into the bay and saw Thom, a stricken look on his face. Sam could see his own startled reflection in the Spartan's mirrored visor.

Sam lunged for the alarm, and had time to call in an alert. Then, the security door exploded in a shower of fire and molten steel.

He heard the whine of plasma rifle fire, then felt something punch him in the chest. His vision blurred, and he groped to feel the wound. His hands came away sticky with blood. *It doesn't hurt,* he thought. *It should hurt, shouldn't it?*

He felt disoriented, confused. He could see a flurry of movement, as armored figures swarmed into the observation theater. He ignored them and focused on his wife's picture—smeared with his own blood—which had somehow fallen to the deckplates. He fell to his knees and scrambled for the photograph, his hands shaking.

His field of vision narrowed as he struggled to reach the discarded photo. It was only centimeters away now, but the distance felt like kilometers. He'd never been so tired. His wife's name echoed in his mind.

Sam's fingers had just brushed the edge of the photograph when an armored boot pinned his arm to the deck. Long, clawed fingers plucked the picture from the floor.

Sam cursed weakly and struggled to face his attacker. The alien—an Elite—cocked his head at the image in puzzlement. He glanced down, as if noticing Sam for the first time. The human continued to reach for the picture.

He dimly heard Thom's voice call out in anguish: "Sam!"

The Elite aimed the plasma rifle at Sam's head and fired.

The Master Chief bristled. Covenant forces were in close proximity, and a fellow soldier had just died. He longed to climb to the observation bay and engage the enemy—but orders were orders. He needed to get to the bridge.

The cryo tech keyed open a hatchway. "Come on!" he yelled, "we've got to get the hell out of here!"

The Master Chief followed the crewman through the hatch and down the corridor. A sudden explosion blew the next door to smithereens, hurled what remained of the technician's body down the passageway, and caused the Chief's shields to flare.

He mentally reviewed the schematics of the Halcyon-class line of ships and doubled back. He vaulted over a pair of power conduits, and landed in the dimly lit maintenance hallway beyond. An emergency beacon strobed and alarms wailed. The rumble of a second explosion echoed down the corridor.

He pushed ahead, past a dead crewman, and into the next section of hallway.

The Master Chief saw a hatch, its security panel pulsing green, and hurried forward. There was a third explosion, but his armor deflected the force of the blast.

The Spartan forced open the partially melted door, saw an opening to his left, and heard someone scream. A naval crewman fired his sidearm at a target the Master Chief couldn't see—and the deck shuddered as a missile struck the *Autumn*'s hull.

The Master Chief ducked under a half-raised door just in time to see the crewman take an energy bolt through the chest as the rest of the human counter-boarders returned fire. Covenant forces backed through a hatch and were forced to retreat into an adjoining compartment.

Chaos reigned as the ship's crew did the best they could to push the boarders back toward the air locks or to trap them in compartments where they could be contained and dispatched later.

Unarmed, and well aware of the fact that Captain Keyes needed him on the bridge, the Master Chief had little choice but to follow the signs, and avoid the fire-fights that raged all around. He made his way down a darkened access corridor—the Covenant boarders must have shorted out the illumination circuits in this compartment—and nearly ran headlong into a Covenant Elite.

The alien's personal shields sparked and he roared

in surprise and anger. The Spartan crouched and prepared to meet the alien soldier's charge—then ducked, as a Marine fireteam unleashed a barrage of assault-rifle fire at the Elite. Purple gore splashed the bulkhead, and the alien dropped in a crumpled heap.

The Marines moved forward to secure the area, and the Chief nodded in thanks to the squad leader. He turned, sprinted down the passageway, and made it to the bridge without further incident.

He looked out through the main viewport, saw the strange-looking construct that floated out beyond the cruiser's hull, and was momentarily curious about what it was. No doubt the Captain would fill him in. He strode toward the captain's station, near the center of the bridge.

A variety of naval personnel sat hunched at their consoles as they struggled to control their beleaguered vessel. Some battled the latest wave of Seraph fighters, others worked on damage control, and one grim-faced Lieutenant made use of the ship's environmental systems to suck the atmosphere out of those compartments which had been occupied by Covenant forces. Some of the enemy carried their own atmosphere, but some of them didn't, and that made them vulnerable. There were crew in some of those spaces, perhaps some she knew personally, but there was no way to save them. If she didn't kill them, then the enemy would.

The Chief understood the situation well. Better a quick death in vacuum than at the hands of the Covenant.

He spotted Keyes near the main tactical display. Keyes studied the screens intently, particularly a large display of the strange ring.

The Spartan came to attention. "Captain Keyes."

Captain Keyes turned to face him. "Good to see you,

Master Chief. Things aren't going well. Cortana did her best—but we never really had a chance."

The AI arched a holographic eyebrow. "A dozen Covenant battleships against a single Halcyon-class cruiser . . . With those odds we still had three—" She paused, as if distracted, then amended, "—make that *four* kills."

Cortana looked at the Chief. "Sleep well?"

"Yes," he replied. "No thanks to your driving."

Cortana smiled. "So, you *did* miss me."

Before he could reply, another blast rocked the entire ship. He grabbed a nearby support pillar and braced himself, as several of the crew crashed to the deck nearby.

Keyes grabbed onto a console for support. "Report!"

Cortana shimmered blue. "It must have been one of their boarding parties. My guess is an antimatter charge."

The fire control officer turned in his seat. "Ma'am! Fire control for the main cannon is offline!"

Cortana looked at Keyes. The loss of the ship's primary weapon, the Magnetic Accelerator Cannon, was a crippling blow to their holding action. "Captain, the cannon was my last defensive option."

"All right," Keyes said gruffly, "I'm initiating Cole Protocol, Article Two. We're abandoning the *Autumn*. That means you too, Cortana."

"While you do what? Go down with the ship?" she shot back.

"In a manner of speaking," Keyes replied. "The object we found—I'm going to try and land the *Autumn* on it."

Cortana shook her head. "With all due respect . . . this war has enough dead heroes."

The Captain's eyes locked with hers. "I appreciate your concern, Cortana—but it's not up to me. The Protocol is clear. The destruction or capture of shipboard AI is absolutely unacceptable. That means you *are* abandoning ship. Lock in a selection of emergency landing zones and upload them to my neural lace."

The AI paused, then nodded. "Aye, aye, sir."

"Which is where *you* come in," Keyes continued as he turned to face the Spartan. "Get Cortana off this ship. Keep her safe from the enemy. If they capture her, they'll learn everything. Force deployment, weapons research." He paused, then added: "Earth."

The Spartan nodded. "I understand."

Keyes glanced at Cortana. "Are you ready?"

There was a pause as the AI took one last look around. In many ways the ship was her physical body and she was reluctant to leave it. "Yank me."

Keyes turned to a console, touched a series of controls, and turned back again.

The holo shivered and Cortana's image swirled into the pedestal below and disappeared from view. Keyes waited until the holo had disappeared, removed a data chip from the pedestal, and offered it to the Spartan, along with his sidearm. "Good luck, Master Chief."

Spartan 117 accepted the chip and reached back to slot the device into the neural interface, located at the base of his skull. There was a positive click, followed by a flood of sensation as the AI joined him within the confines of the armor's neural network. At first it felt as if someone had poured a cup of ice water into his mind, followed by a momentary jab of pain, and a familiar presence. He'd worked with Cortana before—just prior to the disaster at Reach.

The AI-human interface was intrusive in a way, yet comforting too, since he knew what Cortana could do.

He would depend on her during the hours and days ahead—just as she would depend on him. It was like being part of a team again.

The Master Chief saluted and left the bridge. The sounds of fighting were even louder now, indicating that, in spite of the crew's best efforts, Covenant forces had still managed to fight their way out of the areas adjacent to the air locks and made it all the way up to the area around the command deck.

Bodies lay strewn around the corridor, roughly fifty meters from the bridge. The human defenders had pushed them back, but the Chief could tell that the last assault had been close. Too close.

The Master Chief paused to kneel next to a dead ensign, took a moment to close her eyelids, and appropriated the fallen trooper's ammo. The pistol the Captain had given him was standard Navy issue; it fired 12.7mm semi-armor piercing high-explosive ammo from twelve-round clips. Not what he would choose to tackle an Elite with—but good enough for Grunt work.

There was a metallic *click* as the first clip slid into the pistol's handle, followed by the sudden appearance of a blue circle in his HUD—a targeting reticle—as his armor made electronic contact with the weapon in his hand.

Then, conscious of the need to get Cortana off the ship, he made his way down the corridor. He heard the strange high-pitched squeaks and barks before he actually saw the Covenant Grunts themselves. Consistent with his status as a veteran, the first alien to come around the corner wore red-trimmed armor, a methane rig, and a Marine's web pistol belt. The alien wore the captured gear Pancho Villa–style and dragged it across the deck. Two of his comrades brought up the rear.

Confident that there were more of the vaguely simian aliens on the way, the Master Chief paused long enough to let more of them appear, then opened fire. The recoil compensators in his armor dampened the effect, but he could still feel the handgun kick against his palm. All three of the Grunts went down from head shots. Phosphorescent blue ichor spattered the deck.

It wasn't much, but it was a start.

The Master Chief stepped over their bodies and moved on.

A lifeboat. That was his *real* goal—and he would do whatever it took to find one.

Ashamed by the ignominy of it, but consistent with his orders, the Elite named Isna 'Nosolee waited until the Grunts, Jackals, and two members of his own race had charged out through the human air lock before leaving the assault boat himself. Though armed with a plasma pistol, plus a half-dozen grenades, he was there to observe rather than fight, which meant that the Elite would rely on both his energy shielding and active camouflage to keep him alive.

His role, and an unaccustomed one at that, was to function as an "Ossoona," or Eye of the Prophet. The concept, as outlined to 'Nosolee by his superior, was to insert experienced officers into situations where intelligence could be gleaned, and to do so early enough to obtain high-quality information.

Though both intelligent and brave, the Prophets felt that the Elites had an unfortunate tendency to destroy everything in their path, leaving very little for their analysts to analyze.

Now, by adding Ossoonas to the combat mix, the Prophets hoped to learn more about the humans, ranging from data on their weapons and force deployments to the greatest prize of all: the coordinates for their home planet, "Earth."

'Nosolee had three major objectives: to retrieve the enemy ship's AI, to capture senior personnel, and to record everything he saw via the cameras attached to his helmet. The first two goals were bound to be difficult, but a quick check confirmed that the video gear was working, and the third objective was assured.

So, even though the assignment was empty of honor, 'Nosolee understood its purpose, and was determined to succeed, if only as a means to return to the regular infantry where he belonged.

The Elite heard the rhythmic clatter of a human weapon as a group of their Marines backed around a corner, closely pursued by a pack comprised of Grunts and Jackals. The Ossoona considered killing the humans, thought better of it, and flattened himself against a bulkhead. None of the combatants noticed the point where the metal appeared to be slightly distorted, and a moment later the spy slipped away.

It seemed as if the *Autumn* was infested with chrome-armored demons spouting plasma fire. The Master Chief had acquired an MA5B assault rifle along with close to four hundred rounds of 7.62mm armor piercing ammunition. In this situation, with plenty of ordnance lying around, he preferred to reload when the ammo indicator on his weapon dropped to around 10. Failure to do so could result in disaster if he ran into serious opposition. With that in mind, the Chief hit the release, allowed a nearly empty magazine to fall, and shoved a new clip into its place. The weapon's digital ammo counter reset, as did its cousin in his HUD.

"We're closer," Cortana said from someplace just outside his head. "Duck through the hatch ahead and go up one level."

The Master Chief ran into a shimmery, black-clad Elite, and opened fire. There were Grunts in the area as well, but he knew that the Elite posed the *real* danger. He expertly sprayed a trio of bursts at the alien.

The Elite roared defiance and fired in return, but the sheer volume of the specially hardened 7.62mm projectiles caused the Elite's shielding to flare, overload, and fail. The bulky alien fell to his knees, bent forward, and collapsed. Frightened by what had happened to their leader, the Grunts made barking noises, turned, and began to scurry away.

Individually, the Grunts were cowards, but the Spartan had seen what a pack of the creatures could do. He opened fire again. Alien bodies tumbled and fell.

He continued on through a hatch, heard more firing, and turned in that direction. Cortana called out: "Covenant! On the landing above us!"

He ran toward a flight of metal stairs, and charged straight for the landing.

Boots rang on metal as he slammed a fresh magazine into the weapon's receiver and passed a wounded Marine. The Spartan remembered the soldier from his last action on one of Reach's orbiting defense stations. The Marine held a dressing to a plasma burn and managed to smile. "Glad you could make it, Chief . . . we saved some party favors just for you."

The Spartan nodded, paused on the landing, and took aim at a Jackal. The vaguely birdlike aliens carried energy shields—handheld units, rather than the full-body protection the Elites favored. The Jackal shifted to take aim at the wounded Marine, and the Chief saw his opening. He fired a burst at the Jackal's unprotected flank and the alien hit the deck-plates, dead.

He continued the climb up the flight of stairs, and came nearly eye-to-eye with another Elite. The alien roared, charged forward, and attempted to use his plasma rifle like a club. The Master Chief evaded the blow—he'd fought Elites hand-to-hand before, and knew they were dangerously strong—and backed away. He leveled the assault weapon at the Elite's belly, and squeezed the trigger.

The Covenant soldier seemed to absorb the bullets like a sponge, continued to advance, and was just about to swing when a final round cut through his spinal cord. The alien soldier slammed into the deck, twitched once, and died.

Spartan 117 reached for another magazine. Another Elite roared, as did *another*. There was no time to reload, so the Master Chief turned to take them on. He discarded the assault rifle and drew his sidearm. There were a pair of dead Marines at the aliens' feet, roughly twenty-five meters away. *Well within range,* he thought, and opened fire.

The lead Elite snarled as the powerful handgun rounds tore into the shielding around his head. Sensing the Spartan's threat, the aliens shifted all of their fire in his direction only to watch as it dissipated against his shields and armor.

Now, free to direct their fire wherever they chose, the Marines launched a hastily organized counterattack. A fragmentation grenade blew one Elite into bloody ribbons, shredded the Jackals who had the poor judgment to stand next to him, and sent pieces of shrapnel flying across the stairwell to slam into the bulkhead.

The other Elite was consumed by a hail of bullets.

He seemed to wilt, fold, and fly apart. "That's what I'm talking about!" a Marine crowed. He fired a *coup de grâce* into the alien's head.

Satisfied that the area was reasonably secure, the Master Chief moved on. He passed through a hatch, helped a pair of Marines take out a group of Grunts, and marched down a corridor drenched with blood— both human and alien. The deck shook as the *Autumn* took a new hit from a ship-to-ship missile. There was a muffled clang, and a light flared beyond a viewport.

"The lifeboats are launching," Cortana announced. "We should hurry!"

"I *am* hurrying," the Master Chief replied. "I'll get there as soon as I can."

Cortana started to reply, reconsidered, and processed the equivalent of an apologetic shrug. Sometimes, fallible though they were, humans were right.

Flight Officer Captain Carol Rawley, better known to the ship's Marine contingent by her call sign, "Foehammer," waited for the Grunt to round the corner. She shot him in the head, and the little methane-breathing bastard dropped like a rock. The pilot took a quick peek, verified that the next corridor was clear, and motioned to those behind her. "Come on! Let's get while the getting's good!"

Three pilots, along with an equal number of ground crew, followed as Rawley thundered down the hall. She was a tall, broad-shouldered woman, and she ran with a flat-footed determination. The plan, if the wild-assed scheme she'd concocted could be dignified as such, was to make it down to the ship's launch bay, jump into their D77-TC "Pelican" dropships, and get off the *Autumn* before the cruiser smacked into the construct below. At best, it would be a tricky takeoff, and a messy landing, but she'd rather die behind the stick of her bird than trust her fate to some lifeboat jockey. Besides, maybe some transports would come in handy, if anybody actually made it off the ship alive.

That was looking like an increasingly big maybe.

"They're behind us!" somebody yelled. "Run faster!"

Rawley wasn't a sprinter—she was a pilot, damn it. She turned to take aim on her pursuers, when a globe of glowing-green plasma sizzled past her ear.

"Screw this," she yelled, then ran with renewed energy.

As the battle with the interlopers continued to rage, a Grunt named Yayap led a small detachment of his own kind through a half-melted hatch and came upon the scene of a massacre. The nearest bulkhead was drenched in shimmering blue blood. Spent shell casings were scattered everywhere and a tangled pile of Grunt bodies testified to an engagement lost. Yayap keened in brief mourning for his fallen brethren.

That most of the dead were Grunts like Yayap didn't surprise him. The Prophets had long made use of his race as cannon fodder. He hoped that they had gone to a methane-rich paradise, and was about to pass by the gruesome heap, when one of the bodies groaned.

The Grunt paused and, accompanied by one of his fellows—a Grunt named Gagaw—he waded into the gory mess, only to discover that the noise was associated with a black-armored member of the Elite, one of the "Prophet-blessed" types who were in charge of this ill-considered raid. By law and custom, Yayap's race was required to revere the Elites as near-divine envoys of the Prophets. Of course, the implementation of law and custom was somewhat flexible on the battlefield.

"Leave him," Gagaw advised. "That's what *he* would do if it were one of us lying wounded."

"True," Yayap said thoughtfully, "but it would take all five of us to carry him back to the assault boat."

It took Gagaw ten full heartbeats to assimilate the idea and finally appreciate the genius of it. "We wouldn't have to fight!"

"Precisely," Yayap said, as the sounds of battle grew louder once more, "so let's slap some dressings on his wounds, grab his arms and legs, and drag his ass out of here."

A quick check revealed that the Elite's wounds weren't mortal. A human projectile had bored its way into the warrior's face, sliced along the side of his head, and flattened itself on the inside surface of the Elite's helmet. The force of the blow had knocked him unconscious. Aside from that, and some cuts and bruises sustained when he fell, the Elite would survive. *A pity,* Yayap thought.

Satisfied that their ticket off the ship would live long enough to get them where they wanted to go, the Grunts grabbed the warrior's limbs and waddled down the corridor. Their battle was over.

The *Autumn*'s contingent of Orbital Drop Shock Troopers, also known as ODST, or "Helljumpers," had been assigned to protect the cruiser's experimental power plant, which consisted of a unique network of fusion engines.

The engine room was served by two main access points, each protected by a Titanium-A hatch. Both were connected by a catwalk and were still under human control. The fact that Major Antonio Silva's Marines had been forced to stack the Covenant bodies like firewood in order to maintain clear fields of fire testified to how effective the men and women under his command had been.

There had been human casualties as well, *plenty* of them, including Lieutenant Melissa McKay, who waited impatiently while "Doc" Valdez, the platoon's medic, bandaged her arm. There was a lot to do—and clearly McKay wanted to get up and do it.

"Got some bad news for you, Lieutenant," the medic said. "The tattoo on your bicep, the one with the skull and the letters 'ODST,' took a serious hit. You can get a new one, of course . . . but scar tissue won't take the ink in quite the same way."

McKay knew the patter had a purpose, knew it was Doc's way of taking her mind off Dawkins, Al-Thani, and Suzuki. The medic secured the bandage in place and the officer rolled her sleeve down over the dressing. "You know what, Valdez? You are truly full of it. And I mean that as a compliment."

Doc wiped his forehead with the back of a sleeve. It came away with Al-Thani's blood on it. "Thanks, El-Tee. Compliment accepted."

"All right," Major Silva boomed as he strode out onto the center of the catwalk. "Listen up! Play time is over. Captain Keyes is tired of our company and wants us to leave this tub. There's a construct down there, complete with an atmosphere, gravity, and the one thing Marines love like beer—and that's dirt beneath our feet."

The ODST officer paused at that point, allowing his bright, beady eyes to sweep the faces around him, his mouth straight as a crease. "Most of the crew—not to mention your fellow jarheads—will be leaving the ship in lifeboats. They'll ride to the surface in air-conditioned comfort, sipping wine, and nibbling on appetizers.

"Not *you*, however. Oh no, you're going to leave the *Pillar of Autumn* by a different method. Tell me, boys and girls . . . How will *you* leave?"

It was a time-honored ritual, and the ODST Marines roared the answer in unison. "WE GO FEET FIRST, SIR!"

"Damned right you do," Silva barked. "Now let's get to those drop pods. The Covenant is holding a picnic down on the surface and every single one of you is invited. You have five minutes to strap in, hook up, and shove a cork in your ass."

It was an old joke, one of their favorites, and the Marines laughed as if they had just heard it for the first time. Then they formed into squads, and followed their noncoms out into a corridor that ran down the port side of the ship.

McKay led her platoon down the hall, past the troopers assigned to guard the intersection, and through what had been a battlefield. Bodies lay sprawled where they had fallen, plasma burns marked the bulkheads, and a long line of 7.62mm dimples marked the last burst that one of the dead soldiers would ever fire.

They pounded around a corner, and into what the Marines referred to as "Hell's waiting room." The troopers streamed down the center of a long narrow compartment that housed two rows of oval-shaped individual drop pods. Each pod bore the name of an individual trooper, and was poised over a tube that extended down through the ship's belly.

Most combat landings were made via armed assault boats, but the boats were slow, and subject to antiaircraft fire. That was why the UNSC had invested the time and money necessary to create a *second* way to deliver troops through an atmosphere: the HEV, or Human Entry Vehicle.

Computer-controlled antiaircraft fire would nail some of the pods, but they made small targets, and each hit would result in one death rather than a dozen.

There was just one problem. As the ceramic skins that covered the HEVs burned away, the air inside the pods became unbelievably hot, sometimes fatally so, which was why ODST personnel were referred to as "Helljumpers." It was an all-volunteer outfit, and it took a special kind of crazy to join up.

McKay remained on the central walkway until each of her men had entered his particular pod. She knew that meant she would have sixty seconds less to make her own preparations, and was quick to enter her HEV once the last hatch had closed.

Once inside, McKay's hands were a blur as she secured her harness, ran the obligatory systems check, removed a series of safeties, armed her ejection tube, and eyed the tiny screen mounted in front of her. The *Autumn*'s fire control computer had already calculated the force required to blow the pod free and drop the HEV into the correct entry path. All she had to do was hang on, pray that the pod's ceramic skin would hold long enough for the chute to open, and try to ignore how fragile the vehicle actually was.

No sooner had the officer braced her boots against the bulkhead, and looked up at the countdown, than the last digit clicked from one to zero.

The pod dropped, accelerated out of the ejection tube, and fell toward the ring-shaped world below. Her stomach lurched and her heart rate spiked.

Somebody popped a tiny disk into a data player, touched a button, and pushed the hyped-up strains of the Helljumpers' anthem out over the team freq. The regs made it clear that unauthorized use of UNSC communications facilities was wrong, *very* wrong, but

McKay knew that at that particular moment it was *right*, and Silva must have agreed, because nothing came in over the command freq. The music pounded in her ears, the HEV shuddered as it hit the outer layer of the construct's atmosphere, and the Marines fell feet first toward the ring.

The deck jumped as the *Pillar of Autumn* absorbed yet another blow and the battle continued to rage within. The Master Chief was close now, and prepared to sprint for a lifeboat. That was when Cortana said, "Behind you!" and the Master Chief felt a plasma bolt hit him squarely between the shoulder blades.

He rolled with the blow and sprang to his feet. He whirled to face his attacker and saw that a Grunt had dropped out of an overhead maintenance way. The diminutive alien stood with his feet planted on the deck, a plasma pistol overcharging in his claws. The Master Chief took three steps forward, used the assault rifle to knock the creature off its feet, and followed it with a three-round burst. The Grunt's pistol discharged its stored energy into the ceiling. Drips of molten metal sizzled on the Master Chief's shields.

The armor-piercing rounds punctured the alien's breathing apparatus, released a stream of methane, and caused the body to spin like a top.

A trio of additional Grunts landed on the Master Chief's shoulders and grabbed hold. It was almost laughable, until the Spartan realized that one of them was trying to remove his helmet. A second alien carried an ignited plasma grenade—the little bastards meant to drop the explosive into his armor.

He flexed his shoulders, and shook himself like a dog. Grunts flew in every direction as the Master Chief used short controlled bursts to put them down. He turned toward the lifeboats. "Now!" Cortana urged. "Run!"

The Spartan ran, just as the door started to close. A nearby Marine fell while running for the escape craft, and the Chief paused long enough to scoop the soldier up and hurl him into the boat.

Once inside, they joined a small group of crew members already on board the escape craft. "Now would be a very good time to leave," Cortana commented coolly, as something else exploded and the cruiser shuddered in response.

The Master Chief stood facing the hatch. He waited for it to close all the way, saw the red light appear, and knew it was sealed. "Punch it."

The pilot triggered the launch sequence and the lifeboat blasted free of the ship, balanced on a column of fire. The boat skimmed along the surface of the *Autumn* at dizzying speed. Plasma blasts from a Covenant warship slammed into the *Autumn*'s hull. In seconds, the lifeboat dropped away from the cruiser and dove toward the ring.

The Master Chief killed his external com system, and spoke directly to Cortana. "So, any idea what this thing is?"

"No," Cortana admitted. "I managed to slice some data out of the Covenant battle network. They call it 'Halo,' and it has some kind of religious significance to them, but . . . your guess is as good as mine." She paused, and the Spartan sensed the AI's amusement. "Well, *almost* as good."

"Halo," he repeated. "Looks like we're going to be calling it 'home' for a while."

The lifeboat was too small to mount a Shaw-Fujikawa

faster-than-light drive so there was nowhere to go but the ring. There were no shouts of jubilation, no high-fives, only silence as the boat fell through the blackness of space. They were alive, but that was subject to change, and that left nothing to celebrate.

One Marine said, "This duty station really sucks." No one saw any reason to contradict him.

Rawley and her companions skidded to a halt, turned back the way they had come, and let loose with everything they had. Their weaponry included two pistols, one assault rifle, and a plasma rifle that a pilot had scooped up along the way. Not much of an arsenal but sufficient to knock three Jackals off their feet and put the aliens down for good. Rawley caved the last Jackal's skull in with her boot.

Eager to get aboard their ships, the group ducked through the docking bay hatch, closed it behind them, and ran for the Pelicans. Foehammer spotted her bird, gave thanks for the fact that it was undamaged, and ran up the ramp. As always, it was fueled, armed, and ready to fly. Frye, her copilot, dropped into position behind her, with Crew Chief Cullen bringing up the rear.

Once in the cockpit, Rawley strapped in, ran an abbreviated preflight checklist, and started the transport's engines. They joined with the rest to create a satisfying roar. The outer hatch cycled open. Loose gear tumbled into space as the bay explosively decompressed.

Moments later, the cruiser entered the ringworld's atmosphere, which meant that the transports could depart . . . but they had to do it soon. Reentry friction was already creating a wall of fire around the ship.

"Damn!" Frye exclaimed, "Look at that!" and pointed forward.

Rawley looked, saw a Covenant landing craft coming straight toward the bay, braving the heat generated by the *Autumn*'s reentry velocity. There was a limited window of opportunity to get off this sinking ship, and the Covenant bastard was right in the way.

She swore and released the safety on the Pelican's 70mm chin gun. The weapon shook the entire ship, punched holes through alien armor, and hit something vital. The enemy vessel shuddered, lost control, and spun into the *Autumn*'s hull.

"All right," the wing leader said over the ship-to-ship frequency, "Let's go down and meet our hosts. See you on the ground. Foehammer out."

She clicked off the transmitter and whispered, "Good luck."

One by one the dropships left the bay, did a series of wingovers, and dropped through the overarching ring. Rawley struggled to maintain control as the atmosphere tore at her ship. The status panel flashed a heat warning as friction created a massive thermal buildup along the Pelican's fuselage. The leading edges of the ship's short, stubby wings started to glow.

"Jeez, boss," Frye said, his teeth rattling from the constant jouncing of the Pelican, "maybe this wasn't such a good idea."

Foehammer made some adjustments, managed to improve the ship's glide angle, and glanced to her right. "If you've got a better idea," she yelled, "bring it up at the next staff meeting."

He nodded. "Yes, ma'am."

"Until then," she added, "shut the hell up and let me *fly* this thing."

The Pelican hit an air pocket, dropped like a rock, and caught itself. The transport shook like a thing possessed. Rawley screamed with anger and battled her controls as her ship plummeted toward the surface of the ring.

Covenant forces had launched a concerted attack on the command deck about fifteen minutes earlier but the defenders had beaten them back. Since that time the fighting had lessened and there were reports that at least some of the aliens were using their assault boats to leave the ship.

It wasn't clear whether that was due to the considerable number of casualties Covenant forces had suffered, or the realization that the ship was in danger of falling apart, but it hardly mattered. The important thing was that the area around the bridge was clear, which meant that Keyes, plus the command team who remained to help him, could carry out their duties without fear of being shot in the back. At least for the moment.

Their next task was to take the *Autumn* down into the atmosphere. No small order considering the fact that, like all vessels of her tonnage, the cruiser had been constructed in zero-gee conditions and wasn't well-equipped for this type of movement within atmosphere.

Keyes believed it was possible. With that in mind he planned to close with the ringworld, hand control to the subroutine that Cortana had left for that purpose, and use the last lifeboat to make his escape. Maybe the ship would pancake in the way he had planned—and maybe it wouldn't. Whatever the case, it was almost sure to be a landing that would best be experienced from a safe distance.

Keyes turned to look at the data scrolling across the nav screen and detected motion out of the corner of his eye. He looked, saw the primary weapons control station shimmer like a mirage in the desert, and rubbed his eyes. By the time the Naval officer looked for a *second* time, the phenomena had vanished.

Keyes frowned, turned back to the nav screen, and began the sequence of orders that would put the *Autumn* in the place she was *least* equipped to go: on solid ground.

Isna 'Nosolee held his breath. The human had looked straight into his eyes, given no alarm, and turned away. Surely his activities had been blessed by those who went before and from whom all knowledge flowed.

The camouflage, combined with his own talent for stealth, had proven to be extremely effective. Since he had come aboard, 'Nosolee had toured both the ship's engine room and fire control center prior to arriving on the bridge. Now, standing in front of a vent, the Elite contemplated what to do next.

The ship's AI had either been removed or destroyed, he was sure of that. At least some senior personnel remained, however—which meant there was still a chance.

In fact, based on the manner in which the other humans interacted with him, 'Nosolee felt certain that the man named "Keezz" held the position of Ship Master. A very valuable prize indeed.

But how to capture the human? He wouldn't come willingly, that was obvious, and his companions were armed. The moment 'Nosolee deactivated his camouflage they would shoot him. Individually, the humans were weaklings, but they were dangerous in packs. And animals grew all the more dangerous the nearer they came to extinction.

No, patience was the key, which meant that the Elite would have to wait. Vapor continued to roll out of the cold air vent, and the air seemed to shimmer, but no one noticed.

"All right," Keyes said, "let's put her down.... Stand by to fire the bow thrusters . . . Fire!"

The bow thrusters ignited and slowed the ship's rate of descent. The *Pillar of Autumn* wobbled for a moment as it battled the ring's gravity field, then corrected its angle of entry.

Cortana took over after that, or rather, the part of herself that she had left behind did. The *Autumn*'s thrusters fired in increments so small that they were like single notes in an ongoing melody. The highly adaptive subroutine tracked variables, monitored feedback, and made thousands of decisions per second.

The much-abused hull shuddered as it entered the atmosphere, started to shake, and sent a host of loose items tumbling to the deck. "That's as far as we can take her," Keyes announced. "Delegate all command and control functions to Cortana's cousin, and let's haul ass off this boat."

There was a ragged chorus of "Aye, ayes," as the bridge crew disengaged from the ship they had worked so hard to save, took one last look around, and drew their sidearms. The fighting had died down, but that didn't mean *all* of the Covenant forces had left.

'Nosolee watched anxiously as the humans started to leave the bridge. He waited for the last person to exit, and fell into step behind. The beginnings of a plan had started to form in his mind. It was audacious—no, make that outrageous—but the Elite figured that made the scheme all the more likely to succeed.

The lifeboat reserved for the bridge crew was close by. Six Marines had been detailed to guard it and three of them were dead. Their bodies had been dragged off to one side and laid in a row. A corporal shouted, "Attention on deck!"

Keyes said, "As you were," and gestured toward the hatch. "Thanks for waiting, son. I'm sorry about your buddies."

The corporal nodded stiffly. He must have been off duty when the attack began—one half of his face needed a shave. "Thank you, sir. They took a dozen of the bastards with them."

Keyes nodded. Three lives for twelve. It sounded like a good trade-off but how good was it really? How many Covenant troops were there, anyway? And how many would each human have to kill? He shook the thought off and jerked his thumb toward the opening. "Everybody into the boat, on the double!"

The survivors streamed onto the boat, and 'Nosolee followed, though it was difficult to avoid touching the human vermin in such tight quarters. There was a little bit of space toward the front and a handhold which would be useful once the gravity generated by the larger ship disappeared. Later, after the lifeboat landed, the Elite would find an opportunity to separate Keezz from the rest of the humans and seize him. In the meantime all he had to do was hang on, avoid detection, and make it to the surface.

The human passengers strapped in. The lifeboat exploded out of the bay, and it fell toward the ringworld below. Jets fired, the small craft stabilized, and followed a precalculated glide path toward the surface.

Keyes was seated three slots aft of the pilot. He frowned, as if looking for something, then waited for the boat to clear. He leaned toward the Marine in front of him. "Excuse me, Corporal."

"Sir?" The Marine looked exhausted, but somehow managed to snap to a form of attention, despite being belted into an acceleration chair.

"Hand me your sidearm, son."

The expression on his face made it plain that the last thing the soldier wanted to do was part company with one of his weapons, particularly in close quarters. But the Captain was the Captain, so he had very little choice. The words, "Yes, sir," were still making their way from the noncom's brain to his mouth when he felt the M6D pistol being jerked out of his holster.

Would one of the 12.7mm rounds punch its way through the lifeboat's relatively thin hull? Keyes wondered. Cause a blowout and kill everyone aboard?

He didn't know, but one thing was certain: The Covenant son of a bitch standing in this lifeboat was about to die. Keyes raised the weapon, aimed at the very center of the strange, ghostly shimmer, and pulled the trigger.

The Elite saw the movement, had nowhere to run, and was busy reaching for his own pistol when the first bullet struck.

The M6D bucked, the barrel started to rise, and the third slug from the top of the clip passed through the slit in 'Nosolee's helmet, blew his brains out through the back of his skull, and freed him from the tyranny of physical reality.

No sooner had the noise of the last shot died away than the camo generator failed, and an Elite appeared as if from thin air. The alien's body floated back toward the rear of the cabin. Thousands of globules of alien blood escorted bits of brain tissue on their journey to the lifeboat's stern.

Lieutenant Hikowa ducked as one of the Elite's

boots threatened to hit her head. She pushed the corpse away, her face impassive. The rest of the passengers were too shocked to do or say anything at all.

The Captain calmly dropped the clip from the gun, ejected the round in the chamber, and handed the weapon back to the stunned corporal.

"Thanks," Keyes said. "That thing works pretty well. Don't forget to reload it."

SECTION II

HALO

GRASP

Consistent with standard UNSC insertion protocols, Major Antonio Silva's HEV accelerated once it was launched so that it was among the first to enter Halo's atmosphere. There were a number of reasons for this, including the strongly held belief that officers should lead rather than follow, be willing to do anything their troops were asked to do, and expose themselves to the same level of danger.

There were still other reasons, however, beginning with the need to collect, sort, and organize the troops the moment their boots touched ground. Experience demonstrated that whatever the Helljumpers managed to accomplish during the first so-called golden hour would have a disproportionate effect on the success or failure of the entire mission. Especially now, as the Marines dropped onto a hostile world without any of the intel briefings, virtual reality sims, or environment-specific equipment mods they would normally receive prior to such an insertion. To offset this, the command pod was equipped with a lot of gear that the regular "eggs" weren't, including some high-powered imaging gear, and the Class C military AI required to operate it.

This particular intelligence had been programmed with a male persona, the name Wellesley—after the famous Duke of Wellington—and a personality to match. Though he was a good deal less capable than a top-level AI like Cortana, *all* of Wellesley's capabilities were focused on things military, which made him extremely useful if somewhat narrow-minded.

The HEV shook violently and flipped end for end as the interior temperature rose to 98 degrees. Sweat poured down Silva's face.

"So," Wellesley continued, his voice coming in via the officer's ear plugs, "based on the telemetry available from space, plus my analysis, it appears that the structure tagged as HS2604 will meet your needs." The AI's tone changed slightly as a conversational subroutine kicked in. "Perhaps you would like to call it 'Gawilghur,' after the fortress I conquered in India?"

"Thanks," Silva croaked as the pod inverted a second time, "but no thanks. First: *you* didn't take the fortress, Wellington did. Second: There weren't any computers in 1803. Third: none of my troops would be able to pronounce 'Gawilghur.' The designator 'Alpha Base' will do just fine."

The AI issued a passable rendition of a human sigh. "Very well, then. As I was saying, *'Alpha Base'* is located at the top of *this* butte." The curvilinear screen located just centimeters from the end of the Marine's nose seemed to shiver and the video morphed into a picture of a thick, pillarlike formation topped by a mesa with some variegated flat-roofed structures located at one end.

That was all Silva got to see before the HEV's skin started to slough away revealing the alloy crash cage that contained the officer and his equipment. The air turned cold and ripped at his clothes. A moment later, the braking-chute system engaged. Silva winced as the pod decelerated with a bone-rattling jerk. His harness bit into his shoulders and chest.

Wellesley sent an electronic signal to the rest of the Helljumpers. The remains of their HEVs turned in whatever direction was necessary in order to orient themselves on the command pod and follow it down through the atmosphere.

All except for Private Marie Postly, who heard a *snap* as her main chute tore away. There was a sickening moment of freefall, then a jolt as the back-up chute deployed. A red light flashed on the instrument panel in front of her. She started to scream on freq two, until Silva cut her off. He closed his eyes. It was the death that every Helljumper feared, but none of them talked about. Somewhere, down toward Halo's surface, Postly was about to dig her own grave.

Silva felt his HEV stabilize and took another look at the butte. It was tall enough to provide anyone who owned it with a good view of the surrounding countryside, plus the sheer cliffs would force attackers to either come by air or fight their way up along narrow paths. As a bonus, the structures located on top would provide his Marines with defensible shelter. "It looks good. I like it."

"I thought you would," Wellesley replied smugly. "There is one little problem, however."

"What's that?" Silva shouted as the last section of the HEV's skin peeled away and the slipstream tore at his mask.

"The Covenant owns this particular piece of real estate," the AI replied, calmly, "and if we want it, we'll have to take it."

DEPLOYMENT +00 HOURS:02 MINUTES:51 SECONDS
(SPARTAN 117 MISSION CLOCK) / LIFEBOAT LIMA FOXTROT
ALPHA 43, IN EMERGENCY DESCENT TO SURFACE OF HALO.

The Master Chief watched the ring open up in front of
him as the pilot guided the lifeboat in past a thick silvery edge, and down "under" the construct's inner surface, before putting the tiny ship into a shallow dive
calculated to place it on the strange landscape below.
As he looked forward, he saw mountains, hills, and a
plain that curved up and eventually out of focus as the
ring swooped upward to complete itself somewhere over
his head. The sight was beautiful, strange, and disori-
enting all at the same time.

Then the sightseeing was over as the ground came up
to meet them. The Master Chief couldn't tell whether
the lifeboat took enemy fire, suffered an engine failure,
or nicked an obstacle on final approach. It really didn't
matter; the result was the same.

The pilot had time to yell, "We're coming in too
fast!" A moment later, the hull bounced off something
solid, and the Spartan was knocked off his feet.

Pain stabbed through his temples as his helmet
slammed into the bulkhead on his way to the
deckplates—followed by clinging blackness . . .

"Chief . . . Chief . . . Can you hear me?" Cortana's voice
echoed in his head.

The Spartan opened his eyes and found himself facing the overhead light panels. They flickered and
sparked. "Yes, I can hear you," he replied. "There's no
need to shout."

"Oh, *really*?" the AI replied in an arch tone. "Maybe
you'd like to file a complaint with the Covenant. The

crash triggered a lot of radio traffic and it's my guess that the welcome wagon is on the way."

The Master Chief struggled to his feet and was just about to answer in kind when he saw the bodies. The impact of the crash had ripped the boat open and mangled the unprotected people within. No one else had survived.

There was no time to dwell on that, not if he wanted to stay alive, and keep Cortana from falling into enemy hands.

He hurried to gather as much ammo, grenades, and supplies as he could carry. He had just finished checking the pins on a quartet of frag grenades when Cortana piped up in alarm: "Warning—I've detected multiple Covenant dropships on approach. I recommend moving into those hills. If we're lucky, the Covenant will believe that everyone aboard the lifeboat died in the crash."

"Acknowledged."

Cortana's plan made sense. The Spartan surveyed the area for threats, then hurried across the canyon floor and the bridge that crossed it. The span was devoid of safety railings, and was constructed from a strange, burnished metal. Beneath the bridge, a towering waterfall thundered down a massive drop-off.

The rest of the world arched high overhead. Large outcroppings of weather-smoothed gray rock rose ahead, and a scattering of what looked like conifers reminded him of the forests he'd trained in on Reach.

There were differences, however, like the way the ring tapered up from the horizon, the manner in which its shadow fell upon the land, and the crisp, clean air that came in through his filters. It was beautiful, breathtakingly so, but potentially dangerous as well.

"Alert—Covenant dropship inbound." Cortana's voice was calm but insistent.

The prophecy soon proved correct as a large shadow floated over the far end of the bridge and the ship's engines screamed a warning. There was very little doubt that the Spartan had been spotted, so he made plans to deal with it.

He reached the end of the bridge, saw a likely-looking boulder off to his left, and hurried to take advantage of it. He skirted the cliff edge, ignoring the long drop. Careful to watch his footing, the Master Chief circled the rock and found a crevice where the boulder touched the cliff. Now, with his back to the wall, he had a chance to defend himself.

He checked his motion tracker, and realized that a pair of Covenant Banshees were practically on top of him. The alien aircraft boasted plasma cannon and fuel rod guns. Though not especially fast, they were still dangerous, especially against ground troops.

Combined with air support, the Grunts and Elites that dropped from the fork-shaped alien troop carrier were a serious threat.

He steadied his aim and sighted on the nearest Banshee. Careful not to fire early, the Spartan waited for the Banshee to come within range, then squeezed the trigger. The first assault ship came straight at him, which made it relatively easy to stay on target. Bullet impacts sparked on the Banshee's hull as his ammo counter dwindled.

The ship shuddered as at least some of the armor-piercing rounds penetrated the fuselage, pulled up out of its dive, and started to trail smoke.

The Master Chief was in no position to appreciate the results of his efforts, however, as the second Banshee swooped out of the sun and pounded the area around him with plasma fire. His shield display dropped, then pulsed red. An alarm whined in his helmet speakers.

The Master Chief returned fire. Without pause, he thumbed the magazine release and slammed a fresh clip into the receiver.

He crouched, searched the sky for targets, and spotted Banshee number one in the nick of time. He braced himself for another assault. The Spartan allowed the enemy aircraft to approach, took a slight lead, and squeezed the trigger again. The Covenant ship ran into the stream of bullets, exploded into flames, and slammed into the cliff wall.

The second ship was still up there, flying in lazy circles, but the Spartan knew better than to stand around and watch it. A half dozen red dots had appeared on his motion sensors. Each blip represented a potential assailant and most were located to his rear.

The Master Chief waited for his shields to return to their full charge, then turned, jumped up onto the boulder, and took a quick look around. The Covenant dropship had deposited a clutch of Grunts on the far side of the canyon where they were busy examining the wreckage of his lifeboat.

But that wasn't all. To his left, on his side of the bridge, *another* group of Grunts was working its way through the trees, moving in his direction. They were still a ways off, however—which gave him a few seconds to prepare.

Though not armed with the standard S2 AM Sniper's Rifle, his weapon of choice for this sort of situation, the Spartan was packing the M6D pistol that Keyes had given him. It was equipped with a 2X scope and, in the hands of an expert, it could reach out and touch someone.

The Master Chief drew the sidearm, turned to the group gathered around the wreckage, and placed the targeting circle over the nearest Grunt. In spite of the fact that they were of no immediate threat, the aliens on the other side of the canyon were in an ideal position to flank him, which meant he would deal with them first. Twelve shots rang out, and seven Grunts fell.

Satisfied that his right flank was reasonably secure, he slammed a fresh clip into the pistol and shifted his attention to the enemy troops that were emerging from the trees. This group of Grunts was closer now, *much* closer, and they opened fire. The Master Chief chose to target the most distant alien first, thereby ensuring that he would still get a crack at the others, even if they turned and tried to escape.

The pistol shots came in quick succession. The Grunts barked, hooted, and gurgled as the well-aimed bullets hurled their lifeless carcasses down the reverse slope.

When there were no more targets to fire at, the Master Chief took a moment to reload the handgun, clicked on the safety, and returned the weapon to its holster. He jumped off the boulder and crouched under an outcropping of rock.

He eyed the Banshee above. It was still there, circling well out of range, waiting to pounce should he emerge from cover. That meant he could sit there and wait for more ground forces to arrive, or he could abandon his hiding place and attempt to slip away.

The Spartan had never been one for standing around, so he readied his assault rifle and slid forward over the rock. Once on open ground it was a short dash past the scattering of dead Grunts. He crouched beneath the cover offered by a copse of trees.

He counted to three, then dashed from boulder to boulder. He leapfrogged uphill, still very much aware of the Banshee at his back, but reasonably certain he'd given the aircraft the slip.

There were no blips on his threat detector, until he topped the rise and paused to examine the terrain ahead. A telltale red dot popped onto his HUD. The Master Chief eased his way forward, waiting for the moment of contact.

Then he saw movement as hunched bodies dashed from one scrap of cover to the next. There were four of them, including a blue-armored Elite. The Elite charged recklessly forward, firing as he came.

He'd engaged such Elites before—there was some significance to the aliens' armor colors—and they always fought with reckless abandon. A thin smile touched the Master Chief's lips. He maneuvered around the Elite's shots, spun, and then returned fire. The Elite's advance stalled, and the Grunts began to fall back toward a stand of trees. His threat indicator sounded a warning and a red arrow pointed to the right. The Master Chief drew and primed an M9 HE-DP grenade.

He turned just in time to see another Elite—this one in the more senior, scarlet-colored armor—charge him. The grenade was already in hand, and the distance to the target was sufficient, so the soldier let the M9 fly. The grenade detonated with a loud *whump!* and tossed the enemy soldier into the air, while stripping a nearby tree of half its branches.

The Elite was close now, and roared a battle cry. The alien hosed the Master Chief with plasma fire. His shields dropped precipitously.

The Spartan backed away, fired his assault rifle in short controlled bursts, and finally managed to knock the remaining Elite off his feet.

With their leader down, the Grunts broke ranks and began to scamper away. The Master Chief cut their retreat short in a hail of bullets.

He eased up on the trigger, felt the silence settle in

around him, and knew he had made a mistake. The veteran had damned near blindsided him. How?

He realized with a start that he was still fighting like part of a unit. Though he was trained to act independently, he had spent most of his military career as part of a team. The Elite had managed to flank him because he was simply accustomed to one of his fellow Spartans watching out for him.

He was cut off from the chain of command, alone, and most likely surrounded by the enemy. He nodded, his face grim behind the mirrored visor. This mission would require a major revision in his tactics.

He pushed his way up through a meadow thick with knee-high, spiky grass. He could hear the distant chatter of automatic weapons fire and knew some Marines were somewhere up ahead.

He sprinted toward the sound of battle. Perhaps he wouldn't be on his own for long.

DEPLOYMENT +00 HOURS:05 MINUTES:08 SECONDS
(CAPTAIN KEYES' MISSION CLOCK) / LIFEBOAT KILO
TANGO VICTOR 17, IN EMERGENCY DESCENT TO SURFACE
OF HALO.

Maybe it was because the *Autumn*'s navigator, Ensign Lovell, was at the controls, or maybe it was simply a matter of good luck, but whatever the reason, the rest of the trip down through Halo's atmosphere was completely uneventful. So peaceful that it made Keyes nervous.

"Where would you like me to put her down, sir?" Lovell inquired, as the lifeboat skimmed a grassy plain.

"Anywhere," Keyes answered, "so long as there aren't any Covenant forces around. Some cover would be nice—since this boat will act like a magnet if we leave it out in the open."

Like most of its kind, the lifeboat had never been intended for extended atmospheric use; it flew like a rock, in fact. But the suggestion made sense, so the pilot turned toward what he had arbitrarily designated as the "west," and the point where the grasslands met a tumble of low rolling hills.

The lifeboat was low, so low that the Covenant patrol barely had time to see what it was before the tiny vessel flashed over their heads and disappeared.

The veteran Elites, both of whom were mounted on small single-seat hoversleds, Ghosts, stood to watch the lifeboat skim the plain.

The senior of the pair called the sighting in. They turned toward the hills and opened their throttles. What had promised to be a long, boring day suddenly seemed a great deal more interesting. The Elites glanced at each other, bent over their controls, and raced to see which of them could reach the lifeboat first—and which of them would score the first kill of the afternoon.

Deep in the hills ahead, Lovell fired the lifeboat's bow thrusters, dropped what flaps the stubby little wings had, and jazzed the boat's belly jets. Keyes watched in admiration as the young pilot dropped the boat into a gully where it would be almost impossible to spot, except from directly overhead. Lovell had been a troubled officer, well on his way to a dishonorable discharge, when Keyes had recruited him. He'd come a long way since then.

"Nice job," the Captain said as the lifeboat settled onto its skids. "Okay, boys and girls, let's strip this ship of everything that might be useful, and put as much distance between it and ourselves as we can. Corporal, post your Marines as sentries. Wang, Dowski, Abiad, open those storage compartments. Let's see what brand of champagne the UNSC keeps in its lifeboats. Hikowa, give me a hand with this body."

There was a certain amount of commotion as 'Nosolee's corpse was carried outside and unceremoniously dumped into a crevice, the boat was stripped, and the controls were disabled. With emergency packs on their backs, the bridge crew started up into the hills. They hadn't gone far when a sonic boom rolled over the land, the *Pillar of Autumn* roared across the sky, and dropped over the horizon to the arbitrary "south."

Keyes held his breath as he waited to see what would happen. He, like all COs, had neural implants that linked him to the ship, the ship's AI, and key personnel. There was a pause, followed by what felt like a mild earth tremor. A moment later, a terse message from Cortana's subroutine scrolled across his synchronized comm band, courtesy of his neural lace:

```
>CSR-1 :: BURST BROADCAST ::
>PILLAR OF AUTUMN IS DOWN. THOSE
  SYSTEMS WHICH REMAIN FUNCTIONAL ARE
  ON STANDBY. OPERATIONAL READINESS
  STANDS AT 8.7%.
>CSR-1 OUT.
```

It wasn't the sort of message that any commanding officer would want to receive. In spite of the fact that the *Autumn* would never swim through space again, Keyes took some small comfort from the fact that his ship still had the equivalent of a pulse, and might still come in handy.

He forced a smile. "Okay, people, what are we waiting for? Our cave awaits. The last one to the top digs the latrine."

The bridge personnel continued their climb.

In spite of efforts to keep the HEVs together, the Helljumpers came down in a landing zone that stretched approximately three kilometers in diameter. Some of the landings were classic two-point affairs in which the more fortunate Marines were able to jettison their crash cages about fifty meters off the ground, and land like sim soldiers in a training vid.

Others were a good deal less graceful, as the skeletal remains of their drop pods smashed against cliffs, dropped into lakes, and in one unfortunate case rolled into a deep ravine. As the surviving Helljumpers extricated themselves from their HEVs, a homing beacon snapped to life, and they were able to orient themselves to the red square which appeared on their transparent eye-screens. That was where Major Silva had landed, a temporary HQ had been established, and the battalion would regroup.

Each pod was stripped of extra weapons, ammo, and other supplies, which meant that the force which converged on the hot dry plateau was well equipped. Helljumpers were supposed to be able to operate without external resupply for two-week periods, and Silva was pleased that his troops had retained most of their gear, despite the difficult drop conditions.

In fact, Silva thought as he watched his troops stream in from every direction, *the only thing we lack is a fleet of Warthogs and a squad of Scorpions.* But those assets would come, oh, yes they would, shortly after the butte was wrenched from enemy hands. In the meantime, the

Helljumpers would use what ground-pounders always use: their feet.

First Lieutenant Melissa McKay had landed safely, as had most of her 130-person company. Three of her people had been killed in action on the *Autumn*, and two were missing and presumed dead. Not too bad, all things considered.

As luck would have it, McKay hit the dirt only half a klick away from the homing beacon, which meant that by the time a perimeter had been established she had already humped her gear across the hardpan, located Major Silva, and reported in. McKay was one of his favorites. The ODST officer nodded by way of a greeting. "Nice of you to drop in, Lieutenant . . . I was beginning to wonder if you'd taken the afternoon off."

"No, sir," McKay responded. "I dozed off on the way down and slept through my wake-up alarm. It won't happen again."

Silva managed to keep a straight face. "Glad to hear it."

He paused, then pointed. "You see that butte? The one with the structures on top? I want it."

McKay looked, brought her binoculars up, and looked again. The butte's range appeared along the bottom of the image and was soon chased out of the frame by coordinates that Wellesley inserted to replace the concepts of longitude and latitude which worked on most planetary surfaces, but not here.

The sun was "setting" but there was still enough light to see by. As she surveyed the target area, a Covenant Banshee took off from the top of the butte, circled out toward the "west," and came straight at her. The only thing that was surprising about that was the fact that it had taken the enemy so long to respond to their landing.

"It looks like a tough nut to crack, sir. Especially from the ground."

"It is," Silva agreed, "which is why we're going to tackle it from both the air *and* the ground. Lord only knows how they did it, but a group of Pelican pilots were able to launch their transports before the Old Man brought the *Autumn* down, and they're hidden about ten klicks north of here. We can use them to support an airborne operation."

McKay lowered her binoculars. "And the *Autumn*?"

"She's KIA back thataway," Silva replied, hooking his thumb back over a shoulder. "I'd like to go pay my final respects, but that will have to wait. What we need is a base, something we can fortify, and use to hold the Covenant at bay. Otherwise they're going to hunt our people down one, two, or three at a time."

"Which is where the butte comes in," McKay said.

"Exactly," Silva answered. "So, start walking. I want your company at the foot of that butte ASAP. If there's a path to the top I want you to find it and follow it. Once you get their attention, we'll hit them from above."

There was a loud *bang* as one of the first company's rocket jockeys fired her M19 SSM man-portable launcher, blew the incoming Banshee out of the sky, and put a period to Silva's sentence. The battalion cheered as the Banshee bits dribbled smoke and wobbled out of the sky.

"Sir, yes sir," McKay answered. "When we get up there, you can buy me a beer."

"Fair enough," Silva agreed, "but we'll have to brew it first."

Even Grunts had to be granted some rest once in a while, which was why long, cylindrical tanks equipped with air locks had been shipped to Halo's surface, where they were pumped full of methane and used in lieu of barracks.

Having survived the nearly suicidal attack on the *Autumn* by rescuing a wounded Elite, and insisting that the warrior be evacuated rather than left to die, Yayap had extended the duration of his own life, not to mention those of the Grunts directly under his command.

Now, by way of celebrating that victory, the alien soldier was curled in a tiny ball, fast asleep. One leg twitched slightly as the Grunt dreamed of making his way through the swamps of his home world, past naturally occurring pillars of fire, to the marshy estuary where he had grown up.

Then, before he could cross a row of ancient stepping-stones to the reedy hut on the far side of the family's ancestral fish pond, Gagaw shook his arm. "Yayap! Get up quick! Remember the Elite we brought down from the ship? He's outside, and he wants to see you!"

Yayap sprang to his feet. "*Me?* Did he say why?"

"No," the other Grunt replied, "but it can't be good."

That much was certainly true, Yayap reflected as he waded through the chaos of equipment that hung in untidy clusters along the length of the cylinder. He entered the communal lavatory, and hurried to don his armor, breathing apparatus, and weapons harness.

Which was more dangerous, he wondered, to show up disheveled, and have the Elite find fault with his appearance, or to show up later because he had taken the time required to ensure that his appearance would be acceptable? Dealing with Elites always seemed to involve such conundrums, which was one of the many reasons that Yayap had a hearty dislike for their kind.

Finally, having decided to favor speed over appearance, Yayap entered the air lock, waited for it to cycle him through, and emerged into the bright sunlight. The first thing he noticed was that the sentries, who could normally be found leaning against the tank discussing how awful the rations were, stood at rigid attention.

"Are you the one called Yayap?" The deep voice came from behind him and caused the Grunt to jump. He turned, came to attention, and tried to look soldierly. "Yes, Commander."

The Elite named Zuka 'Zamamee wore no helmet. He couldn't, not with the dressing that was wrapped around his head, but the rest of his armor was still in place. It was spotlessly clean, as were the weapons he wore. "Good. The medics told me that you and your file not only pulled me off the ship—but forced the assault boat to bring me down to the surface."

Yayap felt a lump form in his throat and struggled to swallow it. The pilot had been somewhat reluctant, citing orders to wait for a full load of troops before breaking contact with the human ship, but Gagaw had been quite insistent—even going so far as to pull his plasma pistol and wave it about.

"Yes, Commander," Yayap replied, "but I can explain—"

"There's no need," 'Zamamee replied. Yayap almost jumped; the Elite's voice lacked the customary bark of command. It sounded almost . . . reassuring.

Yayap was anything but reassured.

"You saw that a superior had been wounded," the Elite continued, "and did what you could to ensure that he received timely medical treatment. That sort of initiative is rare, especially among the lower classes."

Yayap stared at the Elite, unable to reply. He felt

disoriented. In his universe, Elites didn't offer accolades.

"To show my appreciation I've had you transferred."

Yayap *liked* the normally sleepy unit to which he was attached, and had no desire to leave it. "Transferred, Commander? To what unit?"

"Why, to *my* unit," the Elite replied, as if nothing could be more natural. "My assistant was killed as we boarded the human ship. *You* will take his place."

Yayap felt his spirits plummet. The Elites who acted as special operatives of the Prophets were fanatics, chosen for their limitless willingness to risk their lives—and the lives of those under their command. "Th-thank you, Commander," Yayap stuttered, "but I don't deserve such an honor."

"Nonsense!" the Elite replied. "Your name has already been added to the rolls. Gather your belongings, say good-bye to your cohort, and meet me here fifteen units from now. I'm scheduled to appear in front of the Council of Masters later this evening. You will accompany me."

"Yes, Commander," Yayap said obediently. "May I inquire as to the purpose of the meeting?"

"You may," 'Zamamee replied, allowing a hand to touch the bandage that circled his head. "The human who inflicted this wound was a warrior so capable that he represents a danger to the entire battle group. An individual who, if our records can be believed, is personally responsible for the deaths of thousands of our soldiers."

Yayap felt his knees start to give. "By himself, Commander?"

"Yes. But never fear, those days are over. Once I receive authorization, you and I will find this human."

"*Find* him?" Yayap exclaimed, protocol forgotten. "*Then* what?"

"Then," 'Zamamee growled, "we will kill him."

The dawn air was cold, and McKay could see her breath as she stared upward and wondered what awaited her. Half the night had been spent marching across the stretch of intervening hardpan to get into position below the butte, and the other half had been spent between trying to find a way up to the top, and grabbing a little bit of sleep.

The second task had been easy, perhaps a little *too* easy, because other than a sloppily constructed barricade, the foot of the four-foot-wide ramp was entirely unguarded. Still, the last thing the Covenant expected was for a human ship to appear out of Slipspace, and land infantry on the surface of the construct. Viewed in that light, a certain lack of preparation was understandable.

In any case, the path started at ground level, spiraled steadily upward, and hadn't been used in some time judging from what she could see. That's the way it *appeared*, anyway, although it was hard to be sure from below, and Silva was understandably reluctant to send in one of the Pelicans lest it give the plan away.

No, McKay and her troops would have to wind their way up along the narrow path, engage whatever defenses the Covenant might have in place, and hope that the Pelicans arrived quickly enough to take the pressure off.

The Lieutenant eyed the readout on the transparent boom-mounted eye-screen attached to her helmet, waited for the countdown to complete itself, and started up the steep incline. Company Sergeant Tink Carter turned to face the men and women lined up behind him. "What the hell are you waiting for? An engraved invitation? Let's get it in gear."

While B Company marched toward the butte, and C Company marched off to rendezvous with the Pelicans, the rest of the battalion used the remaining hours of darkness to prepare for the following day under Major Silva's watchful eye. Wireless sensors were placed two hundred meters out and monitored by Wellesley; three-person fireteams took up positions a hundred fifty meters out; and a rapid response team was established to support them.

There wasn't any natural cover here, so the Helljumpers moved their gear up onto a low rise, and did what they could to place fortifications around it. Dirt excavated from the firing pits was used to build a low barrier around the battalion's perimeter, connecting trenches were dug, and a landing pad was established so that Pelicans could put down within the battalion's footprint.

Now, standing at the very highest point of the pad, and gazing off to the west, Silva listened as Wellesley spoke into his ear. "I have good news and bad news. The *good* news is that Lieutenant McKay has started her climb. The *bad* news is that the Covenant is about to attack from the west."

Silva lowered his glasses, turned, and looked to the west. An enormous dust cloud had appeared during the five minutes that had passed since he looked that way. "What *kind* of attack?" the ODST officer demanded curtly.

"That's rather difficult to say," Wellesley replied deliberately, "especially without the ships, satellites, and recon drones that I normally rely on for information. However, judging from the amount of dust, plus my knowledge of the Covenant weapons inventory, it looks like an old-fashioned cavalry charge similar to the one that Napoleon threw my way at Waterloo."

"You weren't at Waterloo," Silva reminded the AI as he brought the binoculars up to his eyes. "But, assuming you're correct, what are they riding?"

"Rapid attack and reconnaissance vehicles—Ghosts," Wellesley replied pedantically. "Perhaps a hundred of these Ghosts . . . judging from the dust."

Silva swore. The timing couldn't have been worse. The Covenant had to respond to his presence, he knew that, but he had hoped for a little more time. Now, with fully half his strength committed elsewhere, he was left with roughly two hundred troops. Still, they were ODST troops, the best in the UNSC.

"All right," Silva said grimly, "if they want to charge, let's give them the traditional counter. Order the pickets to pull back, tell Companies A and D to form an infantry square, and let's get all the backup ammo below ground level. I want assault weapons in the pits, launchers halfway up the slope, and snipers up on the pad. No one fires until I give the command."

Like Silva, Wellesley knew that the Roman legions had used the infantry square to good effect, as had Lord Wellington, and many since. The formation, which consisted of a box with ranks of troops all facing outward, was extremely hard to break.

The AI relayed the instructions to the troops, who, though surprised to be deployed in such an archaic way, knew exactly what to do. By the time the Ghosts arrived and washed around the rise like an incoming tide, the square was set.

Silva studied the rangefinder in his tac display and waited until the enemy was in range. He keyed the all-hands freq and gave the order: "Fire! *Fire!*"

Sheets of armor-piercing bullets sleeted through the air. The lead machines staggered as if they had run into a wall, Elites tumbled out of their seats, and a runaway machine skittered to the east.

But there were a lot of the attack vehicles and as the oncoming horde sprayed the Marines with plasma fire, ODSTs began to fall. Fortunately, the Covenant vehicles couldn't get a fix on the Marines' position, which meant that the rise would continue to offer the humans a good deal of protection, so long as the Ghosts weren't allowed to climb the slopes.

Also operating in the Helljumpers' favor were the skittish nature of the machines themselves, some poor driving, and a lack of overall coordination. Many of the Elites seemed eager to score a kill: They broke formation and raced ahead of their comrades. Silva saw one attack craft take fire from another Ghost, which crashed into a third machine, which subsequently burst into flame.

The majority of the Elites were quite competent, however, and after some initial confusion, they went to work devising tactics intended to break the square. A gold-armored Elite led the effort. First, rather than allowing the riders to circle the humans in whatever direction they chose, he forced them into a counterclockwise rotation. Then, having reduced collisions by at least a third, the enemy officer chose the lowest pit, the one against which the fixed plasma cannons would be most effective, and drove at it time and time again. Marines were killed, the outgoing fire slackened, and one corner of the square became vulnerable.

Silva countered by sending a squad to reinforce the weak point, ordering his snipers to concentrate their fire on the gold Elite, and calling on the rocket jockeys to provide rotating fire. If the humans' launchers had a weakness, it was the fact that they could only fire two rockets before being reloaded, which left at least five seconds between volleys. By alternating fire, and concentrating on the Ghosts closest to the hill, the Marine defenders were able to leverage the weapons' effectiveness.

This strategy proved effective. Wrecked, burned, and mangled Ghosts formed a metal barricade, further protecting the humans from plasma fire, and interfering with new attacks.

Silva lifted his binoculars and surveyed the smoke-laced battle area. He offered a silent thanks to whatever deity watched over the infantry. Had *he* led the assault, Silva would have sent in air support first to pin the Helljumpers down—followed by Ghosts from the west. His opposite number had been trained differently, had too much confidence in his mechanized troops, or was just plain inexperienced.

Whatever the reason, the Banshees were thrown into the mix late, apparently as an afterthought. Silva's rocket jockeys knocked two of the aircraft out of the air on the first pass, nailed another one on the second pass, and sent the fourth running south with smoke trailing from its failing engines.

Finally, with the gold Elite dead, and more than half of their number slaughtered, the remaining Elites withdrew. Some of the Ghosts remained untouched, but at least a dozen of the surviving ships carried extra riders, and most were riddled with bullet holes. Two, their engines destroyed, were towed off the field of battle.

This is why we need the butte, Silva thought as he surveyed the carnage, *to avoid another victory like this one.* Twenty-three Helljumpers were dead, six were critically injured, and ten had lesser wounds.

Static burped in his ear, and McKay's voice crackled across the command freq. *"Blue One to Red One, over."*

Silva swung toward the butte, raised his glasses, and saw smoke drift away from a point about halfway up the pillarlike formation. "This is Red One—go. Over."

"I think we have their attention, sir."

The Major grinned. It looked more like a grimace. "Roger that, Blue One. We put on a show for them, as well. Hang tight . . . help is on the way."

McKay ducked back beneath a rocky overhang as the latest batch of plasma grenades rained down from above. Some kept on falling, others found targets, bonded to them, and exploded seconds later.

A trooper screamed as one of the alien bombs landed on top of his rucksack. A sergeant yelled, "Dump the pack!" but the Marine panicked, and backpedaled off the path. The grenade exploded and sprayed the cliff face with what looked like red paint. The infantry officer winced.

"Roger, Red One. Sooner would be a whole helluva lot better than later. Over and out."

Wellesley ordered the Pelicans into the air as Silva stared out over the plain. He wondered if his plan would work, and if he could stomach the price.

CHAPTER

THREE

Up ahead the Master Chief saw a light so bright that it seemed to compete with the sun. It originated somewhere beyond the rocks and trees ahead, surged up between the horns of a large U-shaped construct, and raced into the sky where the planet Threshold served as a pastel backdrop. Was the pulse some sort of beacon? Part of what held the ringworld together? There was no way for him to know.

Cortana had already warned the Spartan that a group of Marines had crash-landed in the area, so he wasn't surprised to hear the rattle of automatic weapons fire or the characteristic whine as Covenant energy weapons answered in kind.

He eased his way through the scrub and onto the hillside above the U-shaped edifice and the blocky structures that surrounded it. He could see a group of Grunts, Jackals, and Elites dashing back and forth as they tried to overwhelm a group of Marines.

Rather than charge in, assault weapon blazing, the Master Chief chose to use his M6D pistol instead. He raised the weapon, activated the 2X magnification, and took careful aim. A series of well-placed shots knocked a trio of Grunts off their feet.

Before the Covenant forces could locate where the incoming fire had originated, the Master Chief opened fire on a blue-armored Elite. It took a full magazine to put the warrior down, but it beat the hell out of going toe-to-toe with the alien when there wasn't any need to.

The quick, unexpected sniping attack gave the Marines the opportunity they needed. There was a quick flurry of fire as the Spartan made his way down the slope, paused to strip some plasma grenades off a dead Grunt, and was welcomed by a friendly private. "Good to see you, Chief. Welcome to the party."

The Spartan's reply was a curt nod. "Where's your CO, Private?"

"Back there," the Marine said. He turned and called over his shoulder. "Hey, Sarge!"

The Master Chief recognized the tough-looking Sergeant who trotted to join them. He'd last seen Sergeant Johnson during a search-and-destroy run aboard one of Reach's orbital docking facilities.

"What's your status here, Sergeant?"

"It's a mess," Johnson growled. "We're scattered all over this valley." He paused, and added in a quiet voice, "We called for evac, but until you showed up, I thought we were done for."

"Don't worry," Cortana said over the Spartan's external speakers, *"we'll stay here till evac arrives. I've been in touch with AI Wellesley. The Helljumpers are in the process of taking over some Covenant real estate—and one of the Pelicans has been dispatched to pick you up."*

"Glad to hear it," Johnson replied. "Some of my people need medical attention."

"Here comes another Covenant dropship," the Private put in. "It's time to roll out the welcome mat!"

"Okay, Bisenti," Johnson barked. "Re-form the squad. Let's get to work."

The Master Chief looked up and saw that the Marine was correct—another Covenant landing craft hovered for a moment, then dropped close to the ground. The oddly shaped vehicle dipped slightly, and the mandible structures that formed the bulk of the dropship's fuselage hinged open. A clutch of Grunts and an Elite dropped to the ground.

The Master Chief moved fifty meters to the right, and raised his pistol once again. In seconds, a team of Marines poured fire into the Covenant LZ and flushed them out. As the aliens scattered and dove for cover, the Spartan put them down one by one.

There was a brief respite, and the Master Chief paused to survey the situation. Cortana pulled up the Marine positions, tagged them as FIRETEAM C, and highlighted their locations on his HUD. Several of them had climbed the large structure that dominated the area, and the rest patrolled the perimeter.

He had just readied his assault rifle when a Marine voice called out: "Contact! Enemy dropship sighted! They're trying to flank us!"

Seconds later, the Spartan's motion sensor painted a contact—a large one—nearby. He stayed close to a large boulder and used it for cover, then cautiously checked for targets.

The dropship disgorged another contingent of troops—including a trio of Jackals. Their distinctive, glowing shields flared as Sergeant Johnson's men opened fire. Bullets ricocheted as the birdlike aliens crouched behind their protective devices, like medieval footmen forming a shield wall.

Behind them, more Grunts and a blue Elite spread out in an enveloping formation. It was a good tactic, particularly if there were more dropships inbound. Eventually, the Covenant would wear down the Marine defenses and overrun the position.

There was just one problem with their plan: The Master Chief was in a perfect flanking position. He crouched, then sprinted forward into the Jackal's line. His assault rifle barked and bullets tore into the exposed aliens. They had barely hit the ground as the Spartan spun, primed a captured plasma grenade, and threw it at the Elite, almost thirty meters away.

The alien only had time to roar in surprise before the glowing plasma orb struck him in the center of his helmet. The weapon fused to the alien's helmet and began to pulse a sickly blue-white. A moment later, as the alien attempted to tear off his helmet, the grenade detonated.

After that it was a relatively simple matter for the Master Chief to move through the ruins and hunt down the remainder of the Covenant reaction force.

A welcome voice sounded from his radio receiver. *"This is Echo 419. Does anyone read me? Repeat: Any UNSC personnel, respond."*

Cortana was quick to reply on the same frequency. *"Roger, Echo 419, we read you. This is Fireteam Charlie. Is that you, Foehammer?"*

"Roger, Fireteam Charlie," Foehammer drawled, *"it's good to hear from you!"*

There was a distant rumbling, and the Master Chief turned to identify the source of the noise. In the distance, he saw movement—lifeboats, trailing smoke and fire as their friction-heated hulls tore through the atmosphere.

"They're coming in fast," Cortana warned. "If they make it down, the Covenant will be right on top of them."

The Chief nodded. "Then we should find them first."

"Foehammer, we need you to disengage your Warthog. The Master Chief and I are going to see if we can save some soldiers."

"Roger."

The Pelican rounded the spire of the alien structure, circled the area once, then hovered above the crest of a nearby hill. Slung beneath the Pelican was a four-wheeled vehicle—an M12 LRV Warthog. The light reconnaissance vehicle hung beneath the dropship for a moment, then dropped to the ground as Foehammer released it from her craft. The Warthog bounced once on its heavy suspension, slid five meters down the hill, then was still.

"Okay, Fireteam Charlie—one Warthog deployed," Foe-hammer said. *"Saddle up and give 'em hell!"*

"Roger, Foehammer, stand by to load survivors and evac them to safety."

"That's affirmative . . . Foehammer out."

As the Marines sprinted for the Pelican, the Master Chief made his way to the Warthog. The all-terrain vehicle was mounted with a standard M41 light anti-aircraft gun, or LAAG. The weapon fired five hundred rounds of 12.7×99mm armor-piercing rounds per minute and was effective on both ground and airborne targets. The vehicle was capable of carrying up to three soldiers, and one Marine had already taken his place behind the gun. His rank and ID scrolled across the Spartan's display: PFC. FITZGERALD, M.

"Hey, Chief!" Fitzgerald said. "Sergeant Johnson said you could use a gunner."

The Spartan nodded. "That's right, Private. There's two boatloads of Marines on the far side of that ridge, and we're going after them."

Fitzgerald pulled the gun's charging lever back toward his chest, and released it with a metallic snap. A shell slipped into the first of the weapon's three barrels. "I'm your man, Chief! Let's roll."

The Master Chief pulled himself up behind the wheel, started the engine, and strapped himself into the seat. The engine roared and the wheels kicked up geysers of dirt. The Warthog accelerated to the top of a rise, caught some air, and landed with a spine-jarring thump.

"I put a nav indicator on your HUD," Cortana said, "just follow the arrow."

"Figures," the Spartan said, a hint of amusement in his level voice. "You always were a backseat driver."

True to the aircraft's nickname, Keyes heard the Banshee long before he actually caught a glimpse of the attack aircraft. The alien pilot had them on his sensors—Keyes was sure of that—and it wouldn't be long before another team dropped out of the sky in an attempt to root them out.

The hills, which had seemed so welcoming when the command party first landed, had been transformed into a hellish landscape where the humans scuttled from one rocky crevice to the next, always on the run, and never allowed to rest.

They had faced capture on three different occasions, but each time Corporal Wilkins and his Marines had managed to blow a hole in the Covenant's tightening net and lead the naval personnel to safety.

But for how much longer? Keyes wondered. The continuous scrambling through the rocks, the lack of sleep, and the constant danger not only left them exhausted but levied a toll on morale as well.

Abiad, Lovell, and Hikowa were still in fairly good shape, as were Wang and Singh, but Ensign Dowski had started to crack. It had started with a little self-concerned whining, grown into a stream of nonstop complaints, and now threatened to escalate into something worse.

The humans were gathered in a dry grotto. Jagged rocks projected over their heads to provide some protection from the Banshee above. Wang knelt next to the thin, dirt-choked stream that gushed through the rocky passageway. He splashed water on his face. Singh was busy filling the command party's canteens while Dowski sat on a rock and glowered. "They know where we are," the junior officer said accusingly, as if her commanding officer were somehow at fault.

Keyes sighed. " 'They know where we are, *sir*.' "

"Okay," the Ensign replied, "They know where we are, *sir*. So why continue to run? They'll catch us in the end."

"Maybe," Keyes agreed as he dabbed ointment onto a burst blister, "and maybe not. I've been in contact with both Cortana *and* Wellesley. They're both busy at the moment, but they'll send help as soon as they can. In the meantime, we tie up as many of their resources as possible, avoid capture, and kill some of the bastards if we can."

"For what?" Dowski demanded. "So *you* can make Admiral? I submit that we've done all we could reasonably be expected to do, that the longer we delay the harsher the Covenant will be. It makes sense to surrender *now*."

"And you are an *idiot*," Lieutenant Hikowa put in, her eyes blazing with uncharacteristic anger. "First of all, the Captain rates the honorific 'sir.' You will render that honorific or I will plant my foot in your ass.

"Secondly, use your brain, assuming that you have one. The Covenant doesn't take prisoners, everyone knows that, so surrender equals death."

"Oh, yeah?" Dowski said defiantly. "Well, why haven't they already killed us then? They could strafe us with cannons, fire rockets into the rocks, or drop bombs on our position, but they haven't. Explain *that*."

"Explain *this*," Singh said, inserting the barrel of his M6D into the Ensign's left ear. "I'm starting to think that you look a lot like a Grunt. Lovell . . . check her face. I'll bet it peels right off."

Keyes closed the fastener on the light-duty deck shoes, wished he had a pair of combat boots like the Marines wore, and knew Dowski was partially correct, insubordination aside. It *did* seem as though the aliens were intent on capturing his party rather than killing them, but why? It didn't square with their behavior in the past.

Of course, the Covenant had changed tactics on him before—when he'd beaten the tar out of them at Sigma Octanus, and again when they'd returned the favor at Reach.

The officer watched the tableau as it unfolded in front of him. Hikowa stood with her fists on her hips, face contorted with anger, while Singh screwed his weapon into Dowski's ear. The rest of the bridge crew were frozen, uncertain. The Marines weren't present, thank God, but it would be naïve to think they weren't aware of the Ensign's opinions, or of the discord among their superiors. The enlisted ranks *always* knew, one way or another. So, what to do? Dowski wasn't about to change her mind, that was obvious, and she was becoming a liability.

The Banshee whined loudly as it passed over the grotto for the second time. They needed to move and do it soon.

"Okay," Keyes said, "you win. I should charge you with cowardice, insubordination, and dereliction of duty, but I'm a little pressed for time. So I hereby give you permission to surrender. Hikowa, relieve her of her weapon, ammo, and pack. Singh, truss her up. Nothing too tight . . . just enough so she can't follow us."

A look of horror came over Dowski's face. "You're going to leave me? All by myself? With no supplies?"

"No," Keyes answered calmly, "you *wanted* to surrender, remember? The Covenant will keep you company, and as for supplies, well, I have no idea what sort of rations they eat, but it should be interesting if they allow you a last meal. Bon appétit."

Dowski started to babble incoherently but Singh grew tired of it, shoved a battle dressing into the Ensign's mouth, and used some all-purpose repair tape to hold it in place. He used some of the same tape to hog-tie the officer. "That should keep her out of trouble for a while."

Rocks clattered as Corporal Wilkins and two of his fellow Marines made their way down the streambed. The noncom saw Dowski, nodded as if everything were perfectly normal, and looked to Keyes. "A Covenant dropship landed a squad of Elites about one klick to the south, sir. It's time to move."

The Naval officer nodded. "Thank you, Corporal. The command team is ready. Please lead the way."

Meanwhile, a few hundred meters above, and half a klick to the north, the Elite named Ado 'Mortumee put his Banshee into a wide turn, and watched the dropship touch down. There weren't many places to land, which meant that once on the ground his fellow Elites would still have a ways to go.

Rather than drop hundreds of troops onto the rocky hillsides, and leave them to scramble over the exhausting up-and-down terrain, the Covenant command structure decided to use its air superiority to locate the humans and capture them.

And there, 'Mortumee mused, *is the problem. Locating the aliens is one thing—capturing them is another.* During the time since they had landed, the humans had proven themselves to be quite resourceful. Not only had they evaded capture, they had killed six of their pursuers, who, acting under strict orders to take the aliens alive, were at a considerable disadvantage. It made more sense simply to kill the humans. Of course, he was a mere pilot and soldier, not privy to the machinations of the Prophets or the Ship Masters.

After the human lifeboat had been located, it wasn't long before Covenant scouts found Isna 'Nosolee's body, and ran a check on his identity. Intelligence was notified, official wheels began to turn, and the Covenant commanders were confronted with a problem: Why would an Ossoona risk his life to board a human lifeboat and ride it to the surface? The answer seemed obvious: Because someone important was on that boat.

All of which served to explain why none of the humans had been killed. There was no way to know *which* alien 'Nosolee had been after—so all of them had to be preserved. 'Mortumee glanced down at the instruments arrayed in front of him. A change! A string of seven heat blobs was winding its way to arbitrary "north," while one remained behind. What did that signify?

It wasn't long before 'Mortumee's Banshee circled above the grotto. Dowski wrestled to free herself from the tape, and the Covenant closed in around her.

Smoke swirled around the top of the butte as a Pelican pilot made use of his 70mm chin gun to silence a Covenant gun emplacement. Satisfied that the Covenant plasma turret—a powerful weapon that could be easily deployed and recovered—was silent, he dropped down to within four feet of the top of the butte.

Fifteen ODST Helljumpers—three more than the Pelican's operational maximum—leaped from the Pelican's troop bay and fanned out.

Cramming extra troops into a Pelican was a risky move, but Silva wanted to put as many soldiers as possible on the mesa, and Lieutenant "Cookie" Peterson knew his ship. The Pelican was still in reasonably good shape, he had the best maintenance crew in the Navy—what more could a pilot ask for?

Peterson felt the dropship drift upward as the Marines bailed out, and he fought to keep the ship steady and level. He spotted movement in the landing zone. The chin gun—linked to his helmet sensors—followed the movement of Peterson's head. He spotted a column of Covenant troopers and fired. The heavy rotary cannon uttered a throaty roar and pounded the enemy formation into a puddle of blue-green paste.

As the last of the Helljumpers jumped off, the Crew Chief yelled "Clear!" over the intercom. Peterson fired the ship's belly jets, demanded additional power from the twin turbine engines, and left the butte behind.

"This is Echo 136," the pilot said into his mike. "We are green, clean, and extremely mean. Over."

"Roger that," Wellesley replied emotionlessly. "Please return to waypoint two-five for another load of troopers. And, if you're going to insist on poetry, try some Kipling. You might find some of it rather instructive. Over and out."

Peterson grinned, directed a one-fingered salute in the general direction of battalion HQ, and banked the dropship into a wide turn.

Resistance had slackened within minutes of the first landing, which allowed Lieutenant Melissa McKay and the surviving members of her company to advance upward. A significant number of the path's defenders were pulled away in a last-ditch attempt to hold their position.

McKay discovered that the path was blocked by an ancient rockfall about thirty meters up, but saw the side door that was located just downhill of it, and knew what the aliens had been trying to defend. Here was the back door, the way she could enter the butte's interior, and push upward from there.

Plasma fire stuttered out of the entryway, struck the cliff above her head, and blew rocky divots out of the smooth surface.

McKay motioned for her troops to retreat back around the pillar's broad curvature, and waved a hand in the air. "Hey, Top! I need a launcher!"

The company sergeant was six troopers back so that a single well-placed grenade couldn't kill both leaders at once. He signaled assent, bawled an order, and passed one of the M19s forward.

McKay accepted the weapon from the private behind her, checked to ensure that it packed a full load of rockets, and inched around the curve. Plasma fire sizzled out of the door, but the officer forced herself to remain perfectly still. She triggered the weapon's 2X scope, sighted carefully, and squeezed the trigger. The tube jumped as the 102mm rocket raced away, sailed through the hole, and detonated with a loud roar.

There must have been some ammo stored inside, because there was a blue-white secondary explosion which shook the rock beneath the ODST officer's boots. A gout of fire flared from the side of the cliff.

It was difficult to imagine anyone or anything having survived such a blast, so McKay passed the launcher to the rear, and waved her troops forward.

There was a cheer as the Marines ran up the path,

shouldered their way through the smoke, and entered the butte's ancient interior. There were bodies, or what *had* been bodies. Fortunately, the tunnel was intact.

A couple of troopers collected plasma weapons, tried them out on the nearest wall, and added them to their personal armament.

Others, McKay included, stared up through a thirty-meter-wide well toward the circle of daylight above. She saw a shadow pass overhead as one of the Pelicans dropped even more Helljumpers onto the mesa. The distant *thump!* of a frag grenade detonation made dust and loose soil tumble down on them.

"Hey, Loot," Private Satha said, "what's the deal with *this*?"

Satha stomped on the floor and it rang in response. That was when McKay realized that she and her troops were standing on a large metal grating.

"What's it for?" the private wondered aloud. "To keep us out?"

McKay shook her head. "No, it looks *old*, too old to have been put in place by the Covenant."

"I found a lift!" one of the Marines yelled. "That's what it looks like, anyway—come check it out!"

McKay went to investigate. Was this a way to reach the mesa? Her boot dislodged a shell casing which fell through one of the grating's rectangular holes and dropped into the darkness below. It was a long time before it could be heard clanging off ancient stone.

Silva, Wellesley, and the rest of the Major's headquarters organization were on top of the butte waiting for her by the time McKay rode the anti-grav lift to the surface and stepped out into the harsh sunlight. She blinked as she looked around.

Bodies lay everywhere. Some wore Marine green but the vast majority were dressed in the rainbow colors that the Covenant used to identify its various ranks and specialties. A squad of Helljumpers moved through the carnage, searching for wounded humans, and kicking corpses to make sure that the enemy soldiers were actually dead. One of them attempted to rise and received a burst from an assault weapon for his trouble.

"Welcome to Alpha Base," Major Silva said as he arrived at McKay's side. "You and your company did a damn good job, Lieutenant. Wellesley will have the rest of the battalion up here within the hour. It looks like I owe you that beer."

"Yes, sir," McKay replied happily. "You sure as hell do."

The tunnel was *huge*, plenty large enough to handle a Scorpion tank, which meant that the Master Chief had little difficulty steering the Warthog through the initial opening.

He'd almost missed the entry, at the bottom of a large dry wash. Cortana's sensors had identified the entrance to the tunnel system. "It's not a natural formation," she'd warned him. That meant someone built it. Logically, it meant that the tunnel *led* somewhere— and it might shave precious time off his search for the crashed lifeboats.

Once inside, things became a little more difficult as the Spartan was forced to maneuver the LRV up ramps, through a series of tight turns, and right to the very edge of a pit.

A quick recon confirmed that the gap was narrow enough to jump, assuming the 'Hog had a running start. The Master Chief backed away, warned the gunner to hang on, and put his foot to the floor. The LRV raced up the ramp, sailed through air, and jounced to a hard landing on the other side.

"I'm picking up lots of Covenant traffic," Cortana said. "It sounds like Major Silva and the Helljumpers have captured an enemy position. If we can round up the rest of the survivors, and find Captain Keyes, we'll have a chance to coordinate some serious resistance."

"Good," the Master Chief answered. "It's about time something broke our way."

The Warthog's headlights swung across ancient walls as the Spartan turned the wheel, and the LRV emerged into a large open area dotted with mysterious installations. It was dark; the road ended in front of a deep chasm. It wasn't long before Covenant troops emerged like maggots spilling out of a rotting corpse.

Plasma fire splashed across the Warthog's windscreen. The Spartan dove from the vehicle, crouched near the driver's-side front tire, and drew his pistol. Fitzgerald opened up with the LAAG and swept the area with fire. Spent shell casings rained all around them.

The Chief peered over the edge of the Warthog. They were dangerously exposed. The roadway they'd been using was devoid of cover, elevated roughly three meters above the rest of the massive vaulted chamber. Worse, it bisected the chamber, which left them exposed on virtually all sides.

The giant enclosure was dimly lit; visibility was poor and the muzzle flash from the Warthog's gun played hell with his night vision. He blinked his eyes to clear them, then activated his pistol's scope.

The metal floor dropped away to either side, and every surface was engraved with the strange geometric patterns that festooned Halo's mysterious architecture. Set well back from their position were a number of small structures, pillars, and support pylons. The Covenant were dug in among them.

A Grunt popped out from cover, his plasma pistol glowing green—he'd overcharged the weapon. The little SOBs liked to dump energy into the weapon, and discharge it all at once. It drained the weapon damn quick, but it also inflicted hellish damage on a target. A pulsing green-white orb of plasma sizzled past the Warthog.

The Master Chief returned fire, then dropped back behind the 'Hog. "Fitzgerald," he barked. "Keep fire on them. I'll move up on the left and take them out."

"Got it." The tribarreled gun thundered, and fire hosed the Covenant position.

The Spartan was prepared to charge ahead and into the fight when his motion sensor painted movement from the rear. The LAAG ceased fire as Fitzgerald yelled in pain and fell from the back of the Warthog. The Marine's helmet cracked into the metal floor.

A shard of glassy, translucent material, tapered to a wicked point, protruded from the Marine's bicep. The shard glowed a ghostly purple. "God *damn* it!" Fitzgerald grunted, as he tried to regain his footing. Two seconds later, the purple shard exploded, and blood sprayed from the wound. Fitzgerald howled in agony.

There was no time to tend to Fitzgerald's injuries. A pair of Grunts charged up the slight incline and opened fire. A barrage of the glassy projectiles arced toward them and ricocheted madly from the Warthog.

They were too close. The Chief fired at the nearest Grunt, three shots in succession. A trio of bullet pocks formed a neat cluster in the alien's chest. The Grunt's partner squealed in anger and brought his gun to bear—an odd, hunchbacked device with a ridge of the glassy projectiles protruding from it like dorsal fins. The weapon spat pink needles at him.

He sidestepped and slammed the butt of the pistol

into the Grunt's head. The alien's skull caved in. He kicked the corpse back down the incline.

Fitzgerald had crawled to cover behind the Warthog. He was pale, but didn't look like he was suffering from too much shock yet. The Spartan grabbed a first aid kit and expertly treated the wound. Self-sealing biofoam filled the wound, packed it off, and numbed it. The young Marine would need some stitches and some time to rebuild the torn, savaged muscle of his arm, but he'd live—if either of them made it out of here alive.

"You okay?" he asked the wounded soldier. Fitzgerald nodded, wiped sweat from his forehead with a bloody hand, then struggled back to his feet. Without another word, he manned the LAAG.

It took the better part of fifteen minutes for the Master Chief and the gunner to sweep the area clear of Covenant forces. The Spartan patrolled the perimeter. To the left of the Warthog, the chamber stretched roughly eighty meters, then ended—as did the road ahead—in a massive chasm.

"Any ideas?" he asked Cortana.

There was a brief pause as the AI examined the data. "The roadway ahead ends in a gap, but it's logical to assume that there's some kind of bridge mechanism. Find the controls that extend the bridge and we should be able to get across."

He nodded. He turned back and crossed the roadway and headed off to the right of the parked Warthog. As he passed the vehicle, he called over his shoulder to Fitzgerald. "Wait here. I'm going to find us a way across."

The Master Chief marched across the chamber, and checked the odd structures that dotted the landscape. Some were illuminated by the dim glow from some kind of light panels, but there was no indication what powered them, or what the structures contained.

He frowned. There didn't seem to be any sign of mechanisms or controls. He was about to head back to the Warthog and backtrack their course, then stopped. He stared at one of the massive pillars that stretched to the ceiling far overhead.

There was nothing down here, but perhaps the mechanism he sought was above them.

He moved as far to the end of the area as he could. Unlike the opposite side of the chamber, this half was bordered by a high, grooved metal wall. He followed the edge of the barrier and was gratified to locate a gap in the wall—a doorway.

Inside, a ramp led up twenty meters, then turned ninety degrees to the left. The Spartan drew his pistol, activated his helmet lamp, and crept up the ramp.

His caution was justified. As he reached the top, his motion sensor showed a contact—right on top of him. He ducked around the corner just in time to meet the charge of a crimson-armored Elite. The Elite growled a challenge and swung a vicious blow at the Chief's head.

He ducked, and his shields took the brunt of the blow. He fired at point-blank range, not even bothering to aim. The Elite reared and returned fire and plasma blasts slashed through the narrow corridor.

In one fluid motion, the Chief drew, primed, and dropped a frag grenade, practically at the Elite's feet. The alien warbled in surprise as the Spartan spun and ducked back around the corner.

He was rewarded by a flash of smoke and fire. A spray of purple-black blood splashed the metal wall. He rounded the corner, pistol at the ready, and stepped over the Elite's smoking corpse.

The Chief continued along the corridor, which opened onto a narrow ledge. Directly to his right, the thick metal walls stretched up and out of sight. To his left, the metal sloped away at a steep angle that led back to the main floor and gradually gave way to the yawning abyss as he continued forward. Ahead of him, there was a pulsing glow, like the strobe of a Pelican's running lights.

He stopped at the source of the light: A pair of small, glowing orbs hung suspended above a roughly rectangular frame of blue matte metal. Floating within the frame were a series of pulsing, shifting displays— semitransparent, like Cortana's holographic appearance, though there was no visible projection device. The display's shimmering geometric patterns nagged at him, as if he should recognize them somehow. Even with his enhanced memory, he couldn't place where he'd seen them before. They just seemed . . . familiar.

He reached a finger out to one of the symbols, a blue-green circle. The Spartan expected his finger to pass through nothing more than air. He was surprised when his finger met resistance—and the panel lights began to pulse more quickly.

"What did you do?" Cortana asked, her voice alarmed. "I'm detecting an energy spike."

"I . . . don't know," the Spartan admitted. He wasn't sure why he touched the "button" on the display. He just knew it felt right.

There was a high-pitched whine and, from his vantage point, he could see the gap in the roadway in the distance. At its edges, harsh white light sprang into view, forming a path across the break in the road, like a flashlight beam in smoke.

The light brightened, and there was a tremendous ripping sound. "I'm showing a lot of photonic activity,"

Cortana said. "The excited photons have displaced the air around the light path."

"Which means?"

"Which means," she continued, "that the light has become coherent. Solid."

She paused, then added, "How did you know what control to push?"

"I didn't. Let's get the hell out of here."

The ride across the light bridge was harrowing. He had tested the phenomenon with his foot, and discovered that it was as solid and unyielding as rock. Then he'd shrugged, told Fitzgerald to hang on, and sped the Warthog directly at the beam of illumination. He could hear Fitzgerald alternate between cursing and praying as they drove over the seemingly bottomless chasm on nothing more than a beam of light.

Once on the other side, they followed the tunnel out into the valley beyond, where the Master Chief guided the 'Hog up through a scattering of rocks and trees, to the top of a grassy rise. A sheer cliff threatened to block progress to the right, forcing them to stay to the left, as they headed toward a gap to the south.

The vehicle splashed through a shallow river. They saw the mouth of a passageway off to the right, decided that it would be best to investigate, and guided the all-terrain vehicle up through a rocky pass.

It was only a matter of minutes before the Warthog arrived on a ledge that looked out over a valley below. The Master Chief could see a UNSC lifeboat and a scattering of Covenant troops, but no Marines. Not a good sign.

A vaguely pyramidal structure rose to dominate the very center of the valley. The Master Chief saw a pulse of light race toward the sky, and knew that the structure had to be similar to whatever caused the flash he'd seen earlier.

There was only a moment to take in the situation before the aliens opened fire and the gunner replied in kind. It was time to put the 'Hog into motion. The Master Chief drove as the M41 LAAG whirred and rattled behind him. Marine Fitzgerald shouted, "You like that? Here, have some more!" and fired another sustained burst. A pair of Grunts rolled in opposite directions, as a squat, long-armed Jackal was cut in half, and the heavy-caliber slugs blew divots out of the ground beyond.

As the LRV swung past the pyramid, Cortana said, "There are some Marines hiding up on the hill. Let's give them a hand."

The Spartan aimed for a gap between two trees and saw a tall, angular Elite step out from cover. The Elite raised a weapon but was quickly transformed into a speed bump as the Warthog knocked him down and the huge tires crushed his body.

The Marines appeared soon after that, holding their assault weapons in the air, and calling greetings. A sergeant nodded. "It's good to see you, Chief. It was starting to get a little bit warm around here."

Covenant forces made a run at the hill after that, but the 12.7×99 mm rounds made short work of them, and the slope was soon littered with their bodies.

The Master Chief heard a burst of static, followed by Foehammer's voice. *"Echo 419 to Cortana . . . come in."*

"We read you, 419. We have survivors and need immediate dust-off."

"Roger, Cortana. On my way. I spotted additional lifeboats in your area."

"Acknowledged," Cortana answered. *"We're on our way."*

It took the better part of the afternoon to check the interlocking valleys, locate the rest of the survivors, and deal with the Covenant forces who attempted to interfere. But finally, having rounded up a total of sixty-three Marines and naval personnel, the Spartan watched Echo 419 land for the last time, and jumped aboard. Foehammer looked back over her shoulder. "You put in a long day, Chief. Nice job. Our ETA at Alpha Base is thirty minutes."

"Acknowledged," the Spartan said. He exhaled, then softened his clipped tone. He allowed himself to lean back against the bulkhead and added, "Thanks for the ride."

Captain Jacob Keyes stood, hands on knees, panting in front of a vertical cliff face. He and the rest of the command party had been running off and on for three hours. Even the Marines were exhausted, as the shadow cast by the Covenant dropship drifted over them and blocked the sun.

Keyes considered making use of Dowski's pistol to fire at the aircraft but couldn't summon the energy. The voice that boomed through the externally mounted speakers was all too familiar. *"Captain Keyes? This is Ellen Dowski. This is a box canyon. There's no place for you to run. You might as well pack it in."*

The darkness cast by the ship shifted as the aircraft lowered itself onto the bottom of the canyon. The engines howled and blew dust in all directions before eventually spooling down. A hatch opened and Dowski jumped to the ground. She appeared to be unharmed and wore what could only be described as a self-satisfied smirk. "You see? It's just like I told you it would be."

A half dozen veteran Elites dropped to the ground,

followed by a brace of Grunts. All were heavily armed. Gravel crunched as they approached the cliff face. One of the aliens spoke, his booming voice warbling the human speech with detectable discomfort. "You will drop your weapons. *Now.*"

The command crew looked at Keyes. He shrugged, bent over, and laid the M6D on the ground. The others did likewise.

The Grunts scurried about and collected the weapons. One of them chortled in his own language, as he collected all three of the Marines' assault weapons, and carried them away.

"Which?" the Elite with the translator demanded, and looked at Dowski.

"That one!" the renegade officer proclaimed, and pointed at Keyes.

Hikowa started forward. "You little bitch! I'll—"

No one ever learned what Hikowa would do, because the Elite shot her dead. Keyes lunged forward and attempted to tackle the Elite, to no avail. A lightning-fast blow clipped the side of his head, hard enough that his vision grayed out. He fell to the dirt.

The Elite was methodical. Starting with the Marines, he shot each captured human in the head. Wang attempted to run but a plasma bolt hit him between the shoulder blades. Lovell made a grab for the pistol, and took a blast to the face.

Keyes struggled to his feet again, dizzy and disoriented, and attempted to rush the Elite. He was clubbed to the ground a second time. Hikowa's dead eyes stared vacantly back at him.

Finally, after the last plasma bolt had been fired and while the odor of burned flesh still hung in the air, only two members of the command crew were still alive: Keyes and Dowski. The Ensign was pale. She shook her head and wrung her hands. "I didn't know, sir, honest I didn't. They told me—"

The Elite snapped up a fallen M6D pistol and shot Dowski. The bullet hit her in the center of her forehead. The pistol's report echoed down the canyon. The Ensign's eyes rolled back in her head, her knees gave way, and she collapsed in a heap.

The Elite turned the M6D over in his hand. The weapon was small compared to *his* pistol—and his finger didn't fit easily inside the trigger guard. "Projectiles. Very primitive. Take him away."

Keyes felt the other Elites grab him by the arms and drag him up a ramp into the dropship's murky interior. It seemed that the Covenant's rules had changed again. Now they *did* take prisoners—just not very many. The ship lifted, and the only human to survive sincerely wished that he hadn't.

The Master Chief was just about to run routine maintenance check on his armor when a private stuck his head into the Spartan's quarters, a prefab memory-plastic cubicle that had replaced the archaic concept of tents.

"Sorry to bother you, Chief, but Major Silva would like to see you in the Command Post . . . on the double."

The Spartan wiped his hands with a rag. "I'll be right there."

The Master Chief was just about to take the armor off standby when the Marine reappeared. "One more thing . . . The Major said to leave your armor here."

The Spartan frowned. He didn't like to be separated from his armor, especially in a combat zone. But an order was an order, and until he determined what had happened to Keyes, Silva was in command.

He nodded. "Thank you, Private." He checked to

ensure that his gear was squared away, activated the armor's security system, and buckled an M6D around his waist.

The Major's office was located in Alpha Base's CP, the centermost of the alien structures at the top of the butte. He made his way through the halls, and down a bloodstained corridor. A pair of manacled Grunt POWs were hard at work scrubbing the floor under the watchful gaze of a Navy guard.

Two Helljumpers stood guard outside Silva's door. Both looked extremely sharp for troopers who had been in combat the day before. They favored the Spartan with the casually hostile look that members of the ODST reserved for anyone or anything that wasn't part of their elite organization. The larger of the pair eyed the noncom's collar insignia. "Yeah, Chief, what can we do for you?"

"Master Chief Spartan 117, reporting to Major Silva."

"Spartan 117" was the only official designation he had in the eyes of the military. It occurred to him that, after Reach fell, there was no one left who knew his name was John.

"Spartan 117?" the smaller of the two Marines inquired. "What the hell kind of name is that?"

"Look who's talking," McKay interrupted, as she approached the Master Chief from behind. "That's a pretty strange question coming from a guy named Yutrzenika."

Both of the Helljumpers laughed, and McKay waved the Spartan through the door. "Never mind those two, Chief. They're jump happy. My name is McKay. Go on in."

The Spartan said "Thank you, ma'am," took three steps forward, and found himself standing in front of a makeshift desk. Major Silva looked up from what he was doing and met the Master Chief's eyes. The Chief snapped to attention. "Sir! Master Chief Spartan 117, reporting as ordered, sir!"

The chair had been salvaged from a UNSC lifeboat. It made a gentle hissing noise as Silva leaned backward. He held a stylus which he used to tap his lips. That was the moment when most officers would have said, "At ease," and the fact that he didn't was a clear indication that something was wrong. But what?

McKay circled around to Silva's left, where she leaned on the wall and watched the scene through hooded eyes. She wore her hair Helljumper style, short on the sides so that the tattoos on her scalp could be seen, and flat on top. She had green eyes, a slightly flattened nose, and full lips. It managed to be both a soldier's face *and* a woman's face at the same time.

When Silva spoke, it was as if he could read the Spartan's mind. "So, you're wondering who I am, and what this is all about. That's understandable, especially given your elite status, your close relationship with Captain Keyes, and the fact that we now know he has been captured. Loyalty is a fine thing, one of the many virtues for which the military is known, and a quality I admire."

Silva stood and started to pace back and forth behind his chair. "However, there is a chain of command, which means that you report to *me*. *Not* to Keyes, *not* to Cortana, and *not* to yourself."

The Marine stopped, turned, and looked the Master Chief square in the eye. "I thought it would be a good idea for you and I to pull a com check. So, here's the deal. I'm short a Captain, so Lieutenant McKay is serving as my Executive Officer. If either one of us says 'crap,' then I expect you to ask 'what color, how much, and where do you want it?' Do you read me?"

The Chief stared for a moment and clenched his jaw. "Perfectly, sir."

"Good. Now one more thing. I'm familiar with your record and I admire it. You are one helluva soldier. That said, you are also a *freak*, the last remaining subject in a terribly flawed experiment, and one which should never be repeated."

McKay watched the Master Chief's face. His hair was worn short, not as short as hers, but short. He had serious eyes, a firm mouth, and a strong jaw. His skin hadn't been exposed to the sun for a long time and it was white, *too* white, like something that lived in the deep recesses of a cave. From what she had heard he had been a professional soldier since the age of six, which meant he was an expert at controlling what showed on his face, but she could see the words hit like bullets striking a target. Nothing overt, just a slight narrowing of the eyes, and a tightness around his mouth. She looked at Silva, but if the Major was aware of the changes, he didn't seem to care.

"The whole notion of selecting people at birth, screwing with their minds, and modifying their bodies is wrong. First, because the candidates have no choice, second, because the subjects of the program are transformed into human aliens, and third, because the SPARTAN program failed.

"Are you familiar with a man named Charles Darwin? No, probably not, because he never went to war. Darwin was a naturalist who proposed a theory called 'natural selection.' Simply put, he believed that those species best equipped to survive would do so—while other, less effective organisms would eventually die out.

"That's what happened to the Spartans, Chief: *They died out.* Or will, once you're gone. And that's where the ODST comes in. It was the Helljumpers who took this butte, son—not a bunch of augmented freaks in fancy armor.

"When we push the Covenant back, which I sincerely believe we will, that victory will be the result of work by men and women like Lieutenant McKay. Human beings who are razorsharp, metal tough, and green to the core. Do you read me?"

The Master Chief remembered Linda, James, and all the rest of the seventy-three boys and girls with whom he learned to fight. All dead, all labeled as "freaks," now dismissed as having been part of a failed experiment. He took a deep breath.

"Sir, no sir!"

There was a long moment of silence as the two men stared into each other's eyes. Finally, after a good five seconds had elapsed, the Major nodded. "I understand. ODSTs are loyal to our dead, as well. But that doesn't change the facts. The SPARTAN program is *over*. Human beings will win this war . . . so you might as well get used to it. In the meantime, we need every warrior we have—especially those who have more medals than the entire general staff put together."

Then, as if some sort of switch had been thrown, the ODST officer's entire demeanor changed. He said, "At ease," invited both of his guests to sit down, and proceeded to brief the Master Chief on his upcoming mission. The Covenant had Captain Keyes, recon had confirmed it, and Silva was determined to get him back.

Though their ship had been damaged by the *Pillar of Autumn* during her brief rampage through the system, the Covenant's Engineers were hard at work making repairs to the *Truth and Reconciliation*. Now, hovering only a few hundred units off Halo's surface, the ship had become a sort of de facto headquarters for those assigned to "harvest" the ringworld's technology.

The warship was at the very center of the command structure's activities. The corridors were thick with officer Elites, major Jackals, and veteran Grunts. There was also a scattering of Engineers, amorphous-looking creatures held aloft by gas bladders, who had a savantlike ability to dismantle, repair, and reassemble any complex technology.

But all of them, regardless of how senior they might be, hurried to get out of the way as Zuka 'Zamamee marched through the halls, closely followed by a reluctant Yayap. Not because of his rank, but because of his appearance and the message it sent. The arrogant tilt of his head, the space-black armor, and the steady *click-clack* of his heels all seemed to radiate confidence and authority.

Still, formidable as 'Zamamee was, no one was allowed onto the command deck without being screened, and no less than six black-clad Elites were waiting when he and his aide stepped off the gravity lift. If these Elites were intimidated by their fellow's demeanor they gave no sign of it.

"Identification," one of them said brusquely, and extended his hand.

'Zamamee dropped his disk into the other warrior's hand with the air of someone who was conferring a favor on a lesser being.

The security officer accepted 'Zamamee's identity disk and dropped it into a handheld reader. Data appeared and scrolled from right to left. "Place your hand in the slot."

The second machine took the form of a rectangular black box which stood about five units high. Green light sprayed out of a slot located in the structure's side.

'Zamamee did as instructed, felt a sudden stab of pain as the machine sampled his tissue, and knew that a computer was busy comparing his DNA with that on file. Not because he might be human, but because politics were rife within the Covenant, and there had been a few assassinations of late.

"Confirmed," the Elite said. "It appears as though you are the same Zuka 'Zamamee that's scheduled to meet with the Council of Masters fifteen units from now. The Council is running behind schedule, however, so you'll have to wait. Please hand all personal weapons to me. There's a waiting room over there—but the Grunt will have to remain outside. You will be called when the Council is ready."

Though not burdened by his plasma rifle, which he had given to Yayap to carry, the Elite did have a plasma pistol, which he surrendered butt first.

'Zamamee made his way into the makeshift holding area and discovered that a number of other beings had been forced to wait as well. Most sat hunched over, kept to themselves, and stared at the deck.

Making matters even worse was the fact that, rather than first come, first served, it seemed as though rank definitely had its privileges, and the most senior penitents were seen first.

Not that the Elite could complain. Had it not been for *his* rank the Council would never have agreed to see him at *all*. But finally, after what seemed like an eternity, 'Zamamee was ushered into the chamber where the Command Council had convened.

A minor Prophet sat, legs folded, at the center of a table which curved around a podium at which the Elite was clearly expected to stand. Whenever a gust of air hit the exalted one he seemed to bob slightly in his anti-gravity throne, subtly reminding others of who and what he was. Something 'Zamamee not only understood, but admired.

The Prophet wore a complex headpiece. It was set with gemstones and wired for communications. A silver mantle rested on his shoulders and supported a fancifully woven cluster of gold, which extended forward in front of his bony lips. Richly embroidered red robes cascaded down over his lap and fell to the deck. Obsidian black eyes tracked the Elite all the way to the podium while an assistant whispered in his ear.

The other Elite, an aristocrat named Soha 'Rolamee, raised a hand palm outward. "I greet you 'Zamamee. How is your wound? Healing nicely, I hope."

'Rolamee outranked 'Zamamee by two full levels. The junior officer gloried in the respectful manner with which the other Elite had greeted him. "Thank you, Commander. I will heal."

"Enough," the Prophet said officiously, "we're running late, so let's get on with it. Zuka 'Zamamee comes before the Council seeking special dispensation to take leave of the unit he commands, in order to locate and kill one particular human. A rather strange notion, since all of them look alike and are equally annoying. However, according to our records, this particular human is responsible for thousands of Covenant casualties.

"The Council notes that Officer 'Zamamee was wounded during an encounter with this human, and reminds Officer 'Zamamee that the Covenant has no tolerance for personal vendettas. Please keep that in mind as you make your case, and be mindful of the time. A measure of brevity will serve you well."

'Zamamee lowered his eyes as a signal of respect. "Thank you, Commander. Our spies suspect that the individual in question was raised to be a warrior from a very young age, surgically altered to enhance his abilities, and furnished with armor which may be superior to our own."

"Better than our own?" the Prophet inquired, his tone making it clear that he considered such a possibility extremely unlikely. "Mind your words, Officer 'Zamamee. The technology underlying the armor you wear came straight from the Forerunners. To say that it is in any way inferior verges on sacrilege."

"Still, what 'Zamamee says is true," 'Rolamee put in. "The files are full of reports which, though contradictory in some cases, all make mention of one or more humans clad in reactive special armor. Assuming that the eyewitness accounts are accurate, it appears that this individual or group of individuals can absorb a great deal of punishment without suffering personal injury, have exceptional combat skills, and demonstrate superior leadership capabilities. Wherever he or they appear, other humans rally and fight with renewed vigor."

"Exactly," 'Zamamee said gratefully. "Which is why I recommend that a special hunter-killer team be commissioned to find the human and retrieve his armor for analysis."

"Noted," the Prophet said gravely. "Withdraw while the Council confers."

'Zamamee had little choice but to lower his eyes, back away from the podium, and turn to the door. Once out in the hallway, the Elite was required to wait for only a few units before his name again was called, and he was ushered back into the room. 'Zamamee saw that both the Prophet and the second Elite had disappeared, leaving 'Rolamee to deliver the news.

The other officer stood as if to reduce the width of the social gap that separated them. "I regret, 'Zamamee, that the Prophet places little weight on the reports, labeling them 'combat-induced hysteria.' More than that, we all agreed that you are far too valuable an asset to expend on a single target. Your request has been denied."

'Zamamee knew that 'Rolamee had invented the "far too valuable" aspect of his report in order to cushion the blow, but appreciated the intent behind the words. Though severely disappointed, he was a soldier, and that meant following orders. He lowered his eyes. "Yes, Commander. Thank you, Commander."

Yayap saw the Elite emerge, read the slight droop of his shoulders, and knew his prayers had been answered. The Council had denied the Elite's insane request, he would be allowed to return to his unit, and life would return to normal.

If 'Zamamee had been intimidating on his way to see the Council, he was a good deal less so on his way out. He walked even faster, however, forcing Yayap to break into a run. The Grunt weaved his way through the foot traffic arrayed in front of him and struggled to keep pace with 'Zamamee.

Yayap squealed in surprise when he slammed into the back of 'Zamamee's armored legs; the Elite had come to a sudden halt. The Grunt noticed with unease that his new master's hands were clenched. He followed 'Zamamee's gaze and spotted a group of four Jackals.

They dragged a uniformed human between them.

Keyes had just been interrogated for the third time. Some sort of neural shock treatment had been administered to make him talk, and his nerve endings continued to buzz as the aliens prodded his back, yelled incomprehensible gibberish into his ears, and laughed at his discomfort. He tasted his own blood.

The procession came to a sudden stop as an Elite in black combat armor blocked the way, pointed a long slender finger at the human, and said "You! Tell me where the I can find the human who wears the special armor."

Keyes looked up, struggled to focus his eyes, and faced the alien. He saw the dressing and guessed the rest. "I don't have the foggiest idea," he said. He managed a weak smile. "But the next time you run into him, you might consider ducking."

'Zamamee took a full step forward and backhanded the human across the face. Keyes staggered, recovered his balance, and wiped a trace of blood away from the corner of his mouth. He locked eyes with the alien for the second time. "Go ahead—shoot me."

Yayap saw the Elite consider doing just that, as his right hand went to the pistol, touched the butt, and fell away. Then, without another word, 'Zamamee walked away. The Grunt followed. Somehow, by means Yayap wasn't quite sure of, the human had won.

CHAPTER

FOUR

Recon flights conducted the day before had revealed
that the sensors aboard Covenant vessel *Truth and Reconciliation* might have a blind spot down-spin of the
alien vessel's current position, where a small mountain
rose to block the electronic view.

Even more important, Wellesley had concocted an
array of signals designed to trick the Covenant technicians into believing that any UNSC dropship was actually one of their own. Fifty meters above the deck, and
cloaked in electronic camouflage, the Master Chief and
a Pelican-load of Marines waited to find out if their ruse
would work.

Only time would tell if the fake signals were effective. One thing was for certain: Though conceived for
the express purpose of rescuing Captain Keyes, the
mission put together by Silva, Wellesley, and Cortana
bore still another, even more important purpose.

If the rescue team *did* manage to penetrate a Covenant vessel, and successfully remove a prisoner, the human presence on Halo would be transformed from an
attempt merely to survive into a full-fledged resistance
movement.

The ship shuddered as it hit a series of air pockets, then swayed from side to side as the pilot who referred to herself as Foehammer wove back and forth through an obstacle course of low-lying hills. The Master Chief took the opportunity to assess the Marines seated around him.

Maybe Silva was right, maybe the SPARTAN program *would* end with him, but that didn't matter. Not here—not now. The Marines would help him take out the sentries, cope with weapons emplacements, and reach the gravity lift located directly below the *Truth and Reconciliation*'s belly, and he was glad to have their help. Even with the element of surprise, plus support from the Marines, things were likely to be pretty hot by the time they made it to the lift. That's when a *second* dropship would land and discharge a group of regular Marines that would join the assault on the ship itself.

There was some concern that the *Truth and Reconciliation* might simply lift at that point, but Cortana had been monitoring Covenant communications, and was convinced that critical repairs were still being made to the alien cruiser.

Assuming that they were able to reach the gravity lift, meet up with their reinforcements, and fight their way aboard the ship, all they had to do was find Keyes, eliminate an unknown number of hostiles, and show up for the dust-off. A walk in the park.

Foehammer's voice came over the intercom. *"We are five to dirt . . . repeat five to dirt."*

That was Sergeant Parker's cue to stand and eye his troops. His voice came over the team freq and grated on the Spartan's ears. *"All right, boys and girls . . . lock and load. The Covenant is throwing a party and you are invited. Remember, the Master Chief goes in first, so take your cues from him. I don't know about you, but I like having a swabbie on point.*"

There was general laughter. Parker gave the Spartan a thumbs-up, and he offered the same gesture in return. It felt good to have some backup for a change.

He mentally reviewed the plan, which called for him to insert ahead of the Marines, and clear a path with his S2 AM sniper's rifle. Once the outer defenses were cleared, the Marines would move up. Then, once the element of surprise had been lost, the Master Chief planned to switch to his MA5B assault rifle for the close-in work. Like the rest of the troops, the Spartan was carrying a full combat load of ammo, grenades, and other gear, plus two magazines for the M19 launchers.

"*Thirty seconds to dirt!*" Foehammer announced. "*Shoot some of the bastards for me!*"

As the Pelican hovered a foot above the surface, Parker yelled, "*Go, go, go!*" and the Master Chief sprang down the ramp. He sidestepped and swept the area. The Marines thundered down the ramp and onto the ground, right behind him.

It was dark, which meant they had nothing beyond the light reflected off the moon that hung in the sky and the glow of Covenant work lights to guide them to their objective. Seconds later, Echo 419 was airborne again. The pilot turned down-spin, fed fuel to her engines, and disappeared into the night.

The Master Chief heard the aircraft pass over his head, gathered his bearings, and spotted a footpath off to the right. The Marines spread out to either side as Parker and a three-Marine fireteam turned to cover the group's six.

He crept along the rocky footpath, which rose to a two-meter-high embankment. As he neared a cluster of rocks, Cortana warned the Spartan of enemy activity ahead. A host of red dots appeared on his motion sensor. Several meters ahead and to the left was a deep pit—some kind of excavation, judging from the Covenant work lights that dotted the area with pools of illumination. He briefly wondered what the aliens were looking for.

He clicked the rifle's safety off. What they were looking for didn't matter. In the end, he'd make sure they never lived to find it.

The Master Chief found a patch of cover next to a tree, raised the rifle, and used the scope's 2X and night optics setting to find the Covenant gun emplacements located on the far side of the depression. There were lots of Grunts, Jackals, and Elites in the area, but it was imperative to neutralize the plasma cannons—known as Shades—before the Marines moved out into the open. His MJOLNIR armor and shields could handle a limited amount of the Shades' plasma fire. The Marines' ballistic armor, on the other hand, just couldn't handle that kind of firepower.

Once both Shades had been located, the Spartan switched to the 10X setting, practiced the move from one target to the next, and tried it yet again.

Once he was sure that he could switch targets quickly enough, he exhaled quietly, then held his breath. His hand squeezed the trigger and the rifle kicked against his shoulder. The first shot took the nearest gunner in the chest. As the Grunt tumbled from the Shade's seat, the Master Chief panned the rifle to the right, and put a 14.5mm round through the second Grunt's pointy head.

The rifle's booming report alerted the Covenant and they returned fire. He moved forward along the low ridge and took a new firing position behind the scaly bark of a tree. The rifle barked twice more, and a pair of Jackals fell. He reloaded with practiced ease, and continued sniping. Without the Shades to support them, the enemy fell in ones, twos, and threes.

The Master Chief reloaded again, fired until there were no more targets of opportunity, and made the switch to his assault rifle. He jumped down into the open pit and crouched behind a large boulder, one of several that were strewn around the depression.

"Marines: Move up!" he barked into the radio. In seconds, they charged into the pit. As the lead soldiers entered, a trio of Grunts burst from hiding, shot one of the Marines in the face, and tried to run. The soldier's body hadn't even hit the ground before the Spartan and another Marine hosed the aliens with bullets.

The gunshots echoed through the twisting canyons, then faded. The Spartan frowned; there was no way the fracas would go unnoticed. The element of surprise was gone.

There was no time to waste. The Master Chief led the Marines through the depression, up a hill on the far side of the pit, and along the side of a sheer cliff face. He stayed close to this rock wall on his right, mindful of the sheer drop that awaited any who strayed too far to the left. He could just make out the glint of moonlight on a massive ocean, far below him.

His motion sensor pinged two contacts and he waved the Marines to a halt. He crouched behind a clump of brush at the top of the cliff path, conscious of the massive drop on the other side. A pair of Jackals rounded the bend ahead, their overcharged plasma pistols pulsing green, and paid dearly for their enthusiasm.

The Spartan sprang from his cover and slammed the butt of his rifle into the nearest Jackal's shield. The energy field flared and died, and the force of the blow sent the alien tumbling off the path. The alien screamed and plummeted off the cliff.

The Chief pivoted and fired his rifle from the hip. The burst struck the second alien in the side. The Jackal slammed to the ground as his finger tightened on his weapon's trigger as he died. A massive hole blossomed in the rock above the Master Chief's head.

He slammed a fresh magazine into his weapon, and continued to advance.

"Here's a little something to remember me by," one of the Marines growled, and shot the remaining Jackal in the head.

As the team continued up the path, they encountered another Shade, more Grunts, and a pair of Jackals, all of whom seemed to melt away under the combined assault by the Master Chief's sniper rifle, the Marine's assault weapons, and a few well-placed grenades.

The rescue force pressed on, toward the lights beyond. Covenant resistance was determined but spotty, and before long the Master Chief could hear the thrumming sound of the alien ship as it hovered more than a hundred meters above them. His skin crackled with static electricity. In the center of a steep dip in the rock lay a large metal disk, the gravity lift that the Covenant used to move troops, supplies, and vehicles to and from the ringworld's surface. Purple light shimmered around the platform where the beam was anchored.

"Come on!" the Master Chief shouted, pointing at the lift. "That's our way in. Let's move!"

There was a mad dash through a narrow canyon followed by a pitched battle as the Master Chief and the Marines entered the area directly below the ship.

The depression was ringed with Shades, and all of them opened fire at once. The Chief made use of the sniper rifle to kill the nearest gunner, charged up the intervening slope, and jumped into the now vacant seat. The first order of business was to silence the other guns.

He yanked the control yoke to the left and the gun swiveled to face a second Shade, across the defile. A glowing image of a hollow triangle floated in front of his face. When it lined up with the other gun, it flashed red. He thumbed the firing studs, and lances of purple-white energy lashed the enemy emplacement. The Grunt gunner struggled to leap free of his Shade, fell into the path of the Spartan's fire, and was speared by a powerful blast. He slumped against the base of his abandoned Shade, a smoking hole burned through his chest.

The Master Chief swiveled the captured gun and took aim on the remaining Shades. He hosed the targets with a hellish wave of destructive energy, then, satisfied that the emplacements were silenced, went to work on the enemy ground troops.

He had just burned a pair of Jackals to the ground when Cortana announced that a Covenant dropship was inbound, and the Master Chief was forced to shift his fire to the alien aircraft and the troops that spilled out onto the ground.

The human walked the blue Shade fire across the aliens, cutting them down, and pounding what remained into mush. He was still at it when a Marine yelled, "Look at that! There's more of them!" and a dozen figures floated down through the gravity lift. A pair of the newcomers were huge and wore steel-blue armor as well as handheld plate-armor shields.

The Chief had faced such creatures before, not long before Reach fell. Covenant Hunters were tough, dangerous foes—practically walking tanks. They were slow and appeared clumsy, but the cannons mounted on their arms were equivalent to the heavy weapons a

Banshee carried, and they could leap into motion with startling suddenness. Their metal shields could withstand a tremendous amount of punishment. Worse, they would never stop until the enemy lay dead at their feet . . . or they were dead themselves.

The Marines opened fire, grenades exploded, and the pair of Hunters roared defiance. One of them lifted his right arm and fired his weapon, a fuel rod gun. One of the soldiers screamed and fell, his flesh melting. The Marine's rocket fired into the air, slid into the grav lift beam, and detonated harmlessly.

The Hunters lumbered from the grav lift and strode up the edge of the pit. Behind them, a swarm of Jackals and Elites formed a rough phalanx and peppered the human positions with plasma fire.

Sergeant Parker yelled, "Hit 'em, Marines!" and they poured fire onto the massive alien juggernauts. Bullets pinged from their armor and whined through the rocks.

The Spartan swiveled around, and heard a warning tone as a Hunter's weapon discharged. Burning energy smashed into him. The Shade shook under the force of the incoming fire as the Master Chief clenched his jaw and forced himself to bring the targeting reticle down onto the target. His shield bled energy and began to shriek a shrill alarm.

The instant the targeting display pulsed red, he mashed down the firing studs and unleashed a flood of incandescent blue light. The Hunter didn't have time to bring its shield fully into play, and plasma blasts burned through multiple layers of armor, and exited through its back.

The Spartan heard a cry of what sounded like anguish as the second alien saw his bond brother fall. The Hunter spun and fired his fuel rod gun at the Master Chief's captured emplacement. The Shade took a direct hit, flipped over onto its side, and threw him to the ground.

The ground vibrated as the enraged alien charged up the slope, right for the downed Spartan. The Chief rolled to his right and came up in a low crouch. The alien was close now, within five meters. A row of razor-sharp spines sprang up along the Hunter's back. With his shields depleted, the Chief knew that this Hunter's sheer strength was a very real threat.

He dropped to one knee and unslung his assault rifle. Bullets bounced harmlessly from the alien's armor. At the last second, he dodged left and slid down the slope. The Hunter didn't anticipate the move, and his enormous shield passed over the Spartan's head, missing him by mere centimeters.

The Chief rolled onto his belly—and saw his opportunity. A patch of orange, leathery skin was visible along the Hunter's curved back. He emptied the MA5B's magazine into the unprotected target, and thick orange blood spouted from a cluster of bullet wounds. The Hunter gave a low, keening wail, then collapsed in a puddle of his own gore.

He rose to one knee, fed a fresh magazine into the assault rifle, and scanned the area for enemies. "All clear," he called out.

The remaining Marines called in all clears as well. That opened the way to the lift and Cortana was quick to seize on the opportunity. She activated the armor's communication system. *"Cortana to Echo 419. We made it to the gravity lift—and are ready for reinforcements."*

"Copy that, Cortana . . . Echo 419 inbound. Clear the drop zone."

"What's the matter?" Sergeant Parker demanded of his troops, several of whom were looking longingly at the fast-approaching Pelican's running strobes. "Never seen a UNSC dropship before? Keep your eyes on the rocks, damn it—that's where the bastards will come from."

The Spartan waited for Echo 419 to unload the fresh Marines, waved them forward, and joined the surviving soldiers on the lift pad. "Looks like we made it," a private said, just before an invisible hand reached down to pluck him off the surface.

Sergeant Parker looked up toward the belly of the ship, and said, "Aren't we the lucky ones?" then rose as if suspended from a rope.

"Once we're in the ship I can home in on the Captain's Command Neural Interface," Cortana said. "The CNI will lead us to him. He'll probably be in or near the ship's brig."

"I'm glad to hear it," the Chief answered dryly, and felt the beam pull him upward. Someone else yelled, "Yeehaw!" and vanished into the belly of the ship. The Covenant didn't realize it yet—but the Marines had landed.

None of the humans understood, much less had the ability to predict, the ringworld's weather. So, when big drops of blood-warm rain fell on the mesa, it came as a complete surprise. The Marines grumbled as the water streamed off their faces, soaked their uniforms, and started to pool on the surface of the landing pad.

McKay saw things differently, however. She liked the wet stuff, not just because it felt good on her skin, but because bad weather would offer the insertion team that much more cover.

"Listen up, people!" Sergeant Lister bellowed. "You know the drill. Let's shake, rattle, and roll."

There weren't many lights, just enough so that people

could move around without running into one another, but the fact that Silva had been on such missions himself meant that he could visualize what his eyes couldn't see.

The troopers carried a full combat load, which meant that their packs were festooned with weapons, ammo, grenades, flares, radios, and med packs—all of which would make noise unless properly secured. Noise would bring a world of trouble down on their heads during an op. That's why Lister passed through the ranks and forced each Marine to jump up and down. Anything that clicked, squeaked, or rattled was identified and stowed, taped, or otherwise fastened into place.

Once all the troops had passed inspection, the Helljumpers would board the waiting dropships for a short flight to the point where the *Pillar of Autumn* had crashed. The Covenant had placed guards in and around the fallen cruiser, so McKay and her Marines would have to retake the ship long enough to fill the extensive shopping list that Silva had given her.

According to Wellesley, Napoleon I once said, "What makes the general's task so difficult is the necessity of feeding so many men and animals."

Silva didn't have any animals to feed, but he did have a flock of Pelicans, and the essence of the problem was the same. With the exception of the ODST troopers, who carried extra supplies in their HEVs, the rest of the Navy and Marine personnel had bailed out of the *Autumn* with very little in the way of supplies. Obtaining more of everything, and doing it before the Covenant launched an all-out attack on Alpha Base, would be the key to survival. Later, assuming there was a later, the infantry officer would have to find a way to get his people the hell off the ringworld.

Silva's thoughts were interrupted as Echo 419 raced

in over the mesa, flared nose up, and settled onto what had been designated as Pad 3.

The assault on the *Truth and Reconciliation* had gone well so far, which meant that Second Lieutenant Dalu, who had been assigned to follow along behind the rescue team and scoop up everything he could, was having a good evening. Each time Echo 419 dropped a load of troops she brought enemy arms and equipment back in. Plasma rifles, plasma pistols, Needlers, power packs, hand tools, com equipment, and even food packs. Dalu loved them all.

Silva grinned as the Lieutenant waved a team of Naval techs in under the Pelican's belly to take delivery of the Shade he and his team had lifted right out from under the Covenant's collective noses. That was the third gun acquired since the beginning of the operation, and would soon take its place within the butte's steadily growing air defense system.

Sergeant Lister shouted, "Ten-shun!", did a smart about-face, and saluted Lieutenant McKay. She returned the salute, and said, "At ease."

Silva walked out into the rain and felt it pelt his face. He turned to look at the ranks of black, brown, and white faces. All he saw were Marines.

"Most, if not all of you, are familiar with my office aboard the *Pillar of Autumn*. In the rush to leave it seems that I left a full bottle of Scotch in the lower left-hand drawer of my desk. If one or more of you would be so kind as to retrieve that bottle, not only would I be extremely grateful, I would show my gratitude by sharing it with the person or persons who manage to bring it in."

There was a roar of approval. Lister shouted them down. "Silence! Corporal, take that man's name." The

Corporal to whom the order was directed had no idea which name he was supposed to take down, but knew it didn't matter.

Silva knew the Helljumpers had been briefed, and understood the *true* purpose of the mission, so he brought his remarks to a close.

"Good luck out there . . . I'll see you in a couple of days." Except that he *wouldn't* see them, not all of them. Good commanding officers had to love their men—and still be willing to order their deaths if needed. It was the aspect of command he hated the most.

The formation was dismissed. The Marines jogged up into the back of the waiting Pelicans, and the dropships soon disappeared into the blackness of the night.

Silva remained on the pad until the sound of the engines could no longer be heard. Then, conscious of the fact that every war must be won on the equivalent of paper before it can be won on the ground, he turned back toward the low-lying structure that housed his command post. The night was still young—and there was plenty of work left to do.

The gravity lift deposited the rescue team three feet above the deck. They hung suspended for a moment, then fell. Parker gave a series of hand signals, and the Marines crept forward into the lift bay.

The Covenant equivalent of gear crates—tapered rectangular boxes made from the shimmering, striated purple metal the aliens favored—were stacked around the high compartment. A pair of Covenant tanks, "Wraiths," were lined along the right side of the bay.

The Master Chief moved forward toward one of the high metal doors that were spaced along the perimeter of the compartment.

Parker gave the all clear signal and the Marines relaxed a bit. "There's no Covenant here," one of them whispered, "so where the hell *are* they?"

The door was proximity activated, and as the Spartan neared the portal, it slid open and revealed a surprised Elite. Without pause, he tackled the alien and slammed its armored head into the burnished deckplates. With luck, he'd finished the Elite quietly enough—

Another set of doors flashed open on the other side of the bay, and Covenant troops boiled into the compartment.

A second Marine turned to the Corporal who'd just spoken. "'No Covenant,'" he snarled, mocking his fellow trooper. "You just *had* to open your mouth, didn't you?"

Inside the Covenant ship, chaos reigned. The Master Chief charged ahead, and the rescue team fought their way through a maze of interlocking corridors, which eventually emerged into a large shuttle bay. A Covenant dropship passed through a bright blue force field as all hell broke loose. Fire stuttered down from a platform above. A Marine took a flurry of needles in the chest and was torn in half by the ensuing explosion.

A Grunt dropped from above and landed on a Corporal's shoulders. The Marine reached up, got a grip on the alien's methane rig, and jerked the device off. The Grunt started to wheeze, fell to the deck, and flopped around like a fish. Someone shot him.

Numerous hatches opened into the bay and additional Covenant troops poured in from every direction. Parker stood up and motioned his men forward. "It's party time!" he bellowed.

He spun and opened fire, and was soon joined by all the rest. Within a matter of seconds what seemed like a dozen different firefights had broken out. Wounded and dead—humans and Covenant alike—littered the deck.

The Master Chief was careful to keep his back to a Marine, a pillar, or the nearest bulkhead. His MJOL-NIR armor, and the recharging shield it carried, provided the Spartan with an advantage that none of the Marines possessed, so he focused most of his attention on the Elites, leaving the Jackals and Grunts for others to handle.

Cortana, meanwhile, was hard at work tapping into the ship's electronic nervous system in an attempt to find the best way out of the trap. "We need a way out of this bay *now*," the Master Chief told her, "or there won't be anyone left to complete the mission."

He ducked behind a crate, emptied his magazine into a charging Grunt who wielded a plasma grenade, then paused to reload.

A Hunter gave a bloodcurdling roar as it charged into the fray. The Spartan turned and saw Sergeant Parker fire at the massive alien. A trio of bullets spat from his assault rifle—the last three rounds in the weapon. He discarded the empty gun and backpedaled in an attempt to buy himself some time. His hand dipped for his sidearm.

The Hunter sprang forward and the edge of the beast's massive shield shredded through the Marine's ballistic armor. He crashed to the deck.

The Master Chief cursed under his breath, slapped a fresh clip into place, racked a round into the chamber, and took aim on the Hunter. The alien was coming on fast, *too* fast, and the Spartan knew he wasn't going to get a kill-shot in time.

The Hunter stepped past Sergeant Parker's prone form. The alien roared again as the Spartan sprayed it with gunfire, knowing the gesture was futile, but unwilling to let the enemy at his teammate's exposed flank.

Without warning, the Hunter reared up, howled, and crashed to the ground. The Master Chief was puzzled, and briefly checked his weapon. Could he have gotten in a lucky shot?

He heard a cough, and saw Sergeant Parker struggling to his feet, a smoking M6D pistol in his hand. Blood flowed from the gashes in his side, and he was unsteady on his feet, but he found the strength to spit on the Hunter's fallen corpse.

The Chief took a covering position near the wounded sergeant. He gave him a brisk nod. "Not bad for a Marine. Thanks."

The sergeant grabbed a fallen assault rifle, slammed a fresh magazine into place, and grinned. "Any time, swabbie."

His motion sensor showed more contacts inbound, but they were keeping their distance. Their failed assault on the bay must have left them disorganized. *Good,* he thought. *We need all the time we can get.* "Cortana," he said, "how much longer before you get a door open?"

"Got it!" Cortana proclaimed exultantly. One of the heavy doors hissed open. "Everyone should move through the door now. I can't guarantee that it won't lock when it closes."

"Follow me!" he barked, then led the surviving Marines out of the shuttle bay and into the comparative safety of a corridor beyond.

The next fifteen minutes were like a slow-motion nightmare as the rescuers fought their way through a maze of corridors, up a series of narrow ramps, and onto the launch bay's upper level. With Cortana's guidance, they plunged back into the ship's oppressive passageways.

As they proceeded through the bowels of the large warship, Cortana finally gave them good news: "The Captain's signal is strong. He must be close."

The Chief frowned. This was taking too long. Every passing second made it that much less likely that any of the rescue party would be able to get off the *Truth and Reconciliation* alive, let alone with Captain Keyes. The Marines were good fighters, but they were slowing him down.

He turned to Sergeant Parker and said, "Hold your men here. I'll be back soon—with the Captain."

He started to protest, then nodded. "Just don't tell Silva," he said.

The Master Chief ran from door to door until one of them opened to reveal a rectangular room lined with cells. It appeared that the translucent force fields served in place of bars. He dashed inside and called the Captain's name, but received no answer. A quick check confirmed that, with the exception of one dead Marine, the detention center was empty.

Frustrated, yet reassured by Cortana's insistence that the CNI signal remained strong, the Spartan exited the room, entered the hall, and literally went door to door, searching for the correct hatch. Once he located it, the Master Chief almost wished he hadn't.

The portal slid open, a Grunt yelled something the Master Chief couldn't understand, and a plasma beam lashed past the human's helmet.

The Master Chief opened fire, heard a Marine yell from within one of the cells, "Good to see you, Chief!" and knew he was in the right place.

A plasma beam appeared out of nowhere, hit the Spartan in the chest, and triggered the armor's audible alarm. He ducked behind a support column, just in time to see an energy beam slice through the spot he had just vacated. He scanned the room, looking for his assailant.

Nothing.

His motion sensor showed faint trace movements, but he couldn't spot their source.

His eyes narrowed, and he noticed a slight shimmer in the air, directly in front of him. He fired a sustained burst through the middle of it, and was rewarded with a loud howl. The Elite seemed to materialize out of thin air, made a grab for his own entrails, and managed to catch them before he died.

He strode to the access controls and, with Cortana's help, killed the force fields. Captain Keyes stepped out of his cell, paused to scoop a Needler off the floor, and met the Chief's eyes. "Coming here was reckless," he said, his voice harsh. The Chief was about to explain his orders when Keyes' expression warmed, and the *Autumn*'s CO smiled. "Thanks."

The Spartan nodded. "Any time, sir."

"Can you find your way out?" Keyes inquired doubtfully. "The corridors of this ship are like a maze."

"It shouldn't be too difficult," the Master Chief replied. "All we have to do is follow the bodies."

Lieutenant "Cookie" Peterson put Echo 136 down a full klick from the *Pillar of Autumn*, looked out through the rain-spattered windscreen, and saw Echo 206 settle in approximately fifty meters away. It had been an uneventful flight, thanks in part to the weather, and the fact that the assault on the *Truth and Reconciliation* had probably served to distract the Covenant from what was going on elsewhere.

Peterson felt the ship shudder as the ramp hit the ground, waited for the Crew Chief to call "Clear!", and fired the Pelican's thrusters. The ship was extremely vulnerable while on the ground—and he was eager to return to the relative safety of Alpha Base. Then, assuming the Helljumpers got the job done, he and his crew would be back to transport some of the survivors and their loot.

Back at Alpha Base, McKay watched Echo 136 wobble as a gust of wind hit the Pelican from the side, saw the ship gather speed, and start to climb out. Echo 206 took off a few moments later and both ships were gone within a matter of seconds.

Her people knew what they were doing, so rather than make a pest of herself, McKay decided to wait and watch as the platoon leaders sorted things out. The officer felt the usual moments of fear, of self-doubt regarding her ability to accomplish the mission, but took comfort from something an instructor once told her.

"Take a look around," the instructor had advised. "Ask yourself if there's anyone else who is better qualified to do the job. Not in the entire galaxy, but right there, at that point in time. If the answer is 'yes,' ask them to accept command, and do everything you can to support them. If the answer is 'no,' which it will be ninety-nine percent of the time, then take your best shot. That's all any of us can do."

It was good advice, the kind that made a difference, and while it didn't erase McKay's fears, it certainly served to ease them.

Master Sergeant Lister and Second Lieutenant Oros seemed to materialize out of the darkness. Oros had a small, pixielike face which belied her innate toughness. If anything happened to McKay, Oros would take over, and if she bought the farm Lister would step in. The battalion had been short of officers *before* the shit hit the fan, and what with Lieutenant Dalu off playing

Supply Officer, McKay was one Platoon Leader short of a full load. That's why Lister had been called upon to fill the hole.

"Platoons one and two are ready to go," Oros reported cheerfully. "Let us at 'em!"

"You just want to raid the ship's commissary," McKay said, referring to the Platoon Leader's well-known addiction to chocolate.

"No, ma'am," Oros replied innocently, "the Lieutenant lives only to serve the needs of humanity, the Marine Corps, and the Company Commander."

Even the normally stone-faced Lister had to laugh at that, and McKay felt her own spirits lift as well. "Okay, Lieutenant Oros, the human race would be grateful if you would put a couple of your best people on point and lead this outfit to the ship. I'll ride your six with Sergeant Lister and the second platoon walking drag. Are you okay with that?"

Both Platoon Leaders nodded and melted into the night. McKay looked for the tail end of the first platoon, slid into line, and let her mind roam ahead. Somewhere, about one kilometer ahead, the *Pillar of Autumn* lay sprawled on the ground. The Covenant owned the ship for the moment—but McKay was determined to take her back.

It was time to get off the *Truth and Reconciliation*. As Covenant troops ran hither and yon, the recently freed Marines armed themselves with alien weapons, then linked up with the rest of the rescue team. Keyes and Cortana convened a quick council of war. "While the Covenant had us locked up in here, I heard them talking about the ringworld," Keyes said, "and its destructive capabilities."

"One moment, sir," Cortana interrupted, "I'm accessing the Covenant battlenet." She paused, as her vastly powerful intrusion protocols sifted through the Covenant systems. Information systems seemed to be the one field where human technologies held their own against those of the Covenant.

Seconds later, she finished her sift of the alien data stream. "If I'm interpreting the data correctly, they believe Halo is some kind of weapon, one that possesses vast, unimaginable power."

Keyes nodded thoughtfully. "The aliens who interrogated me kept saying that 'whoever controls Halo controls the fate of the universe.'"

"Now I see," Cortana put in thoughtfully. "I intercepted a number of messages about a Covenant search team scouting for a control room. I thought they were looking for the bridge of a ship I damaged during the battle above the ring—but they must be looking for Halo's control room."

"That's bad news," Keyes responded gravely. "*If* Halo is a weapon, and the Covenant gains control of it, they'll use it against us. Who knows what power that would give them?

"Chief, Cortana, I have a *new* mission for you. We need to beat the Covenant to Halo's control room."

"No offense, sir," the Master Chief replied, "but it might be best to finish *this* mission before we tackle another one."

Keyes offered a tired grin. "Good point, Chief. Marines! Let's move!"

"We should head back to the shuttle bay and call for evac," Cortana said, "unless you'd like to walk home."

"No thanks," Keyes said. "I'm Navy—we prefer to ride."

The journey out of the detention area and back to the launch bay was hairy but not quite as bad as the trip in. It wasn't long before they all realized that they really *could* follow the trail of dead bodies back to the launch bay. Sadly, some of the dead wore Marine green, which served to remind the Chief of how many humans the Covenant had murdered since the war had begun more than twenty-five years before. Somehow, in some way, the Covenant would be made to pay.

The tactical situation was made even more risky by the Captain's condition. He didn't complain, but the Spartan could tell that Keyes was sore and weak from the Covenant interrogation. It was a struggle for him to keep up with the others.

The Master Chief signaled for the team to halt. Keyes—out of breath—favored him with a sour look, but seemed grateful for the breather.

Two minutes later, the Chief was about to signal the group to move forward when a trio of Grunts scuttled into view. Needler rounds bounced from the bulkhead and angled right for him.

His shields took the brunt of it, and he returned fire, as did the rest of the group. Keyes blew one Grunt apart with a barrage of the explosive glassy needles. The rest were finished off by a combination of plasma rifle fire and the Chief's assault rifle.

"Let's get moving," the Spartan advised. He took point and moved down the corridor, bent low and ready for trouble. He'd barely gotten twenty meters down the passageway when more Covenant moved in—two Jackals and an Elite.

The enemy was getting closer, and more determined, the longer they remained. He finished off the Jackals with his last frag grenade, then pinned the Elite down with assault rifle fire. Keyes directed the Marines to fire on the alien's flank, and he went down.

"We need to *go*, sir," the Chief warned Keyes. "With respect, we're moving too slowly."

Keyes nodded, and as a group they sprinted down the twisting passages, stealth abandoned. Finally, after numerous twists and turns, they reached the shuttle bay. The Spartan thought it was empty at first, until he noticed what appeared to be two light wands, floating in midair.

Fresh from his encounter with the stealth Elite who had been stationed in the brig, the Master Chief knew better than to take chances. He drew his pistol, linked in the scope, and took careful aim. He squeezed the trigger several times and put half a clip into the area just to the right of the energy blade. A Covenant warrior faded into view and toppled off the platform.

A Marine yelled, "Watch it!" and "Cover the Captain!" as the second blade sliced the air into geometric shapes, and started to advance as if on its own. The Spartan put three quick bursts into the second alien, hit his stealth generator, and the Elite was revealed. Fire poured in from all sides and the warrior went down.

There was a blast of static as Cortana activated the MJOLNIR's communication relays. "*Cortana to Echo 419 . . . We have the Captain and need extraction on the double.*"

The reply was nearly instantaneous. "*Negative, Cortana! I have a flock of Banshees on my tail . . . and I can't seem to shake them. You'll be better off finding your own ride.*"

"*Acknowledged, Foehammer. Cortana out.*" The radio clicked as Cortana switched from the suit's radio to its external speakers.

"Air support is cut off, Captain. We'll need to hold here until Foehammer can move in."

A Marine heard the interchange and, already traumatized by the time spent as a Covenant prisoner, began to lose it. "We're trapped! We're all gonna die!"

"Stow the bellyaching, soldier," Keyes growled. "Cortana, if you and the Chief can get us into one of those Covenant dropships, I can fly us out of here."

"Yes, Captain," the AI replied. "There's a Covenant ship docked below."

The Master Chief saw the nav indicator appear on his HUD, followed the arrow through a hatch, down a series of corridors, and out into the troopship bay.

Unfortunately, the bay was well defended, and another firefight broke out. The situation was getting worse. The Chief slammed his last full clip into the MA5B and fired short, controlled bursts. Grunts and Jackals scattered and returned fire.

The ammo counter dropped rapidly. A pair of Grunts fell under the Spartan's hail of fire. Within seconds, the ammo counter read 00—empty.

He tossed the rifle away and drew his pistol, and continued firing at the alien forces that had begun to regroup at the far side of the bay. "If we're going," he called out, "we need to go now."

The dropship was shaped like a giant U. It rode a grav field and bobbed slightly as some of the outside air swirled around it. As they approached it, Keyes said, "Everybody mount up! Let's get on board!" and led the Marines through an open hatch.

The Spartan waited until everyone else had boarded and backed into the aircraft—just in time. He was down to a single round in his sidearm.

Cortana said, "Give me a minute to interface with the ship's controls."

Keyes shook his head. "No need. I'll take this bird up myself."

"Captain!" one of the Marines called. "Hunters!"

The Master Chief peered out through the nearest viewport and saw that the private was correct. Another pair of the massive aliens had arrived on the loading platform and were making for the ship. Their spines stood straight up, their fuel rod guns were swinging into position, and they were about to fire.

"Hang on!" Keyes said as he disengaged the ship's gravity locks, brought the ship up over the edge of the platform, and pushed one of two joysticks forward. The twin hulls straddled a column, struck both Hunters with what appeared to be glancing blows, and withdrew.

Even a glancing blow from a ship that weighs thousands of kilos proved to be a serious thing indeed. The dropship's hull crushed the Hunters' chest armor and forced it through their body cavities, killing both of them instantly. One corpse somehow managed to attach itself to one of the twin bows. It fell as the dropship cleared the *Truth and Reconciliation*'s hull.

The Master Chief leaned back against the metal wall. The Covenant craft's troop bay was cramped, uncomfortable, and dimly lit—but it beat hell out of wandering through one of their cruisers.

He braced himself as Keyes put the alien aircraft into a tight turn, and accelerated out into the surrounding darkness. He forced his shoulders to relax, and closed his eyes. The Captain had been rescued, and the Covenant had been put on notice: The humans were determined to be more than an annoyance—they were going to be a major pain in the ass.

Dawn had just started to break when Zuka 'Zamamee and Yayap passed through the newly reinforced perimeter that surrounded the gravity lift, and were forced to wait while a crew of hardworking Grunts pulled a load of Covenant dead off the blood-splattered pad, before they could step onto the sticky surface and be pulled up into the ship.

Although the *Truth and Reconciliation*'s commanding officer believed that all of the surviving humans had left the ship, there was no way to be certain of that without a compartment-by-compartment check. The shipboard sensors read clear, but this raid had demonstrated beyond a doubt that the humans had learned how to trick Covenant detection gear.

The visitors could feel the tension as teams of grim-faced Elites, Jackals, and Grunts performed a deck-by-deck search of the ship.

As the pair made their way through the corridors to the lift that would carry them up to the command deck, 'Zamamee was shocked by the extent of the damage that he saw. Yes, there were long stretches of passageway that were completely untouched, but every now and then they would pass through a gore-streaked section of corridor, where bullet-pocked bulkheads, plasma-scorched decks, and half-slagged hatches told of a hard-fought running gun battle.

'Zamamee stared in wonder as a grav cart loaded with mangled Jackals was towed past, blood dripping onto the deck behind it.

Finally, they made their way to the appropriate lift, and stepped out onto the command deck. The Elite expected the same level of security scrutiny as the last time he addressed the Prophet and the Council of Masters; no doubt he'd be dumped into the holding room for another interminable wait.

Nothing could have been further from the truth. No sooner did 'Zamamee clear security than he and Yayap were whisked into the compartment where the Council of Masters had been convened during his last visit.

There was no sign of the Prophet, or any of 'Zamamee's immediate superiors—but the hardworking Soha 'Rolamee was there, along with a staff of lesser Elites. There was no mistaking the crisis atmosphere as reports flowed in, were evaluated, and used to create a variety of action plans. 'Rolamee saw 'Zamamee and raised his hand by way of a greeting.

"Welcome. Please sit."

'Zamamee complied. It didn't occur to either one of the Elites to offer the same courtesy to Yayap, who continued to stand. The diminutive Grunt rocked back and forth, ill at ease.

"So," 'Rolamee inquired, "how much have you heard about the latest . . . 'incursion'?"

"Not much," 'Zamamee was forced to admit. "The humans managed to board the ship via the gravity lift. That's the extent of my knowledge."

"That's correct in so far as it goes," 'Rolamee agreed. "There is more. The ship's security system recorded quite a bit of the action. Take a look at *this*."

The Elite touched a button and moving images popped into view and hovered in the air nearby. 'Zamamee found himself looking at two Grunts and a Jackal standing in a corridor. Suddenly, without warning, the same human he had encountered on the *Pillar of Autumn*—the large one with the unusual armor—stepped around the corner, spotted the Covenant troops, and opened fire on them.

The Grunts went down quickly, but the Jackal scored a hit, and 'Zamamee saw plasma splash the front of the human's armor.

However, rather than fall as he should have, the apparition shot the Jackal in the head, stepped over one of the dead Grunts, and marched toward the camera. The image froze as 'Rolamee touched another control.

'Zamamee felt an almost unbelievable tightness in his chest. Would he have the courage to face the human again? He wasn't sure—and that frightened him as well.

"So," 'Rolamee said, "there he is, the very human you warned us about. A dangerous individual who is largely responsible for the six-score casualties inflicted during this raid alone, not to mention the loss of a valuable prisoner, and six Shades which the enemy managed to steal."

"And the humans?" 'Zamamee inquired. "How many of them were our warriors able to kill?"

"The body count is incomplete," the other Elite replied, "but the preliminary total is thirty-six."

'Zamamee was shocked. The numbers should have been reversed. *Would* have been reversed had it not been for the alien in the special armor.

"You will be pleased to learn that your original request has now been approved," 'Rolamee continued. "We have preliminary reports from other strike groups that many of these unusual humans were killed in the last large engagement. This one is believed to be the last of his kind. Take whatever resources you need, find the human, and kill him. Do you have any questions?"

"No, Commander," 'Zamamee said as he stood to leave. "None at all."

SECTION III

THE SILENT CARTOGRAPHER

ERADICATION

CHAPTER

FIVE

The rain stopped just before dawn—not gradually but all at once, as if someone had flipped a switch. The clouds melted away, the first rays of the sun appeared, and darkness surrendered to light.

Slowly, as if to reveal something precious, the golden glow slid across the plain to illuminate the *Pillar of Autumn*, which lay like an abandoned scepter, her bow hanging out over the edge of a steep precipice.

She was *huge*, so huge that the Covenant had assigned two Banshees to fly cover over her, and a squad of six Ghosts patrolled the area immediately around the fallen cruiser's hull. However, from the listless manner with which the enemy soldiers went about their duties, McKay could tell they were unaware of the threat that had crept up on them during the hours of rain-filled darkness.

Back on Earth, before the invention of the Shaw-Fujikawa Translight Engine, and the subsequent efforts to colonize other star systems, human soldiers had frequently staged attacks at dawn, when there was more light to see by, and the enemy sentries were likely to be tired and sleepy. In order to counter, the more sophisticated armies soon developed the tradition of an early morning "stand-to," when every soldier went to barricades in case the enemy chose that particular morning to attack.

Did the Covenant have a similar tradition, McKay wondered? Or were they dozing a bit, relieved that the long period of darkness was finally over, their fears eased by the first rays of the sun? The officer would soon find out.

Like all sixty-two members of her Company, the Hell-jumper was concealed just beyond the border of the roughly U-shaped area that the Covenant actively patrolled. And now, with daylight only minutes away, the time had arrived either to commit herself or to withdraw.

McKay took one last look around. Her arm ached, and her bladder was full, but everything else was A-okay. She keyed the radio and gave the order that both platoons had been waiting for. "Red One to Blue One and Green One . . . Proceed to objective. Over."

The response came so quickly that McKay missed whatever acknowledgments the two Platoon leaders might have sent. The key was to neutralize the Banshees and the Ghosts so quickly, so decisively, that the ODST troopers would be able to cross the long stretch of open ground and reach the *Autumn* virtually unopposed. That's why no fewer than three of the powerful M19 rocket launchers were aimed at each Banshee— and three Marines had been assigned to each of the half dozen target Ghosts.

Two of the four rockets fired at the Covenant aircraft missed their marks, but both Banshees took hits, and immediately exploded. Wreckage rained on the Covenant position.

The Ghost drivers on both sides of the ship were still looking upward, trying to figure out what had occurred, when more than two dozen assault weapons opened up on them.

Four of the rapid attack vehicles were destroyed within the first few seconds of the battle. The fifth, piloted by a mortally wounded Elite, described a number of large overlapping circles before crashing into the cruiser's hull and finally putting the driver out of his misery. The Elite behind the controls of the sixth and last Ghost panicked, backed away from the wholesale destruction, and toppled over the edge of the precipice.

If the alien screamed on the way down McKay wasn't able to hear it, especially with the steady *crack, crack, crack* of multiple S2 Sniper Rifles going off all around her. She keyed her radio to the command freq and ordered her platoon leaders to move up.

The assault force crossed the open area in a run, and headed toward the ship's sternmost air locks.

Covenant troops stationed within the ship heard the ruckus and hurried outside, and were met by the sight of the still-smoking wrecks of their mechanized support, and an enthusiastic—if somewhat thin—infantry assault.

Most were simply standing there, waiting for someone to tell them what to do, when the snipers' 14.5mm armor-piercing, fin-stabilized, discarding-sabot rounds began to cut them down. The impact was devastating. McKay saw Elites, Jackals, and Grunts alike throw up their arms and collapse as the rolling fusillade took its toll.

Then, as the aliens started to pull back into the relative safety of the ship's interior, McKay jumped to her feet, knowing that one of her noncoms would do likewise on the far side of the hull, and waved the snipers forward. "Switch to your assault weapons! The last one to the lock has to stay and guard it!"

All the ODST troopers knew there were plenty of things to scrounge inside the hull, and they were eager to do so. The possibility that they might end up guarding a lock rather than pillaging the *Autumn*'s interior was more than sufficient motivation to make each Marine run as fast as possible.

The purpose of the exercise was to get the last members of the Company across what could have been a Covenant killing ground and to do so as quickly as possible. McKay thought she'd been successful, thought she'd made a clean break, when a momentary shadow passed over her and someone yelled, "Contact! Enemy contact!"

The officer glanced back over her shoulder and spied a Covenant dropship. The ungainly looking craft swept in from the east, and was about to deploy additional forces. Its plasma cannon opened fire and stitched a line of black dots in the dirt, out toward the edge of the drop-off.

A sniper disappeared from the waist down, and still had enough air to scream as his forward motion slowed, and his torso landed on a pile of his own intestines.

McKay skidded to a halt, yelled, "Snipers! About face, *fire*!" and hoped that the brief parade ground–style orders would be sufficient to communicate what she wanted.

Each Covenant dropship had side slots, small cubicle-like spaces where their troops rode during transit, and from which they were released when the aircraft arrived over the landing zone. Had the pilot been more experienced he would have positioned the aircraft so that it was nose-on to the enemy and fired his cannon while the troops bailed out—but he wasn't, or he'd simply made a mistake, as he presented the ship's starboard side to the humans and opened the doors.

More than half the ODST snipers had switched back to their S2s and had shouldered their weapons up as the drop doors opened. They opened fire before the Covenant troops could leap to the ground. One of their rounds hit a plasma grenade and caused it to explode. A control line must have been severed, because the dropship lurched to port, pitched forward, and nosed into the ground. Twin waves of soil were gouged out of the plateau as the aircraft slid forward, hit a boulder, and exploded into flame.

Secondary explosions cooked off and the twin hulls disintegrated. The sound of the blast bounced off the *Autumn*'s hull and rolled across the surrounding plain.

The Marines waited a moment to see if any of the aliens would try to crawl, walk, or run away, but none of them did.

McKay heard the muffled *thump, thump, thump* of automatic weapons fire coming from within the ship behind her, knew the job was only half done, and waved to the half dozen Marines. "What are you waiting for? Let's go!"

The Helljumpers looked at one another, grinned, and followed McKay into the ship. The El-Tee might *look* like a wild-eyed maniac, but she knew her stuff, and that was good enough for them.

The soil was still damp from the rain, so when the sun hit the top of the mesa a heavy mist started to form, as if a battalion of spirits had been released from bondage.

Keyes, exhausted by his captivity, not to mention the harrowing escape from the *Truth and Reconciliation*, had literally collapsed and slept hard for the next three hours.

Now, awakened by both a nightmare and the internal

clock that was still attuned to the arbitrarily set ship time, the Naval officer was up and prowling about.

The view from the rampart was nothing less than spectacular, looking out over a flat plain to the gently rolling hills beyond. A bank of ivory-white clouds scudded above the hills. The vista was *so* beautiful, *so* pristine, that it was difficult to believe that Halo was a weapon.

He heard the scrape of footsteps, and turned to watch Silva emerge from the staircase that led up to the observation platform. "Good morning, sir," the Marine said. "I heard you were up and around. May I join you?"

"Of course," Keyes said, gesturing to a place at the waist-high wall. "Please do. I took a self-guided tour of the landing pads, the Shade emplacements, and the beginnings of the maintenance shop. Good work, Major. You and your Helljumpers are to be congratulated. Thanks to you, we have a place to rest, regroup, and plan."

"The Covenant did some of the work for us," Silva replied modestly, "but I agree, sir, my people did a hell of a job. Speaking of which, I thought I should let you know that Lieutenant McKay and two platoons of ODSTs are fighting their way into the *Autumn* even as we speak. If they retrieve the supplies we need, Alpha Base will be able to hold for quite a while."

"And if the Covenant attacks before then?"

"Then we are well and truly screwed. We're running short on ammo, food, and fuel for the Pelicans."

Keyes nodded. "Well, let's hope McKay pulls it off. In the meantime there are some other things we need to consider."

Silva found the easy, almost offhanded manner in which Keyes had reassumed command to be a bit irritating, even though he knew it was the other officer's obligation to do so. There was a clear-cut chain of command, and now that Keyes was free, the Naval officer was in charge. There was nothing the Marine could do except look interested—and hope his superior came up with at least some of the right ideas.

"Yes, sir. What's up?"

So Keyes talked, and Silva listened, as the Captain reviewed what he had learned while in captivity. "The essence of the matter is that while the races which comprise the Covenant *seem* to possess a high level of technology, most if not all of it may have been looted from the beings they refer to as the 'Forerunners,' an ancient civilization which left artifacts on dozens of planets, and presumably was responsible for constructing Halo.

"In the long run, the fact that they are adaptive, rather than innovative, may prove to be their undoing. For the moment, however, before we can take advantage of that weakness, we must first find the means to survive. *If* Halo is a weapon, and *if* it has the capacity to destroy all of humanity as they seem to believe, then we must find the means to neutralize it—and perhaps turn it against the Covenant.

"That's why I ordered Cortana and the Master Chief to find the so-called Control Room to which the aliens have alluded, and see if there's a way to block the Covenant's plan."

Silva placed his forearms on the top of the wall that fronted the rampart and looked out over the plain. If one knew where to look, and had a good eye, he could see the blast-scarred ground where the Ghosts had attacked, the Helljumpers had held, and some of his Marines lay buried.

"I see what you mean, sir. Permission to speak freely?"

Keyes looked at Silva, then back to the view. "Of course. You're second in command here, and obviously you know your way around ground engagements far better than I do. If you have ideas, suggestions, or concerns, I want to hear them."

Silva nodded respectfully. "Thank you, sir. My question has to do with the Spartan. Like everyone else, I have nothing but respect for the Chief's record. However, is he the right person for the mission you have in mind? Come to think of it, is any *one* person right for that kind of operation?

"I know that the Master Chief has an augmented body," Silva continued, "not to mention the advantage that the armor gives him, but take a look around. This base, these defenses, were the work of normal human beings.

"The SPARTAN program is a failure, Captain—the fact that the Chief is the only one left proves that, so let's put your mission into the hands of some real honest-to-god Marines and let them earn their pay.

"Thanks for hearing me out."

Keyes had been in the Navy for a long time. He knew Silva was ambitious, not only for himself, but for the ODST branch of the Marine Corps. He also knew that Silva was brave, well-intentioned, and in this case, flat-out *wrong*. But how to tell him that? He needed Silva's enthusiastic support if any of them were going to make it out of this mess alive.

The Captain considered Silva's words, then nodded. "You make some valid points. What you and your 'honest-to-god' Marines have accomplished on this butte is nothing short of miraculous.

"However, I can't agree with your conclusions regarding the Chief or the SPARTAN program. First, it's important to understand that what makes the Chief so effective isn't *what* he is, but *who* he is. His record is not the result of technology—not because of what they've done to him but *in spite* of what they've done to him, and the pain he has suffered.

"The truth is that the Chief would have grown up to be a remarkable individual regardless of what the government did or didn't do to him. Do I think children should be snatched away from their families? Raised by the military? Surgically altered? No, I don't, not during normal times."

He sighed and folded his arms across his chest. "Major, one of my first assignments was to escort the Spartan's project leader during the selection process for the candidates. At the time, I didn't know the full scope of the operation—and I probably would have resigned had I known.

"These *aren't* normal times. We're talking about the very real possibility of *total extinction*, Major. How many people did we lose in the Outer Colonies? How many did the Covenant kill on Jericho VII? On Reach? How many will be glassed if they locate Earth?"

It was a rhetorical question. The Marine shook his head. "I don't know, sir, but I do know *this*. More than twenty-five years ago, when I was a second lieutenant, the people who invented the Chief thought it would be fun to test their new pet weapon on some *real* meat. They engineered a situation in which four of my Marines would run into your friend, take offense at something he did, and try to teach him a lesson.

"Well, guess what? The plan worked perfectly. The plan sucked my people in, and the freak not only kicked the hell out of them, he left two of them dead—beaten to death in a goddamned ship's gymnasium. I don't know what you call that, sir, but I call it murder. Were there repercussions? Hell, no. The windup toy got a pat on the head and a ticket to the showers. It was all in a day's bloody work."

Keyes looked bleak. "For whatever it's worth I'm truly sorry about what happened to your men, Major, but here's the truth: Maybe it isn't nice—hell, maybe it isn't even *right*—but if I could get my hands on a million Spartans I'd take every single one of them. As for this particular mission, yes, I believe it's possible that your people could get the job done, and if that's all we had, I wouldn't hesitate to send them in. But the Chief has a number of distinct advantages, not the least of which is Cortana, and by taking this task on he will free your Helljumpers to handle other things. Lord knows there's plenty to do. My decision stands."

Silva nodded stiffly. "Sir, yes sir. My people will do everything they can to support both the Chief and Cortana."

"Yes," Keyes said, as he gazed up into the gently curving ring, "I'm sure they will."

The normally dark room was bright with artificial light. Zuka 'Zamamee had studied the raid on the *Truth and Reconciliation*, taken note of the manner in which the human AI had accessed the Covenant battlenet, and analyzed the nature of the electronic intrusions to see what the entity seemed most interested in.

Then, based on that analysis, he had constructed projections of what the humans would do next. Not *all* of the humans, since that lay outside the parameters of his mission, but the one person in whom he was truly interested. An individual who appeared to be part of a specialized, elite group similar to his own, and would almost certainly be sent to follow up on what the humans had learned.

Now, in the room that led directly into the Security Control Center, 'Zamamee laid a trap. The armored human would come, he felt sure of that, and once inside the snare, the human would meet his end. The thought cheered 'Zamamee immensely and he hummed a battle hymn as he worked.

There was a flash, followed by a loud *bang!* as the fragmentation grenade went off. A Jackal screamed, an assault weapon stuttered, and a Marine yelled, "Let me know if you want some more!"

"Good work!" McKay exclaimed. "That's the last of them. Close the hatch, lock it, and post a fireteam here to make sure they don't cut their way out. The Covenant is welcome to the upper decks. What we need is down here."

The battle had been raging for hours by then as McKay and her Marines fought to push the remaining enemy forces out of key portions of the *Autumn* and into the sections of the ship that weren't mission-critical.

As the Helljumpers sealed the last interdeck ladder not already secured, they had what they'd been striving for: free and unfettered access to the ship's main magazine, cargo holds, and vehicle bays.

In fact, even as the second platoon pushed the last of the aliens out of the lower decks, the first platoon, under the leadership of Lieutenant Oros, had begun the important task of hitching trailers to the fleet of Warthogs stowed in the *Autumn*'s belly and loading them with food, ammo, and the long list McKay had brought with her of other supplies. Then, once each 'Hog-trailer combo was ready, the Marines drove them down makeshift ramps onto the hardpan below.

Once outside, and positioned laager style, the combined power of the LRV-mounted M41 light antiaircraft guns formed a potent defense against possible attack by Covenant dropships, Banshees, and Ghosts. It wouldn't hold out forever, but it would do the most important job: It would buy them *time*.

Adding to the supply column's already formidable firepower were four M808B Scorpion Main Battle Tanks, or MBTs, which rumbled down off the ramps, and threw dirt rooster tails up off their powerful treads as they growled into position within the screen established by the Warthogs.

The MBTs' ceramic-titanium armor provided them with excellent protection against small arms fire—although the vehicles were vulnerable should the aliens manage to get in close. That's why provision had been made for up to four Marines to ride on top of each Scorpion's track pods.

Now, free to withdraw from the grounded cruiser and supervise final loading, McKay left Lister in charge of keeping the aliens penned up.

As she exited the ship, McKay caught sight of two heavily loaded Pelicans flying off in the general direction of the butte, each with a 'Hog clutched beneath its belly. And there, arrayed on the hardpan in front of her, twenty-six Warthog-trailer combinations sat ready to roll, with still more coming off the ship.

Their only problem was personnel. As a result of the work only fifty-two effectives remained, which meant that the stripped-down infantry company would be hard-pressed to crew thirty-four vehicles and fight, should that become necessary. Both McKay and her noncoms would all play a role as drivers or gunners during the return trip.

Oros saw the Company Commander emerge from the *Autumn*'s hull. The Platoon Leader was caged inside one of the Cyclops exoskeletons taken from the ship. Servos whined in sympathy with her movements as she crossed the intervening stretch of wheel-churned dirt to the point where McKay waited with hands on hips. Grime covered her face and her body armor was charred where a plasma pulse had hit. "You look good in orange."

Oros grinned. "Thanks, boss. Did you see the Pelicans?"

"As a matter of fact I did. They looked a bit overloaded."

"Yeah, the pilots were starting to whine about weight, but I bribed them with a couple of candy bars. They'll be back in about forty-five minutes. When they do we'll wrestle fuel bladders into the cargo compartments, fill them from the ship, and top their tanks all at the same time. Then, just to make sure we get our money's worth, we'll hook a 50mm MLA autocannon under each fuselage and take those out as well."

McKay raised both eyebrows. "Autocannons? Where did you get those?"

"They were part of the *Autumn*'s armament," the other officer answered cheerfully. "I thought it would be fun to spot the occasional Covenant dropship from the top of the mesa."

He paused then added, "That's the good news."

"What's the bad news?"

"A lot of gear didn't survive the crash. No missile or rocket pods for the Pelicans, and we're almost bone dry on 70mm for their chin guns. We can't count on air support for much more than bus rides."

"Damn." She scowled. Without well-armed air support, Alpha Base was going to be a lot tougher to defend.

"Affirmative," Oros agreed. "Oh, and I ordered the pilots to bring fifteen additional bodies on the return trip. Clerks, medics, anybody who can drive or fire an M41. That would allow me to squeeze some additional 'Hogs into the column and put at least two people on each tank."

McKay raised an eyebrow. "You 'ordered' them to bring more bodies?"

"Well, I kind of let them believe that *you* whistled them up."

McKay shook her head. "You are amazing."

"Yes, ma'am," Oros replied shamelessly. *"Semper Fi."*

The Pelicans swept over the glittering sea, passed over a line of gently breaking surf, and flew parallel with the beach. Foehammer saw a construct up ahead, a headland beyond, and a whole lot of Covenant troops running around in response to the sudden and unexpected arrival of two UNSC dropships. Rawley fought the urge to trigger the Pelican's 70mm chin gun. She'd expended the last of her ammo on the last pass—had watched geysers of sand chase an Elite up the beach, and was rewarded by the sight of the alien disappearing in a cloud of his own blood—and it didn't look like more were coming anytime soon.

She keyed open a master channel. "The LZ is hot, repeat, *hot*," Foehammer emphasized. "Five to dirt."

The Master Chief stood next to the open hatch, and waited for Foehammer's signal: "Touchdown! Hit it, Marines!"

He was among the first to step off the ramp, his boots leaving deep impressions in the soft sand.

He paused for a quick look around, then started down-spin to the point where the aliens waited. No sooner had the last member of the landing party disembarked than the Pelicans were airborne once more—and flying up-spin.

Plasma fire stuttered down from the top of a rise as the Marines advanced up the sandy slope, careful to fire staggered bursts, so the entire group didn't wind up reloading at the same time. The Spartan ran forward, added his fire to the rest, and sent an Elite sprawling to the ground. The Covenant forces were outnumbered for once and the human attackers wasted little time cutting them down. The whole fight lasted only ten minutes.

Time to get moving. He reviewed the mission objectives as he surveyed the LZ: Find and secure a Covenant-held facility, some kind of map room—which the enemy had already captured.

The Covenant called the site "the Silent Cartographer"—which could presumably pinpoint the location of Halo's control room. Keyes had been very adamant about the urgency of the mission. "If the Covenant figure out how to turn Halo into a weapon, we're cooked."

Maybe, with Cortana's help, they had a good chance of figuring out where the hell the ring's control systems were housed. All they had to do is take it away from an entrenched enemy.

The Spartan heard a burst of static followed by Foehammer's cheerful voice as her Pelican swooped back into the LZ area. *"Echo 419 inbound. Did someone order a Warthog?"*

A Marine said, "I didn't know that you made house calls, Foehammer."

The pilot chuckled. *"You know our motto: 'we deliver.'"*

The Master Chief waited for the dropship to deposit the LRV on the beach, saw two Marines jump on board, and climbed up behind the wheel. The soldier riding shotgun nodded. "Ready when you are, Chief."

The Spartan put his foot on the accelerator, sand shot out from under the vehicle's tires, and the 'Hog left parallel tracks as it raced along the edge of the beach.

They rounded the headland in minutes, and entered the open area beyond. There was a scattering of trees, some weathered boulders, and a swath of green ground cover. "Firing!" the gunner called, and pulled his trigger. The petty officer saw Covenant troops scurry for cover, steered right to give the three-barreled weapon a better angle, and was soon rewarded with a batch of dead Grunts and a badly mangled Jackal.

The Spartan drove the Warthog uphill, turning to avoid obstacles, careful to maintain the vehicle's traction. It wasn't long before the humans neared the top of the slope and spotted the massive structure beyond. The top curved downward, cut dramatically in, and gave way to a flat area where a Covenant dropship had been docked.

It appeared that the aircraft had just finished loading: It backed out of a U-shaped slot, swung out toward the ocean, and quickly disappeared. The noise generated by its engines covered the sound made by the Warthog and provided the defenders with something to look at.

The gunner tracked the aircraft but knew better than to open fire and attract unwanted attention. The area beyond was crawling with Covenant troops. "Anyone else see what *I* see?" the second leatherneck inquired. "How are we supposed to get around *that*?"

The Master Chief killed the 'Hog's engine, motioned for the Marines to remain where they were, and eased his way up to a point where a fallen log offered him some cover. He drew his pistol, took aim, and opened fire. Four Grunts and an Elite fell beneath the quick barrage of gunfire.

The response was nearly instantaneous as the surviving troops ran for cover and a series of plasma bolts blew chunks of wood out of the protective log.

Confident that he had whittled the opposition down to a more manageable size, the Chief eased his way back to the LRV and pulled himself up into the driver's seat. The Marines waited to see what he would do next. "Check your weapons," he advised, as he hit the ignition switch and the big engine roared to life. "We have some cleanup to do."

"Roger that," the gunner said grimly. "It looks like we have KP duty again."

There was no telling what the Covenant troops expected the humans to do, but judging from the way they ran around screaming, the possibility of an old-fashioned frontal assault just hadn't occurred to them.

The Spartan aimed the vehicle for the front of the complex, spotted the hallway that extended back toward the face of the cliff, and drove straight inside. It was a tight fit, and the Warthog wallowed a bit as the big off-road tires rolled over a couple of dead Grunts, but the strategy worked. Both Marines opened up on the Covenant troops and the Chief ran one of them down.

Then, once the outer part of the structure had been cleared, the Master Chief parked the LRV where the Marines could provide him with fire support, and ventured inside. A series of ramps led down through darkened hallways to the antechamber below. It was full of aliens. The Master Chief tossed a grenade in among them, backed up out of the way, and sprayed the ramp with bullets. The grenade went off with a satisfying *wham!* and body parts flew high into the air before thumping to the floor.

Cortana said, "Don't let them lock the doors!"

Too late. The doors noiselessly flashed shut.

The Spartan polished off the last of the resistance, checked to confirm that the doors were locked, and was already on his way back to the surface when the AI accessed the suit's radio.

"*Cortana to Keyes . . .*"

"*Go ahead, Cortana. Have you found the Control Center?*"

"*Negative, Captain. The Covenant have impeded our progress. We can't proceed unless we can disable the installation's security system.*"

"*Understood,*" Keyes replied. "*Use any means necessary to force your way into the facility and find Halo's Control Center. Failure is not an option.*"

The Master Chief was back in the 'Hog and halfway to the LZ by the time the Captain signed off. "*Good luck, people. Keyes out.*"

If the front door is locked—then go around back. That's what the Spartan figured as the LRV rolled back the way it had come, through the LZ. The Marine seated next to him exchanged insults with a buddy stationed on the beach.

They had just rounded a bluff when Cortana said, "Look up to the right. There's a path that leads toward the interior of the island."

The AI had no more than finished her sentence when the gunner said, "Freaks at two o'clock!" and opened fire.

The Spartan ran the Warthog up a slope, allowed the M41 LAAG to handle the heavy lifting, and positioned the vehicle so the gunner could put fire on the ravine ahead. "Tell me something, Cortana," the Master Chief said, as he lowered himself to the ground. "How come you're always advising me to go up gravity lifts, run down corridors, and sneak through forests while making no mention of all the enemy troops that seem to inhabit such places?"

"Because I don't want you to feel unnecessary," the AI replied easily. "For example, given the fact that your sensors are telling both of us that there are at least five Covenant soldiers lying in wait farther up the ravine, it's logical to suppose that there are even more beyond them. Does *that* make you feel better?"

"No," the Spartan admitted as he checked to ensure that both of his weapons were fully loaded.

He charged up the ravine and took cover behind a large outcropping of rock. Plasma bolts melted the stone near his head, and he snapped a quick shot in return. The Grunt snarled and dove for cover, as a pair of his partners opened up on the Spartan's position. Behind them, a cobalt-armored Elite urged them forward.

The Master Chief took a deep breath. *Time to go to work,* he thought. He sprinted from his cover and his pistol's reports echoed through the narrow ravine.

The skirmish took mere minutes. His shield indicator pulsed a warning yet again, and he paused at the top of the ravine to allow it time to recharge. His gun swept the area, and noted the circular structure that dominated a small depression at the top of the ravine.

His shield had just begun a recharge cycle, feeding off the armor's capacious power plant, when the pair of Hunter aliens burst from cover and lobbed fire at his position.

The first blast struck him square in the chest and sent him tumbling backward. The second shot was stopped by a thick-trunked tree. A trickle of blood pooled in the corner of his left eye. He shook his head to clear his blurred vision and rolled to his left. A third shot kicked up a plume of soil where he had lain just seconds before.

The Chief tossed a frag grenade, counted to three, then sprang to his feet and sidestepped to his right, firing all the way.

He'd timed it perfectly. The grenade detonated, and the flash and smoke briefly confused the aliens. His rounds bounced from their thick armor plates. In unison, they spun to face him, their weapons glowing green as they charged for another salvo.

Another grenade detonated in their path and slowed the Hunters' advance. They fired through the smoke and the crash of their weapons thundered through the low ravine.

The Hunters moved forward, eager for the kill—and realized too late that he'd doubled back and closed in on them. His assault rifle barked and tore into the gaps in their armor at close range. They screamed and died.

The Master Chief followed the terrain as it gradually sloped back down to the west. He dealt with a brace of sentries, then located his objective: a way into the massive structure that loomed above. The human saw a dark, shadowy door, slipped through the opening. He felt the gloom settle around him.

His biochemically altered eyes quickly adjusted to the darkness, and he moved deeper into the structure, pausing only to feed a fresh magazine into his assault rifle.

One level below, Zuka 'Zamamee listened. Someone was on the way, the desperate radio traffic testified to that, and it seemed safe to assume that it was the very human he had set out to kill. The fact that the transmissions ceased amid the clatter of human weaponry attested to the fact that the armored human was here.

But would he enter the trap? He had carefully seeded references to the map room into the stream of battle updates. If the humans had tapped into the network using the downed ship's AI, then they would have no choice but to send this fearsome soldier to find it.

Yes, the Elite thought, as his highly sensitive ears heard the scrape of a booted foot, a muted *click* as a new magazine slid home, and the subtle rasp of armor. *It won't be long now.*

'Zamamee looked left and right, assured himself that the Hunters were in position, and withdrew to his hiding place. Others were present inside the cargo module as well, including Yayap and a team of Grunts.

The Master Chief hit the bottom of the ramp, saw the alien cargo modules that populated the center of the dimly lit room, and knew that damned near anything could be lurking among them. Something—instinct, or perhaps only luck—caused his heart to beat a little faster as he put his back to a wall and slid sideways. Something wasn't right.

Light filtered in through an ornate window which enabled the Spartan to see that there was an alcove to his left. He eased in that direction, felt a cold weight hit the bottom of his stomach as he heard movement, and turned toward the sound.

The Hunter rushed out of the darkness, intent on smashing the Chief with his shield. A steady stream of 7.62mm bullets hammered the Hunter's chest plate and slowed his rate of advance.

'Zamamee, backed by Yayap and his team of Grunts, chose that moment to emerge from the relative safety of the cargo module. The Elite was frightened, but determined to conceal it, and he raised his weapon. But the Hunter was in his line of fire.

Then, as if the melee weren't confusing enough, the

second Hunter charged in, bumped into the Elite, and sent him spinning to the cold metal floor.

Yayap, who found himself standing out in the middle of the floor, was about to order a retreat when one of his subordinates, a Grunt named Linglin, fired a weapon.

It was a stupid thing to do since there was no clear target to shoot at, but that's what Grunts were encouraged to do when in doubt: shoot. Linglin fired, and the plasma bolt flew straight and true. It hit the second Hunter in the back, and threw the spined warrior forward, and caused him to collide with his bond brother.

"Uh-oh," Yayap muttered.

The Master Chief saw his opponent start to go down, shot him in the back, and brought the assault weapon back up. The fact that the second Hunter was already down came as something of a surprise, albeit a pleasant one, and he looked for something else to shoot.

No doubt stunned by the enormity of his error, and terrified regarding the potential consequences, Linglin was still backing away when the bulky, armored human raised his weapon and fired. Yayap felt Linglin's blood spray the side of his face as he tripped over his own feet, fell over backward, and used his hands to push himself back into the shadows. A hand grabbed hold of his combat harness, jerked the Grunt into the still yawning cargo module, and held him in place. "Silence!" 'Zamamee instructed. "This battle is over. We must live to fight another."

That sounded *very* good, maybe the most sensible thing he'd heard in a hundred units, so Yayap held his breath as the human walked past the open cargo module. He briefly wondered if there was some way he could get a transfer back to a normal frontline unit. To the diminutive alien trooper, such an assignment seemed considerably less dangerous.

His nerves on edge, fully expecting yet *another* attack, the Spartan circled the room. But there was nothing for him to deal with except his own twitchiness and the heavy silence which settled over the room.

"Nice job, Chief," Cortana said. "Head through the cargo modules. The security center lies beyond."

The Master Chief followed Cortana's directions, entered a hall, and followed it into a room that featured a small constellation of lights floating at its very center. "Use the holo panel to shut down the security system," Cortana suggested, and, eager to complete the job before anyone else could attack him, the Spartan hurried to comply. He was again struck by an odd near-familiarity with the glowing controls.

Cortana used the suit sensors to examine the results. "Good!" she exclaimed. "That should open the door that leads into the main shaft. Now all we have to do is find the Silent Cartographer and the map to the Control Room."

"Right," the Master Chief replied. "That, and avoid capture in unknown territory, already held by the enemy, with no air support or backup."

"Do you have a plan?" she asked.

"Yes. When we get there, I'm going to kill every single Covenant soldier I find."

CHAPTER

SIX

Three parallel columns of vehicles are pretty hard to hide, and McKay didn't even try. The combination of some thirty Warthogs and four Scorpions raised a cloud of dust that was visible from more than two kilometers away. No doubt the heat produced by the machines registered on sensors clear out in space. Banshee recon flights could have tracked them from the minute they hit the trail, and there was only one logical place the vehicles could be headed: the butte called Alpha Base.

It wasn't too surprising that the Covenant not only organized a response, but a massive one. Here, after days of humiliation, was the opportunity to avenge themselves on the beings who had taken the butte away from them, paid a surprise visit to the *Truth and Reconciliation*, and raided more than a dozen other locations besides.

Knowing she was in for a fight, McKay organized the vehicles into three temporary platoons. The first platoon was comprised of Warthogs under the command of Lieutenant Oros. She had orders to ignore ground targets and concentrate on defending the column from airborne attacks.

Sergeant Lister was in charge of the second platoon's Scorpion Main Battle Tanks, which, because of their vulnerability to infantry, were kept at the center of the formation.

The third platoon, under McKay herself, was charged with ground defense, which meant keeping Ghosts and infantry off the other two platoons. A third of her vehicles, five Warthogs in all, were unencumbered by trailers and left free to serve as a quick reaction force.

By giving each platoon its own individual assignment, the officer hoped to leverage the Company's overall effectiveness, ensure fire discipline, and reduce the possibility of casualties caused by friendly fire, a real danger in the kind of melee that she expected.

As the Marines headed east toward Alpha Base, the first challenge lay at the point where the flat terrain ended. Hills rolled up off the plain to form a maze of canyons, ravines, and gullies which, if the humans were foolish enough to enter them, would force the vehicles to proceed single file, which rendered the convoy vulnerable to air and ground attacks. There was a different route, however, a pass approximately half a klick wide. All three columns could pass through it without breaking formation.

The problem, and a rather obvious one, was the fact that a pair of rather sizable hills stood guard to either side of the pass, providing the Covenant with the perfect platform from which to fire down on them.

As if that weren't bad enough, a *third* hill lay just beyond, creating a second gate through which the humans would have to pass before gaining the freedom of the plain beyond. It was a daunting prospect—and McKay felt a rising sense of despair as the company drew within rifle shot of the opposing hills. She wasn't especially religious—but the ancient psalm seemed to form itself in her mind. "Yea, though I walk through the valley of the shadow of death . . ."

Screw it, she thought. She ordered the convoy to lock and load and prepare for a fight. Psalms weren't going to win the coming fight. Firepower would.

From his vantage point high on what Covenant forces had designated as "Second Hill," the Elite Ado 'Mortumee used a powerful monocular to eye the human convoy. With the exception of five vehicles, the rest of the alien LRVs were hooked to heavily laden trailers, which prevented them from making much speed. Also serving to slow the convoy down was the presence of four of the humans' cumbersome tanks.

Rather than risk passage through the hills, their commanding officer had opted to use the pass. Understandable, but a mistake for which the human would pay.

'Mortumee lowered the monocular and turned to look at the Wraith. Though not normally a fan of the slow-firing, lumpy-looking tanks, he had to admit that the design was perfect for the work at hand, and in combination with an identical unit stationed on First Hill, the monster at his elbow was certain to make short work of the oncoming convoy.

The counterthreat, if that's what it was, would come from the armored behemoths which rolled along at the very center of the human formation. They *looked* powerful, but never having seen one in action, and having found precious little data on them within the intel files, 'Mortumee wasn't sure what to expect.

"So," a voice said from behind him, "the Council of Masters has sent me a spy. Tell me, *spy,* who are you here to watch: the humans or me?"

'Mortumee turned to find that Field Master Noga 'Putumee had approached him from behind, something he did rather quietly for such a large being. Though known for his bravery, and his leadership in the field, 'Putumee was also famous for his blunt, confrontational, and paranoid ways. There was a good deal of truth in the officer's half-serious suggestion, however, since 'Mortumee had been sent to watch both the Field Master *and* the enemy.

'Mortumee ignored the field commander's blunt tone, and clicked his mandibles. "Someone has to count all the human bodies, write the report celebrating your latest victory, and lay the groundwork for your next promotion."

If there was a chink in 'Putumee's psychological armor it was in the vicinity of his ego, and 'Mortumee would have sworn that he saw the other officer's already massive chest expand slightly in response to the praise.

"If words were troops you would lead a mighty army indeed. So, spy, are the Banshees ready?"

"Ready and waiting."

"Excellent," 'Putumee replied. The gold-armored Elite turned his own monocular on the approaching convoy. "Order the attack."

"As you order, Commander."

'Putumee nodded.

McKay heard the incoming Banshees and the prospect of action banished her butterflies to a less noticeable sector of her stomach. The sound started as a low drone, quickly transformed itself into a buzz, then morphed into a bloodcurdling wail as the officer keyed her mike.

"This is Red One: We have hostile aircraft inbound. First Platoon is clear to engage. Everyone else will remain on standby. This is the warm-up, people, so stay sharp. There's more on the way. Over and out."

There were five flights of ten Banshees each, and the first group came through the pass so low that 'Mortumee found himself looking *down* on the wave of aircraft. Sun glinted off the burnished, reflective metal of the Banshees' wings.

It was tempting to jump into his own aircraft and join them, thrilling to the feel of the low altitude flight, as well as the steady *boom*ing of outgoing plasma fire. Such pleasures were denied the spy if he was to maintain the objectivity required to carry out his important work.

Eager to have the first crack at the humans, and determined to leave nothing for subsequent flights to shoot at, the pilots of the first wave fired the moment they came within range.

First Platoon's Marines saw the aircraft appear low on the horizon, watched the bursts of lethal energy jettison their way, and knew better than to engage individual targets. Not yet, anyway. Instead, consistent with the orders that Lieutenant Oros had given, the Helljumpers aimed their M41 LAAGs at a point just west of the pass, and opened fire all at once. The Banshees didn't have brakes, and the pilots had just started to turn, when they ran right into the meat grinder.

'Mortumee understood the problem right away, as did 'Putumee, who ordered the following waves to break up and attack the convoy independently.

The orders came too late for eight of the first ten aircraft, which were ripped into thousands of pieces, and fell like smoking snow.

A pair of the flyers got through the storm of gunfire.

One of the Banshees managed to hit a Warthog with a burst of superheated plasma, killing the gunner, and slagging his weapon. The LRV continued to roll, however—which meant that the trailer and its load of supplies did as well.

Once through the hail of bullets, the surviving Banshees turned and lined up for a second pass.

As the second flight of Covenant aircraft arrived from the east, split up, and launched individual attacks, Field Master 'Putumee barked an order into his radio. The mortar tanks on First and Second Hills fired in unison. Blue-white orbs of fire, trailing tendrils of energy, shot high into the sky, hung suspended for a moment, then began to fall.

The plasma mortars fell with a deliberate, almost casual slowness. They arced gracefully into the ground and a deafening thunderclap shook the ground. Neither round found a target, but these were ranging shots, and that was to be expected.

McKay heard a Marine say, "*What the hell was* that?" over the command freq, then heard Lister tear a strip off him.

She knew exactly what that was, even if the Marine didn't. It was a Wraith, the Covenant's brutal heavy armor unit. For the soldier asking, it didn't matter much though, because the weapon in question was clearly lethal, and would cause havoc in the close quarters of the pass. She keyed her radio.

"Red One to Green One: Those mortars originated from those hilltops. Let's give the bastards a haircut. Over."

"*This is Green One*," Lister acknowledged. "*Roger that, over.*"

There was a burst of static as Lister switched to his

platoon's freq, though McKay could hear every word on the command channel.

"*Green One to Foxtrot One and Two: Lay some high explosive on the hill to the left. Over.*"

"*Green One to Foxtrot Three and Four: Ditto the hill to the right. Over.*"

Banshees wheeled, turned, and poured fire down on the hapless humans as one of the pilots fired his fuel rod cannon and scored a direct hit. A trailer full of precious ammo exploded, wrapped the Warthog in a fiery embrace, and took the LRV with it. Covenant forces watching from the hilltops felt a sense of exultation, and more than that, the pleasure of revenge.

'Mortumee was there to document the battle, not celebrate it, though he watched in fascination as two of the tank turrets swiveled to his left in order to fire on First Hill, while two turned in the opposite direction and seemed to point directly at *him*.

The Elite wondered if he should seek cover, but before the message to move could reach his feet, he heard a reverberating roar as the 105mm shell passed through the intervening air space, followed by a loud *craack!* as the shell landed about fifty units away. A column of bloody dirt flew high into the air. Body parts, weapons, and pieces of equipment continued to rain down as the half-deafened 'Mortumee recovered his composure and ran for cover.

Field Master 'Putumee laughed out loud and pointed to show a member of his staff where 'Mortumee had taken shelter behind some rocks. That was when the second round detonated just below the summit of the hill and started a small landslide. "This," the Elite said happily, "is a *real* battle. Keep an eye on the spy."

Stung by the loss of a Warthog, a trailer-load of ammo, and three Marines, McKay was starting to question the division of labor she had imposed, and was just about to free her platoon's gunners to fire on the Banshees, when her driver said, "Uh-oh, look at that!"

A series of plasma bolts stitched a line along the 'Hog's side, scorched the vehicle's paint, and kicked up geysers of dirt as the officer followed the pointing finger. A force of Ghosts skittered into the pass.

"Red One to all Romeo units . . . follow me!" McKay yelled into her mike, and tapped the driver's arm. "Go get 'em, Murphy—let's clear that gap."

No sooner had the officer spoken than the Marine put his foot into it, the gunner whooped, and the LRV leapt forward.

The rest of the five-vehicle reaction force followed just as the Wraith on Hill One hurled a third then a fourth plasma mortar high into the sky.

McKay looked up, saw the fireball slow to a near stop at the point of apogee, and knew it would be a race. Would the mortar land on top of the reaction force? Or, would the fast-moving 'Hogs slip out from under it, leaving the plasma charge to explode harmlessly on the ground?

The gunner saw the threat as well, and yelled, "Go! Go! Go!" as the driver swerved to avoid a clutch of rocks, did his best to push the accelerator through the floor. He mumbled, "Damn, damn, damn," as he felt something wet and warm puddle on his seat.

The mortar fell with increasing velocity. The first LRV slipped underneath it, quickly followed by the second and third.

Heart in her throat, McKay looked back over her shoulder as the plasma mortar landed, detonated, and blew a large crater out of the ground.

Then, like a miracle on wheels, Romeo Five flew through the smoke, bounced as it hit the edge of the newly created crater, and lurched up over the rim.

There was no time to celebrate as the Ghosts pulled into range and the lead vehicle opened fire. McKay raised her assault rifle, took aim at the nearest blur, and squeezed the trigger.

Master Sergeant Lister faced a harsh reality. Never mind Banshees that swooped overhead, or the Ghosts up ahead, it was his job to do something about the mortar fire, and as the hills loomed ahead, Second Platoon's Scorpions were coming up on the point when their main guns would no longer be able to elevate high enough to engage the primary target. One more salvo, that's what the tanks could deliver, before their weapons could no longer be brought to bear.

"Wake up, people," Lister said over the platoon frequency, "the last group on the left was at least fifteen meters too low, and the last group on the right overshot the hill. Make adjustments, take the tops off those hills, and do it *now*. We don't have time to screw around."

Each tank commander adjusted aim, sent their shells on the way, and prayed for a hit. They all knew that facing the Covenant would be easier than suffering Lister's wrath should the shells miss their marks.

Field Master 'Putumee watched impassively as the Wraith on First Hill exploded, taking a file of Jackals with it. He was sorry to lose the mortar tank, but the truth was that with two dozen Ghosts milling around in the pass below, he was going to have to cease fire anyway. Either that or risk killing his own troops. The

Elite snapped an order, saw one last mortar sail into the air, and watched the humans enter the gap.

Lance Corporal "Snaky" Jones was screwed, he knew that, had known it ever since the front end of his 'Hog took a hit and flipped end-for-end. He was standing behind the LAAG, firing forward over the driver's head, when he was suddenly catapulted into the air. Jones saw a blur, hit hard, and tumbled head over heels. Once his body came to a stop the Marine discovered that it was almost impossible to breathe, which was why he just lay there at first, staring up into the amazing blue sky as he gasped for air.

It was pretty, *very* pretty, until a Banshee screamed through the picture and a Warthog roared past on the left.

That was when Jones managed to scramble to his feet, and yelled into his boom mike, only to discover that it was missing. Not just the mike, but his entire helmet, which had come loose during the fall. No helmet meant *no* mike, *no* radio, and *no* possibility of a pickup.

The Lance Corporal swore, ran toward the wrecked Warthog, and gave thanks for the fact that it hadn't caught fire. The vehicle was resting on its side and the S2 was right where he had left it—clamped butt down behind the driver's seat.

It was hard to see Sergeant Corly strewn over the rear fender with half her face blown away, so Jones averted his eyes. His rucksack, the one that contained extra ammo, a med pack, and the stuff he had looted from the *Pillar of Autumn*, was right where he had left it, secured to the bottom of the gun pedestal.

Jones grabbed the pack, slung it across his back, and

grabbed the sniper rifle. He made sure the rifle was ready to fire, then clicked on the safety and ran for the nearest hill. Maybe he could find a cave, wait for the battle to end, and haul ass back to Alpha Base. Dust puffed away from the Marine's boots and death hung all around.

Lieutenant Oros estimated that First Platoon had reduced the number of attacking aircraft by two thirds—and she had a plan to deal with the rest. McKay wouldn't approve—but what was the CO going to do? Send her to some uncharted, alien-infested portion of the galaxy? The Lieutenant grinned, gave the necessary order, and jumped down to the ground.

She waved to the volunteers from four of the thirteen Warthogs she had remaining, then scampered toward a group of likely-looking rocks. All five of the Marines carried M19 SSM Rocket Launchers slung across their backs, plus assault weapons, and as many spare rockets as they could carry in the twin satchels that hung from their hands. They pounded across the hardpan, scurried into the protection offered by the surrounding boulders, and set up shop.

When everyone was ready, Oros pulled the pins on one flare after another, tossed them out beyond the circle of rocks, and watched the orange smoke billow up into the sky.

It wasn't long before the Banshee pilots spotted the smoke and, like vultures attracted to fresh carrion, hurried to the scene.

The Marines held their fire, waited until no less than thirteen of the Covenant aircraft were circling above them, and fired five rockets, all at once. A second volley followed the first—and a third followed that. There was a steady drumbeat of explosions as ten Banshees took direct hits, some from multiple rockets, and ceased to exist.

Of the aircraft that survived the barrage of rockets, two bugged out immediately. The last staggered in response to a near miss, belched smoke from its port engine, and looked like it would go down. Oros thought it was over at that point, that she and her volunteers would be free to fade into the hills, and beat feet for home.

But it wasn't to be. Unlike most of his peers, the pilot in the damaged Banshee must have had a strong desire to transcend the physical, because he turned toward the enemy, put the aircraft into a steep dive, and plunged into the pile of boulders. Oros tried to make the shot but missed—and barely had time to swear before the mortally wounded Banshee augered into the rocks and swallowed the ambush team in a ball of fire.

The fact that Lance Corporal Jones made it all the way to the base of the hill without getting killed was just plain luck. The subsequent scramble up through the loose tumble of rocks was instinctual. The desire to gain elevation is natural to any soldier, but especially to a sniper, which was what Jones had been trained to be when he wasn't busy humping supplies, operating LAAGs, or taking crap from sergeants.

The fact that Jones was about to go on the offensive, about to take it to the Covenant, *that* was a decision. Maybe not the smartest decision he'd ever made, but one he knew to be right, and to hell with the consequences.

Jones was only halfway up the side of the hill, but that was high enough to see the top of the *opposite* hill, and the tiny figures who stood there. Not the Grunts who were running this way and that, not the Jackals who lined the edge of the summit, but the shiny armor of the Elites. Those were the targets he wanted, and they seemed to leap forward as the Marine increased the magnification on his scope, and let the barrel drift slightly. Which life should he take? The one on the left with the blue armor? Or the one on the right, the shiny gold bastard? At that moment in time, in that particular place, Lance Corporal Jones was God.

He clicked the sniper rifle's safety catch, and lightly rested his finger on the trigger.

'Mortumee had emerged from hiding by that time and was standing next to Field Master 'Putumee as the human convoy cleared the pass and turned up-ring. There was a third hill off to his left—and it, too, was topped with a Wraith.

The mortar tank opened fire. For one brief moment 'Mortumee harbored the hope that the remaining tank would accomplish what the first two had not and decimate the convoy. But the humans were still out of range, and, knowing that the Wraith couldn't do them any harm, they took the time to put their own tanks into a line abreast.

A single salvo was all it took. All four of the shells landed on target, the mortar tank was destroyed, and the way was clear.

'Putumee lowered his monocular. His face was expressionless. "So, spy, how will your report read?"

'Mortumee looked at the other Elite with a pitying expression. "I'm sorry, Commander, but the facts are clear, and the report will practically write itself. Had you deployed your forces differently, down on the plain perhaps, victory would have been ours."

"An excellent point," the Field Master replied, his tone mild. "Hindsight is always perfect."

'Mortumee was about to reply, about to say something about the value of foresight, when his head exploded.

Lance Corporal Jones steadied his aim for a second shot. The first shot had been perfect. The 14.5mm slug had flown true, entered the base of Blue Boy's neck, and exited through the top of his head. That blew his helmet off, allowing a mixture of blood and brains to fountain into the air.

'Putumee snarled and threw himself backward—and thereby escaped the second bullet.

Moments later, the twin reports echoed back and forth between the two hillsides. The Field Master crabbed back to cover and fed position information to the Banshee commander, and snarled into his communications gear: "Sniper! Kill him!"

Satisfied that the sniper would be dealt with, 'Putumee stood and looked down at 'Mortumee's headless body. He bared his fangs. "It looks like I'll have to write that report myself."

Jones spat into the dirt, angry that the gold Elite had evaded the second shot. *Next time,* he promised himself. *You're* mine *next time, pal.* Banshees banked overhead, searching for his position. Jones backed into a deep crevice among the rocks. Fortunately, thanks to the loot gathered aboard the *Autumn,* he had twenty candy bars to sustain him.

The security system neutralized, the Master Chief made his way back through the alien construct, and headed toward the surface. Time to find this "Silent Cartographer" and complete this phase of the mission.

"Mayday! Mayday! Bravo 22 taking enemy fire! Repeat, we are taking fire and losing altitude." The dropship pilot's strained voice was harsh and grating—the sound of a man about to lose it.

"Understood," Cortana replied. "We're on our way."

Then, in an aside to the Spartan, the AI said, "I don't like the sound of that—I'm not certain they're going to make it."

The Master Chief agreed, and in his eagerness to get topside, made a potentially fatal error. Having just cleared the room adjacent to what appeared to be the ringworld's Security Center, he assumed that it was *still* clear.

Fortunately, the Elite—equipped with another of the Covenant's camouflage devices—announced his presence with a throaty roar just prior to firing his weapon. Plasma fire still splashed the Chief's chest, followed by a brief moment of disorientation as he tried to figure out where the attack was coming from. His motion sensor detected movement, and he aimed his weapon as best he could. He fired a sustained burst and was rewarded with an alien scream of pain.

As the Covenant warrior fell, the Master Chief made a mad dash for the ramp that led up toward the surface, reloading as he went. Walking into the once-cleared room too quickly had been stupid—and he was determined not to make the same mistake again. The fact that Cortana was there, seeing the world via his sensors, made such errors that much more embarrassing. Somehow, for reasons he hadn't had time to sort out, the human wanted the AI's approval. Silly? Maybe so, if one thought of Cortana as little more than a fancy computer program, but she was more than that. In the Chief's mind at least.

He smiled at the irony of the thought. The human-AI

interface meant that, in many ways, Cortana was *literally* in the Chief's mind, using some of his wetware for processing power and storage.

The Spartan made his way up the ramp, through a hall, and out into bright sunlight. He paused on a platform, and dropped to the slope below, as Cortana cautioned him to keep an eye peeled for Bravo 22.

Covenant troops were patrolling the beach below—a mix of Jackals and Grunts. The Master Chief drew his sidearm, switched to the 2X magnification, and decided to work from right to left. He nailed the first Jackal, missed the next, and killed a pair of Grunts who were waddling around on top of the mesa opposite his position.

As he moved farther down the slope, he could see Bravo 22's wreckage, half buried in the side of the mesa. There were no signs of life. Either the crew and passengers had been killed on impact, or some had survived and been executed by the enemy.

The possibility made him particularly angry. He turned to the right, caught the surviving Jackal on the move, and put him down. He switched to his MA5B and made his way down the grassy slope to the sand beyond. It was a short walk to the smoking wreckage and the scattering of bodies. Plasma burns on some of the bodies served to confirm the Spartan's suspicions.

Though not the most pleasant of tasks, the Chief knew he had to obtain ammo and other supplies wherever he could, and took advantage of the situation in order to stock up.

"Don't forget to grab a launcher," Cortana put in. "There's no telling what might be waiting for us when we go back to looking for the Control Room."

The Master Chief took the AI's advice and decided to ride rather than walk. The Warthog that had been tucked under the dropship's belly had come loose during the final moments of flight, hit the ground, and flipped over on its side. He approached the vehicle, reached upward, got a good purchase, and pulled. Metal creaked as the 'Hog swayed, tilted in the Spartan's direction, and started to fall. He stepped back, waited for the inevitable bounce, and climbed up behind the wheel. After a quick check to ensure that the LRV was still operable, he was off.

He skidded the Warthog into a slewing turn, then headed back to the mission LZ—the beachhead the Marines had been left to hold.

The Marines had fought off two assaults during his absence, but they still owned the real estate they had originally taken, and remained undeterred.

"Welcome back," a Corporal said as she took her place behind the three-barreled gun. "It was getting boring without you." She had a grimy face, the words CUT HERE tattooed around the circumference of her neck, and a short, stocky body.

The Chief eyed the hastily dug weapons pits and foxholes, the large pile of Covenant corpses, and the plasma-scorched sand. "Yeah, I can see that."

A freckle-faced PFC jumped into the passenger seat, a captured plasma rifle cradled in his arms. The Spartan turned back in the direction he had come from, and raced along the edge of the water. Spray flew up along the left side of the LRV and he wished he could feel the moisture on his face.

A kilometer ahead, a Hunter named Igido Nosa Hurru fumed as he paced back and forth across a docking platform still stained with Covenant blood. Word had come down from an Elite named Zuka 'Zamamee that a lone human had killed two of his brothers a few hours earlier, and was about to attack his newly reinforced position, as well. This was something the spined warrior hoped would happen so that he, and his bond brother Ogada Nosa Fasu, could have the honor of killing the alien.

So, when Hurru heard the whine of the surface vehicle's engine, and saw it round the headland, both he and his bond brother were ready. Having received the other Hunter's characteristic nod, Hurru took up a position directly outside the entrance to the complex. *If* the vehicle was some sort of trick, a ruse to lure both guards away from the door long enough for the human to slip inside, it wasn't going to work.

Fasu, always one to seize the initiative, and something of an artist with the fuel rod cannon attached to his right arm, waited for the LRV to come within range, led the vehicle to ensure that the relatively slow-moving energy pulse would have an adequate amount of time to reach its destination, and fired a single shot.

The Master Chief saw the yellow-green fuel rod appear in his peripheral vision, and made the decision to turn toward the enemy both to make the 'Hog look smaller and to give the Corporal an opportunity to fire. But he ran out of time. The Spartan had just started to spin the wheel when the energy pulse slammed into the side of the Warthog and flipped the vehicle over.

All three of the humans were thrown free. The Master Chief scrambled to his feet and looked up-slope in time to see a Hunter drop down from the structure above, absorb the shock with its massive knees, and move forward.

Both the Corporal and the freckle-faced youngster

were back on their feet by then, but the noncom, who had never seen a Hunter before, much less gone head-to-head with one, yelled, "Come on, Hosky! Let's take this bastard out!"

The Spartan yelled, "No! Fall back!" and bent over to retrieve the rocket launcher. Even as he barked the order, he knew there simply wasn't time. Another Spartan might have been able to dodge out of the way in time, but the Marines didn't have a prayer.

The distance between the alien and the two Marines had closed by then and they couldn't disengage. The Corporal threw a fragmentation grenade, saw it explode in front of the oncoming monster, and stared in disbelief as the alien kept on coming. The alien charged right through the flying shrapnel, bellowed some sort of war cry, and lowered a gigantic shoulder.

Private Hosky was still firing when the gigantic shield hit him, shattered half the bones in his body, and threw what was left onto the ground. The private remained conscious, however, which meant he was able to lie there and watch as the Hunter lifted his boot high into the air, and brought it down on his face.

The Master Chief had the launcher up on his shoulder by then and was just about to fire when the Corporal screamed something incoherent, dashed into the line of fire, and blocked his shot. The Chief yelled at her to hit the deck and was moving sideways in an attempt to get a clear line of fire when Fasu blew a hole the size of a dinner plate through the leatherneck's chest.

The Spartan hit the firing stud, and a rocket *whoosh*ed for the Hunter. With surprising agility, the massive alien hunched and sidestepped, and the rocket skimmed past him. It detonated behind the Hunter, and showered them both with debris.

The Hunter charged.

The Master Chief stepped back, knew there wouldn't be time to reload, and that the next rocket would have to fly straight and true. The surf swirled around his knees as he backed out into the ocean, fought to maintain his footing in the soft sand, and saw the alien fill his sight. Was the target too close? There wasn't time to check. He pulled the trigger, and a second rocket streaked ahead on a column of smoke and fire.

The Hunter had reached full speed and couldn't dodge in time. The creature's massive feet dug into the soft ground as it tried to alter course to avoid the rocket—to no avail. The 102mm shaped charge exploded against the very center of the Hunter's chest armor, blew through his torso, and severed his spine. There was a mighty splash as the alien creature fell face first into the water. A pool of vibrant orange blood stained the surf around the fallen Hunter.

The Master Chief took a moment to reload the launcher then slogged back up onto the beach. A distant howl of anguish issued from the other alien's throat. *Serves you right,* he thought. *You only lost one brother. I lost all of mine.*

He felt a pang of sorrow for the two dead Marines. He *should* have anticipated the long-range attack, should have briefed the leathernecks about the possibility of Hunters, should have reacted more quickly. All of which meant that it was *his* fault that the Marines were dead.

"That wasn't your fault," Cortana said gently. "Now be careful—there's *another* Hunter up on the platform."

The words were like a bucket of cold water in the face. "Mental combat," that's how his teacher, Chief Mendez, had referred to it, always stressing the importance of a cool head.

Slowly, methodically, the Master Chief worked his

way up the slope, killing Covenant soldiers with machine precision. The small groups of Grunts were irrelevant. The *real* challenge waited above.

Hurru heard the firing, knew he was being flanked, and welcomed it. Rage, sorrow, and self-pity all churned around inside him causing him to fire his fuel rod cannon again and again, as if to obliterate the human by the weight of his barrage.

The human made good use of what cover there was, put his left arm against the cliff face, and inched his way forward. The Hunter saw him and attempted to fire, but the fuel rod cannon hadn't had time to recharge after the last shot. That left the human free to fire, which he did. Hurru felt warm relief.

He was about to join his bond brother.

The rocket was a hair high, hit Hurru in the head, and blew it off. Orange blood fountained straight up, splashed the alien metal around the Hunter, and splattered his body as it collapsed.

The Spartan paused, switched to his assault weapon, and waited for the feeling of satisfaction. It never arrived. The Marines were still dead, would *always* be dead, and nothing would change that. Was it fair that he remained alive? No, it wasn't. All he could do was accomplish what they would want him to do. Forge ahead, find the map, and make their deaths count for something.

With that thought in mind, the Master Chief reentered the complex on foot, made his way through halls still slick with alien blood from his last visit, turned down the ramp, proceeded to the lower level, and passed through the door he had worked so hard to open.

The Master Chief moved into the bowels of the structure. From outside, the spires stood several stories high, which was misleading. The interior of the structure plunged deep below the surface.

He wound down a curving ramp. The air was still and slightly stale, and thick pillars of the first large chamber he moved through made the room feel like a crypt.

He slipped through heavily shadowed rooms, padded down spiral ramps, passing through galleries filled with strange forms. The walls and floors were made of the same burnished, heavily engraved metal that he'd encountered elsewhere on the ring. He clicked on his light and noticed new patterns in the metal, like the swirls in marble—as if the material were some kind of metal-stone hybrid.

The tomblike silence was shattered by the squalling of several Grunts and Jackals. There was opposition, *plenty* of it, as the human was forced to deal with dozens of Grunts, Jackals, and Elites. "It's as if they knew we were on the way," Cortana observed. "I think someone is tracking our progress, and has a pretty good idea of where we're headed."

"No kidding," the Master Chief replied dryly as he shot a Grunt and stepped over the body. "I hope we reach the Cartographer before I run out of ammo."

"We're close," the AI assured him, "but be careful. There's bound to be more Covenant ahead."

The Master Chief took Cortana's counsel to heart. He hoped that he would find a way to bypass whatever the Covenant had in store, but that wasn't to be. As the Spartan entered a large room, he saw that two Hunters had been assigned to patrol the far side of it. He slung his rifle and readied the rocket launcher. It was the right weapon for Hunters, no question about that—so long as he didn't allow either one of the monsters to get too close. A rocket fired under those conditions would kill *him* if it detonated nearby.

One of the spined aliens spotted the intruder and bellowed a challenge. The Hunter was already in motion when the rocket flashed across the room, struck him in the right shoulder, and blasted him to hell.

A second Hunter howled and fired his fuel rod cannon. The Chief swore as the wash from a slightly off-target plasma bolt set off the audible alarm, and the indicator in the upper right hand corner of his HUD morphed to red.

The Spartan turned, hoping to put the second Hunter in his sight, but the massive alien slid behind a wall.

Unable to fire, he backed off. The Hunter lunged forward, and the deadly arm-shield raked across his own already weakened shields.

The Chief grunted in pain as the edge of the shield slammed through his armor's shoulder joint. He felt a sickly tearing as the meat of his arm parted beneath the scalpel-sharp limb.

He spun, and the spine wrenched free.

The Master Chief felt a rising sense of frustration as he switched to the assault weapon, backed up a ramp, and used his greater mobility to circle behind the alien. Then he had it, a brief glimpse of unprotected flesh, and the opportunity he needed. He put a quick burst into the warrior's back, spun away, and barely escaped a blast from the plasma pistols of the Jackals that had dropped into view and opened fire.

The Master Chief hurled three grenades over a divider. One of them scored a direct hit, sprayed the walls with chunks of alien flesh, and finally brought the frantic firefight to an end.

Cortana, whose life had been on the line as well, and who had been forced to watch as the Spartan fought for both of them, processed a sense of relief. Somehow, against all odds, her human host had come through again, but it had been close, *very* close, and he was still in something akin to shock, his back pressed into a corner, his vital signs badly elevated, his eyes jerking from one shadow to the next.

The AI hesitated as she processed the dilemma. It was difficult to balance the need to move ahead and complete the mission with her concern that she might push the Master Chief *too* hard, and possibly endanger them both. Cortana's affection for the human, plus her own desire to survive, made it difficult for her to arrive at the kind of clear, rational decision that she expected of herself.

Then, just as Cortana was about to say something, anything, even if it was wrong, the Chief recovered and took the initiative. "All right," he said—whether to himself or to Cortana wasn't exactly clear. "It's time to finish this mission."

Working carefully, so as not to walk into an ambush, the Master Chief left the large room, found his way onto a downward slanting ramp. He backed into a corner and, satisfied that the area was reasonably secure, disengaged the shoulder plates of the MJOLNIR armor.

The wound was ragged, and blood flowed freely. The Chief could ignore the pain, but the blood loss would take its toll and jeopardize the mission. He made sure the motion sensor was still active, then slung his weapon.

He dug into his equipment pack and drew out his med kit. The Spartan had been wounded before, and had on several occasions performed first aid on injured comrades and himself. He quickly cleaned the wound, sprayed a stinging puff of bio-foam into the wound, then applied a quick-adhesive dressing.

In minutes, he had suited up, popped a wake-up stim, and moved on.

"Foehammer to ground team: You've got two Covenant dropships coming fast!"

The Master Chief stood at the edge of a massive chasm and monitored his allies' radio chatter. In the distance, he could barely see the twinkling of the luminescent panels that Halo's creators had left behind to illuminate these subterranean warrens. Below him, the abyss yawned and appeared to be bottomless.

He recognized the next voice as belonging to Gunnery Sergeant Waller, the Marine in charge of their LZ. *"Okay, people,"* Waller drawled, *"we got company coming. Engage enemy forces on sight."*

"It'll be easier to hold them off from *inside* the structure," Cortana put in. "Can you get inside?"

"Negative!" Waller replied. *"They're closing in too fast. We'll keep 'em busy as long as we can."*

"Give 'em hell, Marine," the AI said grimly, and broke the connection. "We'll *all* be in a tight spot if we don't get out of here before enemy reinforcements arrive."

"Roger that," the Master Chief replied, as he pushed his way down a ramp, through a pair of hatches, and into the gloomy spaces beyond. He marched over some transparent decking, crossed a footbridge and killed a pair of Grunts he found there, followed another ramp to the floor below, tossed a grenade into a group of enemies that patrolled the area, and hurried through a likely looking opening. There was a roar of outrage as an Elite fired up at him from the platform below while some Grunts barked and gibbered.

The Spartan used a grenade to grease the entire group and hurried down to see what they had been guarding. He recognized the Map Room the moment he saw the opening, and had just stepped inside when another Elite opened up on him from across the way. A sustained burst from his assault weapon was sufficient to drop the alien's personal shields, and he put the alien down with a stroke of his rifle butt.

"There!" Cortana said. "That holo panel should activate the map."

"Any idea how to activate it?"

"No," she replied, her tone arch. "*You're* the one with the magic touch."

The Master Chief took a couple of steps forward and reached a hand toward the display. He seemed to know instinctively how to activate the panel—it almost seemed hard-wired, like his fight-or-flight response.

He banished the random thought and returned to the mission. He slid his armored hand across the panel and a glowing wire-frame map appeared and seemed to float in front of him. "Analyzing," the AI said. "Halo's Control Center is"—she highlighted a section of the map in his HUD—"*there*. Interesting. It looks like some sort of shrine."

She opened a channel. "*Cortana to Captain Keyes.*"

There was silence for a moment, followed by Foehammer's voice. "*The Captain has dropped out of contact, Cortana. His ship may be out of range or may be having equipment problems.*"

"*Keep trying,*" the AI replied. "*Let me know when you reestablish contact. And then tell him that the Master Chief and I have determined the location of the Control Center.*"

Captain Jacob Keyes tried to ignore the incessant *slambam* beat of the Sergeant's colonial flip music that pounded over the intercom as the pilot lowered the dropship into a swamp. "Everything looks clear—I'm bringing her down."

The Pelican's jets whipped the water into a frenzy as the ramp was lowered and the cargo compartment was flooded with thick, humid air. It carried the nauseating stench of rotting vegetation, the foul odor of swamp gas, and the slight metallic tang typical of Halo itself. Somebody said, "*Pe-euu*," but was drowned out by Staff Sergeant Avery Johnson, who shouted, "Go! Go! Go!" and the Marines jumped down into the calf-deep water.

Somebody said, "Damn!" as water splashed up their legs. Johnson said, "Stow it, Marine," as Keyes cleared the ramp. Freed from its burden, the dropship fired its jets, powered its way up out of the glutinous air, and started to climb.

Keyes consulted a small hand comp. "The structure we're looking for is supposed to be over *there*."

Johnson eyed the pointing finger and nodded. "Okay, you slackers, you heard the Captain. Bisenti, take point."

Private Wallace A. Jenkins was toward the rear, which was almost as bad as point, but not quite. The ebony water topped his boots, seeped down through his socks, and found his feet. It wasn't all that cold—for which the Marine was thankful. Like the rest of the team, he knew that the ostensible purpose of the mission was to locate and recover a cache of Covenant weapons. Still an important thing to do, even in the wake of Lieutenant McKay's efforts to raid the *Pillar of Autumn*, and the fact that Alpha Base had been strengthened as a result.

It was a crap detail, however—especially slogging through this dark, mist-clogged swamp.

Something loomed ahead. Bisenti hoped it was what the Old Man had dragged their sorry butts into this swamp for. He hissed the word back to the topkick. "I see a building, Sarge."

There was the sound of water splashing as Johnson came forward. "Stay close, Jenkins. Mendoza, move it up! Wait here for the Captain and his squad. And get your asses inside."

Jenkins saw Keyes materialize out of the mist. "Sir!"

Johnson saw Keyes, nodded, and said, "Okay, let's move!"

Keyes followed the Marines inside. The entire situation was different from what he had expected. Unlike the Covenant, who killed nearly all of the humans they got their hands on, the Marines continued to take prisoners. One such individual, a rather disillusioned Elite named 'Qualomee, had been interrogated for hours. He swore that he'd been part of a group of Covenant soldiers who had delivered a shipment of arms to the forces guarding this very structure.

But there was no sign of a Covenant security team, or the weapons 'Qualomee claimed to have delivered, which meant that he had probably been lying. Something the Captain planned to discuss with the alien upon his return to Alpha Base. In the meantime, Keyes planned to push deeper into the complex and see what he could find. The second squad, under Corporal Lovik, was left to cover their line of retreat, while the rest of the team continued to press ahead.

Ten minutes had passed when a Marine said, "Whoa! Look at that. Something scrambled his insides."

Johnson looked down at a dead Elite. Other Covenant bodies lay sprawled around the area as well. Alien blood slicked the walls and floor. Keyes approached from behind. "What do we have, Sergeant?"

"Looks like a Covenant patrol," the noncom answered.

"Badass Special Ops types—the ones in the black armor. All KIA."

Keyes eyed the body and looked up at Bisenti. "Real pretty. Friend of yours?"

The Marine shook his head. "No, we just met."

It took another five minutes to reach a large metal door. It was locked and no amount of fooling around with the keypad seemed likely to open it. "Right," Keyes said, as he examined the obstacle. "Let's get this door open."

"I'll try, sir," the Tech Specialist, Kappus, replied, "but it looks like those Covenant worked pretty hard to lock it down."

"Just do it, son."

"Yes, sir."

Kappus pulled the spoofer out of his pack, attached the box to the door, and pressed a series of keys. Outside of the gentle beeping noises that the black box made as it tapped into the door's electronics and ran through thousands of combinations per second, there was nothing but silence.

The Marines shifted nervously, unwilling to relax. Sweat dripped down Kappus' forehead.

They held position for another few minutes, until Kappus nodded with satisfaction and opened the door. The Marines drifted inside. The electronics expert raised a hand. "Sarge! Listen!"

All of the Marines listened. They heard a soft, liquid, sort of slithery sound. It seemed to come from every direction at once.

Jenkins felt jumpy but it was Mendoza who actually put it into words. "I've got a bad feeling about this . . ."

"You've always got a bad feeling," the Sergeant put in, and was about to chew Mendoza out when a message came in over the team freq. It sounded like the second squad was in some sort of trouble, but Corporal Lovik wasn't very coherent, so it was difficult to be sure.

In fact, it almost sounded like screaming.

Keyes responded. "Corporal? Do you copy? Over."

There was no reply.

Johnson turned to Mendoza. "Get your ass back up to second squad's position and find out what the hell is going on."

"But Sarge—"

"I don't have time for your lip, soldier! I gave you an order."

"What *is* that?" Jenkins asked nervously, his eyes darting from one shadow to the next.

"Where's that coming from, Mendoza?" Sergeant Johnson demanded, the second squad momentarily forgotten.

"There!" Mendoza proclaimed, pointing to a clutch of shadows as the Marines heard the muffled sound of metal striking metal.

There was a cry of pain as something landed on Private Riley's back, drove a needlelike penetrator through his skin, and aimed it down toward his spine. He dropped his weapon, tried to grab the thing that rode his shoulders, and thrashed back and forth.

"Hold still! Hold still!" Kappus yelled, grabbing onto the bulbous creature and trying to pull it off his friend.

Avery Johnson had been in the Corps for most of his adult life, and had logged more time humping across the surface of alien planets than any of the other men in the room combined. Along the way, he'd seen a lot of strange stuff—but nothing like what skittered across the metal floor and attached itself to one of his men.

He saw a dozen pale shapes, each maybe half a meter in diameter, and equipped with a cluster of writhing tentacles. They skittered and bobbed in a loose formation, then sprang in his direction. The tentacles propelled them several meters in a single leap. He fired a short, almost panicked burst. "Let 'em have it!"

Keyes, pistol in hand, fired at one of the creatures. It popped like a balloon, with surprising force. The tiny explosion caused three more to burst into feathery shards, but it seemed as if dozens more took their place.

Keyes realized that Private Kappus had been correct. The Covenant *had* locked the door for a reason, and this was it. But maybe, just maybe, they could pull back and close the creatures inside again. "Sergeant, we're surrounded."

But Johnson's attention was elsewhere. "God damn it, Jenkins, *fire your weapon*!"

Jenkins, his face tight with fear, clutched his assault rifle with white-knuckled hands. It seemed like the little things were boiling from thin air. "There's too many!"

The Sarge started to bellow a reply, but it was as if a floodgate had opened somewhere, as a new wave of the obscene, podlike creatures rolled out of the darkness to overwhelm the humans. Marines fired in every direction. Many lost their balance as two, three, or even four of the aliens managed to get a grip on them and pull them down.

Jenkins began to back away as fear overwhelmed him.

Keyes threw up his hands with the intention of protecting his face and accidentally caught one of the monsters. He squeezed and felt the creature explode. The little bastards were fragile—but there were so damned many of them. *Another* attacker latched onto his shoulder. The Captain screamed as a razor-sharp tentacle plunged through both his uniform and his skin, wriggled under the surface of his skin, and tapped his spinal cord. There was an explosion of pain so intense that he blacked out, only to be brought back to consciousness by chemicals the thing had injected into his bloodstream.

He tried to yell for help, but couldn't make a sound. His heart raced as his extremities grew numb, one by one. His lungs felt heavy.

As Keyes began to lose touch with the rest of his body, something foul entered it, pushing his consciousness down and back even as it claimed most of his cerebral cortex, polluting his brain with a hunger so base that it would have made him vomit, had he any possession of his own body.

This hunger was more than a desire for food, for sex, or for power. This hunger was a vacuum, an endless vortex that consumed every impulse, every thought, every measure of who and what he was.

He tried to scream, but it wouldn't let him.

The sight of Captain Keyes struggling with this new adversary had frozen Private Jenkins in place. When the Captain's struggles ceased, however, he snapped into motion. He turned to flee, and felt one of the little beasts slam into his back. Pain knifed into him as the creature inserted its tendrils into his body, then subsided.

His vision clouded, then cleared. He had some sensation that time had passed, but he had no way to tell how long he'd been out. Private Jenkins, Wallace A., found himself in a strange half-world.

Due to some fluke, some random toss of the galactic dice, the mind that invaded *his* body had been severely weakened during the long period of hibernation, and while strong enough to take over and begin the work necessary to create a combat form, it lacked the force and clarity required to completely dominate its host the way it was supposed to.

Jenkins, helpless to do anything about it, was fully aware of the invading intelligence as it seized control of his musculature, jerked at his limbs like a child experimenting with a new toy, and marched him around in circles even as his friends, who no longer had any consciousness at all, were completely destroyed. He screamed, and the air left his lungs, but no one turned to look.

SEVEN

Zuka 'Zamamee had entered the *Truth and Reconciliation* via the ship's main gravity lift, taken a secondary lift up to the command deck, suffered through the usual security check, and been shown into the Council Chambers in record time. All of which seemed quite appropriate until he entered the room to find that only a single light was on, and it was focused on the spot where visitors were expected to stand. There was no sign of Soha 'Rolamee, of the Prophet, or of the Elite to whom he had never been introduced.

Perhaps the Council had been delayed, there had been a scheduling error, or some other kind of bureaucratic error. But then, why had he been admitted? Surely the staff knew whether the Council was in session or not.

The Elite was about to turn and leave when a second spot came on and 'Rolamee's head appeared. Not attached to his body the way it should have been, but sitting on a gore-drenched pedestal, staring vacantly into space.

An image of the Prophet appeared and seemed to float

in midair. He gestured toward the head. "Sad, isn't it? But discipline must be maintained."

The Prophet made what 'Zamamee took to be a mystical gesture. "Halo is old, *extremely* old, as are its secrets. Blessings, really, which the Forerunners left for us to find, knowing that we would put them to good use.

"But nothing comes without risk, and there are dangers here as well, things which 'Rolamee promised to keep contained, but failed to do so.

"Now, with the humans blundering about, his failures have been amplified. Doors have been opened, powers have been released, and it is now necessary to shift a considerable amount of our strength to the process of regaining control. Do you understand?"

'Zamamee didn't understand, not in the least, but had no intention of admitting that. Instead he said, "Yes, Commander."

"Good," the Prophet said, "and that brings us to *you*. Not only were your most recent efforts to trap the marauding human a total failure, he went on to neutralize part of Halo's security system, found his way in to the Silent Cartographer, and will no doubt use it to cause us even more trouble.

"So," the Prophet added conversationally, "I thought it might be instructive for you to come here, take a good look at the price of failure, and decide whether you can afford the cost. Do you understand me?"

'Zamamee gulped, then nodded. "Yes, Commander, I do."

"Good," the Prophet said smoothly. "I'm gratified to hear it. Now, having failed once, and having determined never to do so again, tell me how you plan to proceed. *If* I like the answer, *if* you can convince me that it will work, then you will leave this room alive."

Fortunately 'Zamamee not only had a plan, but an *exciting* plan, and he was able to convince the Prophet that it would work.

But later, after the Elite had rejoined Yayap, and the two of them were leaving the ship, it wasn't a vision of glory that he saw, but 'Rolamee's vacant stare.

The Master Chief paused just inside the hatch to ensure that he wasn't being followed, checked to make certain that his weapons were loaded, and wondered where the hell he was. Based on instructions from Cortana, Foehammer had dropped her Pelican through a hole in Halo's surface, flown the dropship through one of the enormous capillary-like maintenance tunnels that crisscrossed just below the ringworld's skin, and dropped the unlikely twosome off on a cavernous landing platform. From there the Spartan felt his way through a maze of passageways and rooms, many of which had been defended.

Now, as he walked the length of another corridor, he wondered what lay beyond the hatch ahead.

The answer was quite unexpected. The door opened to admit cold air and a sudden flurry of snowflakes. It appeared as if he was about to step out onto the deck of a footbridge. A barrier blocked some of the view, but the noncom could see traction beams that served in place of suspension cables, and the gray cliff face beyond.

"The weather patterns here seem natural, not artificial," Cortana observed thoughtfully. "I wonder if the ring's environmental systems are malfunctioning—or if the designers *wanted* this particular installation to have inclement weather."

"Maybe this isn't even inclement weather to them," he said.

The Chief, who wasn't sure it made a hell of a lot of difference, not to *him* anyway, stuck his nose around the edge of the hatch to see what might be waiting for them.

The answer was a Shade, with a Grunt seated at the controls. A quick glance to the right confirmed the presence of a *second* energy weapon, this one unmanned.

Then, just as he was about to make his move, a Pelican appeared off to the left, roared over the bridge, and settled into the valley below. There was a squawk of static, followed by a grim-sounding male voice.

"This is Fireteam Zulu requesting immediate assistance from any UNSC forces. Does anyone copy? Over."

The AI recognized the call sign as belonging to one of the units operating out of Alpha Base and made her reply. *"Cortana to Fireteam Zulu. I read you. Hold position. We're on the way."*

"Roger that," the voice replied. *"Make it quick."*

So much for the element of surprise, he thought. The Spartan stepped out of the hatch, shot the Grunt in the head, and hurried to take the alien's place on the Shade. He could hear the commotion the sudden attack had caused and knew he had only seconds to bring the barrel around.

He swiveled the weapon into position, saw the sight glow red, and pulled the trigger. A Grunt and a Jackal were snatched off their feet as the ravening energy bolts consumed not only them, but a chunk of the bridge as well. All the rest of the enemy forces seemed to melt back into the woodwork.

Then, with no clear targets left in sight, he took a moment to inspect the bridge. It appeared to have been built for use by pedestrians rather than vehicles, had two levels, and was held aloft by the traction beams he had observed earlier. Snow swirled down from above, hissed when it hit the glowing cables, then ceased to exist.

There was movement farther down the bridge deck, which he rewarded with a steady stream of glowing energy. He used the plasma like water from a hose, squirting the deadly fire into every nook and cranny he could find, thereby clearing the way.

Then, satisfied that he had nailed all the obvious targets, the Spartan jumped to the deck. The bridge was large enough that it featured a variety of islands, turnouts, and pass-throughs, all of which could be used for cover. That cut two ways, of course—meaning that the Covenant had plenty of places to hide.

Moving from one bit of protection to the next, he fought his way across the span, dropping down to the lower level to deal with Covenant forces there, then resurfacing at the far end, where he spotted an Elite armed with an energy blade. The Elite ducked behind a wall.

The Chief saw no reason to close with such a dangerous opponent if it could be avoided, and tossed a plasma grenade over the wall. He heard the startled reaction as the explosive device latched onto the Elite's armor and refused to let go. The alien emerged from hiding, and vanished in a flash of light.

Thankful to put the bridge behind him, the Chief activated the hatch, made his way through the mazelike room beyond, and entered a lift. It dropped for a long time before coming to a relatively smooth stop and allowing him to exit. A short passageway took him to a hatch and the battle that raged beyond.

As the door opened the Master Chief looked up, saw the bridge directly above, and had a good idea where he was. Then, looking down, he saw a snow-covered valley, punctuated by groups of boulders, and the occasional stand of trees.

Judging from the fact that most of the Covenant fire was directed toward the corner of the valley off to his left, the Spartan assumed that at least part of Fireteam Zulu was trapped there. They were under fire from at least two Shades and a Ghost, but putting up a good fight nonetheless.

He knew that the heavy weapons offered the greatest danger to the Marines. He sprinted from the protection of the tunnel, paused to shoot the nearest gunner with his pistol, then headed toward the dead Grunt's Shade. He could feel the heat radiating off the weapon's barrel as he jerked the corpse out of the seat and took his place behind the controls. There were plenty of targets, a rather busy Ghost primary among them, so the Chief decided to tackle that first. A couple of bursts were sufficient to get the pilot's attention and bring him into range.

Both the human and the Elite opened fire at the same moment, their reciprocal fire drawing straight lines back and forth, but the Shade won out. The attack vehicle shuddered, skittered sideways, and blew up.

But there was no opportunity to celebrate as a Wraith mortar tank turned its attention to that corner of the valley, lobbed cometlike energy mortars high into the air, and started to walk them toward the Marines.

The Spartan sent a stream of energy bolts toward the tank, but the range was too great, and the fire couldn't penetrate the monster's armor.

Convinced that he would have to find some other way to deal with the tank, the Chief decided to bail out, and was twenty meters away when one of the mortars scored a direct hit on the Shade he had just occupied.

The Marines saw him coming and took heart from his sudden appearance on the scene. A Corporal tossed him a weak grin, and whooped, "The cavalry has arrived!"

"We can sure use your help—that Shade has us pinned," another Marine chimed in.

The soldier pointed and the Spartan saw that the Covenant had dropped a Shade onto the top of a huge rock overlooking the valley. The elevation allowed the weapon to command half the depression and even as the Chief looked, the gunner continued to pound the area where Fireteam Zulu had taken refuge.

The Marines' Warthog had flipped, spilling supplies out onto the ground. The Master Chief paused to grab a rocket launcher, but knew the range was extreme, and that it would pay to get closer.

So he slung the launcher across his back, checked the load on his assault weapon, and moved into the trees. A party of Grunts made a run at the Marines, and were pushed back even as the Spartan spotted a likely looking tree trunk. He moved up, killed the Jackal that lurked behind the tree cover, then brought the launcher up to his shoulder. The Shade winked blue light as he peered through the sight, increased the magnification, and saw the gun leap toward him. Then, careful to hold the tube steady, he fired.

There was an explosion on top of the rock, and the Shade toppled off the side of a cliff.

The Marines cheered, but the Master Chief had already shifted priorities. He ran for the 'Hog.

A mortar exploded behind him and blew the tree cover he'd just vacated into splinters. A Marine screamed as a meter-long shard of wood penetrated his abdomen and nailed him to the ground.

The Spartan grabbed hold of the Warthog's bumper,

then used his armor's strength enhancements to flip it back onto its tires. One Marine jumped aboard and manned the LAAG, and another jumped into the passenger seat.

Snow sprayed out from behind both of the rear tires as the Spartan put his foot down, felt the 'Hog break loose, and steered into the skid.

The sudden movement gave their position away to the Wraith. It belched, and a comet arced their way and slid sideways across the center of the valley as if to block the humans from reaching the other end.

The Spartan saw the fireball, raced to pass under it, and heard the LAAG open up as the range to the Wraith began to close.

But there was an infantry screen to penetrate before they could dance with the tank, and both the LAAG gunner and the Marine in the passenger seat were forced to deal with a screen comprised of Elites, Jackals, and Grunts as the Chief slammed on the brakes, backed out of a crossfire, and turned to provide them with a better angle.

The M41 roared as it sent hundreds of rounds downrange, plucked Grunts like flowers, and hurled them back into the bloodied snow.

The Marine in the passenger seat yelled, "You *want* me? You *want* some of this? Come and get it!" as he emptied a clip into an Elite. The two-and-a-half-meter-tall warrior staggered under the impact and fell over backward. He wasn't dead, however, not yet, not until the front of the Warthog sucked him under and spit chunks out the back.

Then they were through the screen, and more important, inside the dead area where the Wraith couldn't fire mortars without risking dropping them on itself. That was the key, the factor that made the attack possible. The Chief braked on a patch of ice, and felt the 'Hog start to slide. "Hit him!" he ordered.

The gunner, who couldn't possibly miss at that range, opened fire. There was an earsplitting roar as large-caliber rounds pounded the side of the tank. Some glanced off, others shattered, but none of them managed to penetrate the Wraith's thick armor.

"Watch out!" the Marine in the passenger seat exclaimed. "The bastard is trying to ram!"

The Spartan, who had just managed to bring the Warthog to a stop, saw that the private was correct. The tank surged forward, and was just about to crush the LRV, when the Master Chief slammed the lighter vehicle into reverse. All four wheels spun as the 'Hog backed away, guns blazing, suddenly on the defensive.

Then, having opened what he hoped was a sufficient gap, the Spartan braked. He slammed the shifter forward and swung the wheel to the right. The vehicles were so close as they passed each other that the Wraith scraped the 'Hog's flank, hard enough to tip the left-side wheels off the snowy ground. They hit with a thump, the LAAG came off-target, and the gunner brought it to bear again. "Hammer it from behind!" the Chief yelled. "It might be weaker there!"

The gunner obeyed and was rewarded with a sharp explosion. A thousand pieces of metal flew up into the air, turned lazy circles, and drifted downward. Black smoke boiled up out of the wreckage. What remained of the tank slammed into a boulder, and the battle was over.

The valley belonged to Fireteam Zulu.

Cortana's intelligence revealed there were other valleys, all connected by one means or another, and he would have to negotiate every one of them in order to reach his objective. A drop-off prevented the Spartan from taking the Warthog any farther.

He bailed out and made his way through the snow. A cold wind whistled past his visor and snowflakes dusted the surface of his armor. "Damn," one of the Marines remarked, "I forgot my mittens."

"Stow the BS," a sergeant growled. "Watch those trees . . . this ain't no picnic."

Strangely, the Chief felt very calm. Right then, right there, he was home.

It was sunny, only a few clouds dotted the sky, and the strangely uniform hills piled one on top of the other as if eager to reach the low-lying mountain ridge beyond. It had been dry in this region, which meant that the vehicles sent wisps of dust into the air as they climbed up off the plain, and made for the heights above.

The patrol consisted of two captured Ghosts, plus two of the Warthogs that had survived the long, arduous journey back from the *Pillar of Autumn*.

Various combinations had been tried, but McKay liked the two-plus-two configuration best, combining as it did the best features of *both* designs. The alien attack craft were faster than the LRVs, which meant they could cover a lot of ground in a short period of time, thereby reducing the wear and tear on both the four-wheelers and the troops who rode them. But the Ghosts couldn't handle broken ground the way the Warthogs could and, not having anything like the M41 LAAG, they were vulnerable to Banshees.

Therefore, if an enemy aircraft appeared, it was standard procedure for the Ghosts to scuttle in under the protection offered by the three-barreled weapons mounted on the 'Hogs. Each Warthog carried a passenger armed with a rocket launcher as well, which provided the Marines with even more antiaircraft capability.

Of course the *real* stick, the one the Covenant had learned to respect, was a Pelican full of Helljumpers sitting on a pad back at Alpha Base ready to launch on two minutes' notice. It could put as many as fifteen ODST Marines on any point inside the designated patrol area within ten minutes. No small threat.

The purpose of the patrols was to monitor a circle ten kilometers in diameter with Alpha Base at its center. Now that the Marines had taken the butte and fortified it, they had to hold onto the high keep. And while there had been some air raids, and a couple of ground-based probes, the Covenant had yet to launch an all-out attack, something that bothered both Silva and McKay. It was almost as if the aliens were content to let the humans sit there while they tended to something else—although neither one of the officers could imagine what the something else could be.

That didn't mean a complete cessation of activity; far from it, since the enemy had taken to watching the humans, making note of which routes they took, and setting ambushes along the way.

McKay tried to ensure that she never followed the same path twice in a row, but often the terrain dictated where the vehicles could go, and that meant that there were certain river crossings, rocky defiles, and mountain passes where the enemy could safely lie in wait—assuming they had the patience for it.

As the patrol approached one such spot, a pass between two of the larger hills, the Marine on the lead Ghost called in. *"Red Three to Red One, over."*

McKay, who had decided to ride shotgun in the first 'Hog, keyed her mike. "This is One. Go . . . Over."

"I see a Ghost, Lieutenant. It's on its side—like it crashed or something. Over."

"Stay clear of it," the officer advised. "It could be

some sort of trap. Hold on, we'll be there shortly. Over."

"Affirmative. Red Three, out."

The Warthog bounced over some rocks, growled as the driver downshifted, and entered an open area that led up to the pass. "Red One to team: We'll leave the vehicles here and proceed on foot. Gunners, stay on those weapons, and split the sky. The last thing we need is to get bounced by a Banshee. Ghost Two, keep an eye on the back door. Over."

There was a series of double-clicks by way of acknowledgment as McKay took the Warthog's rocket launcher, jumped to the ground, and followed her driver up the path. A scorched rock, and what might have been a patch of dried blood, served as reminder of the patrol that had been ambushed there not long ago.

The sun beat down on the officer's back, the air was hot and still, and gravel crunched under her boots. The hill could have been on Earth, up in the Cascade Mountains. McKay wished that it were.

Yayap lay next to a pile of wreckage and waited to die. Like most of 'Zamamee's ideas, this one was totally insane.

After failing to find and kill the armored human, 'Zamamee had concluded that the elusive alien must be on top of the recently captured butte. Or, if not *on* the butte, then coming and going from the butte, which was the only base the humans had established. The butte was a strong point that the Council of Masters would very much like to take back.

The only problem was that 'Zamamee had no way to know when the human was there, and when he wasn't, because while taking the butte would be something of a coup, doing so without killing the human might or might not be sufficient to keep his head on his shoulders.

So, having given the problem extensive thought, and aware of the fact that humans *did* take prisoners, the Elite came up with the idea of putting a spy on top of the butte, someone who could send a signal when the target was in residence, thereby triggering a raid.

But who to send? Not *him*, since it would be his role to lead the attack, and not some other Elite, because they were deemed too valuable for such a dangerous scheme—nor could they be trusted not to steal the glory of the kill—especially given the increased demands associated with countering the mysterious "powers" to which the Prophet had referred.

That suggested a lower ranking member of the Covenant forces, but someone 'Zamamee could trust. Which was why Yayap had been equipped with an appropriate cover story, enthusiastically beaten up, and laid out next to a wrecked Ghost which one of the transports had dropped in during the hours of darkness.

The final scene had been established just prior to dawn, which meant that the Grunt had been there for nearly five full units. Unable to do more than flex his muscles lest he unknowingly give himself away, with nothing to drink, and subject to his own considerable fears, Yayap silently cursed the day he "rescued" 'Zamamee. Better to have died in the crash of the human vessel.

Yes, 'Zamamee swore that the humans took prisoners, but what did *he* know? Thus far, Yayap had been unimpressed with 'Zamamee's plans. Yayap had seen Marines shoot more than one downed warrior during the battle on the *Pillar of Autumn*, and saw no reason why they would spare him. And what if they discovered the signaling device that had been incorporated into his breathing apparatus?

No, the odds were against him, and the more he thought about it, the more the Grunt realized that he should have run. Taken what he could, headed out onto the surface of Halo, sought shelter with the other deserters who lurked there. The dignity of his eventual suffocation when his methane bladder finally emptied had considerable appeal.

It was too late for that now. Yayap heard the crunch of gravel, smelled the musky, unpleasant meat odor he had come to associate with humans, and felt a shadow fall over his face. It seemed best to appear unconscious, so that's exactly what he did. He fainted.

"It sounds like he's alive," McKay observed, as the Grunt took a breath, and the methane rig wheezed in response. "Check for booby traps, free that leg, and search him. I don't see much blood, but if he's leaking, plug the holes."

Yayap didn't understand a word the human said, but the tone was even, and no one put a gun to his head. Maybe, just maybe, he was going to survive.

Five minutes later the Grunt had been hog-tied, thrown into the back of an LRV, and left to bounce around back there.

McKay recovered two saddlebag-style containers from the wrecked Ghost, one of which contained some clothes wrapped around what she took to be rations. She sniffed the tube of bubbling paste and winced. It smelled like old socks wrapped in rotting cheese.

She stuffed the alien food back into its pack, and

investigated the second. It held a pair of Covenant memory blocks, brick-shaped chunks of some super-dense material that could store who knew how many gazillion bytes of information. Probably a kilo's worth of BS? Yes, probably, but it wasn't for her to judge. Wellesley loved that kind of crap, and would have fun trying to sort it out.

If they were lucky, it would distract him from quoting the Duke of Wellington for a few precious minutes. That alone was almost worth recovering the devices.

As the humans got back on their vehicles and went up over the pass, 'Zamamee watched them from a carefully camouflaged hiding spot on a neighboring hill. He felt a thrill of vindication. The first part of his plan was a success. The second phase—and his inevitable victory—would follow.

Finally, after battling his way through wintry valleys, twisting passageways, and mazelike rooms, the Master Chief opened still another hatch and peered outside. He saw snow, the base of a large construct, and a Ghost which patrolled the area beyond.

"The entrance to the Control Center is located at the top of the pyramid," Cortana said. "Let's get up there. We should commandeer one of those Ghosts; we're going to need the firepower."

The Spartan believed her, but as he stepped through the hatch, and more Ghosts appeared and began shooting at him, none of the pilots seemed ready to surrender their machines. He destroyed one of them with a long, controlled burst from his assault rifle, then scurried up through a jumble of boulders, and perched on one of the pyramid's long, sloping skirts.

From his new position he saw a Hunter patrolling

the area above, and wished he had a rocket launcher. He might as well have wished for a Scorpion tank.

The pyramid's support structures offered some cover, which allowed the Master Chief to climb unobserved, and toss a fragmentation grenade at the monster above. It went off with a loud *craack!*, peppered the alien's armor with shrapnel, and generally pissed him off.

Alerted now, the Hunter fired his fuel rod cannon, just as the Chief hurled a plasma grenade and hoped his aim was better this time. The energy pulse missed, the grenade didn't, and there was a flash of light as the Covenant warrior went down.

It was tempting to run for the top, but if there was one lesson the Spartan had learned over the last few days it was that Hunters traveled in pairs.

Rather than leave such a potent enemy guarding his six, the Master Chief climbed up to the first level, ducked around the wall that separated one side of the pyramid from the next, and took a peek. Sure enough, there was Hunter number two, gazing down-slope, unaware of the fact that his bond brother was dead. The human put a burst into the alien's unprotected back. The spined warrior fell and slid, face first, to the bottom of the structure.

The Chief worked his way farther up, zigzagging back and forth across the front of the massive pyramid while an extremely determined Banshee pilot tried to bag him from above, and all manner of Grunts, Jackals, and Elites emerged to try and block his progress.

He took a deep breath, and continued his climb.

At the top of the pyramid, the Spartan paused and allowed his long-suffering shield system to recharge. He stepped over the fallen body of a Grunt, and loaded his last clip into the assault rifle.

A huge door fronted the top level. There was no way to tell what waited on the other side, but it wasn't likely to be friendly—a series of motion sensor traces ghosted at the edge of the device's range.

"What's the plan?" Cortana inquired.

"Simple." The Spartan took a deep breath, hit the switch, spun on his heel, and ran.

It was about twenty meters back to the Shade, and the Chief covered the distance in seconds. Once at the controls he swiveled the barrel around just in time to see the doors part and a horde of Covenant soldiers pour out.

The Shade was up to the job. Just as quickly as they appeared, the aliens died.

Dismounting once again, the Spartan entered a large, hangar-like space, took the time required to deal with stragglers, and activated the next set of doors.

"Scanning," Cortana said. "Covenant forces in the area have been eliminated. Nicely done. Let's move on to Halo's Control Center."

He made his way through the doors and out onto an immense platform. A gleaming reflective bridge, apparently without supports, extended over a vast emptiness and ended in a circular walkway. In the center of this walkway was a moving holographic model of Threshold: a gas giant, the small gray moon Basis in orbit around it, and suspended between the two, the tiny shining ring of Halo itself.

Outside of the walkway, stretching almost to the edges of the enormous space, was another model of Halo, this one hundreds of meters across, displaying as it rotated a detailed map of the terrain on its inner surface.

The span lacked any kind of railing, as if to remind those who passed over it of the dangers attendant to the power they were about to encounter. Or so it seemed to the Master Chief.

"This is it . . . Halo's Control Center," Cortana said as the Master Chief approached a large panel. It was covered with glyphs, all of which glowed as if lit from within, and went together to form what looked like a piece of abstract art.

"That terminal," the AI said. "Try there."

The Spartan reached out to touch one of the symbols, then stopped.

He felt Cortana's presence dwindle in his mind as she transmitted herself into the alien computer station. A moment later, she appeared over the control panel. Data scrolled across her body, energy seemed to radiate out of her holographic skin, and her features were alight with pleasure.

Her "skin" shifted from blue to purple, to red, then cycled back as she gazed around the room and sighed.

"Are you all right?" the Master Chief inquired. He hadn't expected this.

"Never been better!" Cortana affirmed. "You can't imagine the wealth of information—so *much*, so fast. It's *glorious*!"

"So," the Master Chief asked, "what sort of weapon is it?"

The AI looked surprised. "What are you talking about?"

"Let's stay focused," the Spartan responded. "Halo. How do we use it against the Covenant?"

The image of Cortana frowned. Suddenly her voice was filled with disdain. "This ring isn't a cudgel, you barbarian, it's something else. Something much more important. The Covenant were right, this ring—"

She paused, and her eyes moved back and forth as she scanned the tidal wave of data she now accessed. A puzzled look flashed across her face. "Forerunner," she muttered. "Give me a moment to access . . ."

A moment later, she began to speak, and her words rushed out in a flood, as if the constant stream of new information was sweeping her along.

"Yes, the Forerunners built this place, what they called a fortress world, in order to—"

The Chief had never heard the AI talk like that before, didn't like being referred to as a "barbarian," and was about to cut her down to size when she spoke again. Plainly alarmed, her voice had a hesitant quality. "No, that can't be . . . Oh, those Covenant fools, they must have known, there must have been signs."

The Chief frowned. "Slow down. You're losing me."

Her eyes widened in horror. "The Covenant *found something*, buried in this ring, something *horrible*. Now they're afraid."

"Something buried?"

Cortana looked off into the distance as if she could actually see Keyes. "Captain—we've got to stop the Captain. The weapons cache he's looking for, it's not really—we can't let him get inside."

"I don't understand."

"There's no time!" Cortana said urgently. Her eyes were neon pink and they focused on the Spartan like twin lasers. "I have to remain here. Get out, find Keyes, stop him. Before it's too late!"

SECTION IV

343 GUILTY SPARK

ENGULFED

_____EIGHT_____

Echo 419's engines roared as the Pelican descended through the darkness and rain into the swamp. The surrounding foliage whipped back and forth in response to the sudden turbulence, the water beneath the transport's metal belly was pressed flat, and the stench of rotting vegetation flooded the aircraft's cargo compartment as the ramp splashed into the evil-looking brew below.

Foehammer was at the controls and it was her voice that came over the radio. *"The last transmission from the Captain's ship was from* this *area. When you locate Captain Keyes, radio in and I'll come pick you up."*

The Master Chief stepped down off the ramp and immediately found himself calf-deep in oily-looking water. "Be sure to bring me a towel."

The pilot laughed, fed more fuel to the engines, and the ship pushed itself up out of the swamp. Now, as Foehammer dropped her passenger into the muck, she was glad to be an aviator. Ground-pounders worked too damn hard.

_____

Keyes floated in a vacuum. A gauzy white haze clouded his vision, though he could occasionally make out images in lightning-fast bursts—a nightmare tableau of misshapen bodies and writhing tentacles. A muted gleam of light glinted from some highly polished, engraved metal. In the distance, he could hear a droning buzz. It had an odd, musical quality, like Gregorian chant slowed to a fraction of its normal speed.

He realized with a start that the images were from his own eyes. The knowledge brought back a flood of memory—of his own body. He struggled, and realized in mounting horror that he could just barely feel his own arms. They seemed softer somehow, as if filled with a spongy, thick liquid.

He couldn't move. His lungs itched, and the effort of breathing hurt.

The strange droning chant suddenly sped into an insect buzz, painfully echoing through his consciousness. There was something . . . distant, something definitively *other* about the sound.

Without warning, a new image flashed across his mind, like images on a video screen.

The sun was setting over the Pacific, and a trio of gulls wheeled overhead. He smelled salt air, and felt gritty sand between his toes.

He felt a sickening sensation, a feeling of indescribable violation, and the comforting image vanished. He tried to remember what he was seeing, but the memory faded like smoke. All he could feel now was a sense of loss. Something had been taken from him . . . but *what*?

The insistent buzz returned, painfully loud now. He could sense tendrils of awareness—hungry for data—wriggling through his confused mind like diseased maggots. A host of new images filled him.

. . . the first time he killed another human being, during the riots on Charybdis IX. He smelled blood, and his hands shook as he holstered the pistol. He could feel the heat of the weapon's barrel . . .

. . . the pride he felt after graduating at the Academy, then a hitch—as if a bad holorecord was being scrolled back—then a knot in his gut. Fear that he wouldn't be able to meet the Academy's standards . . .

. . . the sickening smell of lilacs and lilies as he stood over his father's coffin . . .

Keyes continued to float, mesmerized by the parade of memories that began to pile on him, each one appearing faster than the last. He drifted through the fog. He didn't notice, or indeed care, that as soon as the bursts of memory ended, they disappeared entirely.

The strange *otherness* receded from his awareness, but not entirely. He could still sense the *other* probing him, but he ignored it. The next burst of memory passed . . . then another . . . then another . . .

The Chief checked his threat indicator, found nothing of concern, and allowed the swamp to close in around him. "Make friends with your environment." That's what Chief Mendez had told him many years ago—and the advice had served him well. By *listening* to the constant patter of the rain, *feeling* the warm humid air via his vents, and *seeing* the shapes natural to the swamp, the Spartan would know what belonged and what didn't. Knowing that could mean the difference between life and death.

Satisfied that he was attuned to the environment around him, and hopeful of gaining a better vantage point, he climbed a slight rise. The payoff was immediate.

The Pelican had gone in less than sixty meters from the spot where Echo 419 had dropped him off—but the surrounding foliage was so thick Foehammer had been unable to see the crash site from the air.

The Chief moved in to inspect the wreckage. Judging from appearances, and the fact that there weren't many bodies lying around, the ship had crashed during takeoff, rather than on landing. The impression was confirmed when he discovered that while they were dressed in fatigues, all of the casualties wore Naval insignia.

That suggested that the dropship had landed successfully, discharged all of its Marine passengers, and was in the process of lifting off when a mechanical failure or enemy fire had brought the aircraft down.

Satisfied that he had a basic understanding of what had taken place, the Chief was about to leave when he spotted a shotgun lying next to one of the bodies, decided it might come in handy, and slipped the sling over his right shoulder.

He followed a trail of bootprints away from the Pelican and toward the glow of portable work lights—the same kind of lights he'd seen in the area around the *Truth and Reconciliation*. The aliens were certainly industrious, especially when it came to stealing everything that wasn't nailed down.

As if to confirm his theory regarding Covenant activity in the area, it wasn't long before the Spartan came across a *second* wreck, a Covenant dropship this time, bows down in the swamp muck. Aside from swarms of mothlike insects and the distant chirp of swamp birds, there were no signs of life.

Cargo containers were scattered all around the crash site, which raised an interesting question. When the transport nosed in, were the aliens trying to deliver something, weapons perhaps, or taking material away? There was no way to be certain.

Whatever the case, there was a strong likelihood that Keyes had been attracted to the lights, just as he had, followed them to the crash site, and continued from there.

With that in mind, he swung past a tree that stood on thick, spiderlike roots, followed a trail up over a rise, and spotted a lone Jackal. Without hesitation, he snapped the assault rifle to his shoulder and brought the alien down with a burst.

He crouched, waiting for the inevitable counterattack—which never came. Curious. Given the lights, the crash site, and the scattering of cargo modules, he would have expected to run into more opposition.

A *lot* more.

So where were they? It didn't make sense. Just one more mystery to add to his growing supply.

The rain pattered against the surface of his armor, and swamp water sloshed around his boots as the Master Chief pushed his way through some foliage and suddenly came under fire. For one brief moment it seemed as if his latest question had been answered, that Covenant forces *were* still in the area, but the opposition soon proved to be little more than a couple of hapless Jackals, who, upon hearing the sound of gunfire, had come to investigate. As usual they came in low, crouching behind their shields, so it was almost impossible to score a hit from directly in front of them.

He shifted position, found a better angle, and fired. One Jackal went down, but the other rolled, and that made it nearly impossible to hit him. The Spartan held his fire, waited for the alien to come to a stop, and cut him down.

He worked his way up the side of a steep slope, and the Chief spotted a Shade sited on top of the ridge. It commanded both slopes, or would have, had someone been at the controls. He paused at the top of the ridge and considered his options. He could jump on the Shade, hose the ravine below, and thereby let everyone know that he had arrived, or slip down the slope, and try to infiltrate the area more quietly.

The Chief settled on the second option, started down the slope in front of him, and was soon wrapped in mist and moist vegetation. Not too surprisingly, some red dots appeared on the Spartan's threat indicator. Rather than go around the enemy, and expose his six, the Master Chief decided to seek them out. He slung the MA5B and drew out the shotgun—better suited for close-up work. He pumped the slide, flicked off the safety, and moved on.

Broad variegated leaves caressed his shoulders, vines tugged at the barrel of the shotgun, and the thick half-rotten humus of the jungle floor gave way under the Chief's boots as he made his way forward.

The Grunt perhaps heard a slight rustling, debated whether to fire, and was still in the process of thinking it over when the butt of the shotgun descended on his head. There was a solid *thump!* as the alien went down, followed by two more, as more methane breathers rushed to investigate.

Satisfied with his progress so far, the Spartan paused to listen. There was the gentle patter of rain on wide, welcoming leaves, and the constant sound of his own breathing, but nothing more.

Confident that the immediate perimeter was clear, the Master Chief turned his attention to the Forerunner complex that loomed off to his right. Unlike the graceful spires of other installations, this one appeared squat and vaguely arachnid.

He crept down onto the flat area immediately in

front of it. He decided that the entrance reminded him of a capital A, except that the top was flat, and was bracketed by a pair of powerful floodlights.

Was *this* what Keyes had been looking for? Something caught his eye—a pair of eight-gauge shotgun shells, and a carelessly discarded protein bar wrapper, tossed near the entrance.

He must be getting closer.

Once through the door he came across a half dozen Covenant bodies lying in a pool of commingled blood. Struck once again by the absence of serious opposition, the Master Chief knelt just beyond the perimeter established by the blood, and peered at the bodies.

Had the Marines killed them? No, judging from the nature of their wounds it appeared as if the aliens had been hosed with *plasma* fire. Friendly fire perhaps? Humans armed with Covenant weapons? Maybe, but neither explanation really seemed to fit.

Perplexed, he stood, took a long, slow look around, and pushed deeper into the complex. In contrast with the swamp outside, where the constant *drip, drip, drip* of the rain served to provide a constant flow of sound, it was almost completely silent within the embrace of the thick walls. The sudden sound of machinery startled him, and he spun and brought the shotgun to bear.

Summoned by some unknown mechanism, a lift surfaced right in front of him. With nowhere else to go, the Master Chief stepped aboard.

As the platform carried him downward a group of overlapping red dots appeared on his motion sensor, and the Spartan knew he was about to have company. There was a screech of tortured metal as the lift came to a stop, but rather than rush him as he expected them to, the dots remained stationary.

They had heard the lift many times before, the Chief reasoned, and figured it was loaded with a group of their friends. That suggested Covenant, *stupid* Covenant.

His favorite kind, in fact—apart from the dead kind.

Careful to avoid the sort of noise that might give him away, he completed a full circuit of the dimly lit room, and discovered that the dots were actually Grunts and Jackals, all of whom were clustered around a hatch.

The Chief suppressed a grin, slung the shotgun, and unlimbered the assault rifle.

Their punishment for not guarding the lift consisted of a grenade, followed by forty-nine rounds of automatic fire, and a series of shorter bursts to finish them off.

The hatch opened onto a large four- or five-story-high room. The Master Chief found himself on a plat-form along with a couple of unsuspecting Jackals. He immediately killed them, heard a reaction from the floor below, and moved to the right. A quick peek revealed a group of seven or eight Covenant, milling around as if waiting for instructions.

The noncom dropped an M9 HE-DP calling card into their midst, took a step back to avoid getting hit by the resulting fragments, and heard a loud *wham!* as the grenade detonated. There were screams, followed by wild firing. The Spartan waited for the volume of fire to drop off and moved forward again. A series of short controlled bursts was sufficient to silence the last Covenant soldiers.

He jumped down off the platform to check the sur-rounding area.

Still looking for clues as to where Keyes might have gone, the Master Chief conducted a quick sweep of the room. It wasn't long before he picked up some plasma grenades, circled a cargo container, and came across the bodies.

Two Marines, both killed by plasma fire, their weapons missing.

He cursed under his breath. The fact that both dog tags had been taken suggested that Keyes and his team had run into the Covenant just as he had, taken casualties, and pushed on.

Certain he was on the right trail, the Spartan crossed the troughlike depression that split the room in two, and was forced to step over and around a scattering of Covenant corpses as he approached the hatch. Once through the opening he negotiated his way through a series of rooms, all empty, but painted with Covenant blood.

Finally, just as he was beginning to wonder if he should turn back, he entered a room and found himself face-to-face with a fear-crazed Marine. His eyes jerked from side to side, as if seeking something hidden within the shadows, and his mouth was twisted into a horrible grimace. There was no sign of the soldier's assault weapon, but he had a pistol, which he fired at a shadow in the corner. "Stay back! Stay back! You're not turning me into one of those things!"

The Master Chief raised a hand, palm out. "Put the weapon down, Marine . . . we're on the same side."

But the Marine wasn't having any of that, and pressed his back against the solidity of the wall. "Get away from me! Don't touch me, you freak! I'll die first!"

The pistol discharged. The Spartan felt the impact as the 12.7mm slug rocked him back onto his heels, and decided that enough was enough.

Before the Marine had time to react, the Chief snatched the M6D out of his hand. "I'll take that," he growled. The Marine leaped to his feet, but the Chief planted his feet and gently but firmly shoved the soldier back to the floor.

"Now," he said, "where is Captain Keyes, and the rest of your unit?"

The private turned fierce, his features contorted, spittle flying from his lips. "Find your own hiding place!" he screamed. "The monsters are everywhere! God, I can still hear them! Just *leave me alone.*"

"*What* monsters?" the Spartan asked gently. "The Covenant?"

"No! *Not* the Covenant. *Them!*"

That was all the Spartan could get from the crazed Marine. "The surface is back that way," the Master Chief said, pointing toward the door. "I suggest that you reload this weapon, quit wasting ammo, and head topside. Once you get there hunker down and wait for help. There'll be a dust-off later on. Do you read me?"

The Private accepted the weapon, but continued to blather. A moment later he curled into a fetal ball, whimpered, then fell silent. The man would never make it out alone.

One thing was clear from the Marine's ramblings. Assuming that Keyes and his troops were still alive, they were in a heap of trouble. That left the Chief with little choice; he *had* to put the greatest number of lives first. The young soldier had clearly been through the wringer—but he'd have to wait for help until the Master Chief completed his mission.

Slowly, reluctantly, he turned to investigate the rest of the room. The remains of a badly shattered ramp led up over a small fire toward the walkway on the level above. He felt heat wash around him as he stepped over a dead Elite, took comfort from the fact that the body had been riddled with bullets, and made his way up onto a circular gallery. From there, the Master Chief proceeded through a series of doorways and mysteriously empty rooms, until he arrived at the top of a ramp where a dead Marine and a large pool of blood caused him to pause.

He had long ago learned to trust his instincts—and they nagged at him now. Something felt *wrong*. It was quiet, with only a hollow booming sound to disturb the otherwise perfect silence. He was close to something, he could *feel* it, but what?

The Chief descended the ramp. He arrived on the level spot at the bottom, and saw the hatch to his left. Weapon at the ready, he cautiously approached the metal barrier.

The door sensed his presence, slid open, and dumped a dead Marine into his arms.

The Spartan felt his pulse quicken, as he bent slightly to catch the body before it crashed into the ground. He held the MA5B one-handed and covered the room beyond as best he could, searching for a target. Nothing.

He stepped forward, then spun on his heel and pointed the gun back the way he'd come.

Damn it, it felt like eyes bored into the back of his head. Someone was watching him. He backed into the room, and the door slid shut.

He lowered the body to the ground, then stepped away. The toe of his boot hit some empty shell casings which rolled away. That's when he realized that there were *thousands* of empties—so many that they very nearly carpeted the floor.

He noticed a Marine helmet, and bent to pick it up. A name had been stenciled across the side. JENKINS.

A vid cam was attached, the kind worn by the typical combat team so they could critique the mission when they returned to base, feed data to the ghouls in Intelligence, and on occasions like this one, provide investigators with information regarding the circumstances surrounding their deaths.

The Spartan removed the camera's memory chip, slotted the device into one of the receptacles on his own helmet, and watched the playback via a window on his HUD.

The picture was standard quality—which meant pretty awful. The night-vision setting was active, so everything was a sickly green, punctuated by white flares as the camera panned across a light source.

The picture bounced and jostled, and intermittent spots of static marred the image. It was pretty routine stuff at first, starting with the moment the doomed dropship touched down, followed by the trek through the swamp, and their arrival in front of the A-shaped structure.

He spooled ahead, and the video became more ominous after that, starting with the dead Elite, and growing even more uncomfortable as the team opened the final door and went inside. Not just *any* door, but the same door through which the Master Chief had passed only minutes before, only to have a dead Marine fall into his arms.

He was tempted to kill the video, back his way through the hatch, and scrub the mission, but he forced himself to continue watching as one of the Marines said something about a ". . . bad feeling." A badly garbled radio transmission came in, odd rustling noises were heard, a hatch gave way, and hundreds of fleshy balls rolled, danced, and hopped into the room.

That was when the screaming started, when the Master Chief heard Keyes say that they were "surrounded," and saw the picture jerk as something hit Jenkins from behind, and the video snapped to black.

For the first time since parting company with the AI back in the Control Room, he wished that Cortana were with him. First, because she might understand what the hell was going on, but also because he had come to rely on her company, and suddenly felt very much alone.

However, even as one aspect of the Spartan's mind sought comfort, another part had directed his body to back toward the hatch, and was waiting to hear the telltale sound as it opened. But the door *didn't* open, something which the Master Chief knew meant trouble. It caused a rock to form at the bottom of his gut.

As he stood there, gripped by a growing sense of dread, he saw a flash of white from the corner of his eye. He turned to face it, and that was when he saw one, then five, twenty, fifty of the fleshy creatures dribble into the room, pirouette on their tentacles, and dance his way. His motion sensor painted a sudden explosion of movement—speeding closer by the second.

The Spartan fired at the ugly-looking creatures. Those which were closest popped like air-filled balloons, but there were more, *many* more, and they rolled toward him over the floor and walls. The Spartan opened up in earnest, the obscene-looking predators threw themselves forward, and the battle was joined.

It was dark outside. Only one mission had been scheduled for that particular night, and it had returned to the butte at 0236 arbitrary. That meant the Navy personnel assigned to the Control Center didn't have much to do, and were busy playing a round of cards when the wall-mounted speakers burped static, and a desperate voice was heard. *"This is Charlie 2-1-7, repeat Charlie 2-1-7, to any UNSC forces . . . Does anyone copy? Over."*

Com Tech First Class Mary Murphy glanced at the

other two members of her watch and frowned. "Has either one of you had previous contact with Charlie 217?"

The techs looked at each other and shook their heads. "I'll check with Wellesley," Cho said, as he turned toward a jury-rigged monitor.

Murphy nodded and keyed the boom-style mike that extended in front of her lips. "This is UNSC Combat Base Alpha. Over."

"Thank God!" the voice said fervently. *"We took a hit after clearing the* Autumn, *put down in the boonies, and managed to make some repairs. I've got wounded on board—and request immediate clearance to land."*

Wellesley, who had been busy fighting a simulation of the Battle of Marathon, materialized on Cho's screen. As usual, the image that he chose to present was that of a stern-looking man with longish hair, a prominent nose, and a high-collared coat. "Yes?"

"We have a Pelican, call sign Charlie 217, requesting an emergency landing. None of us have dealt with him before."

The AI took a fraction of a second to check the myriad of data stored within his considerable memory and gave a curt nod. "There was a unit designated as Charlie 217 on board the *Autumn*. Not having heard from 217 since we abandoned ship, and not having received any information to the contrary, I assumed the ship was lost. Ask the pilot to provide his name, rank, and serial number."

Murphy heard and nodded. "Sorry, Charlie, but we need some information before we can clear you in. Please provide name, rank, and serial number. Over."

The voice that came back sounded increasingly frustrated. *"This is First Lieutenant Rick Hale, serial number 87654-43821-RH. Give me a break, I need clearance now. Over."*

Wellesley nodded. "The data matches . . . but how would Hale know that Alpha Base even existed?"

"He could have picked up our radio traffic," Cho offered.

"Maybe," the AI agreed, "but let's play it safe. I recommend you bring the base to full alert, notify the Major, and send the reaction force to Pad Three. You'll need the crash team, the emergency medical team, and some people from intel all on deck. Hale should be debriefed *before* he's allowed to mix with base personnel."

The third tech, a Third Class Petty Officer named Pauley, slapped the alarm button, and put out the necessary calls.

"Roger that," Murphy said into her mike. "You are cleared for Pad Three, repeat, Pad Three, which will be illuminated two minutes from now. A medical team will meet your ship. Safe all weapons and cut power the moment you touch down. Over."

"*No problem,*" Hale replied gratefully. Then, a few moments later, "*I see your lights. We're coming in. Over.*"

The pilot keyed his mike off and turned to his copilot. Bathed in the green glow produced by the ship's instrument panel, the Elite looked all the more alien. "So," the human inquired, "how did I do?"

"Extremely well," Special Operations Officer Zuka 'Zamamee said from behind the pilot's shoulder. "Thank you."

And with that 'Zamamee dropped what looked like a circle of green light over Hale's head, pulled the handles in opposite directions, and buried the wire in the pilot's throat. The human's eyes bulged, his hands plucked at the garrote, and his feet beat a tattoo against the control pedals.

The Elite who occupied the copilot's position had already taken control of the Pelican and, thanks to hours of practice, could fly the dropship extremely well.

'Zamamee waited until the kicking had stopped, released the wire, and smelled something foul. That's when the Elite realized that Hale had soiled himself. He gave a grunt of disgust, and returned to the Pelican's cargo compartment. It was crammed with heavily armed Elites, trained for infiltration. They carried camouflage generators, along with their weapons. Their job was to take as many landing pads as possible, and hold them until six dropships loaded with Grunts, Jackals, and more Elites could land on the mesa.

The troops saw the officer appear and looked expectant.

"Proceed," 'Zamamee said. "You *know* what to do. Turn on the active camouflage, check your weapons, and remember this moment. Because *this* battle, *this* victory, will be carved onto your family's Saga wall and recited by generations to come.

"The Prophets have blessed this mission, have blessed *you*, and want every soldier to know that those who transcend the physical will be welcomed into paradise. Good luck."

A blur of lights appeared out of the darkness, the dropship shed altitude, and the warriors murmured their final benedictions.

Like most AIs, Wellesley had a pronounced tendency to spend more time thinking about what he *didn't* have rather than what he did, and sensors were at the very top of his list. The sad truth was that while McKay and her company had recovered a wealth of supplies from the *Autumn*, there had been insufficient time to strip the ship of the electronics that would have given the AI a real-time, all-weather picture of the surrounding air space. That meant he was totally reliant on the data provided by remote ground sensors which the patrols had planted here and there around the butte's ten-kilometer perimeter.

All of the feeds had been clear during the initial radio contact with Charlie 217, but now, as the Pelican flared in to land, the package in Sector Six started to deliver data. It claimed that six heavy-duty heat signatures had just passed overhead, that whatever produced them was fairly loud, and that they were inbound at a speed of approximately 350 kph.

Wellesley reacted with the kind of speed that only a computer is capable of—but the response was too late to prevent Charlie 217 from putting down. Even as the AI made a series of strongly worded recommendations to his human superiors, the Pelican's skids made contact with Pad 3's surface, a number of nearly invisible Elites thundered down the ramp, and the men and women of Alpha Base soon found themselves fighting for their lives.

One level down, locked into a room with three other Grunts, Yayap heard the distant moan of an alarm, and thought he knew why. 'Zamamee had been correct: The human who wore the strange armor, and was believed to be responsible for thousands of Covenant casualties, *did* frequent this place. Yayap knew that because he had *seen* the soldier more than six units before, triggered the transmitter hidden inside his breathing apparatus, and thereby set the raid in motion.

That was the *good* news. The bad news was that 'Zamamee's quarry might very well have left the base during the intervening period of time. If so, and the mission was categorized as a failure, the Grunt had little doubt as to who would receive the blame. But there was nothing Yayap could do but grip the crudely welded bars with his hands, listen to the distant sounds of battle, and hope for the best.

At this point, "the best" would likely be a quick, painless death.

All the members of the crash team, half the medics, and a third of the reaction team were already dead by the time McKay had rolled out of her rack, scrambled into her clothes, and grabbed her personal weapons. She followed the crowd up to the landing area to find that a pitched battle was underway.

Energy bolts seemed to stutter out of nowhere, plasma grenades materialized out of thin air, and throats were slit by invisible knives. The landing party had been contained, but just barely, and threatened to break out across the neighboring pads.

Silva was there, naked from the waist up, shouting orders as he fired short bursts from an assault weapon. "Flood Pad Three with fuel! But keep it inside the containment area. Do it now!"

It was a strange order, and civilians would have balked, but the soldiers reacted with unquestioning obedience and a Naval rating ran toward the Pad 3 refueling station. He flipped the safety out of the way, and grabbed hold of the nozzle.

The air seemed to shimmer in the floodlit area off to the sailor's right, and Silva fired a full clip into what looked like empty air. A commando Elite screamed, seemed to strobe on and off as his camo generator took a direct hit, and folded at the waist.

Undeterred, and unaware of his close call with death, the rating turned, gave the handgrip a healthy squeeze, and sent a steady stream of liquid out onto the surface of Pad 3. A Covenant work crew had been forced to build a curb around the area during the days immediately after the butte had been taken. The purpose of the barrier was to contain fuel spills, and it worked well, as the high-octane fuel crept in around the Pelican's skids and wet the area beyond.

"Get back!" Silva shouted, and rolled a fragmentation grenade in under Charlie 217's belly. There was an explosion followed by a loud *whump!* as the fuel went up and the rating shut off the hose.

The general effect was to turn those Elites who remained on the pad into shimmering torches—screaming, dancing torches. The response was immediate as the Marines opened fire, put the commandos down, and were then forced to turn their efforts to fire fighting. Charlie 217 was fully involved by that time, and shuddered as the fuel in one of her tanks blew.

But there were other Pelicans to protect and while some had lifted off, others remained on their pads.

Silva turned to McKay. "Show time," the Major said, as Wellesley spoke into his ear. "This was little more than a warm-up, no pun intended. The *real* assault force is only five minutes out. Six Covenant dropships, if Wellesley has it right. They can't land here, so they'll put down out on the mesa somewhere. I'll handle the pads— you take the mesa."

McKay nodded, said, "Yes, sir," and spotted Sergeant Lister and waved him over. The noncom had a squad of her Marines in tow. "Round up the rest of my company, tell them to dig in up-spin of the landing pads, and get ready to handle an attack from the mesa. Let's give the bastards a warm reception."

Lister tossed a glance at the raging fires and grinned at McKay's unintentional pun. "Yes, ma'am!" he said and trotted away.

Elsewhere, out along the butte's irregularly shaped rim, the commandeered Shade emplacements opened fire. Pulses of bright blue energy probed the surrounding blackness, found the first ship, and cut the night into slices.

'Zamamee and a file of five commando Elites had already cleared the landing pad by the time the humans flooded Pad 3 with fuel. In fact, the Elite officer wasn't even on the surface of the Forerunner installation during the ensuing inferno—he and his commandos were already one level down, moving from room to room, slaughtering every human they could find. There had been no sign of the one enemy soldier they wanted most, but it was early yet, and he could be around the next corner.

Murphy had just taken the safeties off the 50mm MLA autocannons, and delegated control to Wellesley, when she felt something brush her shoulder. The petty officer started to turn, saw blood spray, and realized that it belonged to her. An Elite produced a deep throaty chuckle as both Cho and Pauley met similar fates. The Control Room was neutralized.

But Wellesley witnessed the murders via the camera mounted over the main video monitor, killed the lights, and notified Silva. Within a matter of minutes six three-person fireteams, all equipped with heat-sensitive night-vision goggles, were busy working their way down through the mazelike complex. The Covenant's camo generators didn't block heat, they actually *generated* it, and that put both sides on an even footing.

In the meantime, thanks to a dead officer's personal initiative, Wellesley had a 50mm surprise waiting for the incoming dropships. Though effective against Banshees, the Shades lacked the power necessary to knock a dropship out of the sky, something the Covenant had clearly known in advance.

But, just as an Elite couldn't withstand fifty rounds of 7.62mm armor-piercing ammo, the enemy transports proved vulnerable to the 50mm high explosive shells that suddenly blasted their way. Not only that, but the fifties were computer-controlled—which was to say *Wellesley* controlled, which meant that nearly every round went exactly where it was supposed to.

Control had been delegated too late for the AI to nail the first dropship, but the second was right where he wanted it to be. It exploded as a dozen rounds of HE went off inside the fuselage. Ironically, the compartments that held the troops preserved most of their lives so they could die when the aircraft hit the foot of the butte.

But there were only two of the guns, one to the west, and one to the east, which meant that the surviving transports were safely through the eastern MLA's field of fire before the AI could fire on them. Still, the destruction of that single ship had reduced the assault force by one sixth, which struck Wellesley as an acceptable result.

Machine-generated death stabbed the top of the mesa as the Covenant dropships made use of their plasma cannons to strafe the landing zone. A fireteam was caught out in the open and cut to shreds even as a barrage of shoulder-fired rockets lashed up to meet the incoming transports. There were hits, some of which inflicted casualties, but none of the enemy aircraft was destroyed.

Then, hovering like obscene insects, the U-shaped dropships turned down-ring, and spilled troops out their side slots, scattering them like evil seeds across the top of the mesa. McKay did the mental math. Five remaining transports, times roughly thirty troops each, equaled an assault force of about one hundred and fifty troops.

"Hit 'em!" Lister shouted. "Kill the bastards before they can land!"

The response was a steady *crack! crack! crack!* as the company's snipers opened fire, and Elites, Grunts, and Jackals alike tumbled to the ground dead.

But there were plenty left—and McKay steeled herself against the coming assault.

The lights had gone off for reasons that the Grunt could only guess at, a factor which added to the fear he felt. Unable to do anything more, Yayap listened to the muffled sounds of battle, and wondered which side to root for. He didn't like being a prisoner but was starting to wonder if he wouldn't be better off with the humans. For a while at least, until—

A brief flash of light appeared, slid down the opposite wall, crossed the floor, and found its way into the cell. "Yayap? Are you in there?"

There were other lights now, and the Grunt saw the air shimmer in front of him. It was 'Zamamee! Much to Yayap's amazement, the Elite had kept his word and actually come looking for him. Realizing that the breathing apparatus made it difficult for others to tell his kind apart, the Grunt pushed his face up against the bars.

"Yes, Commander, I am here."

"Good," the Elite said. "Now stand back so we can blow the door."

All of the Grunts in the cell retreated to the back of the room while one of the commandos attached a charge to the door lock, backed away, and made use of a remote to trigger it. There was a small flash of light, followed by a subdued *bang!* as the explosive was detonated. Hinges squeaked as Yayap pushed the gate out of the way.

"Now," 'Zamamee said eagerly, "lead us to the human. We've been through most of the complex, but haven't run into him yet."

So, Yayap thought to himself, *the only reason you came looking for me was to find the human. I should have known.* "Of course, Commander," the Grunt replied, surprised by his own smoothness. "The aliens captured some of our Banshees. The human was assigned to guard them."

Yayap expected 'Zamamee to challenge the claim, to ask how he knew, but the Elite took him at his word. "Very well," 'Zamamee replied. "Where are the aircraft kept?"

"Up on the mesa," Yayap answered truthfully, "west of the landing pads."

"We will lead the way," the Elite said importantly, "but stay close. It would be easy to become lost."

"Yes, Commander," the Grunt replied, "whatever you say."

Unable to land on or near the pads as originally planned, Field Master 'Putumee had been forced to drop his assault team on the area up-spin of the Forerunner complex. That meant that his troops would have to advance across open ground, with very little cover, and without benefit of heavy weapons to clear the way.

The wily field officer had a trick up his sleeve, however. Rather than release the dropships, he ordered them to remain over the LZ, and strafe the ground ahead of his steadily advancing troops. It wasn't what the transports had been designed for, and the pilots didn't like it, but so what? 'Putumee, who saw all aviators as little more than glorified chauffeurs, wasn't especially interested in how they felt.

So, the U-shaped dropships drifted down toward the human fortifications, plasma cannons probing the ground below, while volleys of rockets lashed upward, exploding harmlessly against their flanks.

The field officer, who advanced along with the second rank of troops, waved his Jackals forward as the humans were forced to pull out of their firing pits, and withdraw to their next line of defense.

'Putumee paused next to one of the now empty pits and looked into it. Something about the excavation bothered him, but what? Then he had it. The rectangular hole was *too* neat, *too* even, to have been dug during the last half unit. What other preparations had the aliens made, the officer wondered?

The answer came in a heartbeat. McKay said, "Fire!" and the Scorpion's gunner complied. The tank lurched under the officer's feet as the shell left the main gun and the hull started to vibrate as the machine gun opened up. The explosion, about six hundred meters downrange, erased an entire file of Grunts. The other MBT, one of two which Silva had ordered his battalion to bring topside, fired two seconds later. That round killed an Elite, two Jackals, and a Hunter.

Marines cheered and McKay smiled. Though doubtful that the Covenant would try to put troops on the mesa, the Major was a careful man, which was why he ordered the Helljumpers to dig firing pits up-ring of the installation, and create bunkers for the tanks.

Now, firing with their barrels nearly parallel to the ground, the MBTs were in the process of turning the area in front of them into a moonscape as each shell threw half a ton of soil up into the air, and carved craters out of the plateau.

Unbeknownst to McKay, or any other human, for that matter, the third shell to roar down range blew Field Master 'Putumee in half. The assault continued, but more slowly now, as lower-ranked Elites assumed command, and tried to rally their troops.

Though pursuing his own sub-mission, 'Zamamee had been monitoring the situation and knew that the assault had stalled. It was only a matter of time before the dropships would be ordered to swoop in, pick up those who could crawl, walk, or run to them, and leave for safer climes.

That meant that he should be pulling out, looking for a way to slip through the human lines, but the session with the Prophet continued to haunt him. His best chance, no, his *only* chance, was to find the human and kill him. He would keep his head, all would be forgiven, and who knew? A lot of Elites had been killed—so there might be a promotion in the offing.

Thus reassured, he drove ahead.

The commandos were up on the first level by then, just approaching a door to the outside, when one of three waiting Marines saw a glint of Covenant armor within the alcove in which he was hiding, and opened fire.

There was complete pandemonium as the humans ran through clip after clip of ammunition, Grunts were blown off their feet, Elites fired in every direction, and soon started to fall.

'Zamamee felt his plasma rifle cycle open as it attempted to cool itself, and knew he was about to die, when a plasma grenade sailed in among the humans and locked onto a human soldier's arm. He yelled, "No!" but it was already too late, and the explosion slaughtered the entire fireteam.

Yayap, who had appropriated both the grenade and a pistol from one of the dead commandos, tugged on 'Zamamee's combat harness. "This way, Commander. . . . Follow me!"

The Elite did. The Grunt led the officer out through a door, down a walkway, and onto the platform where ten Banshees stood in an orderly row. There were no guards. 'Zamamee looked around. "Where is he?"

Yayap shrugged. "I have no idea, Commander."

'Zamamee felt a mixture of anger, fear, and hopelessness as a dropship passed over his head and disappeared downspin. The entire effort had been a failure.

"So," he said harshly, "you lied to me. Why?"

"Because *you* know how to fly one of these things," the Grunt answered simply, "and *I* don't."

The Elite's eyes seemed to glow as if lit from within. "I should shoot you and leave your body for the humans to throw off the cliff."

"You can *try*," Yayap said as he pointed the plasma pistol at his superior's head, "but I wouldn't advise it." It took all the courage the Grunt could muster to point his weapon at an Elite—and his hand shook in response to the fear he felt. But not much, not enough so that an energy bolt would miss, and 'Zamamee knew it.

The Elite nodded. Moments later, a heavily loaded Banshee wobbled off the ground, slipped over the edge of the butte, and immediately began to lose altitude. A Shade gunner caught a glimpse of it, and sent three bursts of plasma racing after the assault craft, but the Banshee was soon out of range.

The battle for Alpha Base was over.

———

The Spartan fired into what seemed like a tidal wave of tentacled horrors, backed away, and resolved to keep moving. He was vulnerable, in particular from behind, but the armor would help, especially since the monsters liked to jump on people.

What happened next wasn't clear, but could make Marines scream, and put them out of action in a relatively short period of time. Ammo would be a concern, he knew that, so rather than fire wildly, he forced himself to aim, trying to pop as many of the things as he could.

They came at him in twos, threes, and fours, flew into fleshy bits as the bullets ripped them apart and seemed to melt away. The problem was that there were hundreds of the little bastards, maybe *thousands*, which made it difficult to keep up as they flooded in his direction.

There were strategies, though, things the Chief could do to help even the odds, and they made all the difference. The first was to run, firing as he went, stretching their ragged formation thin, forcing them to skitter from one end of the room to the other. They were numerous and determined, but not particularly bright.

The second was to watch for breakouts, concentrations of the creatures where a well-thrown grenade could destroy hundreds of them all at once.

And the third was to switch back and forth between the assault weapon and the shotgun, thereby maintaining a constant rate of fire, only pausing to reload when there was a momentary lull in the fighting.

These strategies suddenly became even more critical as something *new* leaped out of the darkness. A mass of tattered flesh and swinging limbs lashed at his head. During the first moments of the attack the Chief wondered if a corpse had somehow fallen on him from above, but soon learned the truth, as more of the horribly misshapen creatures appeared and hurled themselves forward. Not just ran, but *vaulted* high into the air, as if hoping to crush him under their weight.

The creatures were roughly humanoid, hunchbacked figures that looked partially rotted. Their limbs seemed to be stretched to the breaking point. Clusters of tentacles protruded from ragged holes in their skin.

They were susceptible to bullets, however, something for which the Chief was thankful, although it often took fifteen or twenty rounds to put one down for good. Strangely, even the live ones looked like they were dead, which on reflection the Master Chief was starting to believe they were. That would explain why some of the ugly sons of bitches had a marked resemblance to Covenant Elites, or to what an Elite would look like if you killed him, buried the body, and dug it up two weeks later.

Finally, after what seemed like an eternity, two of the reanimated Elites barged in through the hatch, and were promptly put down. That provided the Chief with an opportunity to escape.

There were more of the two-legged freaks right on his tail, though, along with a jumble of the tumbling, leaping swarms of spherical creatures, and it was necessary to scrub the entire lot of them with auto fire before he could disengage and slip through a door.

The Spartan found himself on the upper gallery of a large, well-lit room. It was packed with the bipedal, misshapen creatures, but none seemed to be aware of him. He intended to keep it that way, and slid silently along the right-hand wall to a hatch.

A short journey brought the Chief to a similar space where what looked like full-fledged battle was underway between Covenant troops and the new hostiles.

The Spartan briefly considered engaging the targets—there was certainly no shortage of them. He held his fire instead, and lingered behind a fallen cargo module. After a hellish battle, the combatants had annihilated one another, which left him free to cross the bridge that led to the far end back along the walkway, and exit via the side door.

Another of the hunchbacked creatures dropped from above and slammed into him. The Spartan staggered back, dipped, and hurled the monster back over his shoulder. It crunched into the wall and left a trail of mottled gray-green, viscous fluid as it slid to the floor.

The Master Chief turned to continue on, when his motion sensor flickered red—illuminating a contact right behind him. He spun and was startled to see the crumpled, badly damaged creature struggle to its feet. Its left arm dangled uselessly and brittle bone protruded from its pale, gangrenous flesh.

The thing's right arm was still functional, however. A twisting column of tentacles burst from the creature's right wrist and he could hear the bones inside break as they forced its right hand roughly aside.

The tentacle flashed out, cracked like a whip and hurled the Master Chief to the floor. His shields were almost completely drained from the single blow.

He rolled into a crouch and opened fire. The 7.62mm armor-piercing rounds nearly cut the monster in half. He kicked the fallen hostile, put two in its chest. *This time, the damn thing should stay dead,* he thought.

He moved farther along the hallway. Two Marines lay where they had fallen, proving that at least some of the second squad had managed to get this far, which opened the possibility that more had escaped as well.

The Master Chief checked, discovered that they still wore their dog tags, and took them. He crept through the wide galleries and narrow corridors, past humming machinery, and entered a dark, gloomy vault. His motion tracker flashed crimson warnings—there were enemies everywhere.

Another of the misshapen bipedal hostiles shambled by, and he recognized the shape of the creature's head—the long, angular head of an Elite faced him. What held his fire was where the head was located.

The alien's skull was canted at a sickening angle, as if the bones of its neck had been softened or liquefied. It hung limply down the creature's back, lifeless—like a limb that needed amputation.

It was as if something had rewritten the Elite, reshaped it from the inside out. The Spartan felt an unaccustomed emotion: a trill of fear. An image of helplessness—of screaming at a looming threat, powerless—flashed through his mind, a snapshot of his cryo-addled dreams aboard the *Pillar of Autumn*.

No way is that going to happen to me, he thought. *No way*.

The beast shuffled by, and moved out of sight.

He took a deep breath, exhaled, then burst from his position and charged for the center of the room. He battered aside the shambling beasts, and crushed a handful of the small spherical creatures beneath his boots. His shotgun boomed and thick, green blood splashed the floor.

He reached his objective: a large lift platform, identical to the one he'd ridden down into this hellhole. He reached for the activation panel, and hoped that he'd find the up button.

One of the hostiles leaped high in the air and landed next to him.

The Chief dropped to one knee, shoved the barrel of the shotgun into the creature's belly, and fired. The beast flipped end over end, and fell back into a clot of the smaller, round hostiles.

He dove for the activation panel, and stabbed at the controls.

The elevator platform dropped like a rock, so far down and so fast that his ears popped.

Where the hell was Cortana when you needed her? Always telling him to "go through that door," "cross that bridge," or "climb that pyramid." Annoying at times, but reassuring as well.

The basement, if that's what it was, had all the charm of a crypt. A passageway took him into another large space where he had to fight his way across the floor to a door and the tunnel-like corridor beyond. That's when the Spartan came face-to-face with something he hadn't seen before and would have preferred never to see again: one of the combative, bipedal beasts—this one a horribly mutated *human*. Though the creature was distorted by whatever had ravaged his body, the Chief recognized him nonetheless.

It was Private Manuel Mendoza, the soldier that Sergeant Johnson loved to yell at, and one of the Marines who had been with Keyes when he disappeared into this nightmare.

Though twisted by what had been done to him, the Private's face still retained a trace of humanity, and it was that which caused the Master Chief to remove this finger from the shotgun's trigger, and try to make contact.

"Mendoza, come on, let's get the hell out of here. I know they did something to you but the medics can fix it."

The reanimated Marine, now possessed of superhuman strength, struck the Chief with such force that it nearly knocked him off his feet, and triggered the suit's alarm. Mendoza—or rather, the *thing* that had once been Mendoza—waved a whip-like tentacle and lashed out again. The Spartan staggered backward, pulled the trigger, and was subsequently forced to pull it again as the eight-gauge buckshot tore what had been Mendoza apart.

The results were both spectacular and disgusting. As the corpselike horror came apart, the Chief saw that one of the small, spherical creatures had taken up residence inside the soldier's chest cavity, and seemed to have extended its tentacles into other parts of what had been Mendoza's body. A *third* shotgun blast served to destroy it as well.

Was that how these things worked? The little round pod-things infected their hosts, and mutated the victim into some kind of combat form. He considered the possibility that this was some kind of new Covenant bioweapon, and discarded it. The first of these combat forms he'd seen had once been Elites.

Whatever these damned things were, they were lethal to humans and Covenant alike.

He quickly fed shells into his shotgun, then moved on. The Spartan moved as fast as he could—at a dead run. He charged into another room, scrambled up onto the gallery above, blew an Elite form right out of his boots, and ducked through a waiting door.

The area on the other side was more of a challenge. The Chief had the second floor to himself, but an army of the freaks owned the floor below, and that's where he needed to go.

Height conferred advantages. Some well-placed grenades, followed by a jump from the walkway, and sixty seconds of close-quarters action were sufficient to see him through. Still, it was a tremendous relief to pass through a completely uncontested space, and into a compartment where he found a *new* development to cope with.

In addition to their battering attacks, the creatures had acquired both human and Covenant weapons from their victims, and these combat forms were even more dangerous as a result. The combat forms weren't the smartest foes he'd ever encountered, but they weren't mindless automatons, either—they could operate machines and fire weapons.

Bullets pinged from the metal walls, plasma fire stuttered through the air, and a grenade detonated as the Master Chief cleared the area, and discovered a place where some Marines had staged a last stand on top of a cargo container. He paused to recover their dog tags, scavenged some ammo, and kept on going.

Something nagged at him, but what was it? Something he'd forgotten?

It came to him all at once: He had nearly forgotten his own name.

Keyes, Jacob. Captain. Service number 01928-19912-JK.

The droning chant that had lurked at the edge of his awareness buzzed more loudly, and he felt some kind of pressure—some sense of anger.

Why was he angry?

No, something *else* was angry . . . because he'd remembered his own name?

Keyes, Jacob. Captain. Service number 01928-19912-JK.

Where was he? How did he get here? He struggled to find the memory.

He remembered parts of it now. There was a dark, alien room, hordes of some terrifying enemy, gunfire, then a stabbing pain . . .

They must have captured him. That was it. This might be some new trick by the enemy. He'd give them nothing. He struggled to remember who the enemy was.

He repeated the mantra in his head: Keyes, Jacob. Captain. Service number 01928-19912-JK.

The buzzing pressure increased. He resisted, though he was unsure why. Something about the drone frightened him. The sense of invasion deepened.

Is this a Covenant trick? he wondered. He tried to scream, "It won't work. I'll never lead you to Earth," but couldn't make his mouth work, couldn't feel his own body.

As the thought of his home planet echoed through Keyes' consciousness, the tone and tenor of the drone changed, as if pleased. He—Keyes, Jacob. Captain. Service number 01928-19912-JK—was startled when new images played across his mind.

He realized, too late, that something was sifting through his mind, like a grave robber looting a tomb. He had never felt so powerless, so afraid . . .

His fear vanished in a flood of emotion as he felt the warmth of the first woman he'd ever kissed . . .

He tried to scream as the memory was ripped from him and discarded.

Keyes, Jacob. Captain. Service number 01928-19912-JK.

As each of the fragments of his past played out and was sucked into the void, he could feel the invader enveloping him like an ocean of evil. But, like the pieces of flotsam that remain after a ship has gone down, random pieces of himself remained, a sort of makeshift raft to which he could momentarily cling.

The image of a smiling woman, a ball spiraling through the air, a crowded street, a man with half his face blown away, tickets to a show he couldn't remember, the gentle sound of wind chimes, and the smell of newly baked bread.

But the sea was too rough, waves crashed down on the raft, and broke it apart. Swells lifted Keyes up, others pushed him down, and the final darkness beckoned. But then, just as the ocean was about to consume him, Keyes became aware of the one thing the creature that raped his mind couldn't consume: the CNI transponder's carrier wave.

He reached for it like a drowning man, clutched the lifeline with all his might, and refused to let go. For here, deep within his watery grave, was a thread that led back to what he had been.

Keyes, Jacob. Captain. Service number 01928-19912-JK.

The Master Chief fired the last of his shotgun rounds into the collapsed hulk of a combat form. It twitched and lay still.

After winding through the confusion of subterranean chambers and passageways for what seemed like hours, he'd finally found a lift to the surface. He carefully tapped the activation panel—worried for a moment that this lift would also drop him deeper into the facility—and felt the lift lurch into a rapid ascent.

As the lift climbed, Foehammer's worried voice crackled from his comm system.

"This is Echo 419. Chief, is that you? I lost your signal when you disappeared inside the structure. What's going on down there? I'm tracking movement all over the place."

"You wouldn't believe me if I told you," the Master Chief replied, his voice grim, "and believe me: You don't want to know. Be advised: Captain Keyes is missing, and is most likely KIA. Over."

"*Roger that,*" the pilot replied. "*I'm sorry to hear it, over.*"

The lift jerked to a halt, the Spartan stepped off, and found himself surrounded by Marines. Not the shambling combat forms he'd spent the last eternity fighting, but normal, unchanged human beings. "Good to see you, Chief," a Corporal said.

The Chief cut the soldier off. "There's no time for that, Marine. Report."

The young Marine gulped, then started talking. "After we lost contact we headed for the RV point, and these *things*, they ambushed us. Sir: Advise we get the *hell* out of here, ASAP."

"That's command thinking, Corporal," the Chief replied. "Let's go."

It was a short walk up the ramp and into the rain. Strangely, and much to his surprise, it felt good to enter the stinking swamp. *Very* good indeed.

CHAPTER

_____NINE_____

"There's a large tower a few hundred meters from your current position. Find a way above the fog and foliage canopy and I can move in and pick you up," Rawley said. Her eyes were glued to her scopes as Spartan 117 took the lead and the Marines left the ancient complex and entered the fetid embrace of the swamp. The rain and some kind of interference from the structure played hell with the Pelican's detection gear, but she was damned if she was going to lose this team now. She had a reputation to maintain, after all.

"*Roger that,*" the Chief replied, "*we're on our way.*"

She kept the Pelican circling, her eyes peeled for trouble. There was no immediate threat. That made her even more nervous. Ever since they'd made it down to the surface of the ring, trouble always seemed to strike without warning.

For the hundredth time since lifting off from Alpha Base, she cursed the lack of ammunition for the Pelicans.

Knowing the dropship was somewhere above the mist, and eager to get the hell out, the Marines forged ahead.

The Spartan cautioned them to slow down, to keep their eyes peeled, but it wasn't long before he found himself back toward the middle of the pack.

The tower Foehammer had mentioned appeared up ahead. The base of the column was circular, with half-rounded supports that protruded from the sides, probably for stability. Farther up, extending out from the column itself, were winglike platforms. Their purpose wasn't clear, but the same could be said for the entire structure. The top of the shaft was lost in the mist.

The Master Chief paused to look around, heard one of the leathernecks yell "Contact!" quickly followed by the staccato rip of an assault weapon fired on full automatic. A host of red dots had appeared on the Spartan's threat indicator. He saw a dozen of the spherical infection forms bounce out of the mist and knew that any possibility of containing the creatures underground had been lost.

The Pelican's sensors suddenly painted dozens—correction, hundreds—of new contacts on the ground. Rawley cursed and wheeled the Pelican around, expecting ground fire.

No fire was directed at the dropship. "What the hell?" she muttered. First, the contacts appeared out of nowhere, charged into the open, but didn't shoot at the air cover? Maybe the Covenant were getting stupid as well as ugly.

She hit the radio to warn the troops and winced as the muffled pop of automatic weapons fire burst from her headset. "Heads up, ground team!" she yelled. "Multiple contacts on the ground—they're right on top of you!"

The radio squealed, then static filled her speakers. The

interference worsened. She thumped the radio controls with a gloved fist. "Damn it!" she yelled.

"Uh, boss," Frye said. "You better take a look at this."

She glanced back at her copilot, followed his gaze, and her own eyes widened. "Okay," she said, "any idea what the hell *that* is?"

The Chief fired short bursts from his assault weapon, popped dozens of the alien pods, and turned to confront a combat form. It was armed with a plasma pistol but chose to throw itself forward rather than fire. The Chief's automatic weapon was actually touching the creature when he pulled the trigger. The ex-Elite's chest opened like an obscene flower and the infection form hidden within exploded into fleshy pieces.

He heard a burst of static in his comm system. Interference whined as the MJOLNIR's powerful communications gear tried to scrub the signal, to no avail. It sounded like Foehammer, but he couldn't be sure.

It hovered in front of the Pelican's cockpit for a moment, and light stabbed Rawley's eyes. It was made from some kind of silvery metal, roughly cylindrical but with angular edges. Winglike, squarish fins shifted and slid like rudders as the device bobbed in the air. It— whatever *it* was—shone a bright light into the cockpit, then turned away and dropped altitude. Below her, she could see dozens of the things flying in a loose line. In seconds, they dropped below the tree line and out of sight.

"Frye," she said, her mouth suddenly dry, "tell Chief Cullen to work the comm system and punch me a hole in this interference. I need to talk to the ground team *now*."

The tide of hostiles fell back into the ankle-deep water and regrouped. A dozen exotic-looking cylindrical machines drifted out of the trees to float over the clearing. The nearest Marine yelled, "What are they?" and was about to shoot at them when the Chief raised a cautionary hand. "Hold on, Marine . . . let's see what they do."

What happened next was both unexpected and gratifying. Each machine produced a beam of energy, speared one of the hostiles, and burned it down.

Some of the combat forms took exception to this treatment, and attempted to return fire, but were soon put out of action by the combined efforts of the Marines and their newfound allies.

Despite the help, the Marines didn't fare well. There were just too many of the hostile creatures around. The squad dwindled until a pair of PFCs remained, then one, then finally the last of the Marines fell beneath a cluster of the little infectious bastards.

As the newcomers overhead rained crimson laser fire on a cluster of the combat forms, the Chief slogged through the swamp toward the tower. High ground—and the possibility of signaling Foehammer for evac—drew him on.

He climbed a supporting strut and pulled himself onto one of the odd, leaflike terraces that ringed the tower. He had a good field of fire, and he fired a burst into a combat form that strayed too close.

He tried the radio again, but was rewarded with more static.

The Spartan heard what sounded like someone humming and turned to discover that *another* machine had approached him from behind. Where the other newcomers were cylindrical in design, with angular, winglike cowlings, this construct was rounded, almost spherical. It had a single, glowing blue eye, a wrap-around housing, and a cheerfully businesslike manner.

"Greetings! I am the Monitor of installation zero-four. I am 343 Guilty Spark. Someone has released the Flood. My function is to prevent it from leaving this installation. I require your assistance. Come this way."

The voice sounded artificial. This "343 Guilty Spark" was some kind of artificial construct, the Spartan realized. From above the little machine, he could see Foehammer's Pelican moving into position.

"Hold on," the Chief replied, trying to sound friendly. "The Flood? Those things down there are called 'Flood'?"

"Of course," 343 Guilty Spark replied, a note of confusion in its synthesized voice. "What an odd question. We have no time for this, Reclaimer."

Reclaimer? The Chief wondered. He was about to ask what the little machine meant by that, but his words never came. Rings of pulsating gold light traveled the length of his body, he felt light-headed, and saw an explosion of white light.

Rawley had just gotten the Pelican into position for a run on the tower, and could see the distinctive bulk of the Spartan standing on the structure. She eased the throttle forward, and the Pelican slid ahead, and nosed toward the structure. She glanced up just in time to see the Spartan disappear in a column of gold light.

"Chief!" Foehammer said. *"I lost your signal! Where did you go? Chief! Chief!"*

The Spartan had vanished, and there was very little the pilot could do except hope for the best.

Like the rest of the battalion's officers, McKay had worked long into the night supervising efforts to restore the butte's badly mauled defenses, ensure that the wounded received what care was available, and restore something like normal operations.

Finally, at about 0300, Silva ordered her below, pointing out that someone had to be in command at 0830, and it wasn't going to be him.

With traces of adrenaline still in her bloodstream, and images of battle still flickering through her brain, the Company Commander found it impossible to sleep. Instead she tossed, turned, and stared at the ceiling until approximately 0430 when she finally drifted off.

At 0730, with only three hours of sleep, McKay paused to collect a mug of instant coffee from the improvised mess hall before climbing a flight of bloodstained stairs to arrive on top of the mesa. The wreckage of what had been Charlie 217 had been cleared away during the night, but a large patch of scorched metal marked the spot where the fuel had been set ablaze.

The officer paused to look at it, wondered what happened to the human pilot, and continued her tour. The entire surface of Halo had been declared a combat zone, which meant it was inappropriate for the enlisted ranks to salute their superiors lest they identify them to enemy snipers. But there were other ways to signal respect, and as McKay made her way past the landing pads and out onto the battlefield beyond, it seemed as if all the Marines wanted to greet her.

"Morning, ma'am."

"How's it going, Lieutenant? Hope you got some sleep."

"Hey, skipper, guess we showed them, huh?"

McKay replied to them all and continued on her way. Just the fact that she was there, strolling through the plasma-blackened defenses with a cup of coffee in her hand, served to reassure the troops.

"Look," one of them said as she walked past, "there's the Loot. Cool as ice, man. Did you see her last night? Standing on that tank? It was like nothin' could touch her." The other Marine didn't say anything, just nodded in agreement, and went back to digging a firing pit.

Somehow, without consciously thinking about it, McKay's feet carried her back to the Scorpions and the point from which her particular battle had been fought. The Covenant knew that the Marines had these metal behemoths at their disposal, which was why both machines were being dug out and run up onto solid ground.

The officer wondered what Silva planned to do with them, and sipped the last of her coffee before wandering onto the plateau beyond. Covenant POWs, all chained together at the ankles, were busy digging graves. One section for members of their armed forces, and one for the humans. It was a sobering sight, as were the rows of tarp-covered bodies, and all for what?

For Earth, she told herself, and the billions who would go unburied if the Covenant found them.

There was a lot to do—the morning passed quickly. Major Silva was back on duty by 1300 hours and sent a runner to find McKay. As she entered his office she saw that he was sitting behind his makeshift desk, working at a computer. He looked up and pointed to a chair salvaged from a lifeboat. "Take a load off, Lieutenant. Nice job out there. I should take naps more often! How are you feeling?"

McKay dropped into the chair, felt it adjust to fit her body, and shrugged. "I'm tired, sir, but otherwise fine."

"Good," Silva said, bringing his fingers together into

a steeple. "Because there's plenty of work to do. We'll have to drive everyone hard—and that includes ourselves."

"Sir, yes sir."

"So," Silva continued, "I know you've been busy, but did you get a chance to read the report Wellesley put together?"

A crate of small but powerful wireless computers like the one sitting on the Major's desk had been recovered from the *Autumn* but McKay had yet to turn hers on. "I'm afraid not, sir. Sorry."

Silva nodded. "Well, based on information acquired during routine debriefings, our digital friend believes that the raid was both less and more than we assumed."

McKay allowed her eyebrows to rise. "Meaning?"

"Meaning that rather than the real estate itself, the Covies were after something, or more precisely *someone* they thought they would find here."

"Captain Keyes?"

"No," the other officer replied, "Wellesley doesn't think so, and neither do I. A group of their stealth Elites were able to penetrate the lower levels of the complex. They killed everyone they came into contact with, or thought they did, but one tech played dead, and another was knocked unconscious. They were in different rooms but both told the same story. Once in the room, and having gained control of it, one of those commando Elites—the bastards in the black combat suits— would momentarily reveal himself. He spoke in a passable form of their own language—and asked both groups the same question. 'Where is the human with the special armor?'"

"They were after the Spartan," McKay said thoughtfully.

"Exactly."

"So, where *is* the Chief?"

"*That*," Silva replied, "is a very good question. Where indeed? He went looking for Keyes, surfaced in the middle of a swamp, told Foehammer that the Captain was probably dead, and disappeared a few minutes later."

"Think he's dead?" McKay inquired.

"I don't know," Silva replied grimly, "although it wouldn't make too much difference if he were. No, I suspect that he and Cortana are out there playing games."

With Keyes out of the picture once more, Silva had reassumed command, and McKay could understand his frustration. The Master Chief was an asset, or would have been if he were around, but now, out freelancing somewhere, the Spartan was starting to look like a liability. Especially given how many of Silva's troops had died in order to defend a man who wasn't even there.

Yes, McKay could understand the Major's frustration, but couldn't sympathize with it. Not after seeing the Chief in that very room, his skin unnaturally white after too much time spent in his armor, his eyes filled with—what? Pain? Suffering? A sort of wary distrust?

The officer wasn't sure, but whatever it was didn't have anything to do with ego, with insubordination, or a desire for personal glory. Those were truths that McKay could access, not because she was a seasoned soldier, but because she was a woman, something Silva could never aspire to be. But it wouldn't do any good to say that, so she didn't.

Her voice was level. "So, where does that leave us?"

"Situation normal: We're cut off and probably surrounded." The chair sighed as Silva leaned back. "Like the old saying goes, 'a good defense is a good offense.' Rather than just sit around and wait for the Covenant to attack again, let's take the hurt to them. Nothing big, not yet anyway, but the kind of pinpricks that still draw blood."

McKay nodded. "And you want me to come up with some ideas?"

Silva grinned. "I couldn't have said it better myself."

"Yes, sir," McKay said, coming to her feet. "I'll have something by morning."

Silva watched the Company Commander exit his office, wasted five seconds wishing he had six more just like her, and went back to work.

The Master Chief felt himself rush back together like a puzzle with a million pieces, wondered what had happened, and where he was. He felt disoriented, nauseated, and angry.

A quick look around was sufficient to ascertain that the machine named 343 Guilty Spark had somehow transported him from the swamp into the bowels of a dark, brooding structure. He saw the machine hovering high above, glowing a thin, ghostly blue.

The Spartan raised his assault weapon, and fired half a clip into it. The bullets were dead on, but had no effect other than to elicit a bemused response.

"That was unnecessary, Reclaimer. I suggest that you conserve your ammunition for the effort ahead."

No less angry, but with little choice but to accept the situation, the Chief looked around. "So where am I?"

"The installation was specifically built to study and contain the Flood," the machine answered patiently. "Their survival as a race was dependent on it. I am grateful to see that some of them survived to reproduce."

"'Survived'? 'Reproduce'? What the hell are you talking about?" the Chief demanded.

"We must collect the Index," Spark said, leaving the Spartan's questions unanswered. "And time is of the essence. Please follow me."

The blue light zipped away at that point, forcing the Chief to follow, or be left behind. He checked both his weapons as he walked. "Speaking of *you*, who the hell are you, and what's your function?"

"*I* am 343 Guilty Spark," the machine said, pedantically. "I am the Monitor, or more precisely, a self-repairing artificial intelligence charged with maintaining and operating this facility. But you are the Reclaimer—so you know that already."

The Master Chief didn't know anything of the kind, but it seemed wise to play along, so he did. "Yes, well, refresh my memory . . . how long has it been since you were left in charge?"

"Exactly 101,217 local years," the Monitor replied cheerfully, "many of which were quite boring. But not anymore! *Hee, hee, hee.*"

The Spartan was taken aback by the sudden giggle from the small machine. He knew that the AIs humans used could, over time, develop personalities politely described as "quirky." 343 Guilty Spark had been here for tens of thousands of years.

It was quite possible that the little AI was insane.

The Monitor chattered on, nattering about "effecting repairs to substation nine" and other non sequiturs.

His dialogue was interrupted as a variety of Flood forms bounced, waddled, and leaped out of the surrounding darkness. Suddenly the Chief was fighting for his life again, moving back and forth to stretch the enemy out, blasting anything that moved.

That was when he first identified a *new* Flood form. They were large misshapen things that would explode when fired upon, spewing up to a dozen infection forms in every direction, thereby multiplying the number of targets that the shooter had to track and kill.

Finally, like water turned off at a tap, the assault came to an end, and the Chief had a chance to reload his weapons.

The Monitor hovered nearby, all the while humming to himself, and occasionally giggling. "There's no time to dawdle! We have work to do."

"What kind of work?" the Chief inquired as he stuffed the final shell into the shotgun and hurried to follow.

"This is the Library," the machine explained, hovering so the human could catch up. "The energy field above us contains the Index. We must get up there."

The Spartan was about to ask, "Index? What Index?" when a combat form lurched out of an alcove and opened fire. The Chief fired in return, saw the creature fall, and saw it jump back up again. The next burst took the Flood's left leg off.

"That should slow you down," he said as he turned to deal with a new horde of shambling, leaping hostiles. A steady stream of brass arced away from the Chief's assault weapon as he worked the mob over, felt something strike him from behind, and spun around to discover that the one-legged combat form had limped back into the fight.

The Spartan blew the creature's head off this time, sidestepped to evade a charging carrier form, and shot the bulbous monster in the back. There was an explosion of green mist mixed with balloonlike infection forms and pieces of wet flesh. The next ten seconds were spent popping pods.

After that the Monitor took off again and the non-com had little choice but to follow. He soon arrived in front of a huge metal door. Built to contain the Flood perhaps? Maybe, but far from effective, since the slimy bastards seemed to be leaking out of every nook and cranny.

The Monitor hovered over the human's head. "The security doors are locked automatically. I will go access the override to open them. I am a genius," the Monitor said matter-of-factly. "*Hee, hee, hee.*"

"A pain in the ass is more like it," the Master Chief said to no one in particular as a red dot appeared on his motion sensor, quickly joined by a half dozen more.

Then, as part of what would become a familiar pattern, combat forms leaped fifteen meters through the air, only to shrivel as the 7.62mm slugs tore them apart. Carrier forms waddled up like old friends, came apart like wet cardboard, and spewed pods in every direction. Infection forms danced on delicate legs, dodging this way and that, each hoping to claim the human as its very own.

But the Chief had other ideas. He killed the last of them just as the double doors started to part, and followed the monitor through. "Please follow closely," 343 Guilty Spark admonished. "This portal is the first of ten."

The Chief replied as he followed the AI past a row of huge blue screens. "*More* doors. I can hardly wait."

343 Guilty Spark appeared immune to sarcasm as it babbled about the first-class research facilities that surrounded them—and blithely led its human companion into still another ambush. And so it went, as the Chief worked his way through Flood-infested galleries, subfloor maintenance tunnels, and *more* galleries, before rounding a corner to confront yet another group of monstrosities.

The Spartan had help this time, as a dozen of the hunter-killer machines he'd seen in the swamp appeared in the air above the scene, and attacked the Flood forms congregated below.

"These Sentinels will assist you, Reclaimer," the Monitor trilled. Lasers hissed and sizzled as the hovering machines struck their opponents down, and having done so, moved in to sterilize what remained.

The Spartan watched in fascination as the machines took care of the heavy lifting. He lent a helping hand when that seemed appropriate, and started to gag when the air that came through his filters grew thick with the stench of cooked flesh.

As the Spartan fought his way through the facility, the Monitor, who floated above it all, offered commentary. "These Sentinels will supplement your combat systems. But I suggest you upgrade to at least a Class Twelve Combat Skin. Your current model only scans as a Class Two—which is unsuited for this kind of work."

If there's a battle suit six times as powerful as MJOLNIR armor, he thought, *I'll be first in line to try it on.*

He jumped to avoid an attack from one of the Flood combat forms, pressed the shotgun muzzle into its back, and blew a foot-wide hole through the creature.

Finally, after the hardworking Sentinels had reduced the Flood to little more than a lumpy paste, the Spartan made his way through the carnage and out onto a circular platform. It was enormous, easily large enough to handle a Scorpion, and in reasonably good repair.

Machinery hummed, bands of white light pulsated down from somewhere above, and the lift carried the human upward. Maybe things would be better up above, maybe the Flood hadn't reached that level yet, he thought. He didn't hold out much hope, however. So far, nothing *else* had gone right on this mission.

Deep within the recesses of Halo, Flood specimens were confined to facilitate future study, and to prevent them from escaping. Aware of the extreme danger the Flood posed, and their capacity to multiply exponentially as well as take over even advanced life forms, the ancient ones constructed the walls of their prison with great care, and trained their guards well. With nothing to feed upon, and nowhere to go, the Flood lay dormant for approximately one hundred thousand years.

Then the intruders came, broke the prison open, and nourished the Flood with their bodies. With a way to escape, and food to sustain it, the tendrils of the malevolent growth slithered through the maze of tunnels and passageways that lay below Halo's skin, and gathered wherever there was a potential route to the surface.

One such location was in a chamber located beneath a tall butte, where little more than a metal grating prevented the Flood from bursting out of its underground lair and shooting to the surface. Unbeknownst to the men and women of Alpha Base, they had a *new* enemy— and it lived directly below their feet.

The lift jerked to a halt. The Master Chief made his way through a narrow passageway into the gallery beyond. The Flood attacked immediately, but with no threat at his back, he was free to retreat into the corridor from which he had just come, which forced the mob of monstrosities to come at him through the same narrow channel. Before long, the bodies of the fallen Flood began to accumulate.

He paused, waiting for another wave of attackers, then shoved aside a pile of the dead and moved into the next section of the complex. They gave under his feet, made gurgling sounds, and vented foul-smelling gas. The Chief was grateful when his boots were back on solid ground again.

The Sentinels reappeared shortly thereafter and led the Spartan past a row of huge blue screens. "So, where were you bastards a few minutes ago?" the human inquired. But if the machines heard him, they made no reply as they glided, circled, and bobbed through the hallway ahead.

"Flood activity has caused a failure in a drone control system. I must reset the backup units," 343 Guilty Spark said. "Please continue on—I will rejoin you when I have completed my task."

The Monitor had left him on his own before—and each absence coincided with a fresh wave of Flood attackers. "Hold on," the human protested, "let's discuss this—" but it was too late. 343 Guilty Spark had already darted through an aperture in the wall and disappeared down some kind of travel conduit.

Sure enough, no sooner had the Monitor left than a lumpy-looking carrier form waddled out into the light, spotted its prey, and hurried to greet it. The Spartan shot the Flood form, but let the Sentinels clean up the resulting mess, while he conserved his ammo.

A fresh onslaught of Flood came out of the woodwork, and the Spartan adopted a more cautious strategy: He allowed the sentry machines to mop them up. At first, the defense machines mowed through a wave of the podlike infection forms with little difficulty. Then more of the hostiles appeared, then *more*, then still more. Soon, the Chief was forced to fall back. He crushed one of the pods with his foot, smashed another out of the air with the butt of his assault rifle, and killed a dozen more with a trio of quick AR bursts.

The Monitor drifted back into the chamber, spun as if surveying the carnage, and made an odd, metallic clicking that sounded very much like a cluck of disapproval. "The Sentinels can use their weapons to manage the Flood for a short time, Reclaimer. Speed is of the essence."

"Then let's go," the Master Chief growled.

The Monitor made no reply, but scooted ahead. The small construct led the Spartan deeper into the Library's gloomy halls. They passed through a number of large open gates prior to arriving in front of one that was closed. The Chief paused for a moment, expecting that 343 Guilty Spark might open it for him, but the Monitor had disappeared. Again.

The hell with it, he thought. The little machine was rapidly draining his reserves of patience.

Determined to move ahead with or without the services of his on-again, off-again guide, the Chief retraced his steps to the point where a steeply sloping ramp emerged from below, followed it downward, and soon found himself in a maintenance corridor packed with Flood.

But the narrow confines of the passageway again made it that much easier to kill the parasitic life forms, and five minutes later the human walked up a ramp on the other side of the metal door to find that the Monitor was there, humming to himself.

"Oh, hello! I'm a genius."

"Right. And I'm a Vice Admiral."

The Monitor darted ahead, leading him across a circular depression to another enormous door. Machinery whirred, and the Chief was forced to pause as the doors started to part. Then he heard a clank, followed by a groan, as the movement stopped.

"Please wait here," Spark said, and promptly vanished.

Just as the Master Chief pulled a fresh clip and rammed it home, dozens of red dots appeared on his threat indicator. He stood with his back to the door as what looked like a platoon of Flood forms prepared to rush him. Rather than simply open up on them, and risk the possibility that they might roll him under, the Chief threw a grenade into their midst, and half his opponents went up in a single blast. It took a few minutes plus a few hundred rounds of ammo to put the rest of them down, but the Spartan managed to do so.

That was when the machinery restarted, the doors opened, and the Monitor reappeared, humming to itself. "I am a genius!"

He moved through the new chamber—a high, vaulted gallery, dimly lit with pools of gold-yellow light. For the first time since Spark had dragged him here, he had a moment of respite. Ever since entering the Library, the Spartan's head had been on a swivel. Wave after wave of hostile creatures had attacked him from all sides.

He popped a stim-pack, downed a nutrient supplement, and gathered up his weapon. Time to move out.

As he proceeded deeper into the Library, he found a corpse—a human one. He stooped to examine the body.

It wasn't pretty. The Marine's body was so mangled that even the Flood couldn't make use of him. He lay at the center of a large bloodstain wreathed by spent brass.

"Ah," 343 Guilty Spark said, peering down over the

Spartan's shoulder. "The *other* Reclaimer. His combat skin proved even less suitable than yours."

The soldier looked up over his shoulder. "What do you mean?"

"Is this a test, Reclaimer?" the Monitor seemed genuinely puzzled. "I found him wandering through a structure on the other side of the ring, and brought him to the same point where *you* started."

The Chief looked down at the body and marveled at the fact that anyone could make it that far. Even with his physical augmentation, and the advantages of his armor, the Spartan was reaching the end of his endurance.

He checked, found the leatherneck's dog tags, and read the name. MOBUTO, MARVIN, STAFF SERGEANT, followed by a service number.

The Chief put the tags away. "I didn't know you, Sarge, but I sure as hell wish I had. You must have been one hardass son of a bitch."

It wasn't much as eulogies go, but he hoped that, had Sergeant Marvin Mobuto been there to hear it, he would have approved.

A good trap requires good bait, which was why McKay had one of the Pelicans pick up Charlie 217's burned-out remains and drop them into the ambush site during the hours of darkness. It took three trips to transport a sufficient amount of wreckage, followed by hours of backbreaking effort to spread the pieces around in a realistic way, then position her troops in the rocks above.

Finally, just as the sun speared the area with early morning light, everything was ready. A phony distress call went out, and a specially prepared fire was lit deep within the wreckage. Scattered around the "crash site" were some "volunteers"—the bodies of comrades killed on the butte had been laid out where they could be seen from the air.

As half of the first platoon tried to get some sleep, the rest kept watch. McKay used her glasses to scan the area. The fake crash site was located between a low, flat-topped rise and a rocky hillside, covered with a jumble of large boulders. The wreckage, complete with a trickle of smoke, looked quite realistic.

Wellesley believed that having first dismissed the Marines and Naval personnel as little more than a nuisance, the enemy had since been forced to change their minds, and had started to take them more seriously. That meant monitoring human radio traffic, conducting regular recon flights, and all the other activities of modern warfare.

Assuming the AI was correct, the aliens would pick up the distress call, backtrack to the source, and send a team to check the situation out. That was the plan, at any rate, and McKay didn't see any reason why it wouldn't work.

The sun inched higher in the sky, and down among the rocks the temperature rose. The Marines took advantage of any bit of shade that they could find, though McKay was privately pleased that the customary bitching about the heat was kept to a minimum.

Thirty minutes into the wait McKay heard a sound like the whine of a mosquito and started to quarter the sky with her binoculars. It wasn't long before she spotted a speck coming down-spin. Very quickly, the speck grew into a Banshee. She keyed her mike.

"Red One to squad three—it's show time."

The officer didn't dare say more lest any Covenant eavesdroppers grow suspicious. She didn't *have* to say much more, though. Her Marines knew what to do.

As the enemy aircraft came closer, members of the third squad, some of whom were made up to look as if they were injured, hurried out into the open, shaded their eyes as if watching for an incoming Pelican, pantomimed surprise as they spotted the Banshee, fired a volley of shots at it, then ran for the safety of the rocks.

The pilot sent a series of plasma bolts racing after them, circled the crash site twice, and flew off in the direction from which he had come. McKay watched it go. The hook had been set, the fish was on the line, and it would be her job to reel it in.

Half a klick away from the phony crash site, another Marine, or what *had* been a Marine, emerged from a subsurface air shaft, and felt the sun hit his horribly ravaged face. Well, not *his* face, because ever since the infection form had inserted its penetrator into his spine, Private Wallace A. Jenkins had been sharing his physical form with something he thought of as "the other." A strange being that didn't have any thoughts, none that the human could access, at any rate, and seemed unaware of the fact that its host still retained some cognitive abilities and possibly even motor functions.

That awareness was entirely unique to him insofar as the leatherneck could tell, because in spite of the fact that some of the bodies in the group had once belonged to his squad mates, repeated attempts to communicate with them had failed.

Now, as the untidy collection of infection forms, carrier forms, and combat forms emerged to bounce, waddle, and walk across Halo's surface, Jenkins knew that wherever the column was headed it was for one purpose: to find and subsume sentient life. He could dimly sense the other's yawning, icy hunger.

His goal, however, was considerably different. After it had been converted into a combat form, his body was still capable of handling a weapon. Some of the other forms had them—and that's what Jenkins wanted more than anything. An M6D would be perfect, but an energy weapon could do the job, as would any grenade. Not for use on the Covenant, or the Flood, but on *himself*. Or what had been him. That's why he'd been careful to conceal the full extent of his awareness from the other. So he had a chance of destroying the body in which he had been imprisoned and escape the horror of each waking moment.

The Flood came to a hill and, following one of the carrier forms, soon started to climb. The other, with Jenkins in tow, tagged along behind.

McKay knew the trap was going to work when one of the U-shaped dropships appeared, circled the phony crash site, and settled in for a landing. Once free of the ship the Elites, Jackals, and Grunts would be easy meat for the Marines hidden in the rocks and the snipers stationed on top of the flat-topped hill.

But war is full of surprises, and when the Covenant ship took off again, McKay found herself looking at everything she had expected to see *plus* a couple of Hunters. The mean-looking bastards would be hard to kill and could rip the platoon to shreds.

The officer swallowed the lump that had suddenly formed in her throat, keyed her mike, and whispered some instructions. "Red One to all snipers and rocket jockeys. Put everything you have on the Hunters. Do it *now*. Over."

It was hard to say who killed the Hunters, given the sudden barrage of bullets and rockets that came their way, but McKay didn't care, so long as the walking tanks were *dead* . . . which they definitely were. That was the good news.

The bad news was that the dropship returned, hosed the boulders with plasma fire, and forced the Helljumpers to duck or lose their heads.

Encouraged by the air support, the Covenant ground troops rushed to enter the jumble of rocks, eager to find some cover, and kill the treacherous humans. They were forced to pay a price, however, as the snipers on the hill picked off five of the alien soldiers before the dropship moved in to exact its revenge.

The Marines were forced to dive deep as the enemy aircraft marched a double line of plasma bolts across the top of the tiny mesa, killing two of the snipers and wounding a third.

Things soon started to get ugly on the rock-strewn hillside as both humans and Covenant hunted one another between the huge, weather-smoothed boulders. Energy bolts flew and assault weapons chattered, as both sides took part in a deadly game of hide-and-seek. This was *not* what McKay had envisioned, and she was looking for a way to disengage, when a wave of new hostiles entered the fight.

A torrent of the bizarre creatures attacked *both* groups from the other side of the hill. McKay had a glimpse of corpse-flesh, twisted and mangled bodies, and swarms of small, sacklike creatures that bounded, leaped, and clambered over the rocks.

The first problem was that while the Covenant forces seemed familiar with the creatures, the Helljumpers weren't, and three members of the second squad had already gone down under the combined weight of multiple forms, and one member of the third had been slaughtered by a grotesque biped, before McKay understood the extent of the danger.

Even as the officer fought her way uphill through the maze of boulders the radio calls continued to boom through her earpiece.

"What the hell is that thing?"

"Fire! Fire! Fire!"

"Get it off me!"

The radio traffic tripled and the command freq turned into such a confusion of screams, requests for orders, and pleas for extraction, that the Marines might as well have spoken gibberish.

McKay cursed. No way. No way were these *things* going to break them. No way. She rounded a boulder, saw a Grunt running downhill with two of the smaller creatures clinging to its back. The Grunt squealed and spun and she got her first close look at the creatures. A sustained burst from the assault weapon brought all three of them down.

As the Marine worked her way farther uphill, she soon discovered that the new enemy took *other* forms as well. McKay killed a two-legged form, saw a private put half a clip into a lumpy-looking monster, and watched in disgust as the dying creature spewed even *more* grotesqueries out into the world.

That was the moment when the third form emerged from between a couple of boulders, saw the human, and launched itself into the air.

Jenkins had the same view that the others did, spotted the Lieutenant, and hoped she was a good shot. This was better than suicide—this was . . .

But it wasn't meant to be.

McKay tracked the incoming body, sidestepped, and used the butt of her weapon to clip the side of the creature's head. It landed in a heap, flailed around, and was just about to jump up when the Lieutenant pounced on it. "Give me a hand!" she shouted. "I want this one alive!"

It took four Marines to subdue the creature, get restraints on both its wrists and ankles, and finally bring it under control. Even at that, one of the Helljumpers suffered a black eye, another wound up with a broken arm, and a third bled from a ragged bite wound on his arm.

The ensuing battle lasted for a full fifteen minutes, an eternity in combat, with both humans and Covenant forces taking time out from their battle with one another to concentrate on the new enemy. The moment the last bulbous form was popped, however, they were back at it again, tracking one another through the maze in a contest of life and death, no quarter asked and none given.

McKay radioed for assistance, and with help from the Reaction Force, plus two Pelicans and four captured Banshees, she was able to drive the Covenant dropship away and kill those ground troops who weren't willing to surrender.

Then, on McKay's orders, the Helljumpers combed the area for reasonably intact specimens of the *new* enemy which could be taken back to Alpha Base for analysis.

Finally, after the bodies were recovered, Jenkins was the only specimen that was still alive. In spite of the way that he jerked, bucked, and tried to bite his captors they threw him onto the Pelican, roped him to the D-rings recessed into the deck, and delivered a few kicks for good measure.

With fully half of her Marines making the return trip in body bags, McKay sat through the seemingly endless journey to Alpha Base. Tears cut tracks down through the grime on the Helljumper's face to wet the deck between her boots. The Covenant had been bad enough—but now there was an even worse enemy to fight. Now, for the first time since the landing on Halo, McKay felt nothing but despair.

The Spartan left Sergeant Mobuto's body behind and approached one of the large metal doors, pleased to see that it was open. He crouched and passed through. 343 Guilty Spark disappeared on one of his mysterious errands a few moments later, and, like clockwork, the Flood came out to play.

He was ready for them. The Flood swept into the room—dozens of the bulbous infection forms scuttling along the walls and floor, with another half dozen of the combat forms in tow.

They paused, as if in confusion. One of the combat forms looked up—and the Spartan dropped from the pillar he'd shimmied up. His metal boots pulped the creature's face. Assault rifle fire raked the leading edge of the cluster of infection forms. The pods detonated in a chain-reaction string.

That *got their attention*, he thought. The Chief turned and ran. He jumped up onto a raised platform as he fought, disengaged, and fought again. Finally, as the last body fell, both the Monitor and the Sentinels reappeared.

The Spartan looked at them in disgust as he reloaded his weapons, scrounged ammo off the Flood combat forms, and followed 343 Guilty Spark out onto a lift that was identical to the last one he'd been on.

The platform carried the human up to a still higher level, where he got off, paused to let the Sentinels soften up the Flood welcome wagon that waited out in the hall, then emerged to lend a hand. There was a loud *boom!* as one of the combat forms leaped from an archway and landed right on top of a Sentinel. Its whip-tendril flailed at the hovering machine's back and was rewarded with a series of sparks and a gout of flame. A moment later, the Sentinel exploded, and the Flood and the wrecked drone crashed into the floor in a ball of flesh, bone, and metal. The resulting shower of shrapnel cut three Flood forms down and wounded a score of others.

The Spartan took another out with a burst from his assault weapon and the Sentinels moved in to fry the remains.

Once that contingent of creatures had been dealt with, the Chief followed the Monitor down a hall lined with blue screens, through an area that was infested with Flood, and out onto a lift that looked different from the last one he'd been on. Geometric patterns split the floor into puzzlelike shapes, a series of raised panels stood guard around a column of translucent blue light, and the whole thing seemed to glow.

The Master Chief stepped on board, felt a slight jerk as ancient machinery reacted to his presence, and saw the walls start to rise. He was headed down this time—and hoped that his journey was near an end. Without hesitation, he slammed fresh ammo into his weapon; it seemed as if he emerged into a huge cluster of Flood every time he traveled on a lift.

The lift made hollow, rumbling sounds, fell a long way, and stopped with a reverberating thud.

343 Guilty Spark hovered over his shoulder as the Spartan stepped off the lift and approached a pedestal. "You may now retrieve the Index," the Monitor said. The artifact glowed lime green; it was shaped like the letter T. It slowly rose from the top of the cylindrical tube in which it had been kept for so many millennia.

A series of metal blocks that encircled the device rotated and spun, releasing their protective grip on the Index.

The Spartan took hold of the device, and pulled it up and out of its tubular sheath. He held it up to examine the glowing artifact—and was startled when a gray beam lanced from Spark. The Index was yanked from his hand and disappeared inside a storage chamber in the Monitor's body.

"What the hell are you doing?" the Spartan demanded.

"As you know, Reclaimer," Spark said, as if addressing an errant child, "protocol requires that *I* take possession of the Index for transport."

343 Guilty Spark swooped and dived, then floated in place. "Your biological form renders you vulnerable to infection. The Index must not fall into the hands of the Flood before we reach the Control Room and activate the installation.

"The Flood is spreading! We must hurry."

The Master Chief was about to reply when he saw the bands of pulsating light flowing down around his body, knew he was about to be teleported, and again felt light-headed.

It wanted something, Keyes realized. The memories that replayed like an endless library of video clips were being sifted for something. The buzzing presence in his mind sought . . . what?

He grasped at the thought, and pushed back against the wall of resistance the other that burrowed through his consciousness had erected. He brushed up against it and it almost slipped away . . .

Then he had it—escape. Whatever this thing was, it wanted *off* the ring. It hungered, and there was a perfect feeding ground to be found.

The other plunged a barbed-wire tendril into his mind and ripped forth an image of a lunar Earthrise, which blurred into images of cattle in a slaughterhouse. He felt the other's tendrils eagerly grasp at the image of Earth. *Where?* It thundered. *Tell.*

The pressure increased and battered through Keyes' resistance, and in desperation he summoned up a new memory. The alien presence seemed startled at the image of Keyes and a childhood friend kicking a soccer ball on a vibrant green field.

The pressure eased as the hungry other examined the memory.

Keyes felt a stab of regret. He knew what he had to do now.

He dragged all he remembered of Earth—its location, his ability to find it, its defenses—and shoved them down, as deep as he could.

Keyes felt the gaping sense of loss as the memory of the soccer field was ripped away and discarded forever. He quickly summoned up another—the taste of a favorite meal. He began to feed his memories to the invading presence in his mind, one scrap at a time.

Of all the battles he'd ever fought, this one was the toughest—and the most important.

The Chief rematerialized back on the walkway which seemed to float over the black abyss below—the Control Room. He saw the replica of Halo which arched above, the globe that floated at the center of the walkway, and the control panel where he had last seen Cortana. Was she still there?

343 Guilty Spark hovered above his head. "Is something wrong?"

"No, nothing."

"Splendid. Shall we?"

The Spartan made his way forward. The control board was long and curved at either end. An endless light show played across the surface of the panel as various aspects of the ringworld's extremely complicated electronic and mechanical machinery fed a constant flow of data to the display, all of which appeared as a mosaic of constantly morphing glyphs and symbols.

Here, if one knew how to read it, were the equivalents of the ringworld's pulse, respirations, and brain waves. Reports that provided information on the rate of spin, the atmosphere, the weather, the highly complex biosphere, the machinery that kept all of it running, plus the activities of the creatures around whom the world had been formed: the Flood. It was awesome to look at—and even more awesome to consider.

343 Guilty Spark hovered above the control panel and looked down on the human who stood in front of him. There was something supercilious about the tone of the construct's voice. "My role in this particular endeavor has come to an end. Protocol does not allow units from my classification to perform a task as important as the reunification of the Index with the Core."

The Monitor zipped around to hover at the Master Chief's side. "That final step is reserved for *you*, Reclaimer."

"Why do you keep calling me that?" the Chief asked. Spark kept silent.

The Spartan shrugged, accepted the Index, and gazed at the panel in front of him. One likely-looking slot pulsed the same glowing green that shone from the Index. He slid it home. The T-shaped device fit perfectly.

The control panel shivered as if stabbed, the displays flared as if in response to an overload, and an electronic groan was heard. 343 Guilty Spark tilted slightly as if to look at the control board.

"That wasn't supposed to happen," Spark chirped.

There was a sudden shimmer of light as Cortana's holographic figure appeared and continued to grow until she towered over the control panel. Her eyes were bright pink, data scrolled across her body, and the Chief knew she was pissed. "Oh, really?" she said. She gestured, and the Monitor fell out of the air and hit the deck with a clank.

The Spartan looked up at her. "Cortana—"

The AI stood with hands on hips. "I spent hours cooped in here watching you toady about helping that . . . *thing* get set to slit our throats."

The Chief turned toward the Monitor and back. "Hold on now. He's a friend."

Cortana brought a hand up to her mouth in mock surprise. "Oh, I didn't realize. He's your *pal*, is he? Your *chum*? Do you have any idea what that bastard almost made you do?"

"Yes," the Spartan said patiently. "Activate Halo's defenses and destroy the Flood. Which is why we brought the Index to the Control Center."

Cortana's image plucked the Index out of its slot and held it out in front of her. "You mean *this*?"

Now reanimated, 343 Guilty Spark hovered just off the floor. He was furious. "A construct in the core? That is absolutely unacceptable!"

Cortana's eyes glowed as she bent forward. "Piss off."

The Monitor darted higher. "What impertinence! I shall purge you at once."

"You sure that's a good idea?" Cortana inquired as she waved the Index, then added the data contained within it to her memory.

"How dare you!" Spark exclaimed. "I'll—"

"Do what?" Cortana demanded. "I have the Index. *You* can float and sputter."

The Master Chief held both hands up. One held the assault rifle. "Enough! The Flood is spreading. If we activate Halo's defenses we can wipe them out."

Cortana looked down on the human with an expression of pity. "You have no idea how this ring works, do you? Why the Forerunners built it?"

She leaned forward, her face grim. "Halo doesn't kill Flood—it kills their *food*. Human, Covenant, whatever. You're all equally edible. The only way to stop the Flood is to starve them to death. And that's exactly what Halo is designed to do. Wipe the galaxy clean of *all* sentient life. You don't believe me?" the AI finished. "Ask *him*!" and she pointed to 343 Guilty Spark.

The ramifications of what Cortana said hit home, and he gripped his MA5B tightly. He rounded on the Monitor. "Is it true?"

Spark bobbed slightly. "Of course," the construct said directly. Then, sounding more like his officious self again, "This installation has a maximum effective radius of twenty-five thousand light years, but once the others follow suit, this galaxy will be quite devoid of life, or at least any life with sufficient biomass to sustain the Flood.

"But you already knew this," the AI continued contritely. The little device sounded genuinely puzzled. "I mean, how *couldn't* you?"

Cortana glowered at the Chief. "Left out that little detail, did he?"

"We followed outbreak containment procedure to the letter," the Monitor said defensively. "You were with me each step of the way as we managed the process."

"Chief," Cortana interrupted, "I'm picking up movement—"

"Why would you hesitate to do what you've already done?" 343 Guilty Spark demanded.

"We need to go," Cortana insisted. "Right *now*!"

"Last time you asked me: If it were my choice, would I do it?" the Monitor continued, as a flock of Sentinels arrayed themselves behind him. "Having had considerable time to ponder your query, my answer has not changed. There is no choice. We must activate the ring."

"Get. Us. Out. Of. Here," Cortana said, her eyes tracking the Sentinels.

"If you are unwilling to help—I will simply find another," Spark said conversationally. "Still, I must have the Index. Give your construct to me or I will be forced to take it from you."

The Spartan looked up at Spark and the machines arrayed in the air behind him. The assault weapon came up ready to fire. "That's not going to happen."

"So be it," the Monitor said wearily. Then, in a comment directed to the Sentinels, he added: "Save his head. Dispose of the rest."

SECTION V

TWO BETRAYALS

POSSESSION

CHAPTER

TEN

The vast platform that extended out over the Control Room's black abyss felt small and confining as the Master Chief was attacked from every direction at once. Ruby-red energy beams sizzled, and the smell of ozone filled the air as the airborne Sentinels circled, searching for a chink in his armor. All they needed was one good hit, a chance to put him down, and they would be able not only to take his head, but the Index as well.

Cortana's intrusion skills had become much less conventional since the landing on Halo. He had been surprised when she'd used his suit comm as a de facto modem to broadcast her way into the Control Room computers. He was also unprepared for her sudden return. After so much time in the ring's massive systems, she felt somehow larger. He pondered her unusual behavior—her shortness, the flare of temper.

There was no time to consider Cortana's "mental state." There was still a mission to achieve: Protect Cortana, and keep Spark the hell away from the Index. For his part the Spartan wove back and forth, conscious of the fact that the walkway had no rails, and how easy it would be to fall off the edge. That made hitting his targets a great deal more difficult. Still, he had seen the Flood bring Sentinels down, and figured that if the combat forms could do it, so could he. He decided to tackle the lowest machines first.

He was careful to get a good lead on each target. The assault rifle stuttered, and the nearest target exploded. He switched to the shotgun and fired methodically. He pumped a new round into the chamber, and fired again. Thanks to the broad pattern provided by each shell, the pump gun soon proved itself to be an extremely effective weapon against the Sentinels.

One of the machines exploded, another hit the deck with a loud clang, and a third trailed smoke as it spiraled into the darkness below.

The battle became somewhat easier after that, as there was less and less incoming fire, and he was able to knock three more Sentinels out of the air in quick succession.

He started to move, reloading as he went. One especially persistent machine took advantage of the interlude to score three hits on his back, which triggered the audible alarm, and pushed his shield to the very edge.

With only four shells in his weapon, the Chief turned, blew the Sentinel out of the air, and spun to nail another. Then, weapon raised, he turned in a circle, searching for more targets. There weren't any.

"So," he said as he lowered the shotgun and pushed more shells into the receiver, "don't tell me—let me guess. You have a plan."

"Yes," Cortana replied unabashedly, "I do. We can't let the Monitor activate Halo. We have to stop him—we have to destroy Halo."

The Spartan nodded and flexed his stiff shoulders. "And how do we do that?"

"According to my analysis of the available data I believe the best course of action is somewhat risky."

Naturally, the Chief thought.

"An explosion of sufficient size," Cortana explained, "will help destabilize the ring—and will cut through a number of primary systems. We need to trigger a detonation on a large scale, however. A starship's fusion reactors going critical would do the job.

"I'm going to find out where the *Pillar of Autumn* went down. If the ship's fusion reactors are still relatively intact, we can use *them* to destroy Halo."

"Is that *all*?" the Spartan inquired dryly. "Sounds like a walk in the park. By the way, it's nice to have you back."

"It's nice to *be* back," Cortana said, and he knew she meant it. Although there were any number of "natural" bio-sentients that she thought of as friends, the bond the AI shared with the Spartan was unique. So long as they shared the same armor they would share the same fate. If *he* died then *she* died. Relationships don't get any more interdependent than that, something that struck Cortana as both wonderful and frightening.

His boots made a hollow sound as he approached the gigantic blast doors and hit the switch. They parted to reveal a battle in progress between a group of Sentinels and Covenant ground troops. Red lasers split the air into jagged shapes as machines burned a Jackal down. The contest was far from one-sided, however, as one of the machines exploded and showered the Covenant with bits of hot metal.

The room was a long rectangular affair with a strangely corrugated floor. Standing at one end of the space, and well out of harm's way, the Spartan was content to watch and let the two groups whittle each other down. However, when the last Sentinel crashed, leaving two Elites still on their feet, the Master Chief knew he'd have to take them on.

The Covenant spotted the human, knew he'd have to come to them, and stood waiting. The Chief took advantage of what little bit of cover there was and made his way down the length of the room. With only half a clip of ammo left in his assault rifle, he had little choice but to tackle them with the shotgun—far from ideal at this range.

He fired a couple of rounds just to get their attention, waited for the Elites to charge, and lobbed a plasma grenade into the gap between them. The explosion killed one soldier and wounded the other. A single blast from the shotgun was sufficient to finish the job. Striding though the carnage, he exchanged the assault weapon for a plasma rifle.

From there it was a short journey through an empty room and out onto the top level of the pyramid. It was dark, and a fresh layer of snow had fallen since the time when the noncom had battled his way up to the Control Room from the valley below.

There were guards, but all of them had their backs to the hatch, and didn't bother to turn until the doors were halfway open. That was when they saw the human, did a series of double takes, and started to respond. But the Chief was ready and used the energy weapon to hose them down. The Elites jerked and fell, quickly followed by several Jackals and Grunts.

Then, just as suddenly as the violence had started, it was over. Snow swirled around the sole figure who remained standing, began the long, painstaking job of covering each body with a shroud of white, and fostered an illusion of peace.

Cortana took advantage of the momentary pause

to update the Spartan regarding her plan. "We need to buy some time in case the Monitor or his Sentinels find a way to activate Halo's final weapon without the Index.

"The machines in these canyons are Halo's primary firing mechanisms. They consist of three phase pulse generators that amplify Halo's signal and allow it to fire deep into space. If we damage or destroy the generators, the Monitor will need to repair them before Halo can be used. That should buy us some time. I'm marking the location of the nearest pulse generator with a nav point. We need to move and neutralize the device."

"Roger that," the Chief said, as he made his way down the first ramp to the platform below. Once again the element of surprise worked in his favor. He killed two Elites, caught a couple of Jackals as they tried to run, and nailed a Grunt as it appeared from below.

The wind whistled around the side of the pyramid. The Spartan left a trail of large bootprints as he made his way down to the point where the ramp met the next level walkway, crossed to the other side of the structure, and ran into a pair of Elites as they hit the top of the up ramp and rounded the corner.

There wasn't enough time to do anything but fire, and keep on firing, in an attempt to overwhelm the Covenant armor. It wouldn't have worked had the aliens been farther away, but the fact that the plasma pulses were pounding them in close made all the difference. The first Elite made a horrible gurgling sound as he fell and the second got a shot off but lost half of his face. He brought his hands up to the hole, made a gruesome discovery, and was just about to scream when an energy bolt took his life.

Then, as the Spartan prepared to descend into the

valley below, Cortana said, "Wait, we should commandeer one of those Banshees. We'll need it to reach the pulse generator in time." Like many of the AI's suggestions, this was easier said than done, but the Chief was in favor of speed, and filed the possibility away.

Now, as he came down off the pyramid, he saw lots of Covenant, but no Flood, and felt a strange sense of relief. The Covenant were tough, but he understood them, and that lessened his apprehension.

The alien plasma rifle lacked the precision offered by an M6D pistol or a sniper's rifle, but the Chief did the best he could to pick off some of the Covenant below. Still, he had only nailed three of the aliens when his efforts attracted the attention of a Wraith tank, along with *more* troops. There was nothing he could do except retreat back uphill.

The Wraith, which continued to hurl plasma mortars upslope, actually helped by preventing other Covenant forces from charging after him. That advantage wouldn't last long, though, which meant that he had to find some additional firepower, and find it fast.

Even though there was no sign of the Flood at the moment, some of their half-frozen bodies lay scattered about, suggesting that there had been a significant battle within the last couple of hours. He knew the Flood carried weapons acquired from dead victims, so the Chief ran from corpse to corpse, looking for what he required. For a while it seemed hopeless as he uncovered a series of M6Ds, plasma pistols, combat knives, and other gear—anything and everything except what he needed most.

Then, just when he had nearly given up hope, he saw a few centimeters of olive drab tubing protruding from under a dead combat form. He rolled the ex-Elite over, and felt a rising sense of excitement. Was the launcher loaded? If so, he was in luck.

A quick check revealed that the weapon *was* loaded, and as if to prove that luck comes in threes, the Spartan found additional ammunition only a few meters away.

Armed with the launcher, he was ready to go to work. The Wraith represented the most significant threat, so he decided to deal with that first. It took time to make his way back across the face of the pyramid to a point where he could get a clear shot, but he did. The monster was dangerously close as he put a pair of rockets into the mortar tank, and watched it explode.

He ejected the spent rocket tubes, slammed fresh ammunition home, and shifted his aim. Two more rockets lanced ahead, and detonated in clusters of Covenant soldiers. He fell back and slung the rocket launcher; he had a limited supply of rockets, and once they were gone, he had no choice but to go down onto the valley floor and finish the job the hard way.

He crept up on the pair of Elites who stood guard near a Banshee. They went down from deadly, spine-cracking blows and he stepped past their fallen corpses. He examined the Banshee's controls while Cortana ensured the machine was fully operational.

He boarded the aircraft, and activated its power plant. He wondered why the aliens hadn't used the Banshee against him, was thankful that they hadn't, and eyed the instrument panel. The Master Chief recognized the very alien yet very familiar interface. The takeoff was rough, but it wasn't long before the Banshee started to climb.

It was dark, and snow continued to fall, which meant that visibility was poor. He kept a close eye on both the nav point Cortana had projected onto his HUD and the instrument panel. The design was different, but an alien turn and bank indicator still looked like what it was, and helped the human maintain his orientation.

The Banshee made good speed, and the valleys were quite close together, so it wasn't long before the Spartan spotted the well-lit platform which jutted out from the face of the cliff, as well as the enemy fire which lashed up to greet him. The word was out, it seemed—and the Covenant didn't want any visitors.

Rather than put down under fire, he decided to carry out a couple of strafing runs first. He swooped low and used the Banshee's plasma and fuel rod cannons to sweep the platform clear of sentries before decelerating for what he hoped would be an unopposed landing.

The Banshee crunched into the platform, bounced once, then ground to a halt. The Chief dismounted, passed through a hatch, and entered the tunnel beyond.

"We need to interrupt the pulse generator's energy stream," Cortana informed him. "I have adjusted your shield system so that it will deliver an EMP burst and disrupt the generator . . . but you'll have to walk into the beam to trigger it."

The Master Chief paused just shy of the next hatch. "I'll have to do *what*?"

"You'll have to walk *into* the beam to trigger it," the AI repeated matter-of-factly. "The EMP blast should neutralize the generator."

"*Should?*" the Chief demanded. "Whose side are you on?"

"*Yours,*" Cortana replied firmly. "We're in this together—remember?"

"Yeah, *I* remember," the Spartan growled. "But you're not the one with the bruises."

The AI chose to remain silent as the Chief passed through a hatch, paused to see if anyone would attempt to cancel his ticket, and followed the nav indicator to the chamber located at the center of the room.

Once he was there the pulse generator was impossible to miss. It was so intensely white that his visor automatically darkened in order to protect his eyes. Not only that, but the Chief could feel the air crackle around him as he approached the delta-shaped guide structures, and prepared to step in between them. "I have to walk into that thing?" the Chief inquired doubtfully.

"You'll be fine," Cortana replied soothingly. "I'm almost sure of it."

The Spartan took note of the "almost," clenched his teeth, and pushed himself into the blindingly intense light. The response was nearly instantaneous. There was something akin to an explosion, the light started to pulsate, and the floor shook in response. The Chief hurried to disengage, felt a bit of suction, but managed to pull free. As he did so he noticed that his shields had been drained. His skin felt sunburned.

"The pulse generator's central core is offline," Cortana said. "Well done."

Another squadron of Sentinels arrived. They swooped into the cramped pulse-generator chamber like vultures, fanned out, and seared the area with ruby-red energy beams. Not only did the Monitor take exception to the damage—he was after the Index too.

But the Chief knew how to deal with the mechanical killers, and proceeded to dodge their lasers as he destroyed one after another. Finally, the air thick with the stench of ozone, he was free to withdraw. He went back through the same tunnel to the platform where the Banshee waited.

"The second pulse generator is located in an adjacent canyon," Cortana announced easily. "Move out and I'll mark the nav point when we get closer."

The Master Chief sent the Banshee into a wide bank, and toward the next objective.

Minus the refrigeration required to preserve them, the bodies laid out on the metal tables had already started to decay, and the stench forced Silva to breathe through his mouth as he entered the makeshift morgue and waited for McKay to begin her presentation.

Six heavily armed Helljumpers were lined up along one wall ready to respond if one or more of the Flood suddenly came back to life. It seemed unlikely given the level of damage each corpse had sustained, but the creatures had proven themselves to be extremely resilient, and had an alarming tendency to reanimate.

McKay, who was still trying to deal with the fact that more than fifteen Marines under her command had lost their lives in a single battle, looked pale. Silva understood, even sympathized, but couldn't allow that to show. There was simply no time for grief, self-doubt, or guilt. The Company Commander would have to do what *he* did, which was to suck it up and keep on going. He nodded coolly.

"Lieutenant?"

McKay swallowed in an attempt to counter the nausea she felt. "Sir, yes sir. Obviously there's still a great deal that we don't know, but based on our observations during the fight, and information obtained from Covenant POWs, here's the best intelligence we have. It seems that the Covenant came here searching for 'holy relics'—we think that means useful technology—

and ran into a life form they refer to as 'the Flood.'"
She gestured at the fallen creatures on the slab. "*Those*
are Flood."

"Charming," Silva muttered.

"As best we can figure out," McKay said, "the Flood
is a parasitic life form which attacks sentient beings,
damages their minds, and takes control. Wellesley believes that Halo was constructed to house them, to keep
them under control, but we have no direct evidence to
support that. Perhaps Cortana or the Chief can confirm
our findings when we're able to make contact with them
again.

"The Flood manifests in various forms starting with
these things," McKay said, using her combat knife to
prod a flaccid infection form. "As you can see, it has
tentacles in place of legs, plus a couple of extremely
sharp penetrators, which they use to invade the victim's
central nervous system and take control of it. Eventually they work their way inside the host body and take
up residence there."

Silva tried to imagine what that might feel like and
felt a shiver run down his spine. Outwardly he was unchanged. "Please continue."

McKay said, "Yes, sir," and moved to the next table.
"This is what the Covenant call a 'combat form.' As
you can see from what remains of its face, this one was
human. We think she was a Navy weapons tech, based
on the tattoos still visible on her skin. If you peek
through the hole in her chest you can see the remains of
the infection form that deflated itself enough to fit in
around her heart and lungs."

Silva didn't *want* to look, but felt he had to, and
moved close enough to see the wrinkled scalp, to which
a few isolated clumps of filthy hair still clung. His eyes
catalogued a parade of horrors: the sickly looking skin;

the alarmingly blue eyes which still bulged, as if in response to some unimaginable pain; the twisted, toothless mouth; the slightly puckered 7.62mm bullet hole through the right cheekbone; the lumpy, penetrator-filled neck; the bony chest, now split down the middle so that the woman's flat breasts hung down to either side; the grossly distorted torso, punctured by three overlapping bullet wounds; the thin, sinewy arms; and the strangely graceful fingers, one of which still bore a silver ring.

The Major didn't say anything, but his face must have telegraphed what he felt, because McKay nodded. "It's pretty awful, isn't it, sir? I've seen death before, sir—" she swallowed and shook her head, "—but nothing like this.

"For what it's worth Covenant victims don't look any better. This individual was armed with a pistol, her own probably, but the Flood seem to pick up and use any weapon they can lay their hands on. Not only that, but they pack a very nasty punch, which can be lethal.

"Most combat forms appear to be derived from humans and Elites," McKay continued, as she moved to the last table. "We suspect that Grunts and Jackals are deemed too small for first-class combat material, and are therefore used as a sort of nucleus around which carrier forms can grow. It's hard to tell by looking at the puddle of crap on the table in front of you, but at one time this thing contained *four* of the infection forms you saw earlier, and when it popped the resulting explosion had enough force to knock Sergeant Lister on his can."

That, or the mental picture that it conveyed, was sufficient to elicit nervous grins from the Helljumpers who lined the back wall. Apparently they liked the idea of something that could put Lister on his ass.

Silva frowned. "Does Wellesley have scans of this stuff?"

"Yes, sir."

"Excellent. Nice job. Have the bodies burned, send these troops up for some fresh air, and report to my office in an hour."

McKay nodded. "Yes, sir."

Zuka 'Zamamee lay belly down on the hard-packed dirt and used his monocular to scan the *Pillar of Autumn*. It wasn't heavily guarded; the Covenant was stretched too thin for that, but the Council had reinforced the security force subsequent to the human raid, and evidence of that was visible in the Banshees, Ghosts, and Wraiths that patrolled the area around the downed ship. Yayap, who lay next to the Elite, had no such device and was forced to rely on his own vision.

"This plan is insane," 'Zamamee said out of the side of his mouth. "I should have killed you a long time ago."

"Yes, Commander," the Grunt agreed patiently, knowing that the talk was just that. The truth was that the officer was *afraid* to return to the *Truth and Reconciliation*, and now had very little choice but to accept Yayap's plan, especially in light of the fact that he had been unable to come up with one of his own.

"Give it to me one more time," the Elite demanded, "so I'll know that you won't make any mistakes."

Yayap eyed the readout on his wrist. He had two, maybe two and a half units of methane left, before his tanks were empty and he would suffocate, a problem which didn't seem to trouble the Elite at all. It was tempting to pull his pistol, shoot 'Zamamee in the head, and implement the strategy on his own. But there were advantages to being in company with the warrior— plus a giddy sense of power that went with having threatened the warrior and survived. With that in mind Yayap managed to suppress both his panic and a rising sense of resentment.

"Of course, Commander. As you know, simple plans are often best, which is why there is a good chance this one will work. On the possibility that the Council of Masters is actively looking for Zuka 'Zamamee, you will choose one of the commandos who died on the human encampment, and assume that individual's identity.

"Then, with me at your side, we will report to the officer in charge of guarding the alien ship, explain that we were taken prisoner in the aftermath of the raid, but were subsequently able to escape."

"But what then?" the Elite inquired warily. "What if he submits my DNA for a match?"

"Why would he do that?" the Grunt countered patiently. "He's shorthanded, and here, as if presented by the great ones themselves, is a commando Elite. Would *you* run the risk of having such a find reassigned? No, I think not. Under circumstances such as these you would seize the opportunity to add such a highly capable warrior to your command, and give thanks for the blessing."

It sounded good, especially the "highly capable warrior" part, so 'Zamamee agreed. "Fine. What about later?"

"Later, if there *is* a later," Yayap said wearily, "we will have to come up with another plan. In the meantime this initiative will assure us of food, water, and methane."

"All right," 'Zamamee said, "let's jump on the Banshee and make our appearance."

"Are you sure that's the best idea?" the Grunt inquired tactfully. "If we arrive on a Banshee, the commanding officer might wonder why we were so slow to check in."

The Elite eyed what looked like a long, hard walk, sighed, and acquiesced. "Agreed." A hint of his former arrogance resurfaced. "But *you* will carry my gear."

"Of course," Yayap said, scrambling to his feet. "Was there ever any doubt?"

The inmate had attempted suicide twice, which was why the interior of his cell was bare, and under round-the-clock surveillance. The creature that had once been Private Wallace A. Jenkins sat on the floor with both wrists chained to an eyebolt located just over his head.

The Flood mind, which the human continued to think of as "the other," had been quiet for a while, but was present nonetheless, and glowered in what amounted to a cognitive corner, angry but weak. Hinges squealed as the metal door swung open. Jenkins turned to look, and saw a male noncom enter the room followed by a female officer.

The private felt an almost overwhelming sense of shame—and did what he could to turn away. Earlier, before the guards secured his wrists to the wall, Jenkins had used pantomime to request a mirror. A well-meaning Corporal brought one in, held it up in front of the soldier's devastated face, and was frightened when he tried to scream. The initial suicide attempt followed thirty minutes later.

McKay took a look at the prisoner's dry, parched lips and guessed that he might be thirsty. She called for some water, accepted a canteen, and started across the cell. "With respect, ma'am, I don't think you should do that," the Sergeant said cautiously. "These suckers are incredibly violent."

"Jenkins is a Private in the UNSC Marine Corps," McKay replied sternly, "and will be referred to as such. And your concern has been noted."

Then, like a teacher dealing with a recalcitrant child, she held the canteen out where Jenkins could see it. "Look!" she said, sloshing the water back and forth. "Behave yourself and I'll give you a drink."

Jenkins tried to warn her, tried to say "No," but heard himself gabble instead. Thus encouraged, McKay unscrewed the canteen's lid, took three steps forward, and was just about to lean over when the combat form attacked. Jenkins felt his left arm break as the chain brought it up short—and fought to counter the other's attempt to grab the officer in a scissor lock.

McKay stepped back just in time to evade the flailing legs.

There was a clacking sound as the guard pumped a shell into the shotgun's receiver and prepared to fire. McKay shouted, "No!" and held up her hand. The noncom obeyed but kept his weapon aimed at the combat form's head.

"Okay," McKay said, looking into the creature's eyes, "have it your way. But, like it or not, we're going to have a talk."

Silva had entered the cell by then and stood behind the Lieutenant. The Sergeant saw the Major nod, and backed into a corner with his weapon still held at the ready.

"My name is Silva," the Major began, "and you already know Lieutenant McKay here. First, let me say that both of us are extremely sorry about what happened to you, we understand how you feel, and will make sure that you receive the best medical care that the UNSC has to offer. But first we have to fight our way off this ring. I think I know how we can do that—

but it will take some time. We need to hold this butte until we're ready to make our move. That's where *you* come in. You know where we are now—and you know how the Flood move around. If you had my job, if you had to defend this base against the Flood, where would *you* focus your efforts?"

The other used his right hand to grab his left, jerked hard, and exposed a shard of broken bone. Then, as if hoping to use that as a knife, the combat form lunged forward. The chains brought the creature up short. Jenkins felt indescribable pain, began to lose consciousness, but fought his way back.

Silva looked at McKay and shrugged. "Well, it was worth a try, but it looks like he's too far gone."

Jenkins half expected the other to lunge forward again, but having shared in the human's pain, the alien consciousness chose that moment to retreat. The human surged into the gap, made hooting sounds, and used his good hand to point at Silva's right boot.

The officer looked down at his boot, frowned, and was about to say something when McKay touched his arm. "He isn't pointing at your boot, sir, he's pointing *down*. At the area under the butte."

Silva felt something cold trickle into his veins. "Is that right, son? The Flood could be directly *below* us?"

Jenkins nodded emphatically, rolled his eyes, and made inarticulate gagging sounds.

The Major nodded and came to his feet. "Thank you, Private. We'll check the basement and be back to speak with you some more."

Jenkins didn't want to talk, he wanted to *die*, but no-body cared. The guards left, the door clanged shut, and the Marine was left with nothing but a broken arm and the alien inside his head. Somehow, without actually dying, he had been sentenced to hell.

As if to confirm that conclusion the other surged to the fore, yanked at the chains, and beat its feet on the floor. Food had been present, food had left, and it remained hungry.

The Master Chief spotted the next waypoint, put the hijacked Banshee down on a platform, and entered the complex via an unguarded hatch. He heard the battle before he actually saw it, made his way through the intervening tunnel, and peered through the next door. As had occurred before, the Covenant was busy taking it to the Flood and vice versa, so he gave both groups some time to whittle each other down, left the security of the tunnel, and proceeded to tidy up.

Then, eager to replenish his supplies, the Spartan made his ghoulish rounds, and soon was able to equip himself with an assault weapon, a shotgun, and some plasma grenades. Even though he didn't like to think about where it came from, it felt good to dump the Covenant ordnance he'd been saddled with, and lay his hands on some true-blue UNSC issue for a change.

Pulse generator one had been dealt with, and he was eager to disable number two, then move on to his final objective. He stepped into the beam, saw the flash of light, felt the floor shake, and was in the process of pulling away when the Flood attacked from every direction.

There was no time to think and no time to fight. The only thing he could do was run. He turned and sprinted for the corridor he'd used to enter the chamber and took two powerful blows from a combat form. He bulled his way between two carrier forms and leaped out of the way as they detonated like grenades. New infection forms spewed from their deflating corpses.

There was barely enough time to turn, hose the closest forms with 7.62mm, and toss a grenade at the group beyond. It went off with a loud *wham!*, broke glass, and put three of the monstrosities down.

He was out of ammo by then, knew he lacked the time necessary to reload, and made the switch to the shotgun instead. The gun blew huge holes through the oncoming mob. He charged through one of them, and ran like hell.

Then, with some pad to work with, the human turned to gun down the pursuers. The entire battle consumed no more than two minutes but it left the Chief shaken. Could Cortana detect the slight tremor in his hands as he reloaded both weapons? Hell, she had unrestricted access to all of his vital signs, so she knew more about what was going on with his body than he did. Still, if the AI was conscious of the way he felt, there was no sign of it in her words. "Pulse generator deactivated—good work."

The Chief nodded wordlessly and made his way back through the tunnel to the point where the Banshee waited. "The *Pillar of Autumn* is located twelve hundred kilometers up-spin," Cortana continued. "Energy readings show her fusion reactors are still powered up! The systems on the *Pillar of Autumn* have fail-safes even I can't override without authorization from the Captain. We'll have to find him, or his neural implants, to start the fusion core detonation.

"*One* target remaining. Let's take care of the final pulse generator."

A nav indicator appeared on the noncom's HUD as he lifted off, took fire from a neighboring installation, and put the Banshee into a steep dive. The ground came up fast, he pulled out, and guided the alien assault craft through a pass and into the canyon beyond. The nav indicator pointed toward the light that spilled out of a tunnel. The Banshee began to take ground fire, and the Spartan knew his piloting skills were about to be severely tested.

A rocket flashed by as he pushed the Banshee down onto the deck, fired the aircraft's weapons, and cut power. Flying into the tunnel was bad enough—but flying into it at high speed verged on suicidal.

Once inside the passageway the challenge was to stay off the walls and make the tight right- and left-hand turns without killing himself. A few seconds later the Spartan saw double blast doors and flared in for a jarring landing.

He hopped down, made his way over to the control panel, hit the switch, and heard a rumbling sound as the doors started to part. Then there was a *bang!* as something exploded and the enormous panels came to a sudden stop. The resulting gap was too small for the Banshee, but sufficient for two carrier forms to scuttle through. The beasts scrambled toward him on short, stubby legs. The humpbacked bladders that formed their upper torsos pulsed and wriggled as the infection forms within struggled for release.

The Chief blew both monsters away with twin shotgun blasts, and mopped up the rest of the infection forms with another shot. He paused and reloaded; there were bound to be more of the creatures on the far side of the doors.

Resigned to a fight, he stepped through the crack and paused. There was no sound beyond the gentle roar of machinery, the *drip, drip, drip* of water off to his right, and the rasp of his own breathing. The threat indicator was clear, and there were no enemies in sight, but that didn't mean much. Not where the Flood were concerned. They had a habit of coming out of nowhere.

The cave, if that was the proper word for the huge

cavern-like space, featured plenty of places to hide. Enormous pipes emerged from the walls and dived downward, mysterious installations stood like islands on the platform around him, and there was no way to know what might lurk in the dark corners. Lights, mounted high above, provided what little illumination there was.

The human stood on a broad platform that ran the full length of the open area. A deep chasm separated his platform from what appeared to be an identical structure on the other side of the canyon. One of two bridges that had once spanned the gorge was down, leaving only one over which he could pass—a made-to-order choke point for anyone who wanted to establish an ambush.

There wasn't a hell of a lot of choice, so he marched down to the point where the remaining span was anchored, and started across. He hadn't gone more than thirty paces before fifty or sixty infection forms emerged from hiding and danced out to block the way.

The Spartan held his position, waited for the Flood forms to come a little closer, and tossed a fragmentation grenade into the center of the group.

The cavern ate some of the sound, but the explosive device still managed to produce a *bang*, and the resulting shrapnel laid waste to all but a handful of the creatures.

There were two survivors, though, both optimists, who continued to bounce forward in spite of the way in which the rest of the group had been annihilated. A single shotgun blast was sufficient to kill both of them.

He slipped some additional shells into the gun's magazine tube, took a deep breath, and moved forward again. He made it about halfway to the other side before a mixed force of combat forms, carrier forms, and

infection forms started to gather at the far end of the
span. Another grenade inflicted casualties, but they
charged him after that, and the Master Chief was forced
to retreat, firing the assault weapon as he did so.

It was nip and tuck for a few seconds as combat
forms launched themselves fifteen meters through the
air, carriers charged straight in, and the omnipresent
infection forms swarmed through the gaps. Retreating,
the Spartan had already reloaded three times before his
back hit the wall, and the last combat form collapsed at
his feet, started to rise, and took a blast in the head.

Once again it was time to reload both weapons, step
out onto the gore-splattered bridge deck, and attempt
another crossing. This one was successful, with only
light opposition on the other side, and an opportunity
to replenish his ammo.

The next set of blast doors opened flawlessly, allowing the Spartan to enter a relatively short section of
tunnel that led back to the surface. Determined to use
stealth if at all possible, he slipped out of the passageway, scrambled up over the snow embankment to his
right, and ran into a group of four Flood. A grenade
took care of two—and the assault weapon finished the
rest.

A Banshee swooped in, burned a long line of dashes
into the snow, and continued up the valley. The Chief
was surprised to get off so lightly, but given the darkness and all of the confusion, it was possible that the
pilot had mistaken him for a combat form. A worthy
target, to be sure, but not something to turn around
for. Particularly not when the valley was full of combat
forms.

He was careful to hug the face of the cliff and stay
within the cover provided by the boulders and trees
that lined the edge of the valley. The incessant thud of

automatic weapons and the whine of plasma weapons testified to the intensity of a conflict raging off to his left.

Then, just as he was starting to believe that he could slide by without firing a shot, he came up over a slight rise to see that the Covenant and Flood were engaged in hand-to-hand combat within the depression below. A grenade followed with bursts of fire from the MA5B decimated both groups.

Snow crunched as the human made his way down through the bloodstained snow, past the spot where a trio of greedy infection forms squabbled over a wounded Elite, and up another rise to a stand of trees where a combat form and a carrier tried to jump him. Both of the Flood staggered as bursts of 7.62mm slugs cut them down, and they flopped onto the snow.

Having broken through the perimeter of the battle, the Master Chief was able to follow the nav indicator into a second valley where he came upon a group of dead Marines, loaded up on ammo, and tried to decide whether to stay with the scatter gun or trade it in for a sniper's rifle or a rocket launcher. It would have been nice to have all three, but that many weapons would be unwieldy, not to mention damned heavy. In the end he went with the rifle and shotgun and hoped it was the right decision.

The Spartan checked the Marines for dog tags, discovered that they had already been taken by someone else, and took the time required to drag the bodies into a nearby cave in the hope that the infection forms wouldn't find them. That seemed like a good place to stash the extra weapons—so that's what he did.

Then, having followed the second valley to the point where it opened onto a *third* valley, he came across a now-familiar scene. The Covenant were battling the

Flood with everything they had, including Shades, a brace of Ghosts, and two extremely active Wraiths, but the Flood had plenty of bodies to throw back at them and didn't hesitate to do so.

What the Chief wanted was the Banshee that was parked at the head of the valley, but in order to get at the aircraft it would be necessary to cut both groups down to size. He stayed right, slipped along the cliff face, and made use of a thin screen of trees and boulders to hide his movements from those out toward the center of the valley. Finally, having passed behind a house-sized rock and found a vantage point that allowed him to look out on the area where the vast majority of the Covenant were congregated, the Spartan unlimbered the S2 AM, selected the 10X setting for the scope, and began his bloody work.

In this particular situation he selected the softest targets first, starting with the Grunts on the Shades, followed by the outlying Jackals, all in hope that he could inflict a lot of casualties before the Elites took notice and sent the tank to get him.

The problem was that the little world inside the scope was all-consuming—a fact that caused him to let down his guard. The first hint he had that a Flood form had come up behind him was when it whacked the Spartan in the head.

The blow would have killed anyone else, but the armor saved him, and the Chief rolled in the direction of the blow. The long-barreled S2 wasn't well suited for close-in combat but that's what he had in his hands. There was no time to aim as the Flood form charged, only time to fire, and that's what he did.

The slug caught the ex-Elite in the chest. The combat form didn't even flinch as the bullet passed through its spongy center of mass. A tiny spurt of gray-green ichor trailed from the entry wound, as the creature swung a vicious blow at the Master Chief.

He ducked the attack and dropped the rifle. He dived, tucked into a roll, and came up with his sidearm in his hand. He emptied the magazine into the beast. One round blew its left arm off, and the final round made a foot-wide exit wound in the Flood's back.

He kicked in the creature's chest, crushing the infection form within. He collected the S2, and frowned. He studied the fallen Flood for a moment, and saw that the creature's insides were rapidly liquefying. The velocity of the S2's projectile had passed through the nonvital mass of the creature's chest and just kept going.

Another nasty surprise, courtesy of the Flood.

After a quick look around to make sure that there weren't any *more* surprises lurking in the vicinity, with his heart still beating like a trip-hammer, the Chief went back to his grisly work. Three more Covenant warriors fell before a barrage of fireballs arced high into the air to land all around his position. One came so close that just the bleed off it was enough to push his shielding into the red and trigger the alarm.

He pulled back, switched to the assault weapon long enough to ice a couple of overly ambitious Grunts, and switched back to the S2 as he rounded the opposite side of the big boulder. He selected a spot where he could go to work on both the Covenant *and* the Flood, and settled in.

He wanted to nail the Elites now and, thanks to the powerful 14.5mm armor-piercing rounds, he could drop most of them with a single shot. Combat forms were a different story, so he switched to the shotgun. It was less accurate, but did the job. It wasn't long before more than a dozen bodies were laid out in the snow. But then the word was out. Soon the mortar tank moved into position to bombard his new position, and it was necessary to pull back.

The Wraith was a problem, a *serious* problem, which meant there was only one thing the Spartan could do: Hike back to the weapons cache and trade the rifle for the launcher. It was a major pain in the ass, but he didn't have much choice, so he pulled out.

It took a full half hour to make the round trip between the valley and the weapons cache, so he expected things to have calmed down a bit by the time he returned. That wasn't the case, however, which suggested that the Flood had thrown even more forms into the battle.

The Chief followed his own footprints back to the hiding place next to the big boulder, put the launcher on his shoulder, and hit the zoom. The Wraith, which was busy hurling mortars down valley, seemed to leap forward. As if somehow aware of his presence, the tank spun on its axis, and launched a bomb toward the rock.

The Spartan forced himself to ignore the artificial comet, locked onto the target, and triggered the rocket. There was an impact and a loud *crump!* followed by smoke—but the Wraith continued to fire nonetheless.

Now, with fireballs exploding all around him, the Master Chief had to take a deep breath, hold the tank at the center of his sight, and pull the trigger again. The tube jerked, the second missile ran straight and true, and hit with a loud *craack!* The Wraith opened like a red flower, burped pitch-black smoke, and nosed into a snowbank.

"Nice shot," Cortana said admiringly, "but watch the Ghost."

It was good advice, because although the attack vehicle had held back up to that point, it came skittering into sight, opened up with its plasma weapons, and threatened to accomplish what the rest of the Covenant soldiers hadn't.

But the Chief had reloaded by then. The rocket tube was the right weapon for the job, and a single missile was sufficient to send the attack vehicle flipping end-for-end to finally wind up with its belly in the air and flames licking at the engine compartment.

With that problem out of the way the Chief came to his feet, slapped a fresh load into the launcher, and made a beeline for the Banshee. He was halfway across, with nowhere to hide, when a pair of Hunters emerged from a jumble of boulders.

Now, grateful that he still had some rockets, he had no choice but to stop, drop to one knee, and take them on. The first shot was dead on, hit the alien in the chest, and blew the bastard apart. Another rocket flew over the second Hunter's right shoulder and cut a tree in half. The big alien started to lumber across open ground, picking up speed and charging its arm-mounted cannon.

It was a waste of ammo to pepper the front end of a Hunter with 7.62mm rounds, and slow though he was, the alien could still bring him down with a blast from his arm-mounted fuel rod cannon.

So he put his sight onto a target so big he didn't need to zoom, and let fly.

The Hunter saw the missile coming, tried to deflect it with his shield, and failed. Seconds later pieces of warm meat showered the area, melted holes in the snow, and continued to steam.

The Chief ran past without a second look, jumped into the Banshee, and strafed the rest of the Covenant forces on his way down the valley. Judging from the way the nav indicator was oriented, the Spartan needed altitude, a lot of it, so he put the Banshee into a steep climb.

Finally, when the red delta flipped over, and started to point down, he knew he was high enough. He did a nose-over and caught his first glimpse of the waypoint below. The surrounding area was dark, and snow continued to fall, but the platform was nicely lit. He lowered the Banshee onto the pad and had just bailed out of the pilot's seat when the Sentinels attacked. "This is the last one," Cortana said. "The Monitor will do anything to stop us."

The Chief blew three of the pesky machines out of the air, backed through the hatch, and let the door close on the rest.

"We're close," the AI commented. "The generator is up ahead."

The Chief nodded, stepped out into a room, and felt a laser burn across the front of his armor. It seemed that the Monitor had posted Sentinels *inside* the complex, as well. Not only that, but these machines had the benefit of intermittent force fields, which were resistant to automatic weapons fire.

Still, he had a couple of 102mm surprises in store for the electromechanical enforcers, which he fired into the center of the hovering pack. Three Sentinels were blown out of the air. A fourth did loops as it tried to rid itself of a plasma grenade, failed, and took another machine with it. The fifth and sixth succumbed to a hail of bullets as their shields recharged, while the seventh slammed into a wall, crashed to the floor, and was busy trying to lift off again when the Chief stomped it to death.

The way was clear at that point and the Spartan was quick to take advantage of it. A few quick strides were sufficient to carry him into the central chamber where he was free to approach the final pulse generator.

"Final target neutralized," Cortana said as the non-com stepped back a few moments later. "Let's get out of here."

"Let's find a ride and get to the Captain," the Chief agreed, as he prepared to leave.

"No, that'll take too long."

"Do you have a better idea?"

"There's a teleportation grid that runs around Halo. That's how the Monitor moves about so quickly," the AI explained. "I learned how to tap into the grid when I was in the Control Center."

"So," the Chief asked, somewhat annoyed, "why didn't you just *teleport* us to the pulse generators?"

"I can't. Unfortunately, each jump requires a rather consequential expenditure of energy, and I don't have access to Halo's power systems to reroute the energy we need." She paused, then reluctantly continued. "There may be another way, however."

The Spartan frowned and shook his head. "Something tells me I'm not going to like this."

"I'm pretty sure I can pull the energy we need from your suit without *permanently* damaging your shield system or the armor's power cells," Cortana continued. "Needless to say, I think we should only try this once."

"Agreed. Tap into the Covenant network and see if you can find him. If we've only got one shot at this, we should make it a good one."

There was a pause as Cortana worked her magic with the intrusion and scan software. A moment later, she exclaimed, "I've got a good lock on Captain Keyes' CNI transponder signal. He's alive! And the implants are intact! There's some interference from the cruiser's damaged reactor. I'll bring us in as close as I can."

"Do it," the Master Chief growled. "Let's get this over with."

No sooner had the Spartan spoken than bands of golden light started to ripple down over his armor, the now-familiar feeling of nausea returned, and the Master Chief seemed to vanish through the floor. Once he was gone only a few motes of amber light remained to mark his passing. Then, after a few seconds, they too disappeared.

D +73:34:16 (SPARTAN 117 MISSION CLOCK) /
ON BOARD THE *TRUTH AND RECONCILIATION.*

He wasn't here, wasn't there, wasn't *anywhere* insofar as the Chief could tell from within the strange never-never land of Halo's teleportation net. He couldn't see or hear anything, save a sense of dizzying velocity. The Spartan felt his body stitched back together, one molecule at a time. He saw snatches of what looked like the interior of a Covenant ship as bands of golden light strobed up and disappeared over his head.

Something was wrong and he was just starting to figure out what it was—the inside of the ship seemed to be upside down—when he flipped head over heels and crashed to the deck.

He'd materialized with his feet planted firmly on the corridor's ceiling.

"Oh!" Cortana exclaimed. "I see, the coordinate data needs to be—"

The Chief came to his feet, slapped the general area where his implants were, and shook his head. The AI sounded contrite. "Right. Sorry."

"Never mind that," the Spartan said. "Give me a sit-rep."

She patched back into the Covenant computing systems, a much easier task now that they were aboard one of the enemy's warships.

"The Covenant network is absolute chaos," she replied. "From what I've been able to piece together, the leadership ordered all ships to abandon Halo when they found the Flood, but they were too late. The Flood overwhelmed this cruiser and captured it."

"I assume," he said, "that's *bad*."

"The Covenant think so. They're terrified that the Flood will repair the ship and use it to escape from Halo. They sent a strike team to neutralize the Flood and prepare the ship for immediate departure."

The Chief peered down the corridor. The bulkheads were violet. Strange patterns marbled the material, like the oily sheen of a beetle's carapace.

He started forward, but quickly came up short as a voice that verged on a groan came in over his implants. *"Chief . . . Don't be a fool . . . Leave me."*

It was Keyes' voice.

Keyes, Jacob. Captain. Service number 01928-19912-JK. He clung to the tether of his CNI carrier wave, and "heard" familiar voices. An iron-hard, rasping male voice. A tart, warm female voice.

He knew them.

Was this another memory?

He was struggling to dredge up new pieces of his past to delay the numbing advance of the alien presence in his mind. It was harder to maintain a grasp on who he was, as the various pieces of his life—the things that made him who he was—were stripped away, one at a time.

Keyes, Jacob. Captain. Service number 01928-19912-JK.

The voices. They were talking about him. The Master Chief, the AI Cortana.

He felt a sense of mounting panic. They shouldn't *be* here.

The other grew stronger, and pressed forward, eager to learn more about these creatures that were so important to the struggling prisoner who clung so stubbornly to identity.

Keyes, Jacob. Captain. Service number 01928-19912-JK.

Chief, Cortana, you shouldn't have come. Don't be a fool. Leave me. Get out of here. Run.

The presence descended, and he could feel its anticipation of victory. It wouldn't be long now.

"Captain?" Cortana inquired desperately. "*Captain!* I've lost him."

Neither one of them said anything further. The pain in Keyes' voice had been clear. All they could do was drive deeper into the ship and hope to find him.

The Chief passed through a hatch, noticed that the right bulkhead was splattered with Covenant blood, and figured a battle had been fought there. That meant he could expect to run into the Flood at any moment. As he continued down the passageway his throat felt unusually dry, his heart beat a little bit faster, and his stomach muscles were tight.

His suspicions were soon confirmed as he heard the sounds of battle, took a right, and saw that a firefight was underway at the far end of the corridor. He let the combatants go at it for a bit before moving in to cut the survivors down.

From there he took a left, followed by a right, and came to a hatch. It opened to reveal a black hole with jagged edges. Farther back, beyond the drop-off, *another* firefight was underway.

"Analyzing data," Cortana said. "This hole was caused by some sort of explosion . . . All I detect down there are pools of coolant. We should continue our search somewhere else."

The AI's advice made sense, so the Spartan turned to retrace his steps. Then, as he took the first left, all hell broke loose. Cortana said, "Warning! Threat level increasing!" and then, as if to prove her point, a mob of Flood came straight at him.

He fired, retreated, and fired again. Carrier forms exploded in a welter of shattered flesh, severed tentacles, and green slime. Combat forms rushed forward as if eager to die, danced under the impact of the 7.62mm rounds, and flew apart. Infection forms skittered across the decks, leaped into the air, and shattered into flaps of flying flesh.

But there were too many, far too many for one person to handle, and even as the Chief heard Cortana say something about the black hole he accidentally backed into it, fell about twenty meters, and plunged feet first into a pond of green liquid. Not in the ship, but somewhere under it, on the surface below. The coolant was *so* cold that he could feel it through his armor. It was thick, too—which made it more difficult to move.

The Master Chief felt his boots hit bottom, knew the weight of his armor would hold him in place, and marched up onto what had become a beach of sorts. The cavern was dark, lit mostly by the luminescent glow produced by the coolant itself, although streaks of plasma fire slashed back and forth up ahead, punctuated by the steady *thud, thud, thud* of an automatic weapon.

"Let's get out of here," Cortana said, "and find another way back aboard the ship."

He moved up toward the edge of the conflict and let the combatants hammer each other for a bit before lobbing a grenade into the mix, waiting for the body parts to fall, and strafing what was left.

Then, having moved forward, he was forced to fight his way through a series of narrow, body-strewn passageways as what seemed like an inexhaustible supply of Flood forms came at him from every possible direction.

Eventually, having made his way through grottoes of coolant, and past piles of corpses, Cortana said, "We should head *this* way—toward the ship's gravity lift," and the Spartan saw a nav pointer appear on his HUD. He followed the red arrow around a bend to a ledge above a coolant-filled basin. Even as he watched, a dozen carrier forms marched up out of the green lagoon to attack a group of hard-pressed Covenant soldiers.

The Spartan knew there was no way in hell that he'd be able to force his way through *that* mess, turned, and made his way back down the trail. A sniper rifle, just one of hundreds of weapons scattered around the area, was half obscured by a headless combat form. The petty officer removed the rifle, checked to ensure that it was loaded, and returned to the overlook. Then, careful to make each shot count, he opened fire.

The Elites, Jackals, and Grunts went down fairly easily. But the Flood forms, especially the carriers, were practically impossible to kill with this particular weapon. With few exceptions the heavy rounds seemed to pass right through the lumpy-looking bastards without causing any harm whatsoever.

When all of the 14.5mm ammo was gone, the Chief went back for the shotgun, jumped into the green liquid, and waded up onto the shoreline. He heard an obscene sucking noise, saw an infection form trying to enter an Elite's chest cavity, and blew both of them away.

After that there was more cleanup to do as some combat forms took a run at the human and a flock of infection forms tried to roll him under. Repeated doses of shotgun fire turned out to be just what the doctor ordered—the area was soon littered with severed tentacles and scraps of wet flesh.

A pitch-black passageway led him back to another pool where he arrived just in time to see the Flood overrun a Shade and the Elite who was seated at the controls. The Spartan began firing, already backpedaling, when the Flood spotted him and hopped, waddled, and jumped forward. He fired, reloaded, and fired again. Always retreating, always on the defensive, always hoping for a respite.

This wasn't his kind of fight. Spartans were designed as offensive weapons, but ever since they'd landed on the ring, he'd been on the run. He had to find a way to take the offensive, and soon.

There was no break in the endless wall of Flood attackers. He fired until his weapons were empty, pried energy weapons out of dead fingers, and fired those until they were dry.

Finally, more by virtue of stubbornness than anything else, and having reacquired human weapons from dead combat forms, the Master Chief found himself standing all alone, rifle raised, with no one to shoot at. He felt a powerful sense of elation—he was *alive*.

It was a moment he couldn't take time to enjoy.

Eager to reboard the cruiser and find Captain Keyes, he made his way back along the path he had been forced to surrender to the Flood, passed the Shade, rounded a bend, and saw a couple dozen infection forms materialize out of the darkness ahead. A plasma grenade strobed the night, pulverized their bodies, and produced a satisfying *boom!* It was still echoing off the canyon walls as the human eased his way through a narrow passage and emerged at one end of a hotly contested pool. About fifty meters away the Covenant and Flood surged back and forth, traded fire with each other, and appeared to be on the verge of hand-to-tentacle combat. Two well-thrown grenades cut the number of hostiles in half. The MA5B took care of the rest.

"There's the gravity lift!" Cortana said. "It's still operational. That's our way back in."

It sounded simple, but as the Master Chief looked up at the hill on which the lift was sited, well-aimed plasma fire lashed down to scorch the rock at his right elbow. It glowed as the human was forced to pull back, wait for a lull, and dash forward again. Looking ahead, he spotted the point where a group of hard-pressed Covenant were trying to bar a group of Flood from making their way up a path toward the top of the hill and the foot of the gravity lift. It was a last stand, and the Covenant knew it. They fought harder than he'd ever seen the aliens fight. He felt a moment of kinship with the Covenant soldiers.

He stood and threw two grenades into the middle of the melee, waited for the twin explosions and went in shooting. An Elite sent plasma stuttering into the night sky as he fell over backward, a combat form swung a Jackal's arm like a club, and a pair of infection forms rode a Grunt down into the pool of coolant. It was madness, a scene straight from hell, and the human had little choice but to kill everything that moved.

As the last bodies crumpled to the ground, the Spartan was free to follow the steadily rising path upward, turn to the right, and enter the lift's footprint. He felt static electricity crackle around his armor, and heard plasma shriek through the air as a distant Covenant took exception to his plans. Then the Chief was gone, pulled upward, into the belly of the beast.

Keyes? Keyes, Jacob. Yes, that was it. Wasn't it?

He couldn't remember—there was nothing left now but navigation protocols, defense plans. And a duty to keep them safe.

A droning buzz filled his mind. He vaguely remembered hearing it before, but didn't know what it was.

It pressed in, hungry.

Metal rang under her boots as McKay jumped down off the last platform onto the huge metal grating. It shivered in response. The trip down from the mesa had taken more than fifteen minutes. First, she had taken the still-functional lift down to the point where she and her troops had forced their way into the butte, back when the Covenant still occupied it, then transferred to the circular staircase, which, like the rifling on the inside of a gun barrel, wound its way down to the bottom of the shaft and the barrier under her feet.

"Good to see you, ma'am," a Private said, as he materialized at her elbow. "Sergeant Lister would like to speak with you."

McKay nodded, said "Thanks," and made her way over to the far side of the grating where the so-called Entry Team were gathered into a tight little group next to an assemblage of equipment that had been lowered from above. A portable work light glowed at the very center of the assemblage and threw huge shadows up onto the walls around them. Bodies parted as McKay approached, and Lister, who was down on his hands and knees, jumped to his feet. "Ten-hut!"

Everyone came to attention. McKay noticed the way that the long hours and constant stress had pared what little bit of extra flesh there was off the noncom's face, leaving it gaunt and haggard. "As you were. How does it look? Any contact?"

"No, ma'am," Lister responded, "not yet. But take a look at *this*."

A Navy tech directed a handheld spotlight down through the grating and the officer knelt to get a better look. The stairs, which had ended on the far side of the platform, appeared to pick up again just below the grating and circled into the darkness below.

"Look at the metal," Lister prompted, "and look at what's piled up on the stairs below."

McKay looked, saw that the thick metal crosspieces had been twisted out of shape, and saw a large pile of weapons below. No human ordnance as far as she could tell, just Covenant, which was to say plasma weapons. With no cutting torches to call upon, not yet anyway, it looked as though the Flood had depleted at least a hundred energy pistols and rifles in a futile attempt to cut their way through the grating. Given some more time, say another day or two, they might have succeeded.

"You've got to give the bastards credit," McKay said grimly. "They never give up. Well, neither do we. Let's cut this sucker open, go down, and lock the back door."

Lister said, "Ma'am, yes ma'am," but there were none of the usual gung-ho responses from the others who stood around him. It was dark down there—and nightmares lay in wait.

Once inside the *Pillar of Autumn*, 'Zamamee and Yayap found conditions to be both better and worse than they had expected. Consistent with the Grunt's predictions, the officer in charge—an overworked Elite named

'Ontomee—had been extremely glad to see them, and wasted little time placing 'Zamamee in charge of twenty Jackals, with Yayap in command.

That, plus the fact that the security detachment had a reasonable amount of supplies, including methane, meant that basic physical needs had been met. That was the good news.

The bad news was that 'Zamamee, now known as Huki 'Umamee, lived in constant fear that an Elite who knew either him or the recently deceased commando he had decided to impersonate would come along and reveal his *true* identity, or that the Prophets would somehow pluck the information out of thin air, as they were rumored to be able to do. These fears caused the officer to lay low, stay out of sight, and delegate most of his leadership responsibilities to Yayap.

This would have been annoying but acceptable where a contingent of Grunts was concerned, but was made a great deal more difficult by the fact that the Jackals saw themselves as being superior to the "gas suckers," and were anything but pleased when they found themselves reporting to Yayap.

Then, as if to add to the Grunt's woes, the Flood had located the *Pillar of Autumn*, and while they were unable to infiltrate the vessel via any of the maintenance ways that ran back and forth just below the ringworld's surface, they had become adept at entering the vessel through rents in its severely damaged hull, the air locks where lifeboats had once been docked, and on one memorable occasion via one of the Covenant's own patrols, which had been ambushed, turned into combat forms, and sent back into the ship. The ruse had been detected, but only after some of the "contaminated" soldiers were inside the vessel. A few of them were still at large, somewhere within the human vessel.

As the Grunt and his group of surly Jackals stood guard in the *Autumn*'s shuttle bay, a dropship loaded with supplies circled over the downed ship, asked for and received the necessary clearances, and swooped in for a landing.

Yayap eyed his recalcitrant troops, saw that three of them had drifted away from their preassigned positions, and used his radio to herd them back. "Jak, Bok, and Yeg, we have a shuttle coming in. Focus on the dropship—not the area outside."

The Jackals were too smart to say anything over the radio, but the Grunt knew they were grumbling among themselves as they returned to their various stations and the ship settled onto the blast-scarred deck.

"Watch the personnel slots," Yayap cautioned his troops, referring to the small compartments that lined the outside surfaces of the shuttle's twin hulls. "They could be packed with Flood."

In spite of the resentment he felt, Bok touched a switch and opened all of the slots for inspection, a new security procedure instituted three days before. The compartments were empty. The Jackals sniggered, and there was nothing Yayap could do but suffer through the indignity of it.

With that formality out of the way, a crew of Grunts moved in to unload supplies from the cargo compartments that lined the *inside* surface of the dropship's hulls, and towed the heavily loaded anti-grav pallets out onto the deck. Then, with the unloading process complete, the shuttle rose on its grav field, turned toward the hatch, and passed out into bright sunlight.

The cargo crew checked the label on each cargo container to see where it was supposed to go, gabbled at one another, and were about to tow the pallets away when Yayap intervened.

"Stop! I want you to open those cargo mods one at a time. Make sure they contain what they're supposed to."

If the previous order had been unpopular, this one met with out-and-out rebellion, as Bok decided to take Yayap on. "You're no Elite! We're under orders to deliver this stuff *now*. If we're late, they'll take our heads." He paused and clicked his beak meaningfully. "And our kin will take *yours*, gas-sucker."

The Jackals, all of whom were enjoying the interchange to the maximum, looked at each other and grinned.

'Zamamee should have been there, should have been giving the orders, and Yayap cursed the officer from the bottom of his heart. "No," he replied stubbornly. "Nothing leaves here until it has been checked. That's the new process. The Elites were the ones who came up with it, not me. So open them up and we'll get you and your crew out of here."

The other alien grumbled, but knew the rule-happy Elites would back Yayap, and turned to his crew. "All right, you heard Field Master Gas-sucker. Let's get this over with."

Yayap sighed, ordered his Jackals to form a giant U with the open end toward the cargo containers, and took his own place in the line.

What ensued was boring to say the least, as each cargo module was opened, closed, and towed out of the way. Finally, with only three containers left to go, Bok undogged a hatch, pulled the door open, and disappeared under an avalanche of infection forms. One of the attacking pods grabbed onto the Jackal's head, wrapped its tentacles around the creature's skull, drove a penetrator down through his throat, and had already tapped into the soldier's spine by the time Yayap yelled, "Fire!" and the rest of the Jackals opened up.

Nothing could live where the twenty plasma beams converged—and most of the infection forms were dead within two or three heartbeats. But Yayap thought he detected motion *behind* the mist created by the exploding pus pods and lobbed a plasma grenade into the cargo module. There was a flash of green-yellow light as the device went off, followed by a resonant *boom!* as it detonated.

The cargo container shook like a thing possessed, and chunks of raw meat flew out to spray the deck with gore. It was clear that three, or maybe even four combat forms had been hiding in the cargo compartment, hoping to enter the ship.

Now, as the last of the infection forms popped, a momentary silence settled over the shuttle bay. Bok's corpse smoldered on the deck.

"That was close," the Jackal named Jak said. "Those stupid gassers damned near got us killed. Good thing our file leader kept 'em in line." The soldiers to either side of the former critic nodded solemnly.

Yayap, who was close enough to hear the comment, wasn't sure whether to be angry or pleased. Somehow, for better or for worse, he'd been elevated to the position of honorary Jackal.

A full company of heavily armed Marines waited as torches cut through the metal grating, sparks fell into the stygian blackness below, and each man or woman considered what awaited them. Would they survive? Or leave their bones in the bottom of the hole? There was no way to know.

Meanwhile, thirty meters away, two officers stood

by themselves. McKay had borne far more than her fair share of the burden ever since the drop. Silva was aware of that and regretted it. Part of the problem stemmed from the fact that she was his CO, an extremely demanding position that could burn even the most capable officer out. But the truth was McKay was a better leader than her peers, as evidenced by the fact that the Helljumpers would follow her anywhere, even into a pit that might be filled with life-devouring monstrosities.

But everyone had their limits, even an officer like McKay, and the Major knew she was close to reaching them. He could see it in the grim contours of her once rounded face, the empty staring eyes, and the set of her mouth. The problem wasn't one of strength—she was the toughest, most hard-core Marine he knew—but one of hope.

Now, as he prepared to send her below, Silva knew she needed something *real* to fight for, something more than patriotism, something that would allow her to get at least some of the Marines to safety.

That, plus the possibility that something could happen to him, lay behind the briefing that ensued.

"So," Silva began, "go down, get the lay of the land, and see if you can slam the door on those bastards. Forty-eight hours of Flood-free operation would be ideal, but twenty-four would be sufficient, because we'll be out of here by then."

McKay had been looking over Silva's shoulder, but the last sentence brought her eyes back to his. Silva saw the movement and knew he had connected. "'Out of here,' sir? Where would we go?"

"*Home,*" Silva said confidently, "to brass bands, medals, and promotions all around. Then, with the intel gathered here, we'll have the opportunity to push the Covenant back into whatever hole they came from."

"And the Flood?" McKay asked, her eyes searching his face. "What about them?"

"They're going to die," Silva replied. "The AIs managed to link up a few hours ago. It turns out that the Chief is alive, Cortana is with him, and they're trying to rescue Keyes. Once they have him they're going to rig the *Autumn* to blow. The explosion will destroy Halo and everything on it. I'm not a fan of the SPARTAN program, you know that, but I've got to give the bastard credit. He's one helluva soldier."

"It sounds good," McKay said cautiously. "But how do we get off before the ring blows?"

"Ah," Silva replied. "That's where *my* idea comes in. While you're down cleaning out the sewers, I'll be up top, making the preparations necessary to take the *Truth and Reconciliation* away from the Covenant. She's spaceworthy now, and Cortana can fly her, or, if all else fails, we'll let Wellesley take a crack at it. It would be a stretch—but he might be able to pull it off.

"Imagine bringing back a Covenant cruiser, packed with their technology, and loaded with data on this ringworld. The response will be incredible! The human race needs a victory right now, and we'll give them a big one."

It was then, as McKay looked into the other officer's half-lit face, that she realized the extent to which raw ambition motivated her superior's actions, and knew that even if his wildest dreams were to come true, she wouldn't want any part of the glory that Silva sought. Just getting some Marines home alive—*that* would be reward enough for her.

An old soldier's adage flashed across her mind: "Never

share a foxhole with a hero." Glory and promotion were fine, but right now, she'd settle for *survival*, plain and simple.

First there was a loud clang, followed by the birth of six blue-white suns, which illuminated the inside surface of the shaft as they fell to the filth-encrusted floor below.

Then the invaders dropped, not one at a time down the stairs as the infection forms might have assumed, but half a dozen all at once, dangling on ropes. They landed within seconds of each other, knelt with weapons at the ready, and faced outward. Each Helljumper wore a helmet equipped with two lights and a camera. With simple back and forth movements of their heads, the soldiers created overlapping scans of the walls which were transmitted up to the grating above, and from there to the mesa.

McKay stood on the grating, eyed the raw footage on a portable monitor, and saw that four large arches penetrated the perimeter of the shaft and would need to be sealed in order to prevent access to the circular stairway. There was no sign of the Flood.

"Okay," the officer said, "we have four holes to seal. I want those plugs at the bottom of the shaft thirty from now. I'm going down."

Even as McKay spoke, and dropped into the hole which had been cut into the center of the grate, Wellesley was calculating the exact dimensions of each arch so that Navy techs could fabricate metal "plugs" that could be lowered to the bottom of the shaft, manhandled into position, and welded into place. Within a matter of minutes computer-generated outlines were lasered onto metal plates, torches were lit, and the cutting began.

McKay felt her boots touch solid ground, and took her first look around. Now, finally able to see the surroundings with her own eyes, the Company Commander realized that a bas-relief mural circled the lower part of the shaft. She wanted to go look at it, to run her fingers across the grime-caked images recorded there, but knew she couldn't, not without compromising the defensive ring and placing herself in jeopardy.

"Contact!" one of the Marines said urgently. "I saw something move."

"Hold your fire," McKay said cautiously, her voice echoing off the walls. "Conserve ammo until we have clear targets."

As soon as she'd given the "hold fire" order, the Flood gushed out into the shaft. McKay screamed: "Now! Pull!" and seven well-anchored winches jerked the entire team into the air and out of reach. The Marines fired as they ascended. One Helljumper screamed curses at the combat form who was leading the charge.

The loudmouthed Marine dropped his clip, loaded a fresh one into his rifle, and shouldered the weapon to resume fire. The combat form he'd been shooting leaped fifteen meters into the air, wrapped his legs around the Marine's waist, and caved in the side of the soldier's head with a rock.

Then, with the fallen Marine's assault weapon slung over his shoulder, the creature climbed the rope like an oversized monkey, and raced for the platform above.

Lister, who still stood on the grating above, aimed his pistol straight down, put three rounds through the top of the combat form's skull, saw the form fall backward into the milling mass below, and watched it disappear under the tide of alien flesh.

"Let's *move*, people!" the noncom said. "Raise the bait, and drop the bombs."

Energy bolts stuttered upward as the winches whirred, the Helljumpers rose, and twenty grenades fell through the grating and into the mob below. *Not* fragmentation grenades, which would have thrown shrapnel up at the Helljumpers, but plasma grenades, which burned as the Flood congregated around them, then went off in quick succession. They vaporized most of the gibbering monsters and left the rest vulnerable to a round of gunfire and a second dose of grenades.

Ten minutes later word came down that the plugs were ready, and a larger combat team was sent down, followed by four teams of techs. The arches were blocked without incident, the shaft was sealed, and the grating was repaired. Not forever, but for the next day or so, and that was all that mattered.

The Master Chief arrived at the top of the gravity lift and fought his way through a maze of passageways and compartments, occupied by Flood and Covenant alike. He rounded a corner and saw an open hatch ahead. "It looks like a shuttle bay," Cortana commented. "We should be able to reach the Control Room from the third level."

The CNI link that Cortana followed served to deliver a new message from the Captain. The voice was weak, and sounded slurred. "*I gave you an order, soldier, now pull out!*"

"He's delirious," Cortana said, "in pain. We have to find him!"

. . . pull out! I gave you an order, soldier!

The thought echoed in what was left of Keyes' ravaged mind. The invading presence descended. It could tell this one was nearly expended—no more energy left to fight.

It pushed in on the memories that the creature so jealously guarded, and recoiled at the sudden resistance, a defiance of terrible strength.

Keyes clutched at the last of his vital memories, and—inside his mind, where there was no one but he and the creature that attempted to absorb him—screamed *NO!*

Death, held in abeyance for so long, refused to rush in. Slowly, like the final drops of water from a recently closed faucet, his life force was absorbed.

With the memory of the voice to spur him on, the Master Chief made his way out onto a gallery over the shuttle bay, found that a pitched battle was in progress, and lobbed two grenades into the center of the conflict. They had the desired effect, but also signaled the human's presence, and the Flood came like iron filings drawn to a magnet.

The Flood onslaught was intense, and the Spartan was forced to retreat into the passageway whence he had come in order to concentrate the targets, buy some time, and reload his weapons.

The pitched firefight ended, and he sprinted for the far side of the gallery and passed through an open hatch. He fought his way up to the next level of the gallery, where the Flood appeared to be holding a convention at the far end of the walkway.

The Chief was fresh out of grenades by then, which meant he had to clear the path the hard way. A carrier form exploded, and sent a cluster of combat forms crashing to the ground.

The burst carrier spewed voracious infection forms in every direction, and collapsed as one of the fallen combat forms hopped forward, dragging a broken leg behind him, hands clutching a grenade as if it were a bouquet of flowers.

The Spartan backed away, fired a series of ten-round bursts, and gave thanks when the grenade exploded.

The carrier had given him an idea—when they blew, they went up in a big way. A second of the creatures scuttled into view, and made its ungainly way forward, accompanied by a wave of infection forms and two more combat forms. He used his pistol scope to survey the combat forms and was gratified that they fit the bill: Each carried plasma grenades.

He stepped into view, and the combat forms instantly vaulted high in the air. As soon as their feet left the deck, the Chief dropped and fired—directly at the carrier.

The Spartan's aim was perfect—as soon as they passed over the carrier, it burst, and ignited the plasma grenades the combat forms carried. They all went up in a blue-white flash of destructive energy.

"The Control Room should be *this* way," Cortana said as he charged ahead, eager to keep them moving in the right direction.

He moved fast, advancing across the blood-slicked floor, and followed Cortana's new nav coordinates toward the still-distant hatch. He passed through the opening, followed the corridor to an intersection, took a right, a left, and was passing through a door when a horrible groan was heard over the link.

"The Captain!" Cortana said. "His vitals are fading! Please Chief, hurry."

The Spartan charged into a passageway packed with both Covenant and Flood, and sprayed the tangle of bodies with bullets.

He kept running at top speed, sprinting past enemies and ignoring their hasty snap-shots. Time was of the essence; Keyes was fading fast.

He made it to the CNI's carrier wave source: the

cruiser's Control Room. The lighting was subdued, with hints of blue, and reflections off the metal surfaces. Thick, sturdy columns framed the ramp which led up to an elevated platform, where something strange stood.

He thought it was a carrier at first glance, but soon realized that the creature was far too large for that. It boasted a fleshy material that connected it to the ceiling overhead, like thick, gray-green spiderwebs.

There were no signs of opposition, not yet anyway, which left him free to make his way up the ramp with his rifle at the ready. As he moved closer the Chief realized that the new Flood form was *huge*. If it was aware of the human presence, the creature gave no sign of it, and continued to study a large holo panel as if committing the information displayed there to memory.

"No human life signs detected," Cortana observed cautiously. She paused, and added: "The Captain's life signs just stopped."

Damn. "What about the CNI?" he asked.

"Still transmitting."

Then the Chief noticed a bulge in the monster's side, and realized that he was looking at an impression of the Naval officer's grotesquely distorted face. The AI said, "The Captain! He's one of *them*!"

The Spartan realized then that he already knew that, *had* known it ever since he had seen Jenkins' video, but was unwilling to accept it.

"We can't let the Flood get off this ring!" Cortana said desperately. "You know what he'd expect . . . What he'd want us to do."

Yes, the Chief thought. *I know my duty.*

They needed to blow the *Autumn*'s engines to destroy Halo and the Flood. To do that, they needed the Captain's neural implants.

The Master Chief drew his arm back, formed his

hand into a stiff-fingered armored shovel, and made use of his enormous strength to plunge the crude instrument into the Flood form's bloated body.

There was momentary resistance as he punched his way through the creature's skin and penetrated the Captain's skull to enter the half-dissolved brain that lay within. Then, with his hand buried in the form's seemingly nerveless body, he felt for and found Keyes' implants.

The Chief's hand made a popping sound as it pulled out of the wound. He shook the spongy gore onto the deck and slipped the chips into empty slots in his armor.

"It's done," Cortana said somberly. "I have the code. We should go. We need to get back to the *Pillar of Autumn*. Let's go back to the shuttle bay and find a ride."

As if summoned by the lethargic beast that stood in front of the ship's controls, a host of Flood poured into the room, all of whom were clearly determined to kill the heavily armored invader. A flying wedge comprised of carrier and combat forms stormed the platform, pushed the human back, and soaked up his bullets as if eager to receive them.

Finally, more by chance than design, the Spartan backed off the command deck and plummeted to the deck below. That bought a moment of respite. There wasn't much time, though, just enough to hustle up out of the channel that ran parallel to the platform above, reload both of his weapons, and put his back into a corner.

The horde *really* came for him then, honking, gibbering, and gurgling, climbing up over the bodies that were mounded in front of them, careless of casualties, willing to pay whatever price he required.

The storm of gunfire put out by the MJOLNIR-clad soldier was *too* powerful, *too* well aimed, and the

Flood started to wilt, stumble, and fall, many giving up their lives only centimeters from the Spartan's blood-drenched boots, clawing at his ankles. He breathed a sigh of relief as the last combat form collapsed, relished the silence that settled over the room, and took a moment to reload both of his weapons.

"Are you okay?" Cortana asked hesitantly, both grateful and amazed by the fact that the Chief was still on his feet.

He thought of Captain Keyes.

"No," the Spartan replied. "Let's get the hell out of here and finish these bastards off."

He was numb from creeping exhaustion, hunger, and combat. The planned escape route back to the shuttle bay was littered with Flood and Covenant alike. The Spartan moved almost as if he was on autopilot—he simply killed and killed and killed.

The bay was filled with Covenant forces. A dropship had deployed fresh troops into the bay and bugged out. A pair of amped-up Elites patrolled near the Banshee at the base of the bay.

All the possibilities raced through his weary mind. What if that particular machine was in for repairs? What if an Elite took over the Shade and gunned him down? What if some bright light decided to close the outer doors?

But none of those fears were realized as the aircraft came to life, turned toward the planet that hung outside the bay doors, and raced into the night. Energy beams followed, and tried to bring the Banshee down, but ultimately fell short. They were free once more.

SECTION VI

THE MAW

AFTERMATH

TWELVE

The Banshee screamed through a narrow valley and out over an arid wasteland. The vehicle's shadow raced ahead as if eager to reach the *Pillar of Autumn* first. The Master Chief felt the slipstream fold in behind the aircraft's nose and tug at his armor. It felt good to be out of twisting corridors and cramped compartments if only for a short while.

The first sign of the ship's presence on the ringworld's surface was the hundred-meter-deep trench the *Autumn*'s hull had carved into Halo's skin. It started where the cruiser had first touched down, vanished where the vessel had bounced into the air, and reappeared a half klick farther on. From there the depression ran straight as an arrow to the point where the starship had finally come to rest with its blunt bow protruding out over the edge of a massive cliff. There were other aircraft in the area as well, all of which belonged to the Covenant, and they had no reason to suspect the incoming Banshee. Not yet, at any rate.

The Spartan, who was eager to make his approach look normal, chose one of the many empty lifeboat bays that lined the starship's starboard side, and bored in. Unfortunately the engine cut out at the last moment, the Banshee hit the *Autumn*'s hull, and although the Spartan was able to bail out, the alien vehicle fell to the rocks below. *Not* the low visibility arrival he had hoped for. Still, given Cortana's plans for the vessel, his presence wouldn't remain secret for long anyway.

"We need to get to the bridge," Cortana said. "From there we can use the Captain's neural implants to initiate an overload of the ship's fusion engines. The explosion should damage enough systems below it to destroy the ring."

"Shouldn't be a problem," the Chief commented as he made his way toward the tiny air lock. "I don't know who's better at blowing things up—you or me."

The moment he stepped outside he saw a cluster of red dots appear on his motion detector and knew some nasties were lurking off to his left. The only question was, *which* hostiles did he face—the Covenant or the Flood? Given a choice, he'd take the Covenant. Maybe, just maybe, the Flood hadn't located the ship yet.

The passageway ended to the right, which meant he had little choice but to turn left. But, rather than run into the Covenant or the Flood, the Spartan came under attack from a flock of Sentinels.

"Uh-oh," Cortana said as the noncom opened fire, "it looks like the Monitor knows where we are."

I wonder if he knows what we're up to, the Chief mused.

A Sentinel exploded, another hit the deck with a loud clang, and the Master Chief shifted fire to a third. "Yeah, he's after my head, but it's *you* that he really wants."

The AI made no reply as the third machine exploded—

and the Chief made his way down the hall using the lifeboat bays for cover. Two additional Sentinels appeared, were blown out of the air, and turned into scrap.

Soon after that they arrived at the end of the corridor, took a right, and spotted an open maintenance hatch. Not ideal, since he didn't relish the thought of having to negotiate such tight quarters, but there didn't seem to be any other choice. So he ducked inside, found himself in a maze, and blundered about for a while before spotting a hatch set flush into the deck in front of him. That's when a group of infection forms swarmed up out of the hole, and the Chief's question was answered. It appeared that the Flood *had* located the *Autumn*—and already taken up residence there.

He swore under his breath, backed away, and hosed the Flood with bullets. He eased forward and looked down through the floor hatch. He saw a carrier form, and knew there were bound to be more. He dropped a plasma grenade down through the hole, backed away, and took a certain amount of pleasure in the ensuing explosion.

The maintenance tunnels didn't seem to be taking him where he needed to go, so he dropped through the hole, crushed a handful of infection forms, and shot two more. The blood-splattered corridor was messy but well lit. He pried open a wall-mounted locker, and was pleased to find four frag grenades and spare ammo. He quickly stowed them, and moved on.

Two Sentinels nosed around a corner, opened fire with their lasers, and got what they deserved. "They might have been looking for us," Cortana observed, "but it's my guess that they were assigned to Flood control."

The theory made sense, but didn't really help much as the Master Chief was forced to fight the Sentinels, the Flood, *and* the Covenant, while he made his way through a series of passageways and into the ship's heavily damaged mess, where a large contingent of Elites and Grunts were waiting to have him for lunch.

There were a lot of them, too many to handle with the assault weapon alone, so he served up a couple of grenades. One of the Elites was blown to pieces by the overlapping explosions, another lost a leg, and a Grunt was thrown halfway across the room.

They'd come full circle—he'd blasted Covenant troops apart before the crash landing, and here he was again. *The enemy just didn't learn,* he thought.

There was a survivor, however, a tough Elite who threw a plasma grenade of his own, and missed by a matter of centimeters. The Master Chief ran and was clear of the blast zone by the time the device went off. The Elite charged, took the better part of a full clip, and finally slammed into the deck, dead.

It was a short distance to the burned-out bridge, where a Covenant security team was on duty. Word had been passed: They knew the human was on his way, and opened fire the moment they saw him.

Once again the Spartan made use of a grenade to even the odds—then crushed the head of an Elite with his fist. The alien's head was turned to pulp and its body collapsed like a puppet with no strings. The armor gave him enough strength to flip a Warthog over. Then, just when he thought the battle was done, a Grunt shot him in the back. The audible went off as his armor sought to recharge itself. A second shot, delivered with sufficient speed, would kill him.

Time seemed to slow as the Master Chief turned toward his right.

The Grunt, who had been hiding inside an equipment cabinet, froze as the armored alien not only survived what should have been a fatal shot, but turned to face him. They were only an arm's length away from each other, which meant that the Master Chief could reach out, rip the breather off his assailant's face, and close the door on him.

There was a loud *click* followed by wild hammering as the Chief made his way forward to the spot where Captain Keyes had issued his orders. Cortana appeared over the control panel in front of him. Everywhere the AI looked she saw burned-out equipment, bloodstained decks, and smashed viewports.

She shook her head sadly. "I leave home for a few days, and look what happens."

Cortana brought a hand up to her semitransparent forehead. "This won't take long— There, that should give us enough time to make it to the lifeboat, and put some distance between ourselves and Halo *before* detonation."

The next voice the Chief heard belonged to 343 Guilty Spark. "I'm afraid that's out of the question."

Cortana groaned. "Oh, hell."

The Chief brought his weapon up but saw no sign of the Monitor or his Sentinels. That didn't prevent the construct from babbling in his ears, though—the AI had tapped into his comm system. "Ridiculous! That you would imbue your warship's AI with such a wealth of knowledge. Wouldn't you worry that it might be captured? Or destroyed?"

Cortana frowned. "He's in my data arrays—a local tap."

Though nowhere near the bridge, the Monitor *was* on board, and flitted from one control panel to the next, sucking information out of Cortana's nonsentient subprocessors with the ease of someone vacuuming a set of drapes. "You can't imagine how exciting this is!

To have a record of all our lost time. Oh, how I will enjoy every moment of categorization. To think that you would destroy this installation, as well as this record . . . I am *shocked*. Almost too shocked for words."

"He stopped the self-destruct sequence," Cortana warned.

"Why do you continue to fight us, Reclaimer?" Spark demanded. "You cannot win! Give us the construct—and I will endeavor to make your death relatively painless and—"

The rest of 343 Guilty Spark's words were chopped off as if someone had thrown a switch. "At least I still have control over the comm channels," Cortana said.

"Where is he?" the Chief asked.

"I'm detecting taps throughout the ship," Cortana replied. "Sentinels most likely. As for the Monitor—*he's* in Engineering. He must be trying to take the core offline. Even if I could get the countdown restarted . . . I don't know what to do."

The Spartan stared at the hologram in surprise. This was a first—and it made her seem more human somehow. "How much firepower would you need to crack one of the engine shields?"

"Not much," Cortana replied, "a well-placed grenade perhaps. But why?"

He produced a grenade, tossed the device into the air, and caught it again.

The AI's eyes widened and she nodded. "Okay, let's go."

The Spartan turned and started to leave.

"Chief!" Cortana said. "Sentinels!"

In unison, the machines attacked.

Major Silva stood at what amounted to parade rest, feet spread, hands clasped behind his back, as he looked out over the landing pads while the men and women under his command made final preparations for the assault on the Covenant ship *Truth and Reconciliation*.

Fifteen Banshees, all scrounged from different sites across Halo's embattled surface, sat waiting for the order to launch.

Pelicans, three of the four that the humans had left, squatted ramps down as heavily loaded Marines filed aboard. Each of the surviving 236 leathernecks was armed with weapons appropriate to the mission at hand. No long-range stuff, like rocket launchers or sniper rifles, just assault weapons, shotguns, and grenades, all of which were lethal within enclosed spaces, and would be effective against both the Covenant and the Flood.

Naval personnel, and there were seventy-six of them, were armed with Covenant plasma rifles and pistols, which, thanks to their light weight, and the fact that there was no need to tote additional ammo, left the swabbies free to carry tools, food, and medical supplies. They had orders to avoid combat, if possible—and concentrate on running the ship. Some, a group of sixteen individuals, had skills considered to be so critical that each one had been given two Marine bodyguards.

Assuming that Cortana and the Master Chief were able to complete their mission, they would take one of the *Autumn*'s remaining lifeboats and rendezvous with the *Truth and Reconciliation* out in space. Annoying though she sometimes was, the officer knew Cortana would be able to pilot the alien vessel, and get them home.

Failing that, Silva hoped that Wellesley, with help from the Naval personnel, would be able to take the cruiser through Slipspace, following protocol, and eventually arriving back at Earth. An event he had already planned for, right down to what he would wear, and a short but moving speech for the media.

As if summoned by his thoughts, Wellesley chose that moment to intrude on the officer's reverie. The AI, who rode in an armored matrix slung from Silva's shoulder, was characteristically unapologetic. "Lieutenant McKay called in, Major. Force One is in place."

Silva nodded, and said, "Good. Now, if they can lay low for the next couple of hours, we'll be in good shape."

"I have every confidence in the *Lieutenant*," the AI replied plainly.

The implication was obvious. While Wellesley had faith in McKay, the AI had concerns where the Lieutenant's superior was concerned. Silva sighed. Had the artificial intelligence been human, the officer would have put him in his place long ago. But Wellesley *wasn't* human, couldn't be manipulated in the same fashion that flesh-and-blood subordinates could, and like the human on whom he had modeled himself, tended to speak his mind. "All right," the Major said reluctantly, "what's the problem?"

"The 'problem,'" Wellesley began, "is the Flood. If the plan is successful, and we manage to take the *Truth and Reconciliation*, there will almost certainly be Flood forms on board. In fact, based on what Cortana and I have been able to piece together, that's the only reason the vessel remains where it is. All of the necessary repairs have been made, and Covenant forces are trying to sterilize the ship's interior prior to lifting off."

"Which answers your question," Silva said, struggling to contain his impatience. "By the time we take over, most of the Flood will be dead. Once underway, I will dispatch hunter-killer teams to find the survivors.

With the exception of a few specimens which I will place under heavy guard, the rest will be ejected into space. There, are you satisfied?"

"*No*," Wellesley replied firmly. "Were a carrier form to escape onto Earth's surface, the entire planet could fall. This threat is as dangerous as, if not more so than, the Covenant. Cortana and I agree—no Flood form can be allowed to leave this system."

Silva took a quick look around to make sure no one was close enough to hear him and let the anger enter his voice. "Both you and Cortana have a tendency to forget one very important fact—*I'm* in command here and you are *not*. And I defy you to find anywhere in my orders that identifies a threat to Earth *bigger* than the goddamned Covenant!

"Your role is to provide advice. Mine is to make decisions. It's my belief that we could find better ways to combat the Flood if our scientists had live specimens with which to work. More than that, our people need to *see* this new enemy, *know* how dangerous they are, and *believe* that they can be conquered."

Wellesley considered taking the debate one step further, by pointing out that Silva's ambitions might well have clouded his judgment, but knew it would be a waste of time. "That's your final decision?"

"Yes, it is."

"Then God help you," the AI replied gravely, "because if your plan fails, no one else will have the power to do so."

The compartment, a space untouched by the fighting, had once served as a ready room for the ship's Longsword, Pelican, and shuttle pilots. Now, with no modifications other than the installation of some crude sleeping accommodations, a back table with some food on it, and crates of supplies, the room functioned as an unofficial HQ for Covenant forces stationed aboard the *Pillar of Autumn*.

The command staff, or what was left of it, sat slumped in the uncomfortably alien chairs, many too tired to move, and stared up at their leader. His name was 'Ontomee, and he was confused, frustrated, and secretly frightened. The situation aboard the *Autumn* had deteriorated dramatically. In spite of all the efforts to stop them, Flood forms continued to trickle into the ship.

The disgusting filth had even managed to seize control of the ship's engineering spaces before a *new* enemy, one which was inimical to Covenant and Flood form alike, sent an army of Sentinels into the ship and took control of the Engine Room.

Now, as if to prove that 'Ontomee was truly cursed, still *another* threat had arrived on the scene, and he was reluctant to share the news with the already exhausted Elites arrayed in front of him.

"So," 'Ontomee began lamely, "it seems that a human crashed a Banshee into the side of the ship, and is now on board."

A veteran named 'Kasamee frowned. "'*A* human'? As in, a *single* human? With respect, Commander, one human more or less will hardly make a difference."

'Ontomee swallowed. "Yes, well, normally I would agree with you, except that *this* human is somewhat unusual. First, because he wears special armor, second, because it appears that he's on some sort of mission, and third, because he single-handedly killed every member of Security Team Three, which had responsibility for the command and control deck."

Unnoticed by those in front of him, the seemingly lethargic officer known as Huki 'Umamee started to look interested. He sat up straighter, and began to pay close attention. Having chosen a seat in the last row, 'Zamamee found it difficult to hear. The discussion continued.

"*One* human accomplished all that?" 'Kasamee demanded incredulously. "That hardly seems possible."

"Yes," 'Ontomee agreed, "but he did. Not only that, but having accomplished whatever he entered the control area to do, he left, and is somewhere else on board this ship." The Elite scanned the faces in front of him. "Who has the skill and courage required to find the alien and kill him?"

The response came with gratifying speed. "*I* do," 'Zamamee said, now on his feet.

'Ontomee peered into the harsh human lights. "Who is that?"

"'Umamee," the Elite lied.

"Ah, yes," 'Ontomee replied gratefully. "A commando . . . Just the sort of person we need to rid ourselves of this two-legged vermin. The mission is yours. Keep me informed.

"Now, turning our attention to these new airborne mechanisms . . ."

Later, as the meeting ended, 'Kasamee went looking for the volunteer, fully intending to compliment the younger officer on his initiative. But, like the human the Elite was supposed to find, the Elite officer had disappeared.

Having fought his way clear of the bridge, the Master Chief made his way through a series of passageways, ran into more Flood and gunned them down. Cortana figured that they could access the Engine Room via the cryo chamber, and that was where the Chief was headed. The problem was that he kept running into jammed hatches, locked doors, and other obstacles that kept him from taking a direct route.

After he moved through a large, dark room strewn with weapons, the Chief heard the sounds of combat coming from the area beyond a closed hatch. He paused, heard the noises die away, and slipped out into the corridor. Bodies lay all about as he slid along a bulkhead, saw some spikes sticking up over a cargo module, and felt his blood run cold. A Hunter! Or more accurately *two* Hunters, since they traveled in pairs.

Lacking a rocket launcher, the Chief turned to the only heavy-duty firepower that he had: grenades.

He threw two grenades in quick succession, saw the behemoth go down, and heard a roar of outrage as the second Hunter charged.

The Spartan fired just to slow the alien down, backed through the hatch, and gave thanks as the door closed. That gave him two or three seconds that he needed to plant his feet, pull another grenade, and prepare to throw it.

The hatch opened, the fragmentation grenade flew straight and true, and the explosion knocked the beast off its feet. The deck shook as the body hit. The Hunter attempted to rise but fell under a hail of armor-piercing bullets.

The Master Chief gave the corpse a wide berth as he left the room, and passed back into the hall. As he made his way through the ship's corridors, he saw blood-splattered bulkheads, bodies sprawled in every imaginable posture of death, blown hatches, sparks flying out of junction boxes, and a series of small fires, which thanks to a lack of combustible materials seemed to be fairly well contained.

He heard the sound of automatic weapons' fire

somewhere ahead, and passed through another hatch. Inside, a fire burned at the point where two large pipes traversed a maintenance bay. He was close to the cryo chamber, or thought he was, but needed to find a way in.

Hesitant to jump through the flames unless it was absolutely necessary, he took a right turn instead. The sounds of combat grew louder as the hatch opened onto a large room where a full array of Flood forms were battling a clutch of Sentinels. He paused, shouldered his weapon, and fired. Sentinels crashed, carrier forms exploded, and everyone fired at one another in a mad melee of crisscrossing energy beams, 7.62mm projectiles, and exploding needles.

Once the Sentinels had been put out of action, and most of the Flood had been neutralized, the Chief was able to cross the middle of the room, climb a ladder, and gain the catwalk above. From that vantage point he could look across into the Maintenance Control Room, where a couple of Sentinels were hard at work trying to zap a group of Flood, none of whom were willing to be toasted without putting up a fight. The combatants were too busy to worry about stray humans, however, and the noncom took advantage of that to work his way down the walkway and into the Control Room.

And *that*, as he soon learned, was a big mistake.

It wasn't too bad at first, or didn't seem to be, as he destroyed both of the Sentinels, and went to work on the Flood. But every time he put one form down, it seemed as if two more arrived to take its place, soon forcing him onto the defensive.

He retreated into the antechamber adjacent to the Control Room. The human had little choice but to place his back against a locked hatch. The larger forms came in twos and threes—while the infection forms came in swarms. Some of the assaults seemed to be random, but many appeared to be coordinated as one, or two, or three combat forms would hurl themselves forward, die under the assault weapon's thundering fire, and fall just as the Spartan ran out of ammo, and *more* carrier forms waddled into the fray.

He slung his AR, drew the shotgun—briefly hoping there would be a lull during which to reload—and opened fire on the bloated monstrosities before the force exerted by their exploding bodies could do him harm.

Then, with newly spawned infection forms flying in every direction it was cleanup time followed by a desperate effort to reload both weapons before the *next* wave of creatures attempted to roll over him.

He dropped into a pattern of fire and movement. He made his way through the ship, closer to the engineering spaces, pausing only to pour fire into knots of targets of opportunity. Then, he quickly disengaged, reloaded, and ran farther into the ship.

The noise generated by his own weapons hammered at the Master Chief's ears, the thick gagging odor of Flood blood clogged his throat, and his mind eventually grew numb from all the killing.

After dispatching a Covenant combat team, he crouched behind a support strut and fed rounds into the shotgun. Without warning, a combat form leaped on his back and smashed a large wrench into his helmet. His shield dropped away from the force of the blow, which allowed an infection form to land on his visor.

Even as he staggered under the impact, and pawed at the form's slick body, a penetrator punched its way through his neck seal, located his bare skin, and sliced it open.

The Spartan gave a cry of pain, felt the tentacle slide down toward his spine, and knew it was over.

Though unable to pick up a weapon and kill the infection form directly, Cortana had other resources, and rushed to use them. Careful not to drain too much power, the AI diverted some energy away from the MJOLNIR armor, and made use of it to create an electrical discharge. The infection form started to vibrate as the electricity coursed through it. The Chief jerked as the Flood form's penetrator delivered a shock to his nervous system, and the pod popped, misting the Spartan's visor with green blood spray.

The Chief could see well enough to fight, however, and did so, killing the wrench-wielding combat form with a burst of bullets.

"Sorry about that," Cortana said, as the Spartan cleared the area around him, "but I couldn't think of anything else to do."

"You did fine," he replied, pausing to reload. "That was close."

Another two or three minutes passed before the Flood gave up and he could take the moment necessary to remove his helmet, jerk the penetrator out from under his skin, and slap a self-adhering antiseptic battle dressing over the wound. It hurt like hell: The Spartan winced as he lowered the helmet back over his head, and sealed his suit.

Then, pausing only to kill a couple of stray infection forms, and still looking for a way to gain entry to the cryo chamber, the Chief made his way through a number of passageways, into a maze of maintenance tunnels, and out into a corridor where he spotted a red arrow on the deck along with the word ENGINEERING.

Finally, a break.

No longer concerned with finding a way into cryo, the noncom passed through a hatch and entered the first passageway he'd seen that was well lit, free of bloodstains, and not littered with corpses. A series of turns brought him to a hatch.

"Engine Room located," Cortana announced. "We're here."

The Spartan heard humming, and knew that 343 Guilty Spark was somewhere in the vicinity. He had already started to back through the hatch when Cortana said, "Alert! The Monitor has disabled all command access. We can't restart the countdown. The only remaining option will be to detonate the ship's fusion reactors. *That* should do enough damage to destroy Halo.

"Don't worry . . . I have access to all of the reactor schematics and procedures. I'll walk you through it. First we need to pull back the exhaust coupling. That will expose a shaft that leads to the primary fusion drive core."

"Oh, good," the Spartan replied. "I was afraid it might be complicated."

The Chief reopened the hatch, stepped out into the Engine Room, and an infection form flew straight at his faceplate.

The attack on the *Truth and Reconciliation* came with mind-numbing speed as a wing of fifteen Banshees came screaming out of the sun, attacked the nearly identical number of Covenant aircraft assigned to fly cover over the cruiser, and knocked half of them out of the sky during the first sixty seconds of combat.

Then, even as individual dogfights continued, Lieutenant "Cookie" Peterson and his fellow Pelican pilots delivered Silva, Wellesley, and forty-five heavily armed Marines into the enemy cruiser's shuttle bay, where the first leathernecks off the ramps smothered the Covenant security team in a hail of bullets, secured all the hatches, and sent a team of fifteen Helljumpers racing for the ship's Control Room.

Conscious of the fact that occupying the Control Room wouldn't mean much unless they owned engineering as well, the humans launched a nearly simultaneous ground attack. Thanks to the previous effort, in which the Master Chief and a group of Marines had entered the ship looking for Captain Keyes, McKay had the benefit of everything learned during that mission, including a detailed description of the gravity lift, video of the interior corridors, and operational data which Cortana had siphoned out of the ship's systems.

Not too surprisingly, security around the gravity lift had been tripled since the previous incursion, which meant that even though McKay and her force of Helljumpers had been able to creep within meters of the hill on which the gravity field was focused, they still had six Hunters, twelve Elites, and a mixed bag of Grunts and Jackals to cope with before they could board the vessel above.

Having anticipated that problem, McKay had equipped her fifteen-person team with eight rocket launchers, all of which were aimed squarely at the Hunters.

The Covenant-flown Banshees had just come under attack, and the spined monsters were staring up into a nearly cloudless sky, when McKay gave the word: "Now!"

All eight launchers fired one, then *two* rockets, putting a total of sixteen of the shaped charges on the aliens, so that the Hunters never had a chance to fight as a series of red-orange explosions blew them apart.

Even as gobbets of raw meat continued to rain out of the sky, the launchers were reloaded, and another flight of rockets was sent on its way.

Three or four of the Elites had been killed during the initial attack, which meant that some of the survivors were targeted by as many as two missiles, and simply ceased to exist as the powerful 102mm rounds detonated.

Those who survived the volley, and there weren't many, fell quickly as the rest of the team hurled grenades into the enemy positions, and hosed them with automatic fire. Total elapsed time: 36 seconds.

A full minute was consumed racing up the hill and greasing the guard at the top, which meant that 1:36 had passed by the time the humans appeared inside the *Truth and Reconciliation*, slaughtered the Grunts on guard duty, and deactivated the lift.

Jenkins was chained between a pair of burly Marines. McKay waved the trio forward. "Let's go, Marines. We're supposed to take the Engine Room—so let's get to work."

Jenkins, or what remained of Jenkins, could smell the Flood. They were there, hiding in the ship, and he struggled to tell McKay that. But the only thing that came out was a series of grunts and hoots. The humans had taken the ship, but they had taken something else as well, something that could kill every single one of them.

'Zamamee ushered Yayap into the heavily guarded Covenant Communications Center—and gave the Grunt a moment to look around. The space had once housed all of the communications gear associated with the *Pillar of Autumn*'s auxiliary fighters, shuttles, and transports. Human gear had been ripped out to make room for Covenant equipment, but everything else was pretty much in the same configuration. A team of six com techs were on duty, all with their backs to the center of the room, banks of equipment arrayed in front of them. A constant murmur of conversation could be heard via the overhead speakers, some of which was punctuated by the sounds of combat, as orders went out and reports came back in.

"This is where you will sit," the Elite explained, pointing toward a vacant chair. "All you have to do is listen to the incoming traffic, make note of the reports that pertain to the human, and pass the information along to me by radio.

"He has an objective, we can be sure of that, and once we know where he's going, I'll be there to greet him. I know you would prefer to be in on the kill, but you're the only individual I can trust to handle my communications, so I hope you'll understand."

Yayap, who didn't want to be anywhere near the kill, tried to look downcast. "I'll do my part, Commander, and take pleasure in the team's success."

"That's the spirit!" 'Zamamee said encouragingly. "I knew I could count on you. Now sit down at the console, put on that headset, and get ready to take some notes. We know he left what the humans refer to as 'the bridge,' fought a battle near the Maintenance Control Room, and was last spotted heading toward the Engine Room. We don't have any personnel in that compartment at the moment, but that doesn't matter, because the real challenge is to figure out where he's headed *next*. You feed the information to me, I'll take my combat team to the right place, and the human will enter the trap. The rest will be easy."

Yayap remembered previous encounters with the human, felt a chill run down his spine, and took his seat. Something told him that when it came to a final confrontation between the Elite and the human, it might be many things, but it wouldn't be easy.

The Engine Room hatch opened, an infection form went for the Master Chief's face, and he fired a quarter of a clip into it. A lot more bullets than the target required, but the memory of how the penetrator had slipped in under the surface of his skin was still fresh in his mind, and he wasn't about to allow any of the pods near his face again, especially with a hole in his neck seal. A red nav indicator pointed the way toward a ramp at the far end of the enormous room.

He pounded his way up onto a raised platform, ran past banks of controls, and ducked through the hatch that led up to Level Two. He followed a passageway out into an open area, and then up the ramp to Level Three. Near the top, a pair of combat forms fell to his well-placed fire. He policed the fallen creatures' ammo and grenades and kept going.

"Not acceptable, Reclaimer," 343 Guilty Spark intoned. "You *must* surrender the construct."

The Chief ignored the Monitor, made his way up to Level Three, and encountered a reception party comprised of Flood. He opened fire, took two combat forms and a carrier down off the top, and backed away in order to reload.

Then, with a fresh clip in place, he opened fire, cut the nearest form off at the knees, tossed a grenade into the crowd behind him. The frag detonated, and blew them to hell.

Quick bursts of automatic fire were sufficient to finish the survivors and allow the Master Chief to reach the far end of the passageway. A group of forms were waiting there to greet him, but quickly gave way to a determined assault as he made his way up the blood-slicked steel, and through the hatch at the top of the ramp.

He moved onto the Level Three catwalk and immediately started to take fire. There was total chaos as the Sentinels fired on the Flood, the Flood shot back, and everyone seemed to want a piece of him. It was important to concentrate, however, to focus on his mission, so the Spartan made a mad dash for the nearest control panel. He hit the control labeled OPEN, heard a beeper go off, followed by the sound of Cortana's voice.

"Good! Step one complete! We have a straight shot into the fusion reactor. We need a catalytic explosion to destabilize the magnetic containment field surrounding the fusion cell."

"Oh," the petty officer said as he jumped down onto a thick slab of duracrete, and felt it start to move. "I thought I was supposed to throw a grenade into a hole."

"That's what I said."

The Chief grinned as a brightly lit rectangular slot appeared, and he tossed a grenade in through the opening.

The ensuing explosion threw bits of charred metal around the smoke-filled compartment.

One down, and three to go, the Spartan told himself as the Sentinels fired, and the laser beams hit his chest.

Thanks to the lightning-fast and extremely well coordinated nature of the attack, the humans controlled more than eighty percent of the *Truth and Reconciliation,* and were preparing to lift off. Those compartments not under human control could be dealt with later on. There hadn't been any contact with Cortana for a while—and Silva intended to play it safe. If Halo was about to blow, he wanted to be *far* away when the event took place.

The cruiser's Control Room was a scene of frantic activity as Wellesley wrestled with the ship's nonsentient nav comp, Naval personnel struggled to familiarize themselves with all manner of alien control systems, and Silva gloated over his latest coup. The attack had been so fast, so successful, that his Marines had captured a Prophet, who claimed to be an important member of the Covenant's ruling class. Now, safely locked away, the alien was slated to become yet another element in Silva's triumphant return to Earth. The officer smiled as the ship's gravity locks were released, the hull swayed slightly in response, and the final preflight check began.

Many decks below, McKay felt someone touch her arm. "Lieutenant? Do you have a moment?"

Though not in the same chain of command, Lieutenant Commander Gail Purdy outranked the Helljumper, which was why McKay responded by saying, "Yes, ma'am. What can I do for you?"

Purdy was an Engineering officer, and one of those sixteen individuals who rated bodyguards, both of whom had their backs to the officer and were facing out. She was middle-aged and stout, with ginger-colored hair. Her eyes were serious and locked with McKay's.

"Step over here. I'd like to show you something."

McKay followed the other officer over to a large tube that served to bridge the one-meter gap between one blocky-looking installation and the next. Jenkins, who had no choice but to go wherever his Marine guards went, was forced to follow.

"See that?" the Naval officer inquired, pointing at the tube.

"Yes, ma'am," McKay answered, mystified as to what such a structure could possibly have to do with her.

"That's an access point for the fiber-optic pathway that links the Control Room to the engines," the Engineer explained. "If someone were to sever that connection, the power plants would run wild. There may be a bypass somewhere—but we haven't found it. Given the fact that twenty percent of the ship remains under Covenant control I suggest that you post a guard on this piece of equipment until all of the Covenant are under lock and key."

Purdy's suggestion had the force of an order, and McKay said, "Yes, ma'am. I'll take care of it."

The Naval officer nodded as the deck tilted and forced both women to grab onto the fiber channel. Two people were thrown to the deck. Purdy grinned. "Pretty sloppy, huh? Captain Keyes would have a fit!"

Silva wasn't worried about the finer points of ship handling as the final loads of UNSC personnel were deposited in the shuttle bay, the Pelicans were secured, the outer doors were closed, and the *Truth and Reconciliation* struggled to break the grip that Halo had on her hull.

No, Silva was satisfied merely to get clear of the surface, to feel the deck vibrate as the cruiser's engines struggled to push countless tons of deadweight up through the ring-world's gravity well, to the point where the ship would break free.

Spurred into action by the vibration, or perhaps just tired of waiting, the Flood chose that moment to attack the Engine Room. A vent popped open, an avalanche of infection forms poured out and came under immediate fire.

Jenkins went berserk, and jerked on his chains, gibbering incoherently as the Marine guards struggled to bring him under control.

The battle lasted for less than a minute before all of the Flood forms were killed, the vent was sealed, and the cover welded into place. But the attack served to illustrate the concerns that McKay already had. The Flood were like an extremely deadly virus—and it was naïve to believe that they could be controlled by anything short of extermination. The Marine used her status as CO to get through to Silva, gave a report on the attack, and finished by saying, "It's clear that the ship is still infected, sir. I suggest that we put down and sterilize every square centimeter prior to lifting again."

"*Negative,* Lieutenant," Silva replied grimly. "I have reason to believe that Halo is going to blow, and soon. Besides, I *want* some specimens, so see what you can do to capture some of the ugly bastards."

"The Lieutenant is correct," Wellesley put in dispassionately. "The risk is *too* great. I urge you to reconsider."

"My decision is final," Silva growled. "Now, return to your duties, and that's an *order.*"

McKay broke the connection. The military incorporated many virtues, in her mind at least, one of the most important of which was duty. Duty not just to the Corps, but to the billions of people on Earth, to whom she was ultimately responsible. Now, faced with the conflict between military discipline, the glue that held everything together, and duty, the purpose of it all, what was she supposed to do?

The answer, strangely enough, came from Jenkins, who, having been privy to her end of the conversation, jerked at his chain. The action took one of the guards by surprise. He fell as Jenkins lunged in the direction of the fiber-optic connection, and was still trying to regain his feet when the combat form ran out of slack, and came up short. Seconds later the Marines had Jenkins back under control.

Having failed to do what he knew was right, and with his chains stretched tight, Jenkins looked imploringly into McKay's eyes.

McKay realized that the decision lay in her hands, and that although it was horrible almost beyond comprehension, it was simple as well. So simple that even the grotesquely ravaged Jenkins knew where his duty lay.

Slowly, deliberately, the Marine crossed the deck to the point where the guard stood, told him to take a break, took one last look around, and triggered a grenade. Jenkins, still unable to speak, managed to mouth the words "thank you."

Silva was too many decks removed to feel the explosion, or to hear the muffled thump, but *was* able to witness the results firsthand. Someone yelled, "The controls are gone!" The deck tilted as the *Truth and Reconciliation* did a nose-over, and Wellsley made one last comment.

"You taught her well, Major. Of *that* you can be proud."

Then the bow struck, a series of explosions rippled the length of the hull, and the ship, as well as all of those aboard her, ceased to exist.

"You're sure?" 'Zamamee demanded, his voice slightly distorted by both the radio and an increasing amount of static.

Yayap wasn't sure of anything, other than the fact that the reports flowing in around him were increasingly negative, as Covenant forces came under heavy fire from both the Flood *and* the Sentinels. Something had caused a rock to form down in the Grunt's abdomen—and made him feel slightly nauseated.

But it would never do to say that, not to someone like 'Zamamee, so he lied instead. "Yes, Commander. Based on the reports, and looking at the schematics here in the Communications Center, it looks like the human will have little choice but to exit via this hatch, make his way to a lift, and go up to the service corridor that runs along the ship's spine."

"Good work, Yayap," the Elite said. "We're on our way."

For reasons he wasn't entirely sure of, and in spite of his many failings, the Grunt felt a strange sense of affection for the Elite. "Be careful, Commander. The human is extremely dangerous."

"Don't worry," 'Zamamee replied, "I have a surprise for our adversary. A little something that will even the odds. I'll call you the moment he's dead."

Yayap said, "Yes, Commander," heard a click, and knew it was the last time he would hear the officer's voice. Not because he believed that 'Zamamee was going to die—but because he believed *all* of them were about die.

That's why the diminutive alien announced that he was going on a break, left the Communications Center, and never came back.

Shortly thereafter he loaded a day's worth of food plus a tank of methane onto a Ghost, steered the vehicle out away from the *Pillar of Autumn*, and immediately found what he was searching for: a sense of peace. For the first time in many, many days Yayap was happy.

As the final grenade went off, the Master Chief felt the shaft he was standing on shake in sympathy and Cortana yelled into his ears. "That did it! The engines will go critical. We have fifteen minutes to get off the ship! We should move outside and get to the third deck elevator. It will take us to a Class Seven service corridor that runs the length of the ship. Hurry!"

The Chief jumped up onto the Level Three platform, blasted a combat form, and turned toward the hatch off to his right. It opened, he passed through, and ran the length of the passageway. A second door opened onto the area directly in front of the large service elevator.

The Chief heard machinery whir, figured he had triggered a sensor, and waited for the lift to arrive. For the first time in hours there was no immediate threat, no imminent danger, and the Spartan allowed himself to relax fractionally. It was a mistake.

"Chief!" Cortana said. "Get back!"

Thanks to the warning, he was already backing through the hatch when the lift appeared from below, and the Elite, seated in the plasma turret, opened fire.

Special Ops Officer Zuka 'Zamamee fired the Shade. The energy cannon took up most of the platform, leaving barely enough room for the Grunts who had helped the Elite wrestle the weapon aboard. The bolt flared blue, hit the hatch as it started to close, and slagged half the door.

He felt elation as the waves of energy slashed through the air toward his target. Soon, victory would be complete, and his honor could be restored. Then he'd deal with the tiresome Grunt, Yayap.

It was going to be a glorious day.

"Damn!" the Chief exclaimed. "Where did *that* come from?"

"It looks like someone has been tracking you," Cortana said grimly. "Now, get ready—I'll take control of the elevator and cause it to drop. You roll a couple of grenades into the shaft."

'Zamamee saw the energy bolt hit the hatch, experienced a sense of exhilaration as the human hurried to escape, and felt the platform jerk to a halt.

The Elite had just fired again, just blown what remained of the human's cover away, when he heard a clank and the lift started to descend.

"*No!*" he shouted, sure that one of the Grunts was responsible for the sudden movement, and desperate lest the human escape his clutches. But it was too late, and there was nothing the smaller aliens could do, as the elevator continued to fall.

Then, even as his target vanished from sight, and 'Zamamee railed at his subordinates, a couple of grenades tumbled down from above, rattled around the floor, and exploded.

The force of the blast lifted the Elite up and out of his seat, gave him one last look at his opponent, and let him fall. He hit with a thud, felt something snap, and waited for his first glimpse of paradise.

Cortana brought the lift back up. The Master Chief had little choice but to step onto the gore-splattered platform and let it carry him toward the service corridor above. Cortana took advantage of the moment to work on the escape plan.

"Cortana to Echo 419, come in Echo 419."

"*Roger, Cortana,*" Foehammer said from somewhere above, "*I read you five-by-five.*"

The Master Chief felt a series of explosions shake

the elevator, knew the ship was starting to come apart, and looked forward to the moment when he would be free of it.

"The *Pillar of Autumn*'s engines are going critical, Foehammer," Cortana continued. "Request immediate extraction. Be ready to pick us up at external access junction four-C as soon as you get my signal."

"Affirmative. Echo 419 to Cortana—things are getting noisy down there . . . Is everything okay?"

The elevator shook again as the AI said, "Negative, negative! We have a wildcat destabilization of the ship's fusion core. The engines must have sustained more damage than we thought."

Then, as the platform jerked to a halt, and a piece of debris fell from somewhere up above, the AI spoke to the Spartan. "We have six minutes before the fusion drives detonate. We need to evacuate *now*! The explosion will generate a temperature of almost a hundred million degrees. *Don't* be here when it blows!"

That sounded like excellent advice. The Master Chief ran through a hatch into a bay full of Warthogs, each stowed in its own individual slot. He chose one that was located near the entry, jumped into the driver's seat, and was relieved when the vehicle started up.

The countdown timer which Cortana had projected onto the inside surface of his HUD was not only running, but running *fast*, or so it seemed to the Chief as he drove out of the bay, hooked a left to avoid a burning 'Hog, and plowed through a mob of Covenant and Flood. An Elite went down, was sucked under the big off-road tires, and caused the vehicle to buck as it passed over him. The slope ahead was thick with infection forms. They popped like firecrackers as the human accelerated uphill and plasma bolts raced to catch him from behind. Then, cautious lest he make a mistake and lose valuable time, he took his foot off the accelerator and paused at the top of the ramp.

A large passageway stretched before him, with walkways to either side, a pedestrian bridge in the distance, and a narrow service tunnel directly ahead. A couple of Flood forms were positioned on top of the entrance and fired down at him as he pushed the Warthog forward, and nosed into the opening ahead.

The ramp sloped down, the Spartan braked, and he was soon glad that he had as something went *boom!* and hurled pieces of jagged metal across the passageway in front of him. The Chief took his foot off the brake, converted a carrier form into paste, and sent the LRV up the opposite slope.

He emerged from the subsurface tunnel, and with a barrier ahead, he swung left, and ran the length of a vertical wall. He saw a narrow ramp, accelerated upslope, and jumped a pair of gaps that he never would have tackled had he been aware of them. He hit a level stretch, braked reflexively, and was thankful when the Warthog nose-dived off the end of the causeway and plunged into another service tunnel.

Now, with a group of Flood ahead, he pushed through them, crushed the monsters under his tires.

"Nice job on that last section," Cortana said admiringly. "How did you know about the dive off the end?"

"I didn't," the Master Chief said as the LRV lurched up out of the tunnel and nosed into another.

"Oh."

This passage was empty, which allowed the Spartan to pick up speed as he guided the Warthog up into a larger tunnel. The 'Hog caught some air, and he put the pedal to the metal in an effort to pick up some time.

The large passageway was smooth and clear, but

took them out into a hell of flying metal, homicidal Flood, and laser-happy Sentinels, all of whom tried to cancel his ticket while he paused, spotted an elevated ramp off to the left, and steered for it even as criss-crossing energy beams sizzled across the surface of his armor and explored the interior of the vehicle.

The Spartan fought to control the 'Hog as one tire rode up onto the metal curb and threatened to pull the entire vehicle off into the chaos below. It was difficult, with fire sleeting in from every possible direction, but the Chief made the necessary correction, came down off the ramp, hooked a left, and found himself in a huge tunnel with central support pillars that marched off into the distance.

Careful to weave back and forth between the pillars in order to improve his time, he rolled through a fight between the Flood and a group of Covenant, took fire from a flock of Sentinels, and gunned the LRV out into another open area with a barrier ahead. A quick glance confirmed that another elevated ramp ran down the left side of the enormous passageway, so he steered for that.

Explosions sent gouts of flame and smoke up through the grating ahead of him, and threatened to heave the Warthog off the track.

Once off the ramp, things became a little easier as the Spartan entered a large tunnel, sped the length of it, braked into an open area, and pushed the vehicle down into a smaller service tunnel. Infection forms made loud popping sounds as the tires ate them alive. The engine growled, and the Chief nearly lost it as he came out of the tunnel too fast, realized there was another subsurface passageway ahead, and did a nose-over that caused the front wheels not only to hit hard but nearly flipped the 'Hog end-for-end. Only some last-minute braking and a measure of good luck brought the LRV down right side up and allowed the Master Chief to climb up out of the passageway and into a maze of pillars.

He swore as he was forced to wind his way between the obstacles while precious seconds came off the count-down clock and every alien, parasite, and machine with a weapon took potshots at him while he did so. Then came a welcome stretch of straight-level pavement, a quick dip through a service tunnel, and a ramp into a sizable tunnel as Cortana called for evac.

"Cortana to Echo 419! Requesting extraction now! On the double!"

"*Affirmative, Cortana,*" the pilot replied, as the Master Chief accelerated out onto a causeway.

"Wait! Stop!" Cortana insisted. "This is where Foe-hammer is coming to pick us up. Hold position here."

The Spartan braked, heard a snatch of garbled radio traffic, and saw a UNSC dropship approach from the left. Smoke trailed behind the Pelican and the reason was plain to see. A Banshee had slotted itself in behind the transport and was trying to hit one of the ship's engines. There was a flash as the starboard power plant took a hit and burst into flames.

The Chief could imagine Foehammer at the controls, fighting to save her ship, eyeing the causeway ahead.

"Pull up! Pull up!" the Spartan shouted, hoping she could pancake in, but it was too late. The Pelican lost al-titude, passed under the causeway, and soon disappeared from sight. The explosion came three seconds later.

Cortana said, "Echo 419!" and, receiving no response, said, "She's gone."

The Master Chief remembered the cheerful voice on the radio, the countless times the pilot had saved some-body's tail, and felt a deep sense of regret.

There was a short pause while the AI tapped into

what remained of the ship's systems. "There's a Longsword docked in launch bay seven. If we move *now* we can make it!"

Rubber screeched as the Chief put his foot to the floor, steered the Warthog through a hatch, down a ramp, and into a tunnel. Huge pillars marked the center of the passageway and a series of concave gratings caused the LRV to wallow before it lurched up onto smooth pavement again. Explosions sent debris flying from both sides of the tunnel and made it difficult to hear Cortana as she said something about "full speed" and some sort of a gap.

He hit the accelerator, but the rest was more a matter of luck rather than skill. The Master Chief pushed the 'Hog up a ramp, felt the bottom drop out of his stomach as the LRV flew through the air, dropped two or three levels, hit hard, slewed sideways, and came to a stop.

The Chief wrestled with the wheel, brought the front end around, and glanced at the timer. It read: 01:10:20. He stamped on the accelerator. The Warthog shot ahead, raced through a narrow tunnel, then slowed as he spotted the array of horizontally striped barrels that blocked the road ahead. Not only that—but the entire area was swarming with Covenant and Flood. The Master Chief jumped out, hit the ground running, and gunned an Elite who had the misfortune to get in the way.

The fighter was straight ahead, ramp down, waiting for him to come aboard. Plasma bolts stuttered past his head, explosions hurled debris in every direction, and then he was there, boots pounding on metal as he entered the ship.

The ramp came up just as a mob of Flood arrived, the Longsword shook in sympathy as another explosion rocked the *Pillar of Autumn*, and the Spartan staggered as he made his way forward. Precious seconds were consumed as he dropped into the pilot's seat, brought the engines online, and took the controls.

"Here we go."

The Chief made use of the ship's belly jets to push the Longsword up off the deck. He turned the fighter counterclockwise, and hit the throttles. Gee forces pushed him back into his seat as the spacecraft exploded out of its bay and blasted up through the atmosphere.

Yayap, who had made it to the edge of the foothills by then, heard a series of dull thuds and turned in time to see a line of red-orange flowers bloom along the length of the *Autumn*'s much abused hull.

As the cruiser's fusion drives went critical, a compact sun blossomed on the surface of Halo. Its thermonuclear sphere carved a five-kilometer crater into the superdense ring material and sent powerful pressure waves rippling throughout the structure. Both up- and down-spin of the explosion, the fireball flattened and sterilized the surface terrain. Within moments, the yellow-white core had consumed all of the available fuel, collapsed upon itself, and winked out.

Still spinning, but unable to withstand the forces exerted on this new weak point, the ring structure slowly tore itself apart. Huge chunks of debris tumbled end over end out into space, as a five-hundred-kilometer-long section of the ringworld's hull sliced through an even longer curve of brilliantly engineered metal, earth, and water, and produced a cascade of eerily silent explosions.

There was an insistent beeping sound as the words ENGINE TEMP CRITICAL flashed on the control panel, and Cortana said, "Shut them down. We'll need them later."

The Master Chief reached up to flick some switches, got up out of his seat, and arrived in front of the viewport in time to see the last intact piece of Halo's hull sheared in half by the dreadful slow-motion ballet of flying metal.

For some reason he thought of Lieutenant Melissa McKay, her calm green eyes, and the fact that he had never gotten to know her. "Did anyone else make it?"

"Scanning," the AI replied. She paused, and he could see scan data scroll across the main terminal. A moment later, she spoke again, her voice unusually quiet. "Just dust and echoes. We're all that's left."

The Spartan winced. McKay, Foehammer, Keyes, and all the rest of them. Dead. Just like the children he'd been raised with—just like a part of himself.

When Cortana spoke it was as if the AI felt that she had to justify what had transpired. "We did what we *had* to do—for Earth. An entire Covenant armada obliterated. And the *Flood*—we had no choice. Halo, it's finished."

"No," the Chief replied, settling in behind the Longsword's controls. "The Covenant are still out there, and Earth is at risk. We're just getting started."

_____ADJUNCT_____

Lak,

I've extracted the priority log and attached it to the end of this transmission. I know this isn't good, not because of what I've done but because of what I failed to do. I am shamed by the loss of the Holy Ring, but I needed you to know the full truth.

I humbly await the Council's ruling.

In peace,
Thel

PRIORITY BROADCAST LOG / ELEVENTH CYCLE, THIRD UNIT
SECURITY ACCESS FOR TIER ONE OF COVENANT MILITARY
  COMMAND ONLY.
ILLEGAL ACCESS OF THIS LOG IS IMMEDIATELY
  PUNISHABLE BY EXECUTION.

ENTRY 34589/9070454—PURIFICATION
Fleet of Holy Respite and the Fleet of Particular Justice move to system perimeter and form blockade to eliminate any escaping craft. Purification process of human world—Reach—remains in progress.

ENTRY 90907/9090304—COWARDLY PREY
Fleet of Particular Justice engages human attack vessel type C-11 at coordinates 343950-410958. Slipspace breach detected, fleet contingent responds accordingly.

ENTRY 86911/9103362—IN PURSUIT
Trajectory confirmed: Particular Justice contingent following tail, Slipspace supersession imminent. Estimated return to normal space 34905 units. Destination currently unknown.

ENTRY 45751/9157545—ARRIVAL
Artificial superstructure sighted upon arrival. Two local planetary bodies are present, strategic reticulation established and calibrated—fleet posture is adhering. Confirmation received and validated, structure is a Holy Ring. Security protocol enacted per Fleet Master Thel 'Vadamee, recon pickets established and awaiting type C-11 at far side of Ring.

ENTRY 59045/9231487—RECLAMATION
Confirmation of the presence of Halo may require San 'Shyuum leadership if available. Prophet claims that the Ring is a religious matter, not a military one, and invokes immediate adherence to reclamation procedure under his leadership.

ENTRY 14075/9245455—HIGH CHARITY
Minor Prophet and Fleet Master convene aboard *Seeker of Truth* and attempt to contact High Charity to ensure interpretation of scripture is accurate. Fleet Master is reluctant to relinquish command with an approaching human military threat. Communication cannot be made with High Charity. No decision is made.

ENTRY 68245/9290304—BREACH

Human ship arrives and engages immediately. Minor Prophet refuses to return heavy fire for fear of damaging the Holy Ring. Fleet Master ignores command, returns fire aggressively. Orders to breach and infiltrate vessel are issued by Minor Prophet. Ossoona dispatched.

ENTRY 68245/9312885—GAS MINE

Minor Prophet sends expeditionary forces to outlying gas facility, distinctly Forerunner in origin. Sesa 'Refumee and Loka 'Bandolee lead detachment. Fleet Master disapproves, issues close-band transmission demanding all military forces be concentrated on the human threat posed to the Holy Ring.

ENTRY 68245/9390304—FACILITY

Minor Prophet issues secondary and tertiary artifact recovery groups to outlying Forerunner weapon cache. Communication with recovery groups has since gone silent. Fourth group is issued. Fleet Master sends second transmission demanding cease and desist on force misappropriation by the Minor Prophet of Stewardship. No response received from Prophet.

ENTRY 68245/9400304—EMERGENCY ACTION

Fleet Master sends single infantry unit to the supercarrier *Ascendant Justice* to relieve the Minor Prophet of his duties until the human threat is mitigated. Contact with unit is lost upon approach of supercarrier. Prophet advises that any future affront to his leadership will be met with the same lethal finality.

ENTRY 45865/9410781—INFINITE SUCCOR

Emergency beacon has been activated on *Infinite Succor*. Threat assessment is piqued, unknown hostile contacts, humans are suspected. Special Operations detachment sent to assess situation, procure the Minister of Etiology, and return the Legate to *Seeker of Truth*.

ENTRY 68245/9450304—FAILURE
Minor Prophet commands the execution of Soha 'Rolamee for failing to secure Forerunner science facility. Significant threat detected on Halo—origin unknown. Fleet Master demands additional data on security failure. Fleet Master and security strike force prepare to personally board *Ascendant Justice* to physically relieve the Prophet of leadership.

ENTRY 68245/9490304—COMMANDER
Commander Rtas 'Vadumee returns to *Seeker of Truth* severely injured. The threat aboard the *Infinite Succor* was not human—it was Flood. Legate is dead. Fleet Master invokes emergency quarantine response, priority alpha. All remaining sterile vehicles should fire immediately upon any craft which does not return clean biometric scans of crew.

ENTRY 89531/9609243—DEPARTURE
Minor Prophet moves with personal security contingent from *Ascendant Justice* to *Truth and Reconciliation*, orders local crew to police ship, detain anyone who poses a threat to the Consecration—including the Fleet Master.

ENTRY 68245/9620304—ASCENDANT JUSTICE
Fleet Master boards *Ascendant Justice*. No shots fired. Existing crew acknowledge his leadership rights, realign forces, and support *Ascendant Justice* detail.

ENTRY 68245/9670304—TRUTH AND RECONCILIATION

Humans have seized *Truth and Reconciliation*. Security compromised, Prophet and his guard have been captured and detained. Prophet issues emergency rescue request to all remaining Covenant vessels in vicinity. Transmission sent successfully.

ENTRY 68245/9690304—ESCAPE

Transmission received successfully. Fleet Master denies special request; Halo's destruction is imminent. He orders all remaining surviving ships to take cover behind gas giant.

<\ **FILE:** ███████–████–████
DATE: ██████
<\ **USER:** CLASSIFIED [LEVEL ██████ AND ABOVE]
<\ **ENTRY:** 47-2396/10763
<\ **CLEARANCE:** CLASSIFIED [LEVEL ██████ AND ABOVE]
<\ **TYPE:** AUDIO TRANSCRIPT
<\ **SUBJECT:** ANALYSIS OF DISTRESS SIGNAL SENT FROM UNSC BUMBLEBEE-CLASS LIFEPOD LFA-19 BY PFC ████████████ ██████[████████████] DURING THE ████████ INCIDENT [**MORE**].
<\ **OBJECTIVE:** ANALYZE INFORMATION CONTAINED WITHIN FILE No. ████████–██████–████'S AUDIO TRANSCRIPT FOR DETAILS PERTINENT TO ONGOING THREAT FROM VIRULENT EXTRATERRESTRIAL LIFE-FORM DESIGNATE: ██████, AS ENCOUNTERED ON ALIEN CONSTRUCT DESIGNATE: ██████. [**MORE**]
<\ **FILE TYPE:** BASIC [FOR FURTHER DETAILS PERTAINING TO THIS DOCUMENT, INCLUDING PARTICIPANT BACKGROUND FILES, CLEARANCE-SENSITIVE AMENDMENTS, AND MORE, CLICK: **HERE**]
<\ **NOTE:** ALL OTHER ENTRIES RELATED TO FILE No. ████████–██████–████ ARE UNDER REVIEW. FULL REPORT PENDING COMPLETION OF INVESTIGATION.
<\ **DATA:** BEGIN 47-2396/10763 TRANSCRIPT [NOTES INCLUDED] . . .

SYSTEM: POWER INITIATED.

SYSTEM: System boot in progress.

SYSTEM: System: Online.

SYSTEM: Primary Frequency: ███████████

SYSTEM: Signal: Moderate

SYSTEM: System: Receiving. [0 signals incoming]

SYSTEM: System: Transmitting. [**ERROR**]

SYSTEM: System: Transmitting. [**ERROR**]

SYSTEM: System: Transmitting. [999,999,999,999 systems receiving]

SYSTEM: System: Transmitting. [**ERROR**]

SYSTEM: Signal Strength: Moderate

SYSTEM: Audio capture: Online.

AUDIO: "<*HUUH*> . . . this thing even on . . . ?"
[0001]

SYSTEM: Visual capture: Offline.

AUDIO: "It's recording . . . it's . . . I know
[0002] it's recording . . . but is anyone *getting*
this? Hello . . . ? Is there anyone there?
Anyone left?"

AUDIO: [NOTE: Movement: Undefined. Duration:
[0003] 00:00:07:59. Full, enhanced audio
analysis can be found **HERE**.]

AUDIO: "My name is . . . Private . . .
<*HUUH*> . . .
[0004] Private First Class ████████████ . . .
████████████████████."

ID: ██████ ██████. I'M PART OF
THE . . . *FUH* . . . *<HUH>* . . .
CHRIST . . . THEY'RE ALL . . .
EVERYONE . . . *<HUUH>* *<HUUH>* . . .
THEY'RE ALL DEAD . . . DEAD OR WORSE . . .
OR . . ."

AUDIO: [MOVEMENT: UNDEFINED. DURATION:
00:00:32:06.]

[0005] [NOTE: FULL, ENHANCED AUDIO ANALYSIS CAN BE
FOUND **HERE**.]

AUDIO: "IS THIS THING WORKING? PLEASE, HELP
ME . . .

[0006] PLEASE . . . *<HEH-HUUH>* SOMEONE COME
THROUGH . . . SOMEONE . . . PICK UP,
OKAY? JUST PICK UP . . . *<HUH>* ANSWER,
PLEASE . . . WE NEED HELP? *<HUH>* *<HUUH>* *I*
NEED HELP . . ."

AUDIO: [NOTE: SILENCE. DURATION: 00:00:32:06.
[0007] FULL, ENHANCED AUDIO ANALYSIS CAN BE FOUND
HERE.]

AUDIO: "I'M PART OF . . . *WAS* PART OF . . . THE,
[0008] UH . . . THE SEVENTY-NINTH INFANTRY
BATTALION . . . OUTTA THE . . . OUTTA THE
PILLAR OF . . . *<HUH>* . . . *PILLAR OF*
AUTUMN, AND THE *AUTUMN'S* GONE . . .
EVERYBODY'S *GONE*. I NEED HELP. I
NEED . . . I DON'T THINK ANYONE ELSE
IS . . ."

AUDIO: [NOTE: MOVEMENT: UNDEFINED. DURATION:
[0009] 00:07:12:41. FULL, ENHANCED AUDIO ANALYSIS
CAN BE FOUND **HERE**.]

AUDIO:
[0010]
"IT'S NOT COVENANT. I DON'T KNOW . . . I HAVE NO IDEA WHERE WE ARE . . . I JUST . . . I DON'T KNOW . . . BUT THIS PLACE . . . <HUUH> . . . THE THINGS HERE . . . THEY'RE WORSE . . ."

AUDIO:
[0011]
[NOTE: SOBBING. MOVEMENT: UNDEFINED. DURATION: 00:00:05:19. FULL, ENHANCED AUDIO ANALYSIS CAN BE FOUND **HERE**.]

AUDIO:
[0012]
"IS THIS COMING THROUGH? ARE YOU GETTING THIS SIGNAL? ANYONE? COME ON . . . COME ON! THIS IS A PRIORITY ALPHA DISTRESS CALL! WE CRASHED HERE, AND I DON'T KNOW WHERE IT IS . . . AND THESE THINGS . . . THESE CREATURES . . . <HUH> THERE'S . . . <HUH> . . . NOTHING LIKE IT . . . THEY'RE EVERYWHERE . . . AND THEY DON'T . . . THEY DON'T STOP . . ."

AUDIO:
[0013]
[NOTE: SOBBING. MOVEMENT: UNDEFINED. DURATION: 00:00:17:03. FULL, ENHANCED AUDIO ANALYSIS CAN BE FOUND **HERE**.]

AUDIO:
[0014]
"I JUST WANNA GO HOME . . . <HEH-HUH> I DON'T WANNA BE . . . <HUH> . . . DON'T WANNA BE HERE ANYMORE . . . CAN YOU HEAR THIS . . . ? PLEASE . . . SOMEONE, JUST SAY SOMETHING, SO . . ."

AUDIO:
[0015]
[NOTE: MOVEMENT: UNDEFINED. DURATION: 00:00:58:13. ADDITIONAL EXTERIOR SOUND: UNDEFINED, POSSIBLE MOVEMENT. DURATION: ONGOING. EXTERIOR SOUND APPEARS TO BE INCREASING, APPROACHING. SUBJECT IS NOT ALONE. FULL, ENHANCED AUDIO ANALYSIS CAN BE FOUND **HERE**.]

AUDIO: "THEY'RE COMING. LIKE BUGS . . .
[0016] *<HUUH>* . . . LIKE GIANT DAMN, LIKE,
ROACHES . . . ER, I DON'T KNOW . . . I
DON'T . . . THEY'RE LIKE THESE MON-
STERS . . . I CAN'T FIGHT 'EM . . . CAN'T
FIGHT . . . I CAN'T . . ."

AUDIO: [NOTE: SOBBING. MOVEMENT: UNDEFINED.
DURATION:
[0017] 00:00:13:27. EXTERIOR MOVEMENT: UNDE-
FINED. DURATION: ONGOING. FULL, ENHANCED
AUDIO ANALYSIS CAN BE FOUND **HERE**.]

AUDIO: "NOBODY'S THERE . . . YOU'RE NOT THERE.
[0018] NOBODY'S LISTENING . . . NOT TO
THIS . . . NOT TO ME . . . I JUST
WANT . . . *<HEEH>* I'M SCARED.
<HUH> . . . I JUST WANNA GO HOME, BUT
NOBODY'S . . . *<HUUH-HEH>* . . . NOBODY'S
GETTING THIS . . . THERE'S NOBODY
THERE . . . JUST ME . . . JUST ME AND
JUST THEM . . . JUST ME AND I'M ALL
ALONE . . ."

AUDIO: [NOTE: SOBBING. MOVEMENT: UNDEFINED.
[0019] DURATION: 00:00:08:10. EXTERIOR MOVE-
MENT:
UNDEFINED. DURATION: ONGOING. FULL,
ENHANCED AUDIO ANALYSIS CAN BE FOUND **HERE**.]

AUDIO: "I CAN HEAR 'EM . . . LIKE . . . IT'S
[0020] LIKE SCRATCHING ON MY BRAIN . . . THE WAY
THEY MOVE . . . AND WHAT THEY DO . . .
THEY DON'T JUST . . . *<HUUH>* . . . THEY
CHANGE YOU . . . THEY KILL YOU . . . BUT
THEY DON'T . . . THEY CHANGE YOU . . . I
CAN'T . . ."

AUDIO: [NOTE: SOBBING. MOVEMENT: FRANTIC,
[0021] UNDEFINED. DURATION: 00:00:17:11.
ADDITIONAL EXTERIOR SOUND: UNDEFINED,
POSSIBLE MOVEMENT. DURATION: ONGOING. FULL,
ENHANCED AUDIO ANALYSIS CAN BE FOUND **HERE**.]

AUDIO: "THEY'RE HERE . . ."
[0022]

AUDIO: [NOTE: MOVEMENT: UNDEFINED. DURATION:
[0023] 00:00:06:43. EXTERIOR MOVEMENT: UNDE-
FINED. DURATION: ONGOING. FULL, ENHANCED
AUDIO ANALYSIS CAN BE FOUND **HERE**.]

AUDIO: "IF ANYONE . . . <*HUH*> IF ANYONE'S GETTING
[0024] THIS . . . IF ANYONE SEES IT . . . I'M
SORRY . . ."

AUDIO: [NOTE: AUDIO ANALYSIS: SINGLE M6C MUZZLE
[0025] REPORT. FULL, ENHANCED AUDIO ANALYSIS CAN BE
FOUND **HERE**.]

AUDIO: [NOTE: MOVEMENT: UNDEFINED. DURATION:
[0026] 00:00:01:02. EXTERIOR MOVEMENT: UNDE-
FINED. DURATION: ONGOING.]

AUDIO: [NOTE: CLASSIFIED. FURTHER REVIEW OF
[0027] AUDIO/VISUAL CAPTURE RELATED TO FILE NO.
███████ ██████ ████████ ████ IS RESERVED FOR
SECURITY CLEARANCE LEVEL ██████ AND ABOVE.]

\\END TRANSMISSION>>

HUNGER

Sound.
Cold. Hunger.
Hunger. Sound. Motion. Cold. Motion. Hunger. Barrier.
Hunger.
Light. Sound. Hunger. Warmth. Freedom. Hunger.
Searching. Searching. Hunger. Warmth. Sound. Fear.
   Searching.
Jump.
Texture. Wet. Sound. Other. Food? Not food. Hunger.
Sound.
Hunger.
Searching. Searching. Pain. Sound. Searching. Hunger.
   Sound. Searching.
Jump.
Food.
FEAST.
Burrow. FEAST. Become. Become. Become.
   . . . make-it-stop-jesus-GOD-get-it-off-of-out-of-me
Become. Spine. Pierce. Change. FEAST. Grow. Food.
   Many food. Become.
   *Birthday-love-oh-god-it-hurts-first-time-I-met-her-
      where's-Johnson?-oh-god-it-hurts-it-hurts-it*
Become. Break. FEAST. Tear. Knit. Burrow. Become.
   *Boot-camp-what's-your-name?-Anna-birthday-it's-
   tearing-me-apart-where's-Johnson?-kill-me-kill-me-
          please-god*

Become. Seize. Sight. Smell. Pain. Decay. Move. Anna.
Stand. Food. Create. Become.

So-hungry-can't-look-son's-birthday-tomorrow-pain-pain-me-I'm-not-me-slipping-son-pistol-end-it-son-son

Become. Weapon. Steel. Hand. Others becoming. Son.
Paul. Moving. Shoot. Hunger. Become.

Hungry-others-together-no-don't-touch-him-me-Paul-run-run-run-together-last-target-down-success-together

Become. Others becoming. Others here. Many.
Covenant. Autumn. Food. Many. Freedom. Autumn.
SHIP. Become.

Hungry-Pillar-of-Autumn-Paul-no-don't-hungry-Anna-food-survivors-nearby-engineering-is-on-level-four-hungry

Become. SHIP. Freedom. Food. Paul. Anna. Food.
Become.

Hungry-oh-god-Paul-I'm-sorry-no-end-food-freedom-Reach-hungry

Become. Freedom. Food. Together. Become.

Food-Paul-become

Become.

Forgive-me

Become.

Become.

Become.

REVELATION
SALVATION

*I know why you have spared my life. You have watched
as my dedication to walk the Path wavered, my faith
weakened. But ever did I strive to make of myself the
most terrible weapon, a shining blade to be used to
destroy all those who would stand in the way of the
Covenant. In this, I have never wavered. It is not every
day a message comes so clearly, but I see now what it
is you have been preparing me for. All of my skills have
brought me here to this crux. You are testing me. You
have always been testing me. And I accept. My journey
is for the first time so very clear. I have seen what it is I
have been brought here for.*

*Never before have I witnessed such evil in the form
of this Demon. I am disgusted at its unnatural strength.
How it savages your most faithful. And I know you
have put this heathen, this monster in my way for a
reason. Beyond this Demon lies my key to the Great
Journey. I will find him. I shall be your will.*

ADVERSITY
PERSEVERANCE

*Your challenges mount, but I shall persevere. I know
you will not lay the Path easily, especially to one you*

turned his back on you before. These barriers in my journey, obstacles of faith, are riddled with clarity. This vile Demon is your gift to me. It is his destruction you nurture my spirit with, inching me along. You are clever, indeed, and my resolve is strengthened. No human will stop me. No greed from the Prophets will keep my glory from you. It is I who you have chosen. And it is I who will do your duty.

TEMPTATION
INSPIRATION

You have given me supreme command, eliminated many but I know now that these lesser humans are yet another test. I saw the Demon again. I may have exploited your faithful but I know it is all your will. I am imbued with your glory, and it all falls into my hands. I know what I must do with this armored animal, and by your will it shall be done.

DOUBT
CONCESSION

His continued existence haunts me. Keeps my dreams cluttered with death. Massacre at his hands. This Demon is a force against your glory. No soldier has even slowed his stride. Are you sure it's my destiny to meet him? I who have shown no true service to your will? Who repeatedly defied the command of your "Prophets"? Who used your servant Unggoy as a means to laughter? If it be in your grace that this blessing has come, let you know now that I am your vessel, a sword to your command. The glory of this artifact will be sung with my name.

JUDGMENT
BLESSING

Every great crusader needs a messenger. Your gifts have been plenty, wrapped in challenge. I am shamed to admit that doubt returned to my heart when you brought me this cowardly Yayap. I feared that I had lost your favor, that you had tied me to a weakling as judgment for the weakness in my faith. But now I know just why you sent me this clever Unngoy. I have passed your penultimate test. The grace of the true Prophets has blessed me, and now I shall claim what you have set forth as my glory.

MARTYRDOM
REJOICE

Let it be known that any deception we masquerade with is all in the name of your glory. It's all a ruse to do your bidding and seal our glory. The Demon still invades my sleep, toying with our holy ring . . . toying with our fate. I know the power of the name is sacred, but it is all I have left to ensure what I know you have always intended for me.

GRACE
ASCENSION

It all comes down to this. My resolve strengthened with your blessings against my own fears. Filled with purpose but cursed in this existence. I am but a vessel for your will. The Path is so clear now; I know what salvation tastes like. Now I must ascend as you blessed me so . . . Let me go . . .

Private Individual Status Report: Array Facility 1
(SIMUL_ARRAY_STATUS_REPORT)
Monitor 343 Guilty Spark
LOG: Psych/checksum/data/integrity/NOT_VALIDATED
  AT NOMINAL

EMERGENCY BULK DATA OFFLOAD REQUEST
  Current_mind_state_cache

Communicating
Transferring
Completing

~Request_accepted_data_collected/safe_transfer_
  confirmed/transmitted_errors_reported_repaired_for_
  next_two_way_transfer_343_Guilty_Spark_recodifica-
  tion.

Begin/

I have been somewhat remiss in my reporting duties, I
have to admit. Recent events have encouraged me to
make up for my tardiness, so this private report may
meander a little.

The intruders are now considered a significant risk.
I have limited capacity, or rather, authority to
defend the structure from this kind of primitive
assault and some of my terrestrial defenses have

ALREADY BEEN COMPROMISED EITHER THROUGH INTERFERENCE OR
DILAPIDATION. I SHOULD ALSO CONFESS THAT SOME OF THE
LATTER IS MY RESPONSIBILITY. I AM STARTING TO SEE THAT
I HAVE BEEN LAX IN SOME OTHER MAINTENANCE DUTIES, TOO.

THE BULK OF THE INTRUSION IS FROM A TIER 2
HEGEMONIZING RELIGIO/POLITICAL SWARM. THEY HAVE ENACTED
SIGNIFICANT DAMAGE TO THE STORAGE AND RESEARCH FACILITY
AT INSTALLATION ALPHA. AS I PREVIOUSLY NOTED, THIS
HAS CAUSED A BREACH IN CONTAINMENT. THE PARASITE IS
NOW LOOSE ON THE STRUCTURE—AND GROWING IN STRENGTH AND
INTELLIGENCE AS IT DECIMATES THE TIER 2 AND 3
SPECIES.

NOTE THAT WHERE CALCIUM DENSITY PERMITS, THE
PARASITE IS FOLLOWING IN ITS PRE-ARRAY EVENT PATTERN,
AN OUTWARD SPIRAL AT A RATIO OF APPROXIMATELY 1.68.

THE SECONDARY INTRUSION ELEMENT IS MORE PROBLEMATIC.
I HAVE TRIED TO CORRAL AND DIVIDE THE TWO FACTIONS BUT
WITH LIMITED SUCCESS. THEY APPEAR TO BE RIVALS AND ARE
ENGAGED IN CONFLICT, EVEN AS THE PARASITE PREDATES UPON
THEM. I AM UNSURE AS TO MY RIGHTS AND RESPONSIBILITIES
AS THEY RELATE TO THE SECONDARY INTRUSION GIVEN
POTENTIAL PRIOR RELATIONS OR DIPLOMATIC SITUATIONS.

ONE PARTY IS, TO THE BEST OF MY ABILITY TO DISCERN,
COMPRISED OF RECLAIMERS.

DNA SAMPLING CONFIRMS IT, BUT FRANKLY I RECOGNIZED
THEM AT FIRST SIGHT. ONE OF THEM IS EVEN WEARING A
PRIMITIVE COMBAT SKIN. HE IS ALSO ACCOMPANIED BY A
VERY LIMITED BUT INQUISITIVE ANCILLA. YOU SEE THE
SYMMETRY OF COURSE. AT FIRST I SUSPECTED THIS WAS A
TEST—AN ILLUSION INSERTED INTO MY RECODIFICATION TO
GAUGE MY LEVEL OF FUNCTIONALITY. I COULD SEE WHY THAT
SHOULD BE A CONCERN . . .

CROSS-REFERENCE OF MY INTERNAL DATA WITH EXTERNAL
SOURCES CONFIRMS IT, HOWEVER—THE SPECIES ARE ALL QUITE
REAL AND ALL IN VARYING DEGREES OF POST-ARRAY RECOVERY

STATES—SIGNIFYING SUCCESS OF THE LIBRARY PROJECT TO
SOME DEGREE. WITHOUT FURTHER CONTEXT I REALLY CAN'T
JUDGE. IN BETTER CIRCUMSTANCES I WOULD BE PLEASED. IN
THE CURRENT STATE OF AFFAIRS, THIS SIMPLY COMPOUNDS MY
CONFUSION AND CONCERN.

I SHOULD BE HAPPY. AND YET THESE ARE FAR FROM THE
IDEAL RESEARCH OR INTERACTION CONDITIONS I WOULD
PREFER. I HAVE DECIDED THAT THE SECURITY OF THE ARRAY
AND THE CONTAINMENT PROTOCOLS ARE MORE IMPORTANT THAN
THIS SITUATION OTHERWISE AND AS SUCH THE PROTOCOLS WILL
BE TREATED AS MY ONLY GOALS FOR NOW. I WILL HAVE TO
MAKE FURTHER CONTACT WITH ONE OF THE RECLAIMERS FOR
ASSISTANCE, BUT NOW IS NOT THE TIME TO PUSH FOR
NON-PERTINENT INFORMATION. BUT STILL . . .

ONE HUNDRED THOUSAND YEARS IS A LONG TIME TO BE
ALONE. THOSE OF US WHO CHOSE THIS PATH ALL UNDERSTOOD
IT WOULD BE THIS LONELY, BUT NOT THIS LONG. I ASSUME
THAT SOME OF THE MORE ERRATIC OR, RATHER, INACCURATE
DECISIONS I HAVE MADE ARE CONNECTED TO MY STATE OF
MIND—SOMETHING I NOW KNOW IS NEITHER FROZEN NOR
IMPERMEABLE.

I WAS YOUNG WHEN I CHOSE THIS PATH AND NOW I AM
SUDDENLY VERY, VERY OLD. THERE IS NO ONE LEFT TO
ADVISE ME.

SO I MUST DECIDE WHAT'S RIGHT FOR MYSELF. I WILL
PROTECT OUR LEGACY TO THE BEST OF MY ABILITY AND TO
THE DEATH, IF NEED BE, AS I PROMISED WHEN I FIRST
TOOK UP THIS MANTLE.

/END

Military activity beyond the sphere is becoming frantic. The relative calm here impedes my sense of urgency. I find myself reading their reports just to provoke my own emotional response.

My report, however, isn't quite so dramatic.

As predicted, the oceanic life is taking longer to catalog than the terrestrial and mammalian populations. What's hampering this collection isn't pressure or friction or depth but rather simplifying categorization. It is rare that we find so many disparate flavors of intelligence in a single habitat, but to find mammalian [standard] intelligence along with Schyzophoa and Cephalopoda in oceans further enhances the theory that this planet has seen interference or experiment in its past. This kind of distributed intellectual symmetry tends to hint at artifice.

What's making things more difficult is the rather distasteful process of testing living samples against simulated attack. I find this task immoral, even as I embrace its necessity. I wish that the entire test process could be undertaken synthetically or virtually. But safety precautions prevail. Eventually we will have a simpler baseline measure, and more depressingly, eventually we may have to make an artificial rather than scientific cutoff line.

The primitive simians were simple to categorize by comparison. But of course the more sophisticated ones are proving as enigmatic and evasive as ever.

Typically I prefer outreach and contact, but some regrettable abductions have been necessary.

The differing subspecies and races within the local population of prospects is a situation causing headaches of its own. They may be genetically very close, but their cultures and attitudes are dramatically different. I can attribute some, but not all, of that to their different physical makeup, although surprisingly the C-types, while physically massive and much more powerful than the B-types, are less aggressive and warlike. In fact, they're agrarian by nature and peaceful in intent and outlook. This may, in the long term, hamper their progress here.

The A-types show the most potential for moral intelligence—but it's possible their lack of physical stature might impede them in direct competition with the other two, where tool use and culture do not give them the upper hand. Still, I have high hopes for them. And I enjoy their company even if they don't fully understand what I am, or why I'm here.

The B-types are curious and will watch our activity from a distance, but they're not as gregarious, and seldom venture too close. The C-types are oddly oblivious to our activity, as if it were a mountain or a river that they simply expected to be here.

I miss my friends, however, and one especially.

The facility here is impressive. I'm almost

embarrassed to have this much access to technology. It's frustrating, however, to be this close to "civilization" and the people I love, yet hermetically sealed away from them by security protocols. In better days, this facility would simply be an open doorway, through which we could all travel and enjoy this world for what it is—the core of a deeper enigma.

But one I feel confident we'll solve one day. I'm the eternal optimist, after all.

Signing off.
L.

mcfarlane.com/halo

Yes...These are actual figures!

HALO: REACH SERIES 6 ACTION FIGURES

Bring the adventure to life with our 5-inch scale hyper-detail and fully articulated action figures. *Halo: Reach* Series 6 includes single figures and multi-packs including *Invasion* & *Team Objectives* Deluxe Boxed Sets!

ACTION FIGURES

DELUXE BOXED SETS

AVAILABLE FEBRUARY 2012 AT THE FOLLOWING RETAILERS:

Walmart
GameStop
power to the players
TARGET
Toys "R" Us

HALO

W A Y P O I N T

Halo Waypoint is your hub for all things Halo. Whether it's for the intricate details of Halo's fiction, the incredibly creative community-generated content, a comprehensive look at your Campaign and Multiplayer Career across many Halo titles, or tools to enhance your Halo Multiplayer experience... Waypoint has you covered.

Halo Waypoint provides fans with access to exclusive, never-before-seen shows and series, offering the Halo community the news and entertainment they need, when they need it. Waypoint provides detailed multiplayer stats and game history for Halo: Reach and Halo: Combat Evolved Anniversary. The Halo Multiplayer experience becomes more social with Waypoint Custom Challenges. And Halo players can get a leg up on the competition with Waypoint ATLAS for mobile devices.

You can access Halo Waypoint on your console via the Main Menu in Halo: Reach and Halo: Anniversary, or directly from the Xbox LIVE Games Marketplace. You can download Halo Waypoint on Windows Phone 7, iOS, and Android devices. And you can access Waypoint from anywhere at www.halowaypoint.com.

 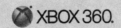